BOOK 2

THE DAILY GRIND

BOOK 2

ARGUS

Podium

To Raven and Quetz, whom I love very much.

All rights reserved. No part of this publication may be reproduced, stored in a retrieval system, or transmitted in any form or by any means electronic, mechanical, photocopying, recording, or otherwise without prior written permission from Podium Publishing.

This a work of fiction. Names, characters, places, and incidents are either products of the author's imagination or used fictitiously. Any resemblance to actual events, locales, or persons, living, dead, or undead, is entirely coincidental.

Copyright © 2023 by Forrest Taylor

Cover design by Paul Ghezzo

ISBN: 978-1-0394-3338-0

Published in 2023 by Podium Publishing, ULC
www.podiumaudio.com

Podium

CHAPTER 1

"You cannot be serious," Anesh said. He was sitting at one of the wire-frame tables outside the coffee shop near their apartment, arm frozen holding a cappuccino halfway to his lips. He wasn't alone; James and Alanna sat around the same table, evenly spaced on the circular edge. Alanna was, just like Anesh himself, wearing an incredulous expression on her face and staring at James. "No, but really, though. What?" He set his cappuccino down, folding his hands and waiting for James to respond.

"I'm serious!" James said, in a voice far more defensive than Anesh's had been accusatory. He cleared his throat and then continued in a normal tone. "It was weak. Like, *way* weaker than the other one I got in a fight with."

They were talking about the stuffed shirt that had torn into the apartment only an hour earlier. It had come up as Anesh was reassuring Alanna that she had, really, not just shot a real person. And that was when James had revealed an awkward fact that he'd noticed.

Alanna rapped her knuckles on the table. "James, it threw me into a patch of blackberry bushes. Like, one-armed, picked me up and flung me twenty feet. Into fucking thorns. I weigh over two hundred pounds. So, before I make you help me go back to your apartment and rip up that entire strip of foliage, explain how the fuck that counts as *weaker?*"

"Well, weaker is typically what you call something that wasn't as strong..." James started.

"Anesh, he's being stupid. Show him your arm again," Alanna said, making a looping gesture with her hand.

Holding up his arm and pointing at it for James to see, Anesh asked, "Are you telling me this is weak?"

"Weaker. Not abstractly weak, come on. It took a chunk out of the damn wall by accident, it's a huge threat," James conceded. "But it just wasn't on par with the one in the dungeon. I was fighting it, toe to toe, and if I'd had more space I think I could have taken it. No help or coffee or anything. And yeah, I've been working out and got some martial arts orbs, but that's not enough. So, yes, I'm serious, I think it was weaker," he concluded.

Alanna leaned back, throwing her head over the back of the chair and looking up at the night sky. "Well, shit, that's horrifying."

"Indeed," Anesh murmured. "But why? Because it was outside the dungeon?"

"Yeah, how the fuck did it do that anyway?" Alanna asked. "Like, did it get a signal when you unleashed your brainpet, and then run all the way there?"

James swallowed a sip of his mocha. "Or was it just waiting?"

"What? Waiting where?" Alanna asked with a snort.

"I dunno, just hiding around somewhere?" James shrugged. "They don't need food or anything, just . . . orbs . . ." He trailed off.

Anesh stepped in. "Say now. That's a good point." James nodded thoughtfully, while Alanna just looked between the two of them.

"What?" she asked shortly.

Motioning to the green orb that she had been rolling around the table, Anesh answered, "It dropped a green, yeah? But the other one dropped a yellow. A *huge* yellow. Why didn't this one? And James, you just said . . ."

". . . that they feed on yellows, yeah," James finished, comprehension dawning on him. "It probably was just sitting out there for who knows how long! It wouldn't need to eat, just avoid detection. Hell, it could have just sat on the roof. Or at the bottom of the little lake!" He slapped the table. "That could be why it was weak. *Weaker*, sorry. But it might have been starving."

Alanna cut short his celebration a bit. "But wait, that leaves a more important question. The fuck tripped it? And why did it still have a green? Does that mean that greens don't 'feed' them?" She leaned back, taking her hand off the orb on the table and looking at it a little suspiciously. "What's the takeaway, I guess?"

"Can't tell you on the green," James said sadly. "You know as much as we do there. But I think that it's safe to say that what activated it was us 'remembering' Sarah."

"But we don't remember Sarah," Alanna reminded him. "We remember Wes, who we never forgot. We just found Sarah's room."

James shrugged, cutting off Anesh before he could respond himself. "We remember Wes because Wes was too unimportant to forget? Honestly, I think that Wes just 'was a roommate,' you know? Like, he lived with us, but we had to not think about him, or we'd have to think about the third bedroom."

Anesh got a chance to cut in. "We could have remembered Wes, we just couldn't have remembered him living with us. Maybe that was the problem, not Sarah. We got too close to remembering that one room, and its contents?"

The three of them sat there quietly, mulling that over for a second. A cool night breeze drifted by, taking away some of the heat of the day. In the distance, frog croaks echoed through the air.

"So . . . does anyone remember anything about Sarah herself?" James asked with a tight voice. He felt a little lost; he was out of his depth entirely. The whole concept of having his memories rewritten was horrifying, and he was really only staying calm thanks to Secret helping him keep the panic at bay. He . . . actually wasn't really sure how he was doing that, honestly. Secret hadn't spelled it out to him. James was a bit curious whether or not his panic was literally being eaten by his imaginary friend. If so, he had concerns about the change in diet, but he wasn't going to complain if it was working.

He snapped out of his thoughts just in time to catch the end of something Alanna was saying. James asked her what she'd said, and she just glared at him but grudgingly repeated, "I said no, but at least months, though, right? Just going by the 'food' in her room. Also her mail, which, uh . . . a lot less guesswork and also less mold there."

"It's a long shot, but it's worth checking. I mean, maybe I just have a massive paladin complex, but I have a hard time thinking that it's okay to leave someone behind in that place. Even if we don't remember them," James told his friends.

Anesh felt more than a little sheepish for thinking almost exactly that. But he agreed; once James spelled it out, it was pretty clear to him what the morally right course of action was. "Okay," he said, "I should have thought of that. Yes. I'm with you, we go try to find her. But! Also make use of any information we can get. We can be pragmatic while also seeing if we can find our . . . friend?"

"Friend," Alanna confirmed. She'd heard the recorded conversations; if Sarah was real, she was a friend, whether they remembered her or not.

"That does bring us to something I'm concerned about," Anesh told them. "If we're going to keep going back in, we're going to need to be better equipped. I know we've talked about this before, but really. I don't know if the stuff we've bought and worked on is going to cut it?"

Alanna slapped the table. "I was gonna ask! Did the maul you ordered for me ever come in?"

"You were gonna ask?" James raised an eyebrow.

"I was! Wait, why am I defending myself to you? That's a legitimate question about my hammer," she retorted. "Anesh! Hammer!"

Choking back a laugh, Anesh turned it into a small cough, and then told her, "Yeah, it's coming in. A lot of stuff is, really. I'm just wondering if there's anything we can add to it?"

"There's such a thing as overpreparing, you know," James told him.

"Lies," Anesh replied without missing a beat.

All of them shared a laugh at that one, started by Alanna as the guys set off her sense of humor with their back-and-forth. After they got past it, though, James carried on. "But really. What more could we need? We both had a dozen things we thought would be helpful, but we got those. We've also got more thermite, for dealing with anything that could be charitably defined as nightmare fuel, and I am . . . mostly . . . done making a new launcher. Do we just start specializing to an extreme?"

"Pressure washer!" Alanna cried out, slapping the table again and causing James to grab at his drink to keep it from tipping over as she upset the table.

After recovering his mocha and settling it back down, he glared over at her and simply asked, "What?"

"I . . . thought it was kind of self-explanatory when I yelled it. We get a pressure washer. You know, for the construction workers," Alanna replied.

"Construction . . . oh, because they're made of paper. I still like 'stuffed shirt' better. Anyway, are they actually enough paper to make it work if we hose them down?" James pondered.

Anesh shook his head. "They only seem to be *full* of paper. And dust. Probably paper dust. *Hopefully* paper dust. I don't see them falling to pieces if they get soggy."

Letting out a small hum and gulping at the drink he'd just sipped, James countered, "I ripped off one of the first ones' arms, though. It kinda had the consistency of paper. If nothing else, a pressure washer might actually be able to ruin a shellaxy or a blackhawk if it turns out they're hostile."

"Sorry, hang on," Alanna interrupted, "blackhawks?"

James turned back to her. "You know those flocks of paper that we see fluttering around like birds?" She nodded in response. "Well, a while back, I made a few paper airplanes, and either they animated or the dungeon just stole the idea. So, now, every now and then, I see one of them up there. And it looks like they hunt the paper flocks, so I call them blackhawks. Since, you know, they're aircraft, and also kinda birds."

"Um . . . James?" Anesh cut in. "Black Hawks aren't airplanes. They're helos."

"I mean, I know that. But the joke doesn't work if I name them after the SR-71 Blackbird, because then I don't get to call them hawks," James sheepishly responded. "Also the Blackbird is the dumbest aircraft. Can I complain about an aircraft? I've been learning weird history trivia."

"Later." Anesh shifted around a bit, settling into his chair. "I'm just saying, the name doesn't work that well."

"Let me have this. It's a paper airplane and I'll name it after the military aircraft of my choice," came the snippish reply from James. "Anyway. Now that I think about it, Alanna has a point that a pressure washer might have use. What's our budget look like? Maybe we could just rent one for a couple days and see if it works. Point it at a flock of paper and see if we get a million orbs from it."

Raising a hand, Alanna cut in. "As amusing as it is to see James get smacked down, do we have anything we want to try to get this week? I know you guys have stuff to take care of, but I find myself with an expanse of free time, so, James, was there anything else on your list that I could try to find around town so we don't have to wait for shipping?"

"Helmets," James said without hesitation. "Seriously, maybe find a better military surplus store and see if they have something with a visor. I'm tired of getting sharp things near my eyes." He pulled his phone out and opened up his list of gear ideas. "I picked up some USB sticks, so that's covered. Anesh, did you order flare guns?"

"Yup," his friend said simply, standing up to go put his empty drink cup in the bus bin. He took a minute to stretch his legs and breathe in the fresh air of the outdoor setting.

"That's all I can really think of. Maybe try to find a riot shield for sale or something. Actually maybe just go ask the police if they'll loan us a riot shield. And a grenade launcher." James shrugged, raising his eyebrows in a comically hopeful expression.

Anesh sat back down. "Your country scares me."

"But yeah, heavily armed police force aside, I don't think we have anything else we need," James said. "Like, there's kind of a limit to how much we can carry, and how far we can specialize."

Alanna considered what she was about to ask for a second, before setting aside her worries and asking anyway. "What about your gun? Can I bring that in?"

"Now that I know it works on the employees, yes." James didn't hesitate. "Even if it's just a last resort, because of the noise."

This did bring up another point in Anesh's mind. They hadn't really had time to just sit down and talk like this, and the relaxed environment was making it a lot easier for him to see more of their options. The scent of clipped grass floating by, the cool iron of his chair, the company of his two closest friends and companions, all of it was going a long way toward letting him relax and get rid of some of his tunnel vision that had been plaguing him ever since James introduced an extra fourteen hours of responsibility into his already busy week.

Granted, it also added eight hours of time to have that responsibility in. But that wasn't really helpful when it ruined his sleep pattern.

Still, now that he wasn't worried about them not dying right now, and with the ability to feel safe just sitting back and enjoying his drink, he was struck with a thought.

"Hey," Anesh said. "We really need to be maximizing our use of the xenotech we find, too. Not just relying on our new income to buy us better gear."

"Good point, I can shoot something with fireballs!" Alanna said, with a lot more cheerful energy than Anesh expected.

James patted her on the shoulder. "You would want to fireball someone, wouldn't you?"

She leaned forward and grumbled, "Everyone wants to fireball someone."

"Yes, fireballs for everything in our way," Anesh said. "We should test to see if we can use other darts in that gun, too. If not, we've only got five shots. But not just that. We've got the map pointer, and those shades that let us see into infrared. We need to be folding those into our tactics."

James grimaced. "Those shades gave me a migraine."

Alanna turned and patted him on the shoulder in a mirror of his previous mocking. "There, there, punchy. We'll get you a magic item someday."

"Xenotech," Anesh corrected.

"Magic. Item," James corrected, tapping the table with one finger to punctuate the words.

Alanna held her hands between the two of them. "Okay, boys, calm down. Flirt later, and in a way that's more fun for me." She pushed them each back a bit. "Can one of you explain to me why we haven't been finding more magic . . . tech . . . fuck it, more doodads? The ones that are useful are *really* useful. Why aren't we looking for them harder?"

"They're hard to spot," James explained. "Like, you've got the pen that can liquefy concrete, and anything less durable than concrete, like people, right? If you set that down on your desk, and it got mixed up, would you be able to tell at a glance it was enchanted?"

"Nnnnnno. No," Alanna said slowly, with growing concern and understanding.

James nodded as she got it. "Exactly. The dungeon has eight billion pens, and two of them are nuclear weapons. Needle in a haystack. Pen in a pen stack, actually."

"We need some way to search faster, then?" she offered.

"There's always Lily," Anesh said, offering up a suggestion. "She can scan objects, too. We don't even have to use her to fully scan the xenotech. Just see if it pops up a progress bar, since the enhanced stuff takes longer for her to understand."

Alanna punched James lightly in the shoulder. "Why didn't you tell me about that?" she demanded.

"Because I forget things!" he cried out, rubbing his arm and ducking away from her assault. "I can't be asked to remember every superpower I've acquired in the last month!"

"Yes, you can!" Alanna and Anesh chorused at him.

He slid down in his chair, wondering if it would be possible to just hide under the table until this all blew over. It wasn't. The plan, much like the table, had holes in it.

"Changing the subject a bit," Alanna said, turning to Anesh while James tried to make a shelter out of their table, "you're the general leader of our little group, right? I wanted to ask you about actual tactics."

From under the table came "Why am I not the leader?" as James overheard them.

"Because Anesh doesn't hide from me when I ask pointed questions." Alanna poked at him with her foot. "Anyway. We brought in JP and Dave, and I don't think that was the worst idea, but five people is kinda awkward in the hallways there. We should consider doing actual practice fights together, instead of just relying on dungeon time to get us up to speed."

Tapping at his chin, Anesh considered it. "That's a good point. But when? I've got school, James works most of the time. JP has to take care of his mom, and Dave is . . . actually, does anyone really know what bollocks Dave does when he's not hanging out at our apartment?"

James plopped himself back in his chair, giving up on the joke. "He works for an animal shelter."

Both of his friends stared at him incredulously. It was Alanna who broke the stunned silence first. "What, seriously?"

"Yeah, you guys never wondered why he talks about his dogs so much?" James turned to look back inside the coffee shop. "I'm thinking of getting a cake. Do either of you guys want cake?"

"No, go back to . . . well, yes, I want cake. But go back to how Dave works in an animal shelter. Dave? *Our* Dave? Dave is . . . trying to say this nicely . . . nope, can't do it. Dave is kind of a dick," Alanna said.

James stood up, reaching his arms up over his head. He paused for a minute in his answer to try to track a bat flying by overhead, but then looked back down at Alanna before going in to purchase some cake. "He's a dick to people, not animals. And even then, I think he's mostly a dick by accident. I'm pretty sure that he'll be the first one to tame a shellaxy, honestly. He just really loves dogs. Anyway, you asked what he does all day. It's mostly that. He puts in, like, twelve-hour days."

"Well, shit," Alanna said to Anesh as James headed off. "Now I feel like a dick."

Anesh shook his head. "Don't. Dave's still a wanker."

She shrugged in response. "Maybe, but no one who takes care of dogs for twelve hours a day can be that bad. I mostly just assumed his entire persona was smoking and playing stupid D&D characters."

"He does have a fascination with stupid ideas, doesn't he?" Anesh mused.

"On that note," Alanna said, "was it actually a good idea to tell Dave and JP? I know I'm the new girl on the team compared to you two, but . . . how secret do we want to keep this?" She'd put quite a lot of thought into this over the last couple weeks. "Do we keep recruiting? And if so, how do we handle things like security and logistics and even just getting everyone into the building? I know Frank gets bribed a ludicrous amount of money to do nothing, but will that last forever?"

Anesh held up his hands. "One question at a time! I'm gonna need more caffeine to handle any more questions." He shot a look inside, wondering if it was too late to get a refill. "First of all, I don't know. Maybe it was jumping the gun a bit to tell them. But . . . it was mostly just a reaction to *not* being able to tell anyone."

The memories of when they'd had their tongues locked by mental invaders they couldn't fight was painful to bring up. The time before Secret was Secret, when it was just another tool that part of the dungeon used to hurt them, wasn't something Anesh looked back on fondly. He wasn't a vindictive person, but he honestly couldn't say he was sorry that his intruder had starved to death.

He wondered if its corpse was still in there somewhere.

"Anyway," he continued, shaking it off. "We did, and have to deal with it now. I don't think we expand right away, though it would be nice to have an even number of people so we could split up properly. You're right that we can't fit five people in a hallway." He thought for a second. "Do you have any names we could put on a short list?" Anesh asked her. "If we did want to start recruiting, that is."

Alanna didn't reply for a second, and Anesh could see that her mouth twisted a bit while she looked down at the ground. "No one really springs to mind," she said with a small hitch in her voice. "I don't have anyone I trust that isn't you guys."

"That's both flattering and kind of sad," Anesh said, and instantly regretted it. His regret was made manifest when Alanna smiled a small bit and also punched him in the arm. "Ow! That . . . that's fair, yeah. But honestly"—he rubbed at his arm, noting that he'd gotten it a lot worse than James—"I'm in the same situation. I don't really have a good roster of options either."

Alanna rolled the green orb around the table a bit, making circles with it, one finger perched right on the top. "So how do we get JP and Dave more practiced? Split up again, but divide them between the three of us, so you don't have to double-babysit?"

Not having to babysit two liabilities at once sounded great to Anesh, and he said as much. "Honestly, when you mentioned practice fights earlier, that sounded good. I'm just not sure where we'd get that kind of experience that would be better than just 'the outskirts of the dungeon,' yeah?"

"I'll see about looking up some training methods and plan something out for next week," Alanna said. "We can at least put in half an hour of practice before starting the real delve. And that's a good chance to do some speed-looting. Since I'm now on payroll for this whole affair, and I find myself lacking gainful employment, I'm a bit more invested than before in stockpiling as much cash as we can from the dungeon."

"Yeah, I'm really sorry you got fired," Anesh said, sympathizing with her. "Do you have enough cash to get you through the week? We still have a bunch left over in the group bank, and I can give you some if you need it."

"Buy me another smoothie, but aside from that, I should be good. I'll just make sure to take home a bit for myself next time we go in, and make sure that I'm secure." She sighed. "I'm just not sure what to do now. I haven't had actual free time in a long, long time. Not since . . . not since I was a kid." Anesh didn't miss the cut sentence, but didn't bring it up. "What do people do when they're not working?"

He shrugged. "Search me. I go to class, then come home and do more schoolwork. Then I plan out the games I run for you guys. Then I sleep. Then sometimes my bloody roommate drags me into a death trap for fun and profit."

The laugh from Alanna rippled through the air, making Anesh smile and helping to further ease away the fear from earlier in the night. "Ah, well," she said. "He might be a bit nuts sometimes, but you love him."

"Yeah," Anesh responded, not really thinking about it. Then he saw Alanna grinning at him, and realized what he'd said. "Wait, no, hang on!"

"Too late!" she yelled out triumphantly. "I fucking knew it! Yes! Vindication!" Her fists pumped into the air in a frenzied dance of victory.

Anesh thunked his head onto the table. "Please no." He knew that Alanna wasn't going to let this go. "If I confess my undying love for you, will that sidetrack this nightmare?"

"Nope! Though it does open up a more interesting prospect for a Friday night date," she replied, continuing to shadowbox the air around her. Less frantic, more just enjoying the feeling of motion, and keeping the joke going. "Really, though. I'm just kidding. And I won't tell."

"Tell what?" James said, coming back to the table with his cake. "Also, who're you dating?"

"I literally just said I wouldn't tell, James. Have some tact," Alanna said, chastising him. "Also, let me have a bite of your cake." She reached over. "Also, *I'm* not dating anyone."

He neither made the connection nor wanted to share his cake. In fact, he took great pains to situate his cake as far from Alanna as possible. And then slid his chair back to hold it in his lap, as Anesh tried to lean in and steal a chunk of it while James had his back turned. "You're both monsters," he scolded them. "What did I miss aside from your romantic lives?"

"Well," Anesh said, "we're thinking we use a half an hour of our time each week to do some basic practice together with the others.

You and I have movement down okay, but we also need to just learn how to coordinate better. Alanna was gonna look into that."

She nodded, still eyeing the chocolate raspberry sugar explosion on James's plate. "I'm thinking of getting some of the squad training manuals from the military surplus store. Or just googling them? Either way, might be useful just to know."

"I like that plan," James said. "It was weird coming back to see you guys hadn't really made progress because of a small mistake."

"Yeah, I think Dave was treating it like a game? We should make it clear that we get injured regularly. Actually, I should just remind them that the month I spent with my arm broken was because of one of the stuffed shirts," Anesh said.

Alanna jerked back a bit. "That's what did it?! Holy shit. I know you said it was the dungeon, but I didn't press it." She shook her head. "I was really worried about you, ya know."

"I know," Anesh said, smiling. "And I appreciate it."

James cut in, "Same here. I sure wasn't going to feed him while he was out of commission."

"James, I could still feed myself. Also, you could absolutely feed me, I know you've got cooking skills," Anesh retorted.

Alanna held up a finger. "Point of order. James once set rice on fire. Oh, wait, you mean dungeon skills. Never mind," she said, seeing James about to respond and shrugging off her own mistake. "So, hey, speaking of dungeon skills, I just thought of something. Can we jump back to a previous topic?"

"Sure, what's up?" James asked, curious.

"What about the yellow orbs?" Alanna asked the two of them.

Anesh and James shared a look with each other. "Do you . . . ?" Anesh motioned to James, and his friend nodded.

He turned to Alanna, he and Anesh folding their hands on the table in front of themselves. "Well, you see, the creatures in the dungeon will often drop small yellow spheres when they . . ."

"I know where they come from, you fuck!" she yelled out. Alanna cleared her throat and adopted a deliberately passive tone. "To elaborate, I should ask, why do the orbs feed the dungeon mobs, but give us skills?"

"Oh, that's easy," James said without thinking. "We're cracking them, not absorbing them." Now Anesh and Alanna both turned to look at *him*, putting James under some curious scrutiny. "What?" he said to their raised eyebrows. "We know that the orbs can be absorbed, because that's what Rufus and Ganesh do, and because I managed to do it once to that one blue. So, clearly, there's just a difference between absorbing and cracking."

"James," Anesh said, tilting his head down and massaging his forehead. "You did what?" Alanna set her elbows on the table, leaned into her hands, and let out a low scream.

In his head, James heard a small whine, as Secret had one of his food sources taken away as the information was shared.

"Ah," James said. "Right. I forgot a number of things. Okay, well, I absorbed a blue orb. It took Secret's help to do it, though. That's why I ended up in the hospital recently, remember? It gave me a limited-use ability. In every sense of that term, yes." He answered the questions about to be asked. "I can sublimate rubber. I didn't tell you because I didn't want anyone to get hurt trying to replicate it, and because Secret literally feeds off of secrets, and it seemed a harmless enough way to keep him happy."

Alanna started headbutting the tabletop while Anesh just leaned over and patted James on the head. "I'm sure you meant well, friend." He sat back in his chair. "This is big, though. This is . . . hm." He pulled out a small yellow orb from his pocket and looked at it. "I wonder . . ."

"Where'd that come from?" Alanna asked from her position spread across the table.

"I save some of mine," Anesh said. "For emergencies." He looked at the orb, gazing into it, rolling it in his fingers. The other two watched him, waiting for him to say what was on his mind. But he stayed silent. James took a bite of cake, Alanna checked the time on her phone, and in the distance, an owl called out.

James was just about to break the stillness when Anesh suddenly let out a small gasp of amazement as the little yellow ball disappeared into the palm of his hand.

"What the fuck!" Alanna barked out.

Jumping out of his chair, James got ready to catch Anesh if his friend convulsed and fell like he did when he absorbed the blue. But, to his surprise, Anesh seemed perfectly fine. "Are you okay?!" he demanded from his friend.

Anesh responded with some kind of affirmative, but he wasn't really paying attention to James at the moment. He'd found it surprisingly easy to put himself in the mindset that the orbs were something he could take inside himself, and while it had felt disturbing at best to drag it under his skin, what happened afterward was what caught his attention. First came a feeling of stability. Of being perfectly content. A thousand small things just went away, and the absence was instantly noticeable in its impact. His foot didn't itch, his back tooth didn't hurt, his eyes weren't tired, and he wasn't feeling that little bit of hunger he'd felt building up over the last hour. The second thing that caught his attention was the notification.

[+2.2 *Operational Hours : Comfortable*]

"Well, that's certainly something," Anesh muttered.

"What . . ." James started to ask, but then Anesh slapped the table and scowled.

Cutting James off, Anesh growled out, "I know this is pretty cool, but I just realized that this is one more thing that is *ruining my sodding sleep schedule!*" He took a deep breath and found that the taste of the air was a little more pronounced. But more than that, he found that he didn't feel like he actually needed the deep breath. Curious, Anesh held his breath and counted. James and Alanna watched as their friend inhaled, held it, and then just sat there for a good minute or two.

James leaned in toward Anesh, curiously poking at his friend. "Did he die?" he asked Alanna, not really worried and sort of amused.

Slapping James's hand away, Anesh resumed breathing normally. "No, I did not die, you wanker. I was just testing this." He tapped at his phone on the table while he talked. "It told me it added 'Operational hours,' which sounds fine. But I think that for the duration, I actually . . . don't have physical needs? If it weren't for how weird it feels, I don't think I'd have to breathe at all. I'm not hungry, a lot of small pains are gone, it's just . . . great, actually."

"So, is this just what we use yellows for now?" Alanna asked, a bit sadly.

"Well," Anesh said, "we'd need to have a lot of them. This only gave me two hours. Also, it seems like a weird trade-off."

Alanna nodded, but James didn't quite get it. "What do you mean?" James asked him.

"Well, skills are permanent, right? But this absolutely isn't," Anesh replied. "So, anytime we want an all-nighter without any aftereffects, we need to sacrifice four random skill levels."

"Harsh trade, I see," James said.

"So," Alanna cut in, "what do I do with this green one, then?" Her words drew the attention of the others to the orb on the table that she'd been casually rolling around throughout the conversation. "I mean, I was going to just crack it, but should I be trying to shove it inside my arm or something?"

That got a cringe from James as he imagined the sensation of the fist-sized orb pushing into flesh. "Nope nope nope," he yelped out. Continuing in a more level tone, he gave an actual answer. "But yeah, I dunno. I mean, it's your orb, I feel like you get to choose?"

"I can already see Anesh vibrating a little at the idea of getting some more data on different uses of orbs," Alanna joked.

James nodded, looking over at Anesh just to make sure that she wasn't being literal about that. "Yeah, well, it's still your choice. Anesh can't make you, no matter how much you glare at me, you bastard." He deliberately turned away from his scowling roommate and focused on talking to Alanna. "Really, though. I don't know how much mental gymnastics Anesh had to do just there to absorb the yellow, but I know that it took help from Secret to pull in a blue. Oh, and it hospitalized me. I can't imagine that a green would be any better."

Covering the orb with her palm while a couple other patrons walked by their table, Alanna thought about it for about three seconds before coming to a conclusion. "I feel like, while I could totally tank something that would hospitalize *you* . . ."

"Hey!"

". . . I still don't want to actually go through that," she finished, ignoring James's protest. "I think my original plan stands. Crack it at that elementary school down the road."

Anesh finished scowling at James to look over at Alanna and ask, "I know you want to use your powers for good, but are you sure you don't want to use it at your house? Or maybe wait until we get some kind of home base workshop thing?"

It wasn't that Alanna hadn't had that thought. She'd actually put a lot of time into considering the best way to use the different stuff that she might one day get to use from the dungeon. And while they hadn't been aware of the effects of the green orbs for very long, it wasn't that hard to realize from what James and Anesh said that they were super useful. But that just reinforced her desire to use them on someone else. They still gave huge skill-ups, and while it would be cool to live in a house where food took twice as long to spoil, or where laundry stayed clean for an extra day regardless of how it was used, she felt like the best way to achieve the most good for the most people was to hit somewhere like a school, hospital, or even just shopping mall.

After all, there were always more orbs. And given how James and Anesh had once run into a shellaxy army, she didn't doubt that there would be more greens. Eventually, she'd use one for herself. But until then, she was content to take her share of the skill points and pay it forward with the area buff.

"Nah, I think I'm good," she told Anesh. "I know it could be useful. But I think that since these are the easiest orbs to 'split' the effects of, I can safely satisfy my pathological desire to do good while still getting something out of it. Like how gainful employment is supposed to work." She ended the sentence with exaggeratedly optimistic cheer in her voice.

James snickered, but also told her, "I meant it, though. It's your orb, and you use it how you want. If we ever do get some kind of office that we use as a workshop and/or meeting place for planning, then I can see us tithing greens to it. But right now, it doesn't seem worth it. Unless one of them will literally keep the stuffed shirts from coming through the door."

"Hey, yeah. What if the dungeon sends more?" Anesh asked. "I don't want to give you an anxiety attack or anything, but what do we do about that?"

"Security system?" James mused. "We have those wireless cameras. Maybe set one of them up by the door and turn on motion detecting on the app? It's not too complicated."

That was something Anesh wished he'd thought of, though he was pretty happy James just had an answer to the problem. "All right. That's a start. We need a way to figure out if they're tracking *us*, or the *room*. Because if this wasn't a one-off, then we may have to move."

"I haaaate movinnnng," James whined. "Can't we just hire Alanna to sit in the living room and shoot anything that isn't supposed to be there?"

"I have reasonable rates!" Alanna said.

Anesh waved away the suggestion. "I'll consider it. I'll also consider that, since we think this one was 'starving,' and had been lying in wait for a while, it might be a one-off thing. Though it does tell us something horrifying."

"That Alanna already knows what she'd charge us to keep us alive?" James asked.

Anesh slowly held an outstretched finger up to James's lips, silencing him. "It tells us that the dungeon can send things outside itself."

"Are we back to assuming that the dungeon is a sentient thing now?" Alanna asked him with a sigh.

"No, but it does indicate some more organization. There's at least a faction in there that we're dealing with, right?" Anesh said. "The dungeon keeps changing as we go farther in, but it always looks like James's office, so it seems like it's just acting on instinct.

Or maybe isn't a 'person,' exactly. But the shirts and maybe the tumblefeeds seem to have some more organization. We should be aware of that."

James held up a hand to ask a question. "Hey, so, going back a step, you remember how I mentioned the blackhawks? Those only really started showing up after I had to make all those paper airplanes. Is it possible the dungeon is stealing ideas from us?"

It wasn't something that they'd ever really considered before. While it made sense that the dungeon continued to change, as it felt like more of a living place than a building, it wasn't something that they felt was guided. Just more effects of the random number generator.

"I think it's probably just . . . coincidence?" Anesh replied. "Maybe not the right word. But more that it's just copying what it has access to, right? Not an intelligent thing." He shrugged. "If it was doing it on purpose, I feel like they'd be murdering us."

"Good point," James said.

Suddenly struck by a different thought, Anesh redirected the conversation a bit. "Hey, going back a second, Alanna. You mentioned splitting up green orbs?"

Looking up from her phone and the dog gifs she'd been looking at, Alanna made a small confused humming noise, then processed what Anesh had said and answered. "Oh, yeah." It took her a second to think of how to explain it. "So, the yellows and blues, and probably also oranges? They all give everything to the person using them. The greens, though, from what you said, they give *you* skill points, and they also change the area around you. So, if you're looking to split an orb, and because none of us can figure out what the fuck Rufus is doing when he splits them, that's the easiest way to divide up the effects. At least, until we find more mixed orbs. The purple wasn't mixed, by the way."

"Mixed?" James cut in.

She nodded. "Yeah, like, the blues also have the effects of yellows in them. Same with the oranges and greens. Though the reds seem to be on their own, same with the purples. So I call them mixed. Honestly, now that we know the yellows actually do just provide power to things they're in, it's . . . probably just that? Like, they're a fuel source? Maybe not, though. Could be that different balances get different effects; like, the oranges need a certain amount of yellow in them to bend space in the right ways or something." Alanna said it like it was the most obvious thing in the world.

"I'm really annoyed that you appear to have put more thought into this than I have," Anesh griped. Alanna just smiled at him and blew him a mocking kiss.

"So, we need to start tracking orb mixes, huh? I bet that's why the huge yellow we have at the house is so weird-looking; we're seeing other colors under the surface, yeah?" James asked the questions back to back but didn't pause for answers. "I wonder if it'll have three or four effects attached. Actually, shit. I don't want any more of the red ones."

Alanna frowned a bit. "Why is that? Isn't it a good thing to understand an emotion more?"

"It's weird, but not that bad," James explained. "It's just that I feel like it's changing how I act, and I don't know if I'm comfortable with it? Like, I can more easily empathize with other people now, but in a way that pushes me to act on it. And yes, I see your face light up at that, but think about it from my perspective; that's basically an outside force rewriting my mind. And in a way that I can't get Secret to kill."

"Hm. Point," Alanna said. "I'd like to try some myself, though. See if that's just a special case or an always thing. We have more in Fort Door, yeah?" she asked Anesh.

He nodded slowly. "We do, though I don't know if Rufus was going to use them. He's been tending that little garden of his with a couple that we got. But we do have more, and we can always get extras from the burnouts or blast roasts."

"You guys spend way too much energy on the pun names," she muttered.

James and Anesh just smiled, and in unison gave her a "Thanks!"

The three of them sat there for a bit, thinking of what to say next. James finished up his cake and collected everything on the table. Alanna shivered a bit and wished she'd brought a coat; it wasn't quite actually summer yet, and the air had dropped in temperature dramatically over the course of their chat here.

"When's the last time we saw a movie?" Alanna mused out loud.

Anesh looked up from his phone, where he was checking on his class assignments. "What?"

"A movie. Or, like, hung out and played games together. Or talked about the news, or the world, or something that wasn't a glittering death trap?" she continued. "Don't get me wrong, I'm enjoying this whole thing. But the dungeon stuff has absolutely consumed our lives. A couple years ago, we'd be sitting here talking about plot holes in the Pokémon universe, or just discussing whatever philosophy book James most recently read. Now it's gear lists and survival tactics. We've turned our own lives into a simulation of how it would be to live in a postapocalyptic wasteland."

"That's an exaggeration, surely," Anesh said.

"Really?" Alanna asked. "Is it? Think about the last conversation we had, the last *real* conversation, that wasn't about James's office. And I've only been here for two weeks! How the hell have you two not burned out on this?"

"I spent a month out for recovery," Anesh responded. "Also, James is really, really into the whole 'risk and reward' thing. Though I see your point. We do need to make sure we still have lives." He sighed. "I moved here for college, but I'm starting to wonder if I even have the energy to get through *that*. It's exhausting, and the dungeon on top of it is really draining. Maybe for me, absorbing the yellows is so easy because it's what I need. Badly."

James, coming back, leaned down and perched himself on Anesh's head. "Aww. Buddy. I didn't realize how bad it was for you! You know you don't need to go delving with us, right? And, hell, you don't need to worry about rent anymore. Take care of yourself first, okay?" he told Anesh.

His roommate shook him off, but with a smile. "I appreciate that. But I *want* to go in with you guys. Maybe it has dominated our lives, but it's just so . . . fascinating! Everything about it is stupid and random and yet I just have to know where it all leads."

The other two nodded. They both understood, of course. Maybe it was a gamer thing, or maybe it was just the shared trait that made them all click as friends, but the desire to see what was around the next corner, to poke under all the rocks, was something they all had. And the dungeon offered so many opportunities to see new things and explore new ideas. Even if it was constantly trying to kill them.

"That does remind me," James said. "I want to check out the decision tree again. I want to see if it tells the future or is just guessing. Also, let's head back to the apartment. I need sleeeeep."

Anesh and Alanna stood up from their chairs to join him, Alanna stretching and Anesh brushing off the rear of his pants. "You'll have to explain how you plan to test that," Anesh said.

"By getting in bed," James replied with a perplexed tone.

Anesh didn't let him out of the headlock until a block later.

The three of them strolled down the quiet streets, lightly chatting and trying to avoid too much more dungeon talk. After a quick reminder from Alanna and a short diversion, though, they stood in front of a public elementary school. Alanna stood at the front of their group, holding up the green orb in her palm.

"So, do I have to be inside for this to work?" she asked.

"I hadn't considered that," James said. "I guess not? On the property, at least, though."

She nodded, and they walked through the opening in the chain-link fence onto the back field of the school. Past mowed grass and a dusty baseball dugout, until they were standing at the back door of the building, just past a playground. "All right, here goes nothing," Alanna said. "I'm sure as hell not breaking into a school right now, so let's see if this works." And she squeezed down on the emerald ball in her hand.

[Local Area Shift : Exercise efficiency, −280 kCal use/hour, +14% muscle development rate]

[+4 Skill Ranks : Juggling - Combat]

"I wonder if they'll let me bring a weight set here . . ." she murmured to herself with a smile.

After they got back to the apartment and Alanna headed home, James took the longest shower of his life. He had a lot of stuff to think about, and his frazzled brain didn't seem to really want to make any useful connections, so he just stood under the hot water and zoned out until he couldn't breathe through the steam filling the bathroom and was forced back to reality.

It wasn't until he was about to get back to his room that he realized they hadn't done anything with the body of the stuffed shirt, and he tactfully shut the door to Sarah's room. While he was still uncomfortable as all hell to have the corpse just lying there on the floor, at least it wasn't going to get up in the middle of the night and strangle him. Especially not now that he'd had that thought, and wouldn't be sleeping. Ever again.

He texted Alanna about helping him dispose of the body the next day, and she just sent him back fire emojis until he gave up and muted his phone.

Flopping back on his bed, he stared up at the ceiling, just letting himself drift off to sleep and process the events of the day. That is, until he felt a small poking at his arm and looked down to see that Lily had crawled up onto the blankets with him.

He smiled a bit and reached down to pet the iLipede that he'd kidnapped and/or adopted, depending on your viewpoint. And while doing so, he noticed that a certain progress bar had finally completed, and there was a notification on the screen. Squealing with delight, he opened up the app to look at exactly what it was that the giant yellow orb on his floor had been identified as. Though he was less interested in the results, and more just super excited that after he showed Anesh, he'd be able to finally crack it for himself, and become . . . well, he didn't really know, did he? God of Making Sandwiches Really Good or something, probably.

James's eyes fell on the words on the screen. It took him a few seconds to understand what he had just read, and then a few more to process it.

And then he stumbled out of his door back into the hallway. Brushing Anesh aside, he lurched into the bathroom and vomited up the remains of his cake, a sickening twisted feeling burning itself in the pit of his stomach and at the back of his mind. He vaguely registered Anesh saying something to him, asking if he was okay. He felt his friend's hands on his head, checking his temperature, and squeezing his shoulders, holding him up. James couldn't respond, though. He could barely stay standing, braced on the bathroom counter. He realized he *hadn't* stayed standing, and he was sitting on the bathroom floor. Anesh said something else, care and concern painted on his face.

He was asking what was wrong.

James couldn't answer. He just held up Lily, still squirming in his grasp, and showed Anesh the screen.

The orb had been scanned. Identified. Thoroughly examined. And the little phone bug had given them a simple output for all those weeks of work.

[Power unit type : Personal. Operational time : 15,670 hrs/1k. Contains : Jerome.]

Anesh dropped Lily back in James's lap.

All he could think to say was, "Well. Bollocks."

CHAPTER 2

James lurched forward, landing hands-first on the oddly smooth concrete sidewalk without pain. Jerking himself upward, he staggered backward, vision suddenly clear and unobscured by panicked tears. Whipping his head around, he saw only gray. Gray buildings, gray roads, gray street signs and fences and vending machines and sky. He felt like his heart should be racing, his breathing should be labored, but instead, even his own body felt gray. Bland. Normal to the extreme.

"It's not that bad, you know." A voice came floating through the gray air to him.

James turned and saw Secret standing at the end of the street. He looked different than normal; instead of his own customized copy of James's own face, it was more like he was wearing that body as a shirt. The rest of him, the parts that James didn't normally talk to, drifted behind the human shape. Scales and fins and teeth, wearing a James-shaped mask.

"What do you mean?" he asked calmly. He tried to scream it, tried to demand answers. But his voice came out placid. "What's going on here?" he inquired, curious. His curiosity hadn't taken a hit at all.

Secret shrugged, and the motion rippled down the body extending behind his visage. "I am keeping you calm," he said. "You were panicking. I didn't want you to injure yourself."

"This is a dream," James said, suddenly realizing. "This is the city you were building." He looked about a bit more, at the buildings without definition or color.

There was a pause that lasted a lifetime before the response came. "This is not a dream," Secret said. "You are not exactly asleep. A human would have blacked out. You, though, have come here. I was not expecting company." He gestured with a hand and a fin, displaying his current state, as if to apologize.

James sighed and sat down on a bus stop bench. "Damn. I'm sorry. Thanks for taking over my heart rate, though," he said. "What do you mean it's not that bad?"

Secret took a seat next to him, somehow fitting eight thousand pounds of deep-sea monster comfortably on the seat in a way that confused James's brain. If he'd been awake, it would have been an optical illusion or an orange orb. If he'd been truly asleep, dream logic would have kept him from worrying. But now, his only real defense against the twisted physics here was to just look away. He figured it was only polite; he'd caught Secret half-dressed, after all.

"You are concerned about the lives in the orbs," Secret said. "You think you've been eating your fellows."

"More or less," James said. "Well, that, and the fact that the large orbs only drop from the ones that look human. Guess I know what happened to all those coworkers, huh? That's the part that really bothers me. I know the creatures in the office aren't stupid, but these ones used to be *people*." He folded his hands on his lap, resisting the anxious urge to pull on his own fingers. "I don't want to be a killer."

Secret nodded. "I understand. The brothers that I have killed while with you have been unenlightened. I mourn the need for it, but they were not like you or me. You do not wish to think you have taken a higher life."

His words cut through to the core of James's worry and fear. "Yeah," he said simply, not knowing how to respond, and caught off guard by the strangely elegant words from his internal companion.

"You are, I have decided, a good person," Secret said abruptly. It shocked James a bit. He wasn't used to thinking of himself as a good person. He tried to do the right thing whenever he could, tried to be kind and caring, tried to be the sort of person that his dad would be proud of. But he never felt like a *good person*. In saying that, Secret cut straight into the core of his fear: that he had done something inexcusable. For some reason, the approval of the memetic life form pretending to be sitting next to him mattered to James. A lot.

He looked up, making eye contact with his friend. Actual eye contact, not just with the shell. "Thank you," James said, quietly but with real weight behind the words. "But it doesn't change the fact that those are people."

"Ah." Secret pronounced the word strangely. Of all the things he'd acquired from James lately, understanding of that particular word was not one of them, and he said it letter by letter. James didn't have time to find it weird, though, as he launched into an explanation. "Those things were not once persons. Like every other life within the expanse, they are awoken with power. Much more power than would be used, for example, to awaken one like my maker. But power nonetheless."

"Your . . . oh, Rufus. Right." James remembered where Secret had come from. "So, they're just creations?"

"Just?" Secret turned one of his real eyes to James. "Every living thing is just a creation. Even you," he said. "We grow up, eventually." If there was a hint of anger in his voice, it faded as he continued. "Yes, though. They are newly minted. No hint of a ghost or a person within them."

James would have flushed red with embarrassment at accidentally degrading Secret, if he weren't still being held in forced calm. "Sorry," he said simply, but honestly. "Also, sorry that I told the others about the blue orb you helped with. I didn't realize until after that you were feeding on that."

Secret smiled with both mouths and shrugged. "It is of no concern. There is food aplenty in your heart. I have found a secret that you insist on keeping even from yourself. It keeps me fed and strong."

Well, that was something James wasn't expecting to hear. "What . . ." he started to ask, and then stopped himself. He didn't need to know, probably. If it was actually dangerous, Secret would just tell him. So he decided to trust him for now. "Never mind. I'm glad you're staying healthy," he settled on saying. "What about the orbs, though? Why did Lily identify it as a person's name? And someone I used to work with, too."

"He may still have been lost to the expanse," Secret said sadly. "Or perhaps it is simply a copy of the idea of that person. I am still young, and have only seen as much as you have. But we may yet find out together, if you can handle future truths with more grace."

Again, James was glad he couldn't blush. Despite being orders of magnitude older than Secret, he felt like he was in the principal's office. And, appropriately enough, he was getting schooled on how to drop casual burns on people.

Feeling a small tug from somewhere outside himself, James looked up at the sky. It was still gray, but with a small splotch of blue and green near the horizon. "I think that's my cue to wake up," he said, standing up from the bench. He looked over at Secret. "Hey, thanks. Again. Really." He took a breath and felt his chest move, inside and out. "I had a question, though, before I go. You're clearly learning more about talking; why are you talking like a character from a high fantasy book?"

This got a wide, fanged smile from Secret. "Because this is how you wish you spoke, all the time," he said, as James opened his eyes.

"Fuck, that makes too much sense" was the first thing James said when he woke up. He was in his bed, and it was pretty comfortable. He considered just going back to sleep but decided he needed to talk to Anesh first before doing so. Just to apologize to his friend for freaking the hell out on him.

Rolling out of bed, he noticed that Lily was back in her pen, but the orb was gone. He also noticed that he'd been undressed at some point, which was either more or less concerning. James didn't have time to decide right now.

Throwing on some sweatpants, he walked out into the hall and peeked into Anesh's room. His friend was currently awake and doing something on his laptop. From the look on his face, it could have been either math that would make James question his place in the universe, or losing at StarCraft to someone half his age. They had very similar facial cues.

"Hey," he said, announcing himself. "I'm up."

Anesh turned to him, leaning back in his plush desk chair. "You weren't out long. Are you okay?" he asked, worry lacing his voice. The ease with which he broke his focus on the monitor made James think that either it was homework after all, or that he was more important to Anesh than a game of StarCraft, which was pretty flattering.

"Yeah, I'm doing better. Secret talked to me a bit about it. He's growing into a pretty Zen guy in here." James tapped his forehead. "Not sure where he gets it from."

His roommate raised a single eyebrow. "I see. So, you're not going to freak out? Even though we've been stealing memories from other humans?"

James slumped against the doorframe. "That's where my mind went too, though apparently I reacted a bit stronger than you. I blame the fact that I was tired," he said, justifying it weakly. "But no. I don't really know how to explain it the way Secret did, but they're not exactly parts of other people. I'm not sure exactly what they *are*, and neither is he, I don't think, but we're both interested in finding out."

"Okay," Anesh said, "as long as you're doing all right. I don't want to have you retching all over the bathroom again every time we have to fight a suit."

"Onetime thing, I promise," James said, raising his hand in an oath taker's gesture. "Oh, on that note, thank you for cleaning up. I'm sorry I was out. Although . . . did you take my pants off?"

James had never seen someone with skin as dark as Anesh's blush quite that shade of red. It made him look almost copper as he looked up at the ceiling to avoid eye contact. "I had to wash your clothes too, since you ruined them! I wasn't trying to be weird about it or anything!" he stammered.

It was hard for James not to laugh at that. "Jesus, man. That's the most anime thing I've ever seen you do. Relax, I'm not mad." He stifled a yawn. "Anyway, I need to go sleep for real. Good night. And... thanks again. Really."

"Of course," Anesh said with a small smile. "Sleep well."

James ducked out, then poked his head back in for one last thought. "Oh, vaguely related to that. Apparently, Secret literally feeds off secrets. So, now that I've ruined the one about the blue orb absorby thing for him, can you think of anything that we could have as a replacement secret? I want to do something nice for him."

Anesh blinked, trying to process the rapid-fire sentence James had just said that included the word *secret* too many times. "Um... how about we keep it between us what his food source is, and promise not to tell JP or Alanna? Would that work?"

"I... think so?" James said. He looked to the side, half opening his mouth to say something and then closing it as he thought. "If nothing else, maybe he can snack on the abstract concept of irony that's going to produce. Okay. Thanks! G'night, friend." And with that, he headed back to his own bed to collapse.

Anesh sighed. "Well, that was productive," he muttered to himself. While he cared about James quite a lot, he was a bit frustrated with how his friend could so easily jump to the worst possible conclusion for everything in his life. This wasn't the first time, though it was the most dramatic so far. Every missed call from an unknown number could have been a family member dying, every time he was ten minutes late to work he was going to get fired, that sort of thing. Anesh knew that James had pretty bad depression, so he tried to be as understanding as possible, but it made it hard to talk to him about stuff like this sometimes. Still, though, it was good to know that Secret was being a good influence. If James continued to stubbornly refuse to get on any kind of antidepressant, maybe the living meme in his brain could tweak some of his biological processes instead.

Anesh shook his head as he tried to figure out how to have a one-on-one chat with an entity that lived literally inside someone else. He gave up on that after about ten seconds, and with an exasperated huff went back to his game of StarCraft. Which he was now losing.

Over the next several days, a lot of stuff piled up in their living room. Boxes arrived for various things purchased off the internet. A few new suits of body armor, one of them properly sized for Alanna. Several individual packages with different helmets in the sizes and formats of everyone's preference. A pair of heavy steel cases with flare guns in them at one point materialized on their table, along with a more modern-looking box of flares. James and JP kept working on and testing (outdoors) the new potato gun, until it was both complete and a little more protected against spontaneous explosions, and that got added to the pile.

Alanna became a more permanent presence at their apartment, too. She was there when James woke up and there when he came back from work. She was also there when her warhammer was delivered, and spent a good deal of time out in the field near the apartment practicing with it. The hammer, about a meter and a half of weapon, topped with a head that was half studded hammer, half curved spike for those things that required a bit more piercing power, fit her hands almost perfectly, and she quickly started to develop solid aim with it. James was concerned that she was a bit too filled with restless energy, what with her sudden onset of joblessness; he was also amused that it seemed like her primary motivation was more that she just wanted to mooch off his food.

And he was finding it was a lot of fun to cook for his friends. Of all the skills he'd acquired, the ability to make food, to find his way around the kitchen and understand recipes and know flavor profiles, that was the most valuable to him so far.

Well, that or the martial arts. He was really starting to enjoy the kinetic feeling of motion in his own body.

Other stuff started showing up as well, further cluttering their living room. Alanna acquired a set of folding bikes for them to bring in: lightweight, compact, and stacked against a wall in a way that was still adding to the growing amount of things they'd have to take in. Someone (James assumed it was Anesh but couldn't be sure) also got them a flat platform cart that they could use to transport all of it. Bonus use, it could also be used to vastly increase their effective load in the dungeon. James had a feeling he was going to need to pay Frank again to get it into the elevator at work, though.

About a dozen new backpacks showed up too, in varying sizes. Along with proper canteens, and harnesses for the armor that had about a thousand clips and slots to hold things. Dave also brought them lunch boxes that they could use to have . . . lunches. Eight hours was a long time to go with only snacking on randomized candy.

James sighed as he looked at his kitchen table. There were currently two spools of copper wire on it that he had *no* idea where they came from, next to a counting machine for dollar bills and the lunch boxes. Piled next to that were about thirty small USB drives that James had picked up for cheap, opting to keep any weird files they found quarantined to their own devices. In the back corner sat a compact electric pressure washer that had been purchased with the last of the group funds, along with two full carboys of water, ready to go. Everything was coming together, everyone was preparing themselves, and he felt really bad that the only thing he could think was that his apartment had never looked messier.

He'd talk to Anesh about getting an actual office space of their own to base their operations out of later.

They'd given up on building a shield for any of themselves after the one they were trying to make for Alanna just . . . didn't hold up. It was weirdly demoralizing to have one part of their whole operation fail, when everything else was going as planned, but Anesh just shrugged, made a note to allocate some funds to going shopping at the next Renaissance faire that was around the area, and kicked everyone back out of their moping.

And then they had a special box. It only had a few things in it, but it was the heaviest on James's mind. A pair of shades, a Nerf gun, a pen, nothing too important to look at, but it was duct-taped shut and meant to not be tampered with or lost in any way until they were back in the dungeon and ready to use what it contained. They'd tested the Nerf gun with regular darts and been disappointed to find that it didn't work. But they still had five more shots with it, and any one of them could save their lives.

That box sat on the flat cart, on top of a longer, flatter, plastic case, which contained Alanna's final contribution to their operation. Her Mossberg 590 shotgun, the sleek metal weapon sitting comfortably in its foam-padded case. A couple boxes of twelve-gauge slugs next to it declaring its intent to be the final line of defense for Fort Door in the event that they ran into too many stuffed shirts to handle. Or, worst-case scenario, something bigger.

And finally, one collapsible metal rod. The iconic ten-foot pole that every good dungeon-delving group needed.

James finished making his sandwich on the kitchen counter and made his way back to his room. It was a rare moment of quiet compared to the last week, and he was planning to sit down, eat his food, watch some random stuff on YouTube, and relax. Deep breaths and inner peace were his plan for the night.

Because tomorrow was Monday. And after the end of his shift at work, it was going to be Tuesday.

And then they were going in.

Ready or not, dungeon, James thought. *Here we come.*

CHAPTER 3

"Alanna, wake up," Anesh said, kicking at the couch in his living room. The couch itself was that smooth, not-quite-leather substance that made for great padding but was never quite right to sleep on. It didn't hold heat that well, Anesh thought, so it was always just a little too cold, no matter how many blankets you bundled up in on it.

Which is why he was a bit surprised to see Alanna asleep on it when he came out to the living room.

She was sprawled out on the couch, still fully dressed. Anesh hadn't heard her come in, so she must have shown up while he was doing homework and decided to take a nap before the delve. But right now, she was taking the nap a bit too far. He kicked the couch again, getting an unsatisfying thump as the pillows dispersed the shock more than he wanted. "Alanna! Time to go!" he said a bit louder.

She rolled over, pushing her face into the corner of the couch. "Fuck off. M'sleeping" were the words that came out of her temporary bed. Anesh didn't relent, though. He grabbed one of the cushions she was lying on and dragged it out, making a hole in her formation that gave Alanna no choice but to try to readjust. And doing so was enough to get her to open her eyes and sit up. "Ugh. Why?" she muttered.

"Because it's two thirty a.m., we're on a schedule, and we need to go. I thought you were going to get there yourself, but now I find you in my living room, so, are you coming?" he asked her. Anesh had, luckily, had a late day with his classes. So he'd slept in and was feeling bright-eyed and energized even at this late hour. He was pretty sure that he'd be more than able to make it through the dungeon tonight without falling asleep. Though he'd actually thought ahead and added a couple cots to their supply list, so that Fort Door could expand into a miniature hotel if any of them needed to nap.

But now, despite being ready to go, despite having prepared everything and loaded the car earlier, and even made fresh coffee to bring along, he found he was still waiting for Alanna to open her eyes all the way.

"Yeah. Yeah." She stayed sitting on the edge of the couch, eyes mostly closed, as if considering falling back asleep. "Sorry. I can . . . I can get up." It looked for a minute as if that would be a lie, but after a long pause, Alanna did manage to haul herself to her feet.

Anesh just shook his head. "How can it possibly be comfortable sleeping in jeans? It's warm enough that I feel too hot and I'm wearing shorts."

"S'not comfortable. I'm just tired," Alanna responded. "I'm gonna use your bathroom, then I'll be ready to go."

"Okay," Anesh told her, opening the front door. "Don't take too long. I'll meet you in my car."

He took his time heading down the wooden steps of the apartment building, the green paint chipped and flaking off in places. The complex was kept up-to-date internally, with all the apartments having modern appliances and no cut corners on basic construction, but the exterior always had this feeling to Anesh of just being a little rundown. Like no one ever had the time or energy to spend just making the stairs look nice. He supposed he couldn't blame the apartment maintenance guys for that; they really were overworked around here. But it was weird to think, as he made his way to his car carrying the thermoses of coffee, that he could tell what step he was on blindfolded by the feeling of the chips in it.

Waiting in his car, a old sedan that never stopped smelling a little odd and that was probably constructed before he was born, Anesh spent the next few minutes fiddling with the radio before settling on the local jazz station just as Alanna opened the passenger door and climbed in. She didn't even say anything, just fired a disappointed look at the radio and immediately started flipping through preset stations herself. Anesh glared at her but found it more amusing than anything else and didn't make a big deal of it.

Hitting the road, the two of them sat in companionable silence for a while as Alanna fully woke up. It didn't take long, driving down dark streets mostly empty of cars, lit only by the orange glow of the streetlights, for Anesh to hit the highway. As they were merging from the on-ramp, Alanna decided to break the silence that had been filling the car.

"So, are we going to get there on time?" she asked him. It wasn't an aggressive question, but it did mildly bother Anesh.

He flicked his eyes over to look at her, just to check if she was being serious or just screwing with him. "We are going to get there on time, yes."

Alanna made an affirmative noise in her throat. "Right, right. I just ask because you've been going *exactly the speed limit* this whole time, and I didn't want you to think you were, you know, required to for my benefit. I don't mind if you open it up."

"First of all," Anesh started, indignant, "it's a small miracle that this car made it up to fifty-five at all. Second, and more important, we wouldn't be running late if it wasn't a 'we.' Why were you sleeping on our couch to begin with?" he asked her, blocking her probing question with his own.

"I was tired, obviously," Alanna retorted, deflecting his question with a nonanswer. She let out a short laugh as she felt Anesh's displeasure with that answer, before turning serious. "But . . . um . . . no. I was just trying to not be at home for a while."

"Oh," Anesh sheepishly replied as he flicked his turn signal to show the empty road that he planned to leave it. "Do you . . . want to talk about it?"

It was amazing that someone like Alanna, who most of the time seemed seven feet tall and made out of two hundred pounds of steel, could look small, sitting there in his passenger seat. "I don't know," she said. "I mean, I don't know what I'm fucking doing. I'm responsible for taking care of three other humans, and one of them hates me, and one of them is my mother, and those two people are the same person. And now, I can't be at work all day, but I still have to explain that we can still eat, but I'm not a sex worker. So I'm taking your couch sometimes, yeah."

"Bloody hell," Anesh muttered, leaning back into his seat as they waited for a uselessly red light. There was another silence now, this one less comfortable and more tense. "I don't know what to say. 'I'm sorry' doesn't seem good enough here." He chewed on his own lip for a minute. "You're welcome over anytime you need, though. And if the couch isn't comfortable, we know we have an extra bed."

Anesh pulled the car into one of the parking spaces outside the office building James worked in. Putting it in park and killing the engine, he checked the time—still on track, a good forty minutes before they needed to be at the door. So he didn't move to get out, and neither did Alanna, and they just sat there together for a bit. "I'm not sleeping in the haunted bed," she told him wryly.

"Oh, come on. It's probably not haunted. Besides, isn't the whole point of this that Sarah might actually be alive? Or at least . . . recoverable?" he asked, grimly.

"Recoverable?" Alanna tasted the word and found it strange. "James told me that the huge orb from the shirt was 'identified' as a person. Do you have some kind of plan to . . . try to bring it back?"

Anesh didn't make eye contact as he answered, "Nope. Also it's *named* like a person, but . . . if you build a table and name it Shivam, that doesn't make it alive. At least, that is how I understand it." He looked up at the stars through his windshield. "But still. The room is there. And from everything we know . . . I don't think Sarah would mind you using it. At least, the person we think she was." His voice was heavy with melancholy. "It's so daft, to know that I have this person-shaped hole in my life, and not be able to see the edges of it."

She tilted back her head to look up at the sky as well. "Yeah. Did you notice that we didn't find any pictures of her in that room? But I found more than a few of me. I looked . . . happy. Or at least amused. And I don't remember those moments. It really pisses me off."

"Of course it does," Anesh said with a grin. Then, after a pause, he added, "James really does think we can get her back. Along with anyone else the dungeon has in it."

Alanna snorted. "James has a paladin complex the size of some small countries. But, well, shit, I get it. This place is seeming less like a treasure trove, and more like the kind of bullshit monster that you tend to cook up for D&D night."

Clearing his throat, Anesh started to say something, then decided to *not* tell Alanna that the genius loci was right there in the *Monster Manual*. Instead, he changed tracks. "Maybe you're right. We do need to keep an eye on it, for sure." He opened his door and started to swing his legs out of the car. "Now, help me get allllll this stuff onto the pallet so we can get it inside. I don't want to be late because we dragged our heels getting too philosophical."

"Getting philosophical is probably the best reason I can think of to be late," Alanna responded as they opened the trunk. Looking at the mass of gear in the back of Anesh's car, she whistled quietly. "Holy shit, this is just a big ol' pile of stuff, isn't it?"

The two of them manhandled out the pallet, attaching the cart handle to it, then began the process of stacking boxes and cases on top of it. With the exception of the cots, which were safely in their own wrappings, they'd decided to box up most of the stuff just so it wasn't quite so suspicious. In theory, only one person was going to see them drag this mountain of material through the door, but just in case, it was probably for the best to not have to answer questions about why they had two hundred feet of rope and a flare gun in an office.

The weight of the cart made navigating the entrance to the office tricky. There were stairs, which were useless. But the access ramp was a strangely long and curved path that cut through the manicured lawn on the right of the stairs. The maneuvering of the cart took them minutes that were quickly becoming precious as the opening of the breach came closer and closer.

"Good evening, sir," Anesh said to Frank as Alanna held the doors open for him and he dragged the cart in.

Frank, with his eternal gray five o'clock shadow and endless cup of coffee, looked up from his crossword. Well, he tilted his head slightly. That kind of attention was essentially full focus from Frank. Alanna also waved at him and smiled. "Hey, Frank. How's the night going?"

"M. Patel. F. Byrne. Stay out of trouble," Frank said, dropping his eyes back to his paper as the two younger people wheeled four hundred pounds of various weaponry and survival tools across the lobby and over to the main elevator bank. He wasn't chastising them, or even warning them. The way he dropped the words was simply that he was informing them that trouble, such as the sort that would require him to stand up, wasn't permissible tonight.

And they were totally fine with that.

As the elevator doors closed, Alanna tilted her head and quietly whispered to Anesh, "Do you find it weird that he knows our last names?"

"I find it weird that you're whispering. He can't hear you," Anesh replied. "I find it more strange that he used Asimov's gendered honorifics. Wait, doesn't he just call James 'Jim' all the time? What is that wanker even doing?"

"You can't prove he can't hear us," Alanna stage-whispered as the elevator doors opened.

They stashed the cart in the hallway, right across from the stairwell doors. Originally, Anesh wanted them to put it in the stairwell itself, but Alanna had pointed out that, if they were even a minute late, they wouldn't be able to retrieve it, short of looping around to get it from inside, taking the elevator down and then running back up the stairs from below.

That had led to the conversation about how they didn't really know what happened if someone tried to come through the door from the other side when it wasn't a door. Did they end up on the other side of the miles-long "exterior" wall that their group always entered from? Did the door just not open? Did it lead somewhere else entirely?

"We should test that sometime," Anesh had said.

"We should maybe not risk being vaporized," Alanna had replied.

It was a fair concern, even if it was mostly unfounded. After all, it wasn't a risk when they went through the door this direction.

Alanna brought up that it was more likely that, since the door itself seemed to be the focus of the warped time, it probably just shunted anyone trying to get through the other way a few minutes in one direction or another. Which would have been reassuring, if Anesh didn't realize that would constitute legitimate time travel. Which was a bit of a problem if it ever moved someone back in time.

"It probably doesn't," Alanna had said. "I'm just guessing, after all." But it was too late, and the seed of worry was planted in Anesh's mind.

They waited in the break room, Anesh getting more and more fidgety as they counted down the minutes to the delve. At thirty minutes to entrance, JP and Dave showed up together and joined them. At fifteen, James finally strolled in.

JP gave him a mock salute as he entered. "We were worried about you," he said. "You weren't in the slave pits."

"You mean at my desk, where a normal employee goes?" James said. "No, I was in the bathroom. A place I recommend you all visit before we go into a realm devoid of common toilets for the next eight hours."

JP and Anesh snorted with laughter, but that didn't stop Anesh and Alanna from both standing and going to take the suggestion. Dave, meanwhile, just gave James a weird look. "Why are you talking like a character from a fantasy novel?" he asked.

"Don't question me, acolyte," James snapped back with a smile.

Exactly seventeen minutes later, five people and one flat cart left their reality for one of too-tall ceilings and burning fluorescent lights.

"Okay! Recap!" Anesh took charge as they dragged the cart in and the door shut behind them, setting an alarm clock down on the desk with a seven-hour timer on it. With no more connection to the real office, there was no more need to keep voices down or constantly check over their shoulders for actual employees or managers. There was, of course, still a need to not alert the whole dungeon they were there, and to check over their shoulders for fake employees, but that was a problem for outside of Fort Door. Anesh was more interested in getting everything sorted, getting everyone geared up, and getting moving. "Dave, Alanna, you're on the cart! JP, grab that hand truck and help me get a couple desks in here that we can use for these maps! James!" James looked up with a half-surprised expression. Looking at his roommate, fresh off an eight-hour shift at work, Anesh rethought what he was going to say, and instead went with "Go say hi to Rufus."

James smiled and clapped Anesh on the shoulder as he walked in to find his strider friend.

Rufus was waiting on the desk where he'd set up his little "garden." "Hey, friend," James greeted the stapler as he walked up. "Got a crop coming in?" He said it half jokingly and got a bit of surprise when Rufus bobbed his head in agreement. "Oh?"

He looked down, and Rufus moved back, sweeping a pen leg out to show off his plot. He had some makeshift planters, made up of actual regular staplers and a couple of bulky gray office phones. Their edges kept in a sea of loose staples and paper clips, into which James was sure Rufus had planted those strange, fractal balls of staples that he'd been moving around a few delves ago. Out of the mess of metal, though, something was growing. It looked like a tangle of USB cables, black plastic bunched together in three places throughout the garden. In the middle of one of them, poking up to the sky, a single copper wire had sprouted.

"This is really something, buddy," James said to Rufus. "I have no idea if it's good or not, but you got something to grow without, you know, dirt or water or sun. So I'm impressed, but also terrified as to what this actually is." Rufus shook himself, and James got the impression he was simultaneously being told not to worry, and also that the strider had no idea what dirt was. "Well, I just wanted to say hi while everyone else did hard work. I should really go get ready for the delve. Are you coming along tonight?"

Rufus thought about it, blinking slowly with his one sparkling yellow eye. He'd not thought about it, since he hadn't really been asked before. Eventually, though, he settled on crossing his forelegs in front of himself. *Not tonight,* he was saying. *But thank you.*

While James and Rufus caught up, Ganesh simply alighted on Anesh's shoulder. The sudden soft weight of the drone was a feeling he'd grown used to, after so many hours in here, and it was a comforting presence to know that he had his smaller counterpart here with him. The relationship between Anesh and Ganesh was a little more stoic than James's with Rufus, but all the same, he reached up a hand to give a small pat to his companion, and the drone in turn gave him a bobbing nod of appreciation.

Distraction handled, Anesh went back to their plan for the night. He'd brought in Sarah's map, and the idea was that he, Alanna, and JP would go scout out the path to the restrooms, while James and Dave went another direction on a general exploration run. They didn't really know if the route was safe, but it was more or less complete and had some notes on traps. It also had a date annotated next to it, as did many other parts of the map, and the bathrooms were the last place that it looked like Sarah had gone while on her own delves.

James had been more than eager to take the whole group there first. It hadn't taken a lot of effort to calm him down, really, but there was a discussion about it. JP himself was the one who reminded him that he and Dave just didn't have the experience yet, let alone any game-changing skills like James himself had, and that they needed time to get their feet here before they went off on a rescue operation. Reluctantly, James agreed, and he and Dave ended up strapping on armor and equipment before the others, planning to stagger their disembarkation times so that they'd be able to call for help if things went bad too quickly.

While James and Dave mock-argued over who got to carry the flare gun, and JP exasperatedly tried to resolve their "argument," Alanna was examining the map. She knew Anesh had been studying it, but hadn't taken the time to do so herself. And one thing jumped out right away that bothered her. "Hey, did you see the dates on here?"

"Yes," Anesh said shortly, dragging the two folded-up cots over to stack near the front fort wall. "It's something we need to start doing. Or at least, keeping a good timeline."

"No, I mean, did you actually look at the dates themselves?" Alanna clarified.

Anesh sighed. "What did I miss?" he asked, defeated.

"These are too close together." Alanna pulled out her phone and brought up the calendar, doing some quick checking. "Yeah, none of these are on Tuesdays. They're all, assuming they're correct, either Friday or Sunday."

"Well, shit," Anesh said. "I'm getting tired of saying that. So, at least three breaches, then?"

"Four. No way she was using the one in the vents."

He shuddered. "Yeah, this place is getting more and more worrying." Anesh already knew that James had found a second breach into the dungeon. But it was a small one, and it was in a really awkward place. No matter what the dungeon felt like doing, it probably wasn't going to have an easy time sending an army through the air vents unnoticed. This wasn't *Die Hard*, after all. But if Sarah's map was to be believed, then there were not one but *two* more openings that a human could reasonably get through. Or at least, one that was open on two different days.

It was looking more and more like they really had lucked into the dungeon's back door.

"So," Alanna said, "what do we do about this?"

Anesh sighed. "Nothing? No, that's not quite right. We keep delving, we do it as safely as possible, and we learn more. Also, we should set up a contingency in case we . . . get lost." He couldn't bring himself to say *die*.

"Nice euphemism," Alanna growled. She wasn't angry at him, though, just annoyed that the whole place was turning out a lot less fun than was originally pitched to her. "How, though? If this place takes us, won't it just wipe all the memories of us, like Sarah?"

"Terrifying," Anesh deadpanned. "We'll have to think of something this week. Maybe just an email set to send if we don't stop it. Can't think who we'd aim it at, though." He looked up toward the entrance to the fort. "All right, looks like James and Dave are ready to go. Want to go make sure they didn't screw up their armor before we see them off?"

"Sure," his friend replied, standing up and dusting off her knees from where she'd been crouched on the ground on the other side of the desk.

Strolling over to the front, the two got there just in time to see JP present James with the flare gun, and for the latter to clip the holster for it to the belt clip on the armor. "I'm giving it to him because he's not going to . . . well, he's less likely to fire it off just for fun," JP told Dave.

"Yesssss," James hissed out. "All right, Davey, ready to go? I've got a tree to show you."

"I have no idea what that means," Dave told him, suspicious.

James nodded. "I know. It's going to be a great surprise. But not a lethal one! I promise!" He turned to Anesh and Alanna. "You guys are gonna give us a fifteen-minute lead time, right?"

"Yeah." Alanna nodded. "We're gonna unpack all the gear and sort it out properly. What are you taking, anyway?"

James looked down at the utility webbing that was layered over his armor. "The standard stuff. I've also got coffee and rope and stuff in the backpack. Oh, and the thermite 'grenades.'"

"Not taking the potato gun? You spent so long on it!" JP asked him, surprised. "And broke your wall."

He shrugged. "Nah. I mean, it's cool, but Anesh"—he nodded at his friend—"says that the impact triggers were kinda risky. So these ones just have timers on them." He gestured over at Dave. "I'm also making him carry a lot of stuff. Leaving the ten-foot pole for you guys, though. It only seems fair."

"How . . ."

"I don't really have a great reason, I just didn't want to carry yet more stuff. Besides, you guys are going to have the cart you can take with you, so you can loot a hell of a lot better," James replied.

Alanna slapped her forehead. "Oh shit, I didn't even think of that! We can steal so much stuff!" she exclaimed with joy.

"*Besides* that," James continued, "I'm taking the pen, and a couple of our saved blues. For emergencies."

"Seems fair. Well, you two have fun. Don't let Dave get killed." Anesh patted him on the armored shoulder one last time and gave James a smile.

The two groups said their final goodbyes and good-lucks then, and Dave and James turned to march off to the right. James really wanted to go see the Decision Tree again, and he also wanted to be the one to show it off to someone new, so that was his plan for introducing Dave to their tactics and basic survival tricks in the dungeon. A quick trip out and back, and then they'd regroup and make a plan for the second half of the night.

Easy as breathing.

James felt the breath flee his lungs as he was slammed back into the desk. Fortunately, his head missed the shelves with their carefully and arbitrarily arranged file folders and supplies and, on one of them, a small terrarium. Pain started to leak through as the small of his back turned into one singular angry bruise.

He'd been slammed back through the door of one of the cubicles, and it took him a second to realign his brain. What the fuck had hit him? One minute, he was showing Dave the standard procedure for looting a desk and discussing methods of identifying magic items, and the next, the pencil sharpener on that same desk had fired to life. But instead of trying to buzzsaw through their fingers, it had simply disgorged a cloud of shaving and dust, throwing up a blinding screen that left the two of them coughing and covering their eyes as they stumbled out into the hallway.

Then James had been clipped by something heavy, moving at high speed.

Coughing, trying to drag in a breath as his body refused to relax his diaphragm, James staggered back to a standing position. His hand went down for the hatchet clipped to his belt, while the other one fumbled open a case that he'd had tucked in a pouch, pulling out the contents and discarding the case itself. With the axe in one hand and the pen in the other, he lurched forward, out into the hallway.

Dave was flat on the ground on the other side of the hall. The cloud of smoke and pencil shavings had cleared up, but there was no sign of what had hit either of them. James ducked over, tapping Dave on the shoulder. "Hey, hey! Are you alive?"

"Ow" was the reply. "Aaaahhh fuck. Fuck! What was that?!" Dave half yelled, grabbing at his ankle. "I think it knocked my brains out. And I sprained my ankle again."

"Okay, that's bad," James said. "Good thing you had the helmet on. Also, did you see what it was?"

Dave shook his head. "It felt metal, though. I tried to grab it, and it felt metal. Hit at about waist height."

"That narrows it down. Couldn't have been a tumblefeed, at least. Can you stand?" He set his axe down and offered Dave a hand up. His friend took a minute to test how much weight could go on his leg. "Okay, can you run?"

"Probably," Dave said. "It's not that bad." He winced as he stood up fully. "Hurts. How come I keep getting hurt here?" he asked.

James shrugged. "We get hurt here sometimes. It's the price we pay for candy and skill points. Okay, watch that way down the hall, I'll keep an eye behind us. Let's find a safe cube to sit in."

The two of them moved, not quite in perfect sync, but staying close together and both on high alert. Dave, having listened to some of James's advice over the course of the last half hour, was checking the cubicles as they passed by. The first one he ignored. There were three lamps on the desk; that was too obvious even for him. The second one he paused at, and James half bumped into him when he stalled to look through it. But seeing the computer tower on the desk shudder and shift itself in its sleep, he decided to abandon that one as well. At the third cube, he tapped James on the shoulder, and the two of them ducked in to take a respite.

"This is way more tense than I was expecting," Dave told him. He was already sweating in the armor, and his brain felt like it was totally burned out. "How do you guys do this?"

"Practice, I suppose," James said. "Also, there's some routines you get into that help. Speaking of . . ." He opened up the desk, the small side drawer sliding out on smoothly oiled rails. "Score," he muttered, pulling out a bag of candied nuts proudly bearing the name of They Are.

Dave looked over as James started munching on them. "They Are what?"

"They are delicious, I'm hoping," James told him. "Also, that's something. The weird names on the candy are really surprisingly relaxing. It lets you laugh, keeps you from going insane being on full alert all the time. It makes it easier to think critically when you need to. You know, let your brain open up and do its job without having to focus on it." He tilted the bag toward Dave with a raised eyebrow, offering his friend some of the candy.

Dave took a second to process, then shrugged and held out a hand. Munching on the nuts, he leaned back in the office chair. "Wow, these are good. Hey, why does the dungeon make exclusively good candy? And, follow up, why does it always seem like stuff that should be in the real world, but isn't? Like, they could sell these in stores."

"Are you implying that the dungeon consumed the idea of good candy?" James asked with a smile, as he pushed Dave's chair out of the way and opened up the laptop.

There was a long pause, before Dave came to a conclusion. "Nah, that's stupid. I just want to be able to buy this stuff normally. Can I have some more?"

"All gone."

"Damn." Dave rolled his shoulders, trying to get his muscles to relax a bit. Looking around the cubicle while James tried to get into the computer, he tried to take James's advice and think a little more critically. What did he see? He thought to himself. An inbox, an outbox, piles of papers in each. A gloved hand reached out to riffle through them, but none of them made any sense. There were binders neatly arranged on one of the shelves, as there almost always were, but half of them were empty despite being labeled, and the other half were full of more gibberish. There was a bunch of pencils scattered across the desk, an absolutely inaccurate calendar hanging on the wall, a confirmed inert stapler, a pencil sharpener . . .

"Hey, James," Dave asked. "How often do you see pencil sharpeners? We went through a lot of cubes, but I think that last one, and this one, were the only ones I've seen. And the last one was . . ."

James snapped his head up, and almost instinctively reached out for the piece of hardware. But as he got too close to it, it made an all-too-familiar buzzing, and a black haze erupted out of it. Dave was already reacting; he'd been paying attention for once, and actually felt pretty good about having spotted it in time to be moving. He was confused, though, when he nimbly backpedaled out the low opening, and James yelled out after him to freeze.

But he didn't stop. James caught one last glimpse of Dave through the smoke screen before it totally eclipsed the entrance and started billowing out into the hallway. He dragged his shirt up out from under the armor to cover his mouth, so he could breathe, and re-armed himself with axe and pen, before shouldering out into the aisle.

He could barely see anything, but he caught sight of Dave ducking into the cube across the hall. James moved to follow him, but a soft metal rattling and a sliver of motion out of the corner of his eye made him pause.

That pause turned out to be a good idea, as something blitzed past him. He felt something hard and unyielding clip him in the stomach, and heard a low hiss over the constant buzzing of the pencil sharpener. Now almost totally blind, and not wanting to breathe in any more graphite than strictly necessary, James ducked across the hall as fast as he could into the cube Dave had taken refuge in. As soon as he was through the door, there was a *whump* from just behind him, and the cubicle wall slid inward a little.

"What was that?!" Dave yelped out.

James glared at him. "It's the ambush predator that apparently lives around here. I'm kind of shocked that we didn't notice it the first time. But then, we didn't trip any smoke screens the first time."

Dave gripped the crowbar he'd insisted on bringing along. "Is it still out there?" he asked, terrified.

The comment earned him a glare. "I mean, I can't see right now, but I think it ran off. It's jumping us every time we trigger one of the smoke clouds." James peeked down the hallway as the smoke cleared. "I think it's a chair? That would be kind of insulting, but yeah, I think it's a swivel chair. Probably covered in spikes, obviously. I don't see it, though."

"Okay." Dave wavered a bit. "Sorry I didn't listen to you fast enough. What's the plan, then?"

"Simple," James told him. "One of us is bait, and the other one jumps it when it tries charging again." The look he gave Dave, a wide grin and raised eyebrows, made his friend acutely aware of which one of them was going to be the bait.

Dave stuttered for a second. "Is there any way I could bribe you to do it?"

"Nope!" James said, doing another check as the cloud finally settled, leaving the carpet and walls covered in a black dust. "Okay, I'm gonna wait here, and I'll move up every three cubes you search. How long is this hall?"

"Thirty-eight," Dave answered without thinking about it.

James did a double take. "Are you just pulling numbers out of your ass?"

"What? No. It's thirty-eight. Didn't you count?" Dave asked him, shocked.

Exhaling through his nose, James pushed up his helmet to rub at his forehead. "Are you secretly actually OCD? You just count that without thinking about it?"

"I thought about it!" Dave objected. "You told me to be more alert! I'm being more alert!"

"No wonder you're exhausted" came the muttered reply from James. "Okay, well, the plan stands. Move up, every three cubes I'll follow. If you see one of the dusters, just set it off, and when I see the thing coming, I'll jump it."

Dave nodded and moved out. James crouched down in the doorway, waiting as his friend picked his way through to the next cube door. He was trying to keep an eye out, and also pay enough attention to be ready to help Dave if something went wrong. So focused on that was he that he didn't notice the strider sneaking up on him until it tried to stab into his leg.

"Gah!" James nearly jumped out of his armor. "What the . . ." He looked down to see the stapler, this one lime green and a bit sparkly, savaging his thigh. "Oh, come on. That's not even doing anything," he told it. But all that he got in return was an indignant hiss. "Go away," he told the strider, but it persisted, trying to scramble up his leg to attack a presumably less armored point on his body. "Okay, fine!" he snapped at it, grabbing it and smashing it to the floor. James didn't want to be cruel, even though he was mad at it, so he went for a quick kill, flipping it backward and snapping it in half at the hinge that seemed to be more like a spine for these creatures. A second later, he plucked up and cracked the yellow orb it dropped without thinking about it.

[+1 Skill Rank : Drive – Hovercraft]

"Well, that's just stupid. Who the hell has ever worked here that knew how to pilot a hovercraft?" he asked no one in particular. "Or maybe that's the point . . ." He didn't have much time to think about it, as a few seconds later, another plume of graphite scraps flooded the air of the hallway.

James steeled himself as Dave rushed through the hallway, coughing, trying to make it to a less polluted zone. A second later, Dave stumbled on his injured ankle, which turned out to be a good thing, since James got a perfect view of a *mail cart* bulldozing its way down the hallway at Mach two. It was a frame of steel bars on a set of four caster wheels; drawers dotted the side of it, baskets that could be pulled out, and James saw that a lot of them were full of . . . something. Not mail, he'd bet. On the top of it, a couple packages sat, alongside a half-dozen disposable coffee cups, a ring of probably lethal lattes that somehow didn't fall off its back as it sped along. James noticed that part as he was midlunge, though, a little too late to uncommit.

His hatchet swing connected with it, then slid down through its skeletal metal frame, hooking onto one of the rear bars near one of the wheels. James almost felt his arm yanked in half as the speed of the thing carried it on down the hall, now with him dragged along behind it like a Saturday morning cartoon made real. "James!" he heard Dave shout out from behind him; had he glanced back, he would have seen him bursting out of the smoke cloud and racing after him, but by that point, the cart was already a dozen cubes away, and gaining ground.

James held on for dear life as the mail cart juked side to side. It clearly knew he was there, and he dug in his feet, trying to slow it down. He didn't want to try to grab any of the cube doors flying by; James actually preferred his wrists intact and not shattered into a million pieces. The cart did a sudden pivot ninety degrees sideways, dislodging the hatchet that James was desperately clinging to.

He lashed out, ditching the axe and gripping onto the cart itself. Even as momentum slammed him into the end wall of the hall hard enough to leave a James-shaped crack in it, he *pulled* as hard as he could to try to cut the charger's momentum before it could race off. It almost worked, but he was losing the fight, and being pulled along like a badly positioned water-skier. James was scared almost to the point of inaction to try to drag himself on top of it. Those coffee cups hadn't gone off yet, but he was paranoid to the extreme that they would if he so much as tapped one. So instead, he clicked open the pen in his left hand, fumbling for a minute through the glove, and then drove the smoking tip of the pen into the back right wheel of the cart. He missed the wheel, but still nailed the leg itself.

Neither James nor Dave had really considered what kind of noise a wounded mail cart would make. It was the sort of thought that didn't tend to come up in daily life. But now, they both got a firsthand experience.

It sounded like a million pieces of paper being run through the world's most rusted paper shredder. It sounded like an office supply store in pain. It sounded like a child screaming, if the sound were impossibly composed of return-to-sender stamps.

James let go of the cart, and Dave collapsed to his knees, covering his ears. It tried to speed off but almost tilted over, its back leg smoldered away in flakes of steel, drifting in the drafts of the dungeon's air conditioning. Staggering on its damaged rear leg, unable to keep its wheel balanced, it turned back on the two of them.

Dave was already on his feet in front of James, crowbar at the ready. James rose to his feet behind him and tapped him on the shoulder, signaling that he was moving up next to him. He didn't have his axe anymore, but he brandished the pen as threateningly as he could, smoke still dripping in strangely liquid wisps from its tip.

"The coffee cups explode," he mentioned to Dave.

Dave shot him a look that pretty accurately said *You are fucking kidding me*, before turning back to the oncoming creature. It rushed them, but slower than it had been hitting them before. Both of them pivoted to the side, and it rushed past, trying to whip itself back around. Dave tried to strike at it with his crowbar, but it just rattled across the handles of the drawers.

"How are we supposed to kill this?!" he demanded.

James pointed back to the cubicle they'd been looting when the first trap had gone off. "Rope in the bag. Hold it down, break it."

Dave started to move for the door, but the cart was already swinging around, driving straight at him. He dodged, but it was restabilizing, and it got up a burst of speed before knocking him off his feet. He let out a *whoomp* of air as he was slammed to the ground, and the cart perched one wheel on his throat. James froze as its drawers opened up along its sides; the small slots for sorting mail contained, instead of letters or parcels, unblinking paper eyes that pivoted to focus on James.

"Oh, fuck, of course you're some Lovecraftian bullshit." He threw the words at the thing. Dave, under it, appeared to be struggling far more than its apparent weight would have made James think was reasonable. "Get off him," he commanded it.

To his surprise, it obliged, wheeling itself backward a bit, over Dave's supine form. James almost wanted to try for a peaceful resolution, before the eyes turned sharp and pointed at him, and the cart tipped itself sideways; one of the coffee cups started smoking and detached from it. James saw some kind of black sinew snap off at its base, and it started tumbling toward Dave.

Eyes wide, heart racing, James shuffle-stepped forward and lashed out with his foot. He caught the cup as softly as he could, while still moving fast enough to hit it before it hit the floor. Cradling it on the slope of his boot, he flung it down the hallway, as far away from them as he could. It got maybe three feet before it airburst, a wave of pressure knocking James backward into the cube wall.

His vision went blurry, and he heard Dave screaming from the floor. When James righted himself again, he saw Dave holding a hand to his face, small drops of coffee sprayed across his skin. "Fuck. Okay, we need to get some burn gel on that," he said.

He knelt down to help Dave up, but his friend shoved him away. "It's coming back!" he shouted, and James turned to see that the cart had gone to the other end of the hallway before turning around. Either it really wanted to build up speed, or it had changed its mind about running and was going to try to finish them off.

The coffee cups on its back started smoking. All of them. Apparently, it had noticed the adverse reaction Dave had and decided to go for all or nothing. "Okay, fuck that," James said. If that thing got too close, they were either dead or wishing they were. So he thought, *Fuck it. I'm supposed to be able to sublimate rubber. Let's see if this works.*

"Secret," he muttered to himself. "I don't actually know to do this, and I could use some help right now." The response was swift. Inside his mind, something moved, a perspective shifted, and James, for just a second, saw the world the way a magic item would.

Then there was a snapping back to reality, and a spike of *something* lashed out of his arm. The plastic shell of his armor turned to powder, motes of black vapor no longer held together by anything. He felt more than saw the power he'd unleashed rush down the hall toward the mail cart, impact it, and wash over it.

The metal frame didn't change. The wire baskets didn't care. The coffee cups on the top shrugged it off. The paper and ichor organs and eyes stored inside it weren't even close to affected.

The wheels exploded.

The cart lost control at once. It tried flexing its legs to regain balance, but without the wheels it was used to, it was about as effective as a human trying to recover from a full sprint when their feet vanished. Trails of vaporized rubber flowed behind it as it slammed into the ground on its side, the coffee blisters on its back detonating one after another at the impact. It let out another bleating cry and just lay there for a second, giving James long enough to haul Dave back to his feet.

The two of them didn't speak as they recovered their weapons and circled around the creature. It was trying to pull itself to its metal legs, the frame warping in strangely organic ways and making it look more like a frightened metal deer now that it was stripped of its mobility and armaments.

It had some of its eyes out, one of them slightly ripped, and it flicked its vision between its two hunters. Dave moved in first, bringing the crowbar down at one of its drawers that was left hanging open. It clanged into it, bending part of it but not breaking anything. In response, the creature proved it wasn't completely defenseless; one of the few still-closed drawers popped open, and a spray of paper came out. Sheet after sheet, crisp and pure white, flew up at Dave's face, aiming to startle or unbalance him.

He just covered his face with one gloved hand, and then smashed down again with the crowbar as soon as the assault ended. On the other side, James grabbed one of the drawers, holding it open while he slammed his hatchet into the paper eye inside. It crumpled right away, black goo seeping out of the side of it, and triggering another hateful cry.

They pressed the attack, not giving it a chance to recover, and, bit by bit, dismantled it. Dave tore out drawers, James laid into it with the pen, and in five minutes, the cart finally gave one last howl and perished. It struggled to the last, though, dragging itself through the hall, kicking at them, and drawing in striders with its screams. But the two of them handled everything it had and emerged victorious.

"Well, that was awful," Dave gasped out.

The two of them stood in the crumpled remains of what was once a metallic life form, panting for breath. Around them, a dozen small yellow orbs dotted the floor where they'd struck down striders trying to scavenge the fight. James had a nasty gash on his right wrist where the armor had simply been wiped away by the use of his ability and something had nailed him in that small weak point. But they were alive, and victorious.

"No kidding. Let's sweep this place, and get patched up. I want to get out of here before a sentient desk decides it's time to show off," James said as he steadied his breathing. "You still up for moving on?"

"Oh, yes," Dave said. "That was insane! But it was also . . . um . . ." He tried to find the words to make it sound like he wasn't crazy.

"Nah, I get it." James smiled. "It actually is a ton of fun, fighting for your life, isn't it?"

His friend nodded in relief that James understood. "Why? I didn't even do anything. I would have died if you weren't here. Why is this so . . . cool?" he asked as James tossed him a packet of burn gel from the medkit and started wrapping up his own cut.

"I think we're just profoundly fucked up," James told him with a sunny smile. "Hey, did you get the orb from the big one?" he asked as they shouldered the backpacks and prepared to move out.

"Oh! Hang on!" Dave turned and trotted back, returning to James with a baseball-sized yellow orb, and also a small package wrapped in brown parcel paper. "Hey, this was still intact. Do you mind if I take it?" he asked.

"I don't . . . isn't that just a corpse bit?" James asked, confused.

Dave shrugged. "I dunno, it just seems reasonable that a wrapped package has something useful in it."

Before they started moving again, James stopped Dave. "All right, tell you what. I'm going to go see if I can find fifty bucks in that cube so we can all go get dinner after this. You open that up, and if it's something useful . . . well, I'll bet you one loot share it's not."

"Deal!" Dave said without hesitation. James shook his head and ducked through the door to do the standard loot sweep. They were far enough in that the cubicles were getting into some weird geometry, and this one had a ceiling that came down in stalactites overhead, giving it the feeling of a cave. He found two rolls of quarters in the cubicle, each one arbitrarily $6.25 worth of coins, and also scored a packet of Gummy Shrocks, which he hadn't seen in a while. Coming back out after the quick sweep, he saw Dave standing there holding a small black box in his hand.

"So . . . ?" James prompted him.

Dave looked up, an uncertain expression on his face. "It's a printer ink cartridge?"

Both of them looked down at it for a minute, before James shrugged. "Okay, we postpone the bet. Pack it up, and let's move. Fifty-fifty odds it's either bizarrely normal, or turns the printer into a swan or some shit."

"What constitutes 'bizarrely normal'?" Dave asked as James checked their map and started them moving on toward the Decision Tree, which should be just around a few more turns.

"I like how you question that and not the swan thing." James smiled. "And I'm thinking, I dunno, only two colors and one of them is puce."

"That would be bizarrely normal," Dave agreed.

Falling back into their pattern of move-and-sweep, they moved on. A little more beat-up, a bit tired, but having a blast, and not ready to turn back yet.

CHAPTER 4

"I don't know what that word means," Dave said as he watched down the halls of the three-way intersection while James poked at the vending machine.

No selection was made; James was just running his fingers down the side, trying to get his brain to more easily accept the non-Euclidean motions while they were passing by a relatively safe example of them. "Oh, it's a weird science term," he told Dave. "It means to turn something from a solid to a gas without liquefying it."

Dave gave James an alarmed look. "Isn't that super dangerous?" he asked in a nasal tone.

"First of all, keep it down. Second of all: no? I mean, it worked on the maul cart, right? And neither of us exploded."

He was answering Dave's questions currently on his ability that had been acquired by absorbing the blue orb. Ideally, he would have kept it as a small secret, for the infomorph that lived in his mind to feed on. Especially since telling Dave generated the risk of Dave trying to replicate it, and James wasn't exactly sure if he wanted to open that can of worms. Best case, Dave wasted some blues. Worst case, he either died or got superpowers. Or both.

"Okay, fine." Dave sulked as he tracked a flock of fluttering crumpled paper sheets through the holes in the cubicle panels overhead. "So, why do you keep mispronouncing 'mail'?"

"Mail?" James asked in response without thinking about it.

Dave nodded, even though James wasn't looking. "Yeah, you keep saying 'mail cart,' but you're sort of slurring the word 'mail.' Is that something I should worry about?"

"Why would you worry about that?" James turned to look at his nominal friend. "Is that really the sort of thing that concerns you?"

Dave got defensive. "I've seen a lot of shows and stuff where weird tics like that are signs of impending doom! Don't pretend you haven't! And you've got an alien *thing* living in your head, so maybe it's a sign of brain damage!"

That was actually a fair point, so James relaxed a bit and told him so. "Oh. No, it's nothing so sinister. I'm trying to say *maul* cart. Like, it mauls us. But then trying to keep the cadence of the word 'mail,' and . . . look, coming up with dumb names for things is a burgeoning tradition here," he said, trying to explain.

Honestly, when he actually said it out loud, it sounded a bit silly to think that they were giving these things weird names like this. If James was going to be honest with himself, then it would probably be more efficient—especially in combat—to have the names be short and snappy. *Tumblefeed* and *camraconda* were hilarious to him, but calling them *ball* and *snake* would save precious seconds in a fight. Still, though. It was a tradition, something that he and Anesh had shared through their early explorations and fumbling adventures. The silly names were a legacy, and a good reminder of just how surreal this place was at times.

Unable to see James's inner thoughts, Dave just shrugged it off. "All right, I mean, I guess that's okay if it's what we do. I was just curious." He let out a long breath as he kept his watch on the halls. "Are we going to go anytime soon?"

James dropped his hand down from the vending machine and turned to Dave with some aggressive frustration. He was about to snap at his friend but then reined himself back. Sighing a bit, he picked up his backpack again and slung it over his shoulder. "Yeah, okay. Break over. Let's get on to the thing, and then head back."

"Yeah, what is this thing anyway?"

"It's a surprise," James told him. Mostly, he'd just wanted to show someone new the Decision Tree, and thought it would make a fun endpoint for Dave's training run. But now he had a lump of irritation in his chest; Dave was running his patience out, sure, but also he really did just want to finish this up and head back, so he could talk to Anesh and Alanna about going through the bathrooms tonight. James knew he was being impatient, but ever since learning that the dungeon had literally erased someone, he was finding it hard to focus on the safe-but-slow approach that they had adopted.

He wanted to rush in. Not sit around wasting time. That wasn't . . . well, it wasn't heroic.

Of course, James knew that was stupid. The right choice really *was* to play it safe. To be careful, a little methodical, and to make sure they could survive before moving forward.

Because if they died, or the dungeon ate them like it had Sarah, then there really wouldn't be anyone to stumble across the artifacts of their memory this time.

This was what was on James's mind as he led Dave through the halls and corridors formed by the increasingly twisted geometry of the cubicles. They were moving quietly, not talking, and it gave James ample time to let his mind wander.

Every now and then, they would hear a noise and take cover until they could figure out what it was or verify that it was far enough away to continue. Sometimes, one of them would point into a cube, and they'd take a short break to rest and loot. But since they were trying to move quickly and avoid too many encounters, they were intentionally only hitting desks that had literally nothing risky near them. It was more time than James expected, but far swifter than actually searching everything.

By the time they made it to the cramped turn that led to the open-air zone that was their destination, they'd picked up three small yellow orbs, a pound of assorted candy, and about twice that weight in cash. Also, season one, episode three, of some kind of post-singularity sitcom directed by Joss Whedon. James was a little disappointed that the file had been alone, but wasted no time sticking it on one of his USB sticks.

"Okay, so, this is where we start to see arrow traps," James was telling Dave as they approached the carpet shift. "Watch for the line where the carpet changes. It's not the colors, it's the panels of flooring. Also, it's got some kind of electromagnetic trigger, so you need either a person or a phone to trip it. I recommend not using your phone."

Dave rolled his eyes. "So, what, we trip it, then run?"

"No, we step over it. It's a line on the floor. Just make sure not to touch it, or we might die," James told him, calmly walking forward and hopping over the line.

Staring after him, Dave hesitated. The line was small, innocuous, and easily avoided, but it scared the hell out of him. "How . . . how fast do the darts go again?"

James looked back. "Like, I dunno, thirty miles an hour or something? They're not like bullets, but they're sharp enough to go through the armor. Come on, let's go."

Dave hesitated again before finally shuffling forward and then stepping over the line on the floor like he was tiptoeing around a nuclear warhead. "I hate this. I really hate this," he muttered as he moved to catch up to his partner. Fortunately for him, James wasn't paying attention and hadn't noticed his apprehension.

He was moving forward with confidence and an excited energy that Dave hadn't really seen in his friend before. As soon as he stepped out of the corridor, Dave was a bit startled at how quickly the walls fell away. This whole area, maybe five hundred feet across, was like a cavern in the mass of tunnels that was the dungeon. No walls here went above five feet, many not even getting up to that height, and he could easily see across the whole expanse. Some of the cubicles even had frosted glass panes in their sides, making this space feel bright and open and free.

There was a second ceiling here, with holes in it feeding in light from above, and through those holes, support beams that were normally disguised by cubicle walls showed through. Some of them were wrapped in tangles of what looked like power cabling.

Overhead, a pair of paper airplanes circled, keeping an eye on the clearing, lower to the ground than Dave had ever seen any of the fluttering birdlike paper creatures.

But none of that interested James. He was here to see something specific, and so Dave followed after him, still keeping alert. There were far more striders visible here, moving up and over the walls of the cubes. But none of them made any aggressive moves, so Dave just kept an eye on them and followed on.

And then his party member stopped in at one of the cubicles. "Here" was all he said, moving in without checking. It was one of the cubicles with the tangled-up support beams, and Dave entered cautiously. He ducked his head to avoid a strider "web" and stepped inside.

"Okay, so, what's . . . ?" Dave trailed off as he looked up. The hole in the ceiling made it hard to spot from any angle but this one, which was why James probably hadn't pointed it out earlier.

Above them, stretching out and casting down the glow that permeated through the hole in the ceiling, was a massive tangle of black cables. Unfolding flowers of LCD screen tilted down toward them, showing dancing colored screen savers. Small lizard-things that looked like they had scales made of shards of those same screens skittered along the branches of the twisted and bound cabling. The whole thing was massive, imposing, and majestic.

"Oh. Huh. That's cool," Dave said.

James, sitting in one of the chairs and staring up, trying to get a monitor lizard to climb onto his outstretched hand, looked down at Dave. "That's cool? That's it? You see a tree that grows computer monitors from cables and fluorescent lights, and all you can say is 'That's cool'? I'm a bit offended!"

Dave moved into the cube, still looking up despite his lack of reaction. "Well, how am I supposed to react, then?" he asked, a bit put off.

The tree answered his rhetorical question. Monitors flickered to life, colors and light splashing together to form words and phrases. "Aww," said one of the screens. "Wonder," another told him. Smaller ones came to life with "Fear," "Worship," "Panic," "Flight," "A little appreciation," and "Heart attack?" That last one was in smaller letters, and for some reason was a question.

"Okay, that's pretty cool," Dave said, nodding. "So, why are we here?" He wasn't upset, but it had felt like James was a little more excited about this than was strictly required.

James leaned back again, now trying to entice the lizard that was crouched on the trunk of the tree into his palm with one of the yellow orbs. "I was going to ask the tree a question," he said. Dave gave him a blank look that quickly turned into one of frustration at the lack of explanation. "Okay, okay. So, everything in here seems like it feeds off the orbs to stay alive. But for the tree, that doesn't make sense, right? It's not hostile, and the lizards on it all seem totally fine. So Anesh and I were talking about where it got its life source from—what it ate, basically."

"And?" Dave prompted, trying to get this to go faster.

"Well, we're pretty sure it works kind of like a plant. It absorbs light from the fluorescents overhead, it takes 'nutrients' through its 'roots,' that sorta thing."

Dave may have been a bit apathetic about the whole tree thing, but he was still smart enough to see the problem there. "There's no way that's enough to support this. Also, what roots?"

"Well, the power cables, and when I say nutrients I mean electricity," James explained, before agreeing. "But still, you're right. So, while we were trying to decide how it worked as a life form, Alanna pointed out that a much more practical issue was what powered it from our point of view. As in, could it produce orbs as maybe a kind of 'fruit.'"

"And?" Dave asked again, feeling like he wasn't really part of this conversation.

James shrugged. "And now we're here, and I was just going to ask?"

"Ask what?" Dave said to him. And overhead, the screens lit up again.

"Food source," one cluster said, while another batch of them said variations on "Gifts" or "Bounty." A single small one in the corner offered up "Secret to happiness," which made James smile when he saw it.

But, ultimately, he knew what he wanted to ask already. "That one." He pointed up. "Hey, tree! What kind of orbs do you produce?" James called up at the construct.

Dave shook his head at his friend's antics. It was almost embarrassing. No matter what the monitors said, it was just a plant. A dungeon plant, sure, but . . .

His shoulders slumped and James let out a smug laugh as one of the monitor lizards paused for a second and then scurried into one of the larger screen lotuses. A second later, it emerged, holding up a tiny, brilliantly shining purple dot.

"I knew it!" James half yelled, while Dave head-butted his fist. "It editorializes too much to not be sentient!" As he jumped up and pumped his fist in the air, the lizard skittered away carrying the orb.

"Okay, so, it actually really hurts to see you be right about this," Dave said, not actually angry, but a little irritated that once again, James had been right about something stupid. "But how does that even work?"

James stroked his chin while he thought. "Well, it clearly 'eats' from the sources we talked about. Maybe it refines them into the purple orbs, somehow? And then the lizards . . . eat those? Process them into yellows, that then go back to the tree? Hm. Okay, the ecosystem doesn't line up quite right. But the point is . . ."

"The point is you were right. Okay, so, now what? And I'm not asking the tree this time." Dave shot that last sentence upward at the monitors that had already started displaying options.

The response was a shrug from James. "I mean, I don't want to fight a swarm of moving monitor shards and also a whole tree. So I was planning on asking nicely if we could have a few. Maybe offer to trade for them?" Overhead, one of the monitors blinked as its suggestion was taken unknowingly.

"Trade what?" Dave inquired.

"Well, we've got a few yellows. Hey, tree!" James called up, fishing around in his pocket. "It's not a whole lot, but we'll give you these for a couple of yours!"

Dave sighed. "Now, there's no way . . . no, you know what? I'm not going to doubt it anymore. That's only making me look bad. Go ahead, go treat the magical lightning tree like it's a vending machine." He stepped back, shoving his hands into his pockets in annoyance.

His hedging of bets was rewarded a minute later, when a couple of the monitor lizards came down the side of the trunk, gripping slivers of bright purple in their spiky mouths. They waited at about head height while a small horde of unburdened lizards, their crystal scales shimmering, scampered down toward James's outreached hand.

Almost daintily, ladylike, one of them unfolded itself off the black plastic shell of the trunk, and with tiny forelegs plucked the first yellow orb out of James's palm. Placing it in its mouth, it curled back up, planted its claws back on the tree, and with the lightest of tapping noises was back up into the branches. The others followed suit, plucking away the orbs James offered and running away as if afraid he was going to try to catch them in his hands. After all the yellows were taken, the two remaining held out the purple orbs his way, and James smiled as he took them in his fingers.

"Well, thank you," he said, as much to the lizards themselves as to the tree. "All right, Dave. Now we can head back, and maybe see if we have an ice pack or something for all the bruises."

"Thanks," Dave said, glad that James actually did seem to care about his own feelings. "I'm not trying to be a downer or anything, just, well, even after this, I don't know if I'm cut out to be here," he confided, trying to open up to James a bit.

"Hey, it's all right," James reassured him. "We're not a cult. You can leave whenever you want. Anyway, let's get going. I'll bet you a hundred bucks we got a better haul than Anesh's squad did." They walked out of the cube, Dave taking the lead and almost unconsciously dropping back into his high-alert mode. Before they turned back to the path to Fort Door, though, James turned around one last time. "Pleasure doing business with you," he said to the tree, with a small bow.

Had he stuck around, he might have seen the "You as well" lit up in the branches.

CHAPTER 5

James and Dave strode back through the entrance of Fort Door to little fanfare, which was sort of a letdown. Ganesh flew out to greet them, doing a quick loop of Dave's head before buzzing back inside, where the other three were sitting around the map-desk that Anesh had dragged out to the center of the main "room."

"I really don't like that he does that," Dave muttered.

James just smiled and replied, "Obviously—that's why he does it." He raised a hand in greeting to Anesh, who looked up as they walked in. "Hey! We're back! I brought shimmering treasures and cryptic hints! We almost got killed by a mail cart!"

Helmets sat on the floor, backpacks were set against desks. The loot table that they'd set up had a big plastic bowl, the kind meant for chips at parties, sitting on it, half-filled with small colored balls.

For a half second, it looked like both Alanna and JP wanted to say something, but the rapid-fire nature of James's greeting left them with vaguely confused and bemused expressions on their face. In that vacuum, Anesh stepped in. "Well, that would have been a weird postmortem," he said, without missing a beat and with a totally straight face.

"Hrgh!" Alanna groaned out through bared teeth. "Ow, fuck, I think I actually took damage from that one." She grasped at her torso theatrically. "My one weakness! Terrible puns!"

"My one weakness is bullets," James said casually, getting a snicker from JP as he walked up to the desk and slung his backpack onto the floor. "So, how was your guys' trip?"

Anesh groaned, and Alanna scowled at the table, avoiding eye contact. It was JP who actually answered, delivering bad news with some grace. "Not great," he said with a shake of his head. "The map has detail to it, but it doesn't match up. Either the terrain changed, or it's just wrong. So we ended up, well, lost."

"How lost?"

"Ganesh-bail-us-out lost," Anesh said, clearing his throat. "It's actually really kind of unsettling, yeh? We just . . ."

Alanna half cut him off. "Well, it was partly our fault for just trusting a random map from someone we don't know." Her tone had a hard edge to it.

". . . Just got a little out of sight of the main aisle, and got totally turned around," Anesh continued as if he hadn't been interrupted. "Ended up being an Escher, so not *entirely* the fault of our misplaced trust, but still. Feels pretty shitty to waste half our night here, and it didn't help that you didn't answer your radio."

James and Dave traded a quick confused look before James turned his gaze back to the rest of the party. "Sorry, half the night? It's been an hour, tops. Also . . . wait, hang on." James pulled out the small handheld radio from one of the pockets on his armor. "No, I *did* remember to turn it on! This one isn't my fault! Finally!"

"An hour?" Alanna asked with suspicion. "So we're now . . ."

Anesh sighed. "Okay, the oranges screw with time too. Good to know."

"Might be what makes the door work, and the three-minutes-to-eight-hours thing we've got going on," JP suggested. "Should we try to dismantle the dooooh—no, nope. I realized what I was suggesting as I said it. Never mind!"

"Yes, please, let's not destroy our exit," Alanna grumbled.

Anesh took over the conversation again to deliver a more complete and less upset report. "So anyway! We have an orange orb, a handful of yellows, one blue from a spreadsheet that told you the favorite colors of people in your social circle, and the usual pile of money and food. Also, confirmation that we still need to find an actual path back to the bathrooms, because Sarah's map isn't... correct, I guess, is the best word? And that's all, I think. JP, Alanna? Anything to add?"

"I got in a swordfight with a plant!" JP burst out with a grin. With the tension of wasted time torn away, and the failure of the map and their misplaced trust now aired, he'd been almost vibrating to tell someone else about this. It wasn't often that JP bragged about anything; bragging, he believed, was almost always done by people who didn't have a damn thing worth bragging about. He preferred to let his actions and attitude speak for him, and for the most part, he did. It was why it was so easy for James and Alanna and Anesh to form comfortable friendships with him, it was why he got along with so many different types of people, and it was the source of his aura of confidence. But sometimes, well...

Sometimes you got in a duel with foliage, and it was hard to not want to share.

"What! That's not fair! I didn't even get a sword, and we just went to see a tree!" Dave bemoaned.

Anesh raised an eyebrow. "You didn't like the Decision Tree?" he asked, surprised.

"It was fine, I guess," Dave said, "as now I know I could have been fighting potted plants. With swords."

It wasn't an entirely unreasonable complaint. But James still rolled his eyes. "We fought a mail cart. You got to eat weird candy. You are living the dungeon life, come on, man," he said, chastising his delving partner. Dave just let out a huff of air and didn't respond. "Well, sounds like you guys got at least something done."

"Yeah, I mean, now that we know we only spent an hour on it, it seems pretty good," Anesh said. "I am starting to get hungry, though. Hungry for something that *won't* give me diabetes." He cut off Alanna as she reached to offer him a Baby Things. "So, what's your report?"

James shrugged as Dave went over to one of the chairs and started peeling off his armor. "Well, we took a trip to go see the Decision Tree. Got jumped by a mail cart, which I am now calling a postmortem, thanks, Anesh. Oh, it was an ambush predator, so you know; there were some pencil sharpeners, the big bricks with motors in them, and they shot out smoke and dust, and it used that as cover for charges." James paused as Anesh made a note of that, his friend starting a new page in the three-ring binder that was becoming their bestiary. "Then we got to the tree, no real issues there, and then I traded it a few yellows for these."

He held up the purple orbs, and everyone stared.

There was no holding back the smug smile on his face. James just couldn't help it.

"Next time lead with that, you fucker," Alanna said, starting to smile herself.

"How?" Anesh asked. "No, wait . . . no, let's stick with how."

"I asked it nicely. It turns out it might be semi-sentient," James replied.

"Did you ask it anything about the dungeon? About Sarah?" JP prompted, curious.

James opened his mouth, then closed it again. "I . . . did not think to do that. We were sort of just dropping by, then heading back. I didn't actually know if it would work."

"Why did it have purples in the first place?" Alanna asked, watching with open greed as James walked over and added them to the bowl, the color splashing against the hotter yellows and reds, and the singular orange.

Dave was the one who answered. "It grows them," he said.

James nodded. "Yeah, turns out, they're what's in those monitor blooms. Like fruit, or maybe seeds? Still not sure what it 'eats,' though."

"We're really assuming that it works like a normal life form, though, aren't we?" JP questioned. "What if it doesn't eat anything? Just casually violating conservation of orbs."

That was a worrying thought. And while it brought some laughter to the group, it still left James and Alanna, and especially Anesh, wondering if maybe they were going down the wrong path in their "studies" of the dungeon. The problem was, the place was all unreal, but still recognizable as real-adjacent. But how much of the foundation could you take out before it started to become unrecognizable? How many assumptions had they made about the basics of life that just didn't apply anymore?

They knew Rufus and Ganesh and the other "life" here had to eat, in a sense. So they had a little bit of the real world to bring with them into the dungeon, in terms of how they thought about the world around them. Really, it was just about how fake the dungeon could get, and how hard it would be to form new assumptions and theories when the basis of their worldview was thrown off like that.

"That's an unpleasant thought," Anesh said. "So, thanks for that."

"No problem." JP gave him a thumbs-up.

Alanna sighed and hopped up onto one of the empty desks braced up against the walls, turning it into a seat for a moment. "So, what now? I'm pretty hungry, and Anesh looks like he's gonna fall asleep soon. Do we just pack it in and head back?"

"I packed food," James said. "So we have that covered, it's in that cardboard box over there with the red tape. Personally, I don't want to go yet. There's so much we can still get done." He was trying not to sound too greedy, but, well, it was a challenge. "We've got those cots, and the expanded 'bedroom wing' of the fort, if you want to take a nap." He aimed that comment at Anesh. "And really, I want to go take one more shot at finding the way to the bathrooms. Get some experience working as a larger group."

That wasn't exactly the only reason. The other, unspoken impetus was the loot. James specifically wanted to go hunting for a tumblefeed, now that they were re-armed with weapons that could kill one. But besides that, just taking the cart out with thousands of dollars' worth of computer hardware, office supplies, and coats was a pretty appealing prospect.

Theoretically, if they acquired enough money, they could just buy out the building's lease, and he could quit his job. Which was almost a more magical prospect than the dungeon itself.

"I also wouldn't mind sticking around," JP said. "I want to try to find an iLipede nest, and make friends with one. Even though I'm not that into Apple products."

"Good news for you, their logos are legally distinct," Alanna told him.

JP gave her a sly smile. "For copyright reasons, that makes me quite happy, thank you!" Dungeon diving was one thing—dangerous, sure, but acceptable. Upsetting a brigade of lawyers? Not on his to-do list.

"Okay, that's two of us going back in. Dave? Alanna?" James asked them, noticing that Anesh really was about to doze off.

"I'm gonna stay here," Dave said. "I haven't hiked that much in a while. So I'll keep an eye on everything, especially if Anesh is gonna be sleeping."

Alanna nodded. "Good call. I'm in, though. Just let me actually eat first."

"Yeah, it'll give me some time to figure out where we're going, and what to bring," James said, unzipping his backpack and beginning the process of preparing for part two of tonight's adventure. "Anesh! Go to bed!" He tried to pick up his friend who was attempting to steal away the bag for use as a pillow, wrapping his arms around his chest and pulling him away from the table. Anesh wasn't totally asleep, and comically ragdolled just to see what James would do, for his own amusement. "We bought beds specifically for this! Also, wake up and tell me what box you put the thermite in!"

"Part of me feels offended that two of us are working while one of us is eating lunch," James commented, as he and JP looked through desk drawers for the password to the computer in the cubicle they were in.

They were about a quarter of a mile down Hallway One, or whatever they were calling it. James had lost track, since they never actually used it that much anymore. It was the first hall, the one that he had first stepped into when he'd found this place. The one that was most thoroughly explored and looted. Well, up until the break room, that is.

James and JP were in one of the cubicles near the breach, the point where hard carpet turned to harder linoleum tile, and brighter lights cut through across cafeteria chairs, vending machines, and a fridge that no one was ever going to open. Currently, they were casually, but thoroughly, looting. The whole routine: drawers and dry cleaning, files off the computer, then hardware out of it, and lightly fiddling with as many objects as possible to look for blue orbs.

Right now, though, it was proving frustrating. Every now and then, they ran across a computer that wouldn't have an obvious answer to its "puzzle." Normally, it was simply social engineering; James had found so many passwords on sticky notes that he was starting to get angry at the staff that didn't exist here. The IT guy in him wanted to start leaving passive-aggressive memos around the office about information security. That said, the dungeon-delver guy in him really didn't mind so much that the keys were always kept within arm's reach of the treasure chests. Sometimes, they'd had to do a little more trial-and-error to get the passwords: looking at any pictures on the desks for pets with names on the collars, checking wallets for IDs with birthdays, that sort of thing. With this one, though, none of that had worked so far, and it was starting to bug James.

"At the risk of violating my oath to the cult of digital security, I'm really starting to get annoyed that they didn't just write their password down," he said aloud, sitting in the cubicle's chair and staring at the desktop in front of him. His brain felt fried, like he was thinking in circles; he knew the solution had to be here, but he couldn't make that last connection.

JP was currently looking through the filing cabinet near the door. "Hm. Maybe we should have brought lunch as well," he commented, nodding out the door to where Alanna was sitting perched on the cart, eating leftover curry while she kept an eye on the break room area for any signs of tumblefeeds. "That looks a lot more relaxing than banging our heads into the monitor."

James considered banging his head into the monitor. "Why is this one so awful! Like, if it's one of the ones that doesn't actually work, or it's a shellaxy, then there just isn't a prompt! Why is this one so stupid?!" He threw his hands out at the monitor on the desktop, surrounded by opened folders and sheaves of paper, as if gesturing at it would cause it to surrender its secrets.

"You know, we don't have to do this one," JP told him warmly. "We could just move on, go a little deeper in. There's no need to get too stressed about one password, friend." He was really trying to help James calm down, without sounding condescending.

"I have decided this computer is my enemy," James stated flatly.

Behind him, JP tried really hard to resist the urge to roll his eyes as he closed the bottom drawer of the filing cabinet, kneeling on the ground. "Well, if you're that dedicated to . . . oh, what about this?" His eyes had found, tucked behind the filing cabinet, a brown leather briefcase. He pulled it out and held it up to James, who raised an eyebrow.

"Well, crack it open, see if it's got the hint in it," James told him, encouragingly.

JP assumed a cross-legged position on the floor, propping the briefcase in front of him. He thumbed the brass latch, but it didn't open. He started turning it over while James watched like an excited hawk. "No number lock. No keyhole? How is this supposed to open?"

"There's a thing on the back." James reached down and pulled off a small folded piece of paper taped to the case. He opened it up and read from the printout of what looked like an email. "Wow, this is weirdly worded. Um . . . okay." James started muttering his way through the words. "'Delivering for the . . . unto on for cubicle of R-4401 . . .' Okay, this is super badly written. But I think it's a work order?"

"Want to just try prying the case open?" JP asked. "There's a crowbar on the cart."

"Sure," James agreed, and the two of them stepped out of the cubicle to where Alanna was finishing her lunch.

She tossed the empty carton of rice and curry into one of the wastebaskets in the cubicles as the two guys came out. "Hey. Find it? I heard you swearing."

"Not yet. Hand me the crowbar," James said, holding up the briefcase to show her his intent.

Alanna shook her head. "Won't work. Anesh and I found one of those . . . last week? Two weeks ago? Anyway, no lock, right? They don't open for anything." She shrugged, somehow making the motion look casual even through the plating of the armor. "We were going to take it with us and try more drastic measures, but then you got in a fight with the cable snake, and we had to go bail you out, and I think it just got forgotten."

JP let a bit of worry show on his face. "Now, when you say drastic measures, are you talking about anything that might get all of us arrested?"

"Probably," James said. "Well, fuck it. Just throw it on the cart, we'll get to it later. I like to think I'm genre savvy enough to know that the note on it is the 'quest' to open the fucking thing, but hell if I know how to find cubicle . . ." He checked the paper. "R-4401." He looked back up at the other two. "Does that sound familiar at all? Have we even seen numbers on the cubicles at all?"

"Not that I've seen," JP said. "I'll pay more attention, though. What now?"

James threw the case onto the wire frame base of the little wheeled hand cart that they'd been bringing along, sticking it between a pair of cardboard boxes that they were using to sort out cash and electronics. "Now we keep hanging out here, I guess. The idea was to take out another tumblefeed. Though if you guys want to keep moving, we can. I don't want to go too far, though, and risk meeting a stuffed shirt."

"I'd still like to find one of the phone bugs, if that's all right," JP offered. He was never one to try to guilt his friends into going with his ideas, so he presented it honestly and cheerfully. "If not, well, maybe we could just circle around the break room and try hunting some of the neon-laser-dog computers."

"They aren't . . ."

"That's how you described them, that's what I'm calling them until proven otherwise," JP sniped back with a smile.

Alanna let out a groan. "Let's just cut through, for fuck's sake. What's it going to do, jump us right in the middle? We just clear the mines, and if the tumblefeed shows up, set it on fire."

It was a pretty simple decision for Alanna. Sometimes, she was a very straightforward person. Most times, really. In her world, there was almost always a direct path to success. That didn't mean that you couldn't apply cunning and guile, but just that moving forward was usually better than sitting still.

And she was sick of sitting still. They'd been here for half an hour, James and JP casually and methodically strip-mining the cubicles around her, and she was *bored*.

James thought about it, then bobbed his head in a nod. "Yeah, okay. How do we do this?"

He almost jumped out of his skin as, just next to him, JP flicked the ten-foot pole out to full length with a metal ratcheting sound. "I'm on it!" he said with childish glee.

"Aahh! Please don't do that!" James said, clutching at his chest. Or at least, the chestplate of his armor, which he couldn't really feel through. "Fuck, man." He tried to breathe while Alanna and JP suppressed smiles. "But yeah, good. Let's do this."

Five dull, bone-rattling thuds later, the break room was more or less clear. There was still a pair of potted plants in the corner, one of them hanging from a pot hooked to the top of one of the high walls around them, the other planted firmly on the ground in a wider ceramic base. The two green chunks flowed together somewhere midway up the wall, creating a verdant column that clearly sent a message. The message was: *Fuck off. This is our break room.*

The three of them made a quick plan and then moved through as a unit. JP pulled the cart at a slow walking pace, while ahead of him, Alanna and James quickly and efficiently shifted coffee-stained tables and chairs out of the way to clear a path.

They didn't speak, and tried to keep the scraping of table legs to a minimum. But the whole time, James was eyeing the coffee machine that had remanifested over on the counter, wondering what the coffee it produced would do. JP was scanning the high walls around them, keeping his ears open for the sound that James had described to him as "like rain, but hostile." That is, when he wasn't stealing glances at the plants and wondering if his sword was sharp enough.

As they finished shoving the last long table off to the side, making a neat corridor through the previously labyrinthian territory of exploding coffee, James took a minute to glance around. He was struck with a quick idea as JP pulled their convenient loot platform through under Alanna's escort, and, seeing no immediate danger, he took the chance to hop over one of the tables to the counter and sink against the wall.

Old green faux-tile countertops and a grimy metal basin, on top of cupboards that looked like they were installed by the lowest bidder. The break room, James realized, was really the most human part of this whole place. Because it didn't look warped or mutated, just kind of dirty and shoddily put together, like a real office. Even the refrigerator, somehow plugged in and running, had that weird click in its hum that let him know it was old, and no one had bothered to fix it for at least a year or two.

He didn't dwell on it, though. Instead, he stepped to the side and opened one of the cabinets. Standing out of the potential zone of doom if anything went wrong, of course. But nothing did, so James ducked his head down to see what was in there. "Score!" he muttered, grabbing a whole box of hot chocolate packets, sliding them back onto the table behind him. JP noticed what he was doing and settled the cart down to a stop long enough to grab the box and situate it in its new home on their treasure truck.

"Really? Really, guys? Now?" Alanna griped, looking back at the two of them handing off a half-full cardboard container full of water bottles. "I mean, I get that it's been a bit dull, but this place is seriously not where I want to waste time."

"It should be fine," JP said calmly, in a low voice. "I'm keeping an ear out, and I'll stop him if he tries to open the fridge." James threw a quiet protest back over his shoulder as he opened the next cabinet. "I know you were the one that told me it was probably a trap, but I've *also* seen that episode of *Cowboy Bebop*, friend. And I know how curious you get." JP clicked his tongue slightly. "I mean, I'm also curious," he said in a quieter tone to Alanna, "it might actually just have some kind of bizarro-world leftover lasagna. But I'll risk that later, and take the bag of coffee grounds now."

A yelp caused both of their heads to snap back to James. JP displayed lightning reflexes, jerking his head at a forty-five-degree angle just as a flailing strider whipped through the air. Alanna hefted her hammer as JP shoved the table out farther to open up a path to where James was now tumbling back on his heels as the entire nest of striders he'd pissed off poured out of the cabinet.

"Gentlemen, please! We can resolve this peacefully!" JP called into the growing pile of hostile staplers as he strode forward.

James disagreed. They'd run across a few varieties of the basic stapler crab/spider species in their time here: the royal fancy type, the sleek and streamlined version, the heavier bricks that preferred falling from the ceiling in ambush, and of course, the occasional strangely intelligent ones, like Rufus or the team that harassed James and Alanna to a standstill. But he had yet to see ones that looked quite as . . . feral . . . as these.

They were old. Not aged, but the models that you'd see in movies from the sixties or seventies. Big solid chrome-steel hulks of things, with the weight to match. No coloring or plastic coating, just bare metal, sometimes not machined quite right, leaving burs and sharp edges in places. In one of those moments of unasked-for clarity through the swarming horde, James noticed that they had more legs than they should, probably to accommodate their longer and heavier frames. Ten or twelve of those click-open pens, actually tilted like crab legs this time, the legs angling up out of the side of the creatures before spiking back down toward the ground. The legs didn't form perfect angles; instead, the connection to the main body met the leg midway up, leaving the "clicker" part extending upward like something from a mecha anime. An exposed piston that drove their steps forward.

And unlike all the other ones that they'd seen, these ones could actually flex open their mechanical jaws wide enough, and hit hard enough, that those staples were threatening to break into James's skin again. An experience he'd really like to avoid living again, if at all possible.

To that end, he grabbed another one of the small monsters that was currently trying to dig furrows out of the plastic shell of his armor, climbing up his chest while he pushed backward with his legs. It hissed in his hand, mad with rage, and he was more than glad for the thick gloves keeping his hands safe from the stabbing motions of the wicked legs. He flung it backward over his head, just trying to put distance on it, and from behind him did not see, but heard, the metallic smash of Alanna taking a batter's stance and slamming the helpless strider into the floor.

JP pinned one of them underfoot and tried to use the metal pole to prod and flick back the rest of the nest, though their weight made it a less-than-effective move. Alanna vaulted over the table, the piece of furniture tilting dangerously as the combined weight of her weapon and armor and her own form pressed down on the edge of it before she landed and started taking long steps toward the mess. And James, well, James just kept kicking. He was flat on his ass now, trying to get clear of them, but there were more than ten, more than twenty, so many of the sharp terrors. So he just kept trying to push himself backward as more and more of them pushed their way out of the cupboard.

"Where the fuck are they all coming from?!" James yelled as Alanna started laying into them with the hammer. Her first two swings were golf: teeing off with biting metal targets, sending multiple members of the packed swarm flying. But after that, she switched to just pounding them into the ground, sending chunks of metallic chitin and tiny splashes of inky blood spraying across the floor near James's legs.

Lashing out with his foot and barking out a yelp, JP skitter-stepped back with a new hole in his sneaker, and a new appreciation for how fucking much it hurt to get stapled in the foot. "How long are those?!" he barked out.

James got his feet under him and shoved himself to his feet. The three of them put some distance between themselves and the growing carpet of staplers, some of which were climbing on top of each other as they snapped at the trio. They didn't rush right away, and between the pole and hammer, and the spear that James quickly snagged off the cart, they managed to create a bit of a barrier between them and the encroaching mass. "Okay, this is fine," James gasped out. "We just hold them back, pick them off one at a time, and . . ."

There was a rattle like falling rain.

James and Alanna shared a half-second terrified glance, before Alanna tapped him on the shoulder, yelling "Go!" and sending him scrambling for more distance to safely yank one of the improvised thermite bombs off his belt. His head was on a swivel, and he only briefly caught a glance of JP catching a stapler to the chest as one dove off the fridge that it had climbed up and threw itself forward as he continued to watch the walls. His friends would be okay, he had to trust in them. Even through JP's lack of experience or real armament for this situation, they could hold off long enough for him to torch a tumblefeed.

The armament problem he could fix, actually. "JP!" He got his friend's attention for a second. "Catch!" And underhand-lobbed him a cool brass pen. JP snapped it out of the air with his left hand, already turning back to the battle line with the striders, and clicked it open. A thin wisp of smoke trailed from the tip where it burned away the thin dust in the air, and that line in the air followed it as JP arced his arm around to stab another lunging strider out of the air. The scent of cooking acrylic filled the air as the black blood of the target boiled away in seconds, leaving a strangely limp metal corpse hanging inches away from JP's face.

JP panted hard, even as he kept tapping the pole into the mass to keep them back. "We didn't have to do this, you idiots," he rasped out as he let the dead strider slide off the pen onto the floor in a heap.

Alanna and JP were both backing up now, and James kicked a chair aside to help give them room to maneuver. If they needed to, they could easily just abandon the cart and run, but these things were moving in shockingly fast bursts sometimes, and James wasn't interested in turning his back on the mass.

But the two of them, while giving ground, were still dishing out punishment on the pile of staplers. If they had an ounce of sense, they'd cut their losses sooner or later. Either that, or just rush them, James thought.

And then he spotted the tumblefeed. It was right on the other side of the mass of striders; James only barely saw the tips of a dozen cables, just starting to snake up over the edge of the wall. He opened his mouth to say something, throwing out one arm to start to pull JP back, but before he could say anything, it flung itself over.

The last tumblefeed had been slow. It rattled and hissed and dragged itself along the ground on its own time. This one, though, launched itself a good foot over the wall; it was a bit smaller, but it lacked the lazy aura the other had. The ball of cables slammed into the ground right in the middle of the striders, not quite totally clearing the counter and sink behind it as some of its bulk rattled against the tile, and there was a moment of quiet and stillness. Then dozens of corded Cat 5 serpents started striking out, piercing through the hide of the striders nearest to it, and hissing screams filled the air.

The striders nearest to the tumblefeed tried to bite into it, and landed staple after staple, but it had thousands of feet of cable in its amorphous mass, and none of them cut any connections that mattered before they were dragged inside and torn apart.

"What the fuck . . ." JP started to say, his pleasant demeanor breaking for a minute as he watched the slaughter, before the tumblefeed began stalking toward them: two massive stalks of power cables bound by tangled headphones serving as mantis legs pulling the tumblefeed forward. James tried to yank him back farther, but he stumbled, and wasn't fast enough to stop the tumblefeed from rolling itself and lashing forward with an uncountable number of cable whips toward JP. He got his arms up in front of his face, and most of the cables were pretty small, but he still felt the impacts a lot more than he was expecting. And when the teeth from the Cat 5 cables started digging into his armor and tugging him toward the bulk, he started panicking.

James turned the activator on the thermite, pushed in the button of the "grenade" Anesh had made them, and threw it into the tumblefeed. Not wasting any time to see if it worked, he grabbed onto JP's arm with one hand and pulled out the sword at his friend's waist with the other, bracing himself to start hacking through the cables. James was actually pretty surprised when the blade went through the first cable pretty easily, though he did have to pull back on it to get the blade to do its job. JP digging in his heels and holding the cords taut was helping.

There was a strangely warbling howl from the tumblefeed as the thermite started to go off, and James almost sighed in relief. But that moment of hope was short-lived, as the creature flung the melting ball of cascading molten sparks off to the side to bounce off Alanna's hammer held in a guard. Seemingly no worse for wear, the ball of cables kept pulling JP in, and also split its attention to keep snapping at striders, and also trying to wrap its cords around Alanna's leg and hammer, though she refused to give ground to it.

As James kept trying to free JP with one hand, while fumbling for another thermite grenade with another one, the striders suddenly scrambled away from the tumblefeed and the team alike, creating a strangely empty space on the dance floor. And before any of them could figure out why, another strider came to the mouth of the cabinet, dragging a black backpack with it. The bag looked empty, and James caught glances of the strider fumbling to unzip the thing while he hacked the last cable tendril away from JP. Good timing, too, because as soon as the strider caught one of its legs under the zipper and started to open it, the whole room seemed to shift.

Lighter things moved first. The flimsy plastic and hollow aluminum chairs, and the corpses of some of the striders shifting first, sliding across the floor toward the row of cabinets to thunk into them. One of the chairs clipped Alanna across the back of the legs, but it was so light, she didn't even budge from her position holding against the tumblefeed.

Then heavier stuff, as the bag was opened wider. A couple of still-living staplers that were on top of the tumblefeed and had gone unassaulted were yanked backward, one of them clattering into the sink. James was starting to feel the pull, too. This one was different; he wasn't being pulled, his feet just weren't attached as much anymore. It was like gravity itself was shifting.

"Everybody back!" he yelled, shoving JP back and off to the side, before throwing himself over toward Alanna and slicing through half of the cables around her ankle. This freed her up to kick out of the rest and yank her hammer back. The two of them pulled back to the sides, James making sure to keep them clear of the plants still alive and now quite active in their corner.

The tumblefeed tried to claw its way after them, but it was too late. The strider's manipulation of local gravity had it stuck. It could hold itself in place, but the looser of its cables began to radiate behind it, pulled backward like it was forcing its way into hurricane winds.

James stood up fully, pushing off of JP, and plucking a toothed USB connector out of his shoulder plate, and casually tossing it into the growing vortex. "Let's try this again," he growled, triggering the second thermite grenade and pitching it into the center of the tumblefeed.

This time, the fountain of melting metal was accompanied not by resistance, but by howling. Sparks flew and the scent of burning plastic filled the air as the weapon melted through the tumblefeed's core. And in seconds, it went limp, released its hold on the floor, and was crushed back against the counter.

Then gravity snapped back to normal, and the pile of plastic slumped to the floor, revealing the strider holding a closed backpack.

"Well, shit. That was pretty cool," James said, nodding at the strider holding the bag as he helped JP back to his feet.

JP let out a deep breath as he looked out at the thinned and not-charging strider nest horde. "Ah, see? No need for us to fight at all," he said. "We can . . ." He didn't get any farther before the strider turned the backpack toward where the two of them had pivoted off to the side of its original fire path and yanked it open again.

James let out a short "Ffffuck!" as he felt himself start to be pulled—dropped, really—toward the cabinet and the awaiting swarm. JP grabbed the doorframe of the break room, holding on to the light cubicle wall for all he was worth, throwing out one arm to grasp onto James's forearm as he started to slide forward.

Then there was an earsplitting crack, and the backpack jerked sideways. Gravity reasserted itself in an eyeblink. The strider holding the bag looked almost surprised for a second, its forward eye blinking for a stunned moment, before a second crack split the air, and it jerked sideways too, with a clean hole through its snout.

Alanna shifted out of her firing stance, reholstering the pistol that she'd borrowed from James. "Enough of that shit," she said, leveling the Nerf gun at the remainder of the swarm that had packed itself to the sides of the cabinet to avoid being crushed by the changing gravity. "You all have five seconds to get out of here." She curtly delivered the ultimatum to the survivors.

The remaining striders, as heavy and sharp and angled as they were, didn't need to think too long on that one.

As soon as the break room was empty, the last of the skittering nightmares over the wall, Alanna and James didn't waste any time. "You get the yellows, I'll grab the cabinet," James called to her, and she nodded and started snapping up the drops from all the striders. "JP! Help her with the tumblefeed!"

"Wha . . ." he gasped out. "What just happened?"

"We won! Now we need to move, because we made a *ton* of noise! So let's get going!" Alanna called back, shoving small yellow beads into her pockets.

James, meanwhile, went straight to the cabinet and stuck his head in. It wasn't too hard to see how thirty striders had made their nest in here; there was an orange orb embedded in the wall down at the end, lengthening the shelf to a couple meters long. The nest itself was covered in bundles of shredded paper, loose staples, and the occasional pencil stabbed into the wall. James leveraged himself in a bit farther, the bulk of his armor making it almost impossible to fit his shoulders inside, but he was still able to reach down far enough to grab at the orb and pry it loose.

Remembering what had happened the last time they'd done this, and from what Anesh had told him of his own experience, he jerked back quickly as the space collapsed. He also tried not to look at the folding ripples in reality as the cabinet went back to just being a cabinet. And then, he was out.

"All right, are we ready to go?" he asked, throwing the orange orb into the box of hot chocolate packets on the cart and following up with the blue orb that the backpack had left behind.

Alanna and JP had rolled the bulk of the tumblefeed sideways, revealing the dozen striders it had dragged in and killed off. There weren't nearly that many yellows, though, so the thing must have eaten some of them while it was busy . . . eating them. "We're good," Alanna said, wiping melted plastic off her gloves and onto the floor. "Let's get the hell out of here before a million more of these show up."

They stuck JP on the cart, and Alanna and James fanned out to the front and back, keeping an eye out and prepared to ruin the day of anything that moved with extreme prejudice, as the three of them made their way back down Hallway One. They moved fast this time, going more for just getting out without any problems, rather than caution.

And after that, they all had enough rattling their nerves to forget about caution just a little bit.

But either they drove everything away, or there wasn't enough left nearby to feel like swarming the trio was a good idea, because after fifteen minutes of jogging, taking it a little easy to make sure nothing spilled off their cart, they managed to get through back to the area near the door where the walls were lower, and Fort Door was in sight.

It was a little strange to James, just how much it felt like coming home.

CHAPTER 6

"Okay, where's Anesh?" James asked as the group sat around the desk that they were now using as their improvised group meeting table.

It was pretty interesting to James that the notion of a "kitchen table" seemed to show up, no matter where their group was. Wherever they went, they found themselves a table to sit around so that they had a place to sit and talk as a group. And, in this case, pile loot on.

The whole thing made James feel almost like a pirate captain, right down to the small cut on his right cheekbone. Here he was, relaxing with other members of his crew, weapons stacked on the table or against the walls of their makeshift fort, and a bowl of reality-warping orbs in the middle of the table surrounded by cash and chocolate. It was practically enough to make him forget that he had to go in to his normal job tomorrow.

"Anesh is still sleeping," Dave said, leaning over the table and casually stacking piles of bills.

Alanna gave out a long and exhausted sigh as she dropped down onto her chair, dropping the last piece of her shell armor onto the floor next to her. "Fucking hell, that stuff is hot. My skin feels like it's turned into sweat." She arched her arms over her head, saying, "I'm taking the longest shower when I get back."

Next to her, James scrunched up his face. "Hurgh. You *smell* like you turned into sweat too."

"Oh, like you're any better. You smell like blood and fear," Alanna retorted, sticking out her tongue.

"What does . . . fear . . ." JP started to ask, and then he brought his hand up to his mouth in thought and corrected himself. "No, no, never mind. I think I can figure it out."

James reached out and started giving Rufus some pets where the strider was curled up with his legs under him on the table. "Okay, so, Alanna's inhuman sense of smell and JP's overactive imagination aside, why is Anesh still sleeping?"

"Because he's tired?" Dave asked sarcastically, looking up from where he was half lying across the desktop. Everyone just kind of paused for a beat and turned to look at Dave, before slowly turning away again.

"Okay, that aside," James said, "someone go wake him up. Actually, Dave! I nominate you!" Dave groaned, but did stand up and head over to the side "room" that they'd built in Fort Door to house the cots.

JP poked through the bowl of orbs, newly refilled with what they'd brought back. "So, I was thinking. It was mentioned to me that you can . . . was it 'eat' the yellow ones?" James and Alanna traded a considering look before shrugging. "Okay, eat or absorb or something the yellow ones. So, we had a few here. Why didn't Anesh just take one of those instead of sleeping?"

"I . . . hm." James stalled his line of thought. "That's a good question. I mean, it burns them up pretty fast. Maybe he just didn't want to waste one? Also, what if it ran out during a fight? That would be . . . well, we don't know what it would look like, I guess. He might just fall over."

Alanna shifted in her chair. "I bet he just didn't think of it."

"Ooh, oh! I bet he has a complaint about not wanting to throw off his sleep schedule!" James excitedly threw back.

Opening her mouth to respond, Alanna stopped and thought for a second, tapping her finger on the table. "You know what? Okay. I bet you one share of loot."

"What, really?" James asked.

"Really."

"Okay, yeah. Yeah! You're on." He reached his arm across himself to shake her hand firmly. "I'm gonna regret this!" James said cheerfully.

Over the course of the week, JP had apparently had a long conversation with Anesh about the nature of their loot-sharing system. The core of it was solid, and they weren't planning to change that. But an argument at game night had brought up the case of trading away shares, and how they broke up some of the items on offer. Was it "fair," really, to have a single small yellow orb be on the table next to a giant green? Or next to stacks of cash? And how did they split up the cash in the first place?

The answers were pretty straightforward, really. The "petty cash" account took half the money they got. The rest got split into one pile per person. The orbs all stood alone, and so did the magic items. If someone wanted to trade that big green to someone else for a dozen small yellows, that was totally their choice. Really, as with the arrangement in the group itself, the unifying principle was less a matter of contract law, and more a matter of *just don't be a dick.*

And so far, it was working out for them. Even Dave, James would grudgingly admit. Dave wasn't always the most pleasant person to be around; he often came across as annoying or overbearing even when he wasn't saying anything stupid or rude. But he wasn't stupid, and he was taking to the dungeon pretty well now that he had some decent direction and a bit of practice.

Anesh chose that moment to stumble out, still blinking sleep out of his eyes, and trying to hit Dave, who was dodging ahead of him. Ganesh buzzed around both of them, doing lazy loops that seemed a little unstable, and James wondered if the drone had been asleep too. The mental image of his friend cuddled up with the little chitinous critter was pretty adorable.

"Anesh!" Alanna called over, causing him to stop trying to strangle Dave for the crime of waking him up. "Why did you take a nap and not just absorb a yellow? This is important."

"Because James already ruined my sleep patter—" He didn't even get to finish the sentence before he was interrupted.

"Yes!" James cut him off, pumping a fist in the air. "I knew it!"

Alanna punched the table in mock anger. "Now see here, young man!" she said to Anesh in her best "stern librarian" voice. "I didn't come all this way to lose bets on you."

"Why are you betting on me?" Anesh said, taking his own seat as he cleared the dust from his eyes. Ganesh took the opportunity of a stable platform to land on his shoulder and settled down for a nap of his own, while Dave took a seat on the other side of the desk, out of range of any retaliation from Anesh. "Wait, no, *what* are you betting on me?"

"Loot shares." JP smoothly filled him in with a grin. "So, that puts James at three, Anesh at two, and the rest of us at one? Does that sound right?"

"I've actually been wondering. How do we do this with this much stuff?" Dave asked. The question was kind of open, but mostly aimed at JP or Anesh, since they were the ones who were "running" the system of divvying up the spoils.

JP leaned back. "We pick who picks first randomly," he started, setting a pair of dice from his pocket on the table, "then we go around in order, picking something off the table. Each pick costs a share. When we *all* run out of shares, we start over."

"Isn't this kind of uneven?" James slowly spoke with concern.

"Well, yes," JP admitted. "But think about it; we can either live as Bill and Ted commanded, and be excellent to each other, or we can spend half our time in here sorting out who 'deserves' what, and generally feel resentful when the system fails us." He looked over at James, steepling his fingers in front of him as he put on a distinguished voice. "Tell me, my friend, how do you feel about overly complex management systems?"

There was a series of *"oooh nos"* as everyone, James included, made gestures of dissent. "Okay, point taken. I'm fine with the imbalance if everyone else is." Nods to that one. "Okay, so, any other business before we do this?"

"Why's there a briefcase on the table?" Anesh asked.

"We can't figure out how to open it, and I wanted something from that stupid cubicle where I couldn't figure out the password. I think 'briefcase that can't take damage' is a pretty fair reward," James told him.

Anesh looked over the briefcase and its attached note. "Did you consider trying R-4401 as the password?" he asked.

". . . Well, fuck," James said. Everyone burst out laughing at that, startling Rufus up to a ready position before he realized there wasn't a threat and settled back down. "I mean, obviously not. Though I'll think of it next time. Anyway! Loot! Come on, let's go!"

"Why are you in such a hurry, man?" Dave asked with an amused huff of breath.

James glared at his teammate. "Because I have to pee, you jackass! And the bathrooms are two miles away, and we lost the path back to them! So loot! Now! Go!"

JP casually rolled the dice, cutting off the chatter. "Eight," he said in an even tone, as if his friends weren't fighting across his seat.

One by one, they rolled. And then, one by one, they started picking things.

"Stack of cash!" Alanna opened with.

"Wow, really? Not an orb?" James asked in response.

"Really. JP, go!" she commanded.

JP snapped up one of the larger yellow orbs and passed to Dave. Dave, on his turn, started to reach for the larger of the blues on the table, but Anesh held up a hand. "Hey, offer for you. I'll give you two shares for that blue."

"That's . . . weird. But okay, sure." Dave handed him the orb, unsure if something weird was going on, and passed to Anesh. "Why not just . . . couldn't you just ask for the blues and we could . . . do that?"

Anesh just shrugged. "This is kinda fun. I'm out of shares for this round. On to you, James."

"Okay, I take the green, then," he said.

The loot started to be separated out as each of them took their choices into their own private pile. The orange went to Alanna, and the other blue disappeared too, followed shortly by the purples, and then the money and yellows started to go, and eventually, they were just grabbing bundles of candy or one of the couple of USB drives with amusingly mundane files on them. The briefcase ended up going to Alanna, and the mysterious printer ink cartridge went to Dave, who muttered about spoils of war. JP, in consolation, grabbed a box full of mundane 8GB RAM sticks, which soothed his loss a bit.

"So, is that everything?" James asked. "We can crack them now or later, I don't care, but I need to get going right now either way, and Dave is so bored he's been building some kind of monster out of folded paper and binder clips."

"And tape!" Dave informed him. He'd sold away almost all his shares for the last purple, and had been just chilling while the rest of them cut the pile into pieces.

Anesh waved James off. "Go, do your thing. I mean, we'll literally catch up to you in no time, since once the door closes, it'll be a couple seconds for you, and we can wrap up here."

"Good point. See you in a bit. Good night, Rufus!" James said, standing up, shoving his winnings into his backpack and heading out in a hurried walk. The dungeon was great, he loved it, but after six hours of hiking, fighting, discussing, and exploring, and staying hydrated through all of it, he felt like his options were find a bathroom, or literally pop. And he wanted to avoid that one.

Anesh waved to him as the door swung shut behind him. Then he turned back to the table. "So, anyone have anything else we need to go over? Do you guys have an after-action report to file?" he asked JP and Alanna.

"Do we do those now?" Alanna asked with mild scorn. Bureaucracy was never her favorite thing, and Anesh was proposing something dangerously close to actual work.

Fortunately, JP was there to sum it up efficiently. "We staked out the break room for a while, then when nothing showed up,

James and I started looting the cupboards. Found a folded space nest of striders, then a tumblefeed engaged. Things you might be interested in: the striders were actively using a magic item, and the tumblefeed was eating the orbs from the striders. Alanna? Anything about the fight?"

This was more where she was able to talk confidently. "Oh, tumbles was less trying to roll us over, and more trying to grapple. It was also a lot smaller, but a lot springier. We should consider that these things actually 'age' in some way." She made air quotes as she said it. "James had to use some of our thermite on it. Oh, I also shot a couple things, normally"—it took Anesh a second to understand she meant "with a real gun" and that she hadn't fireballed them—"and that didn't attract a swarm." She took a deep breath as she ended her explanation. "I think . . . that's all?"

"Oh, all the hot chocolate packets are real," JP said.

Alanna and Anesh both turned to look at him with puzzled faces. "Why . . ."

"I mean, they're real. They're not . . . this." JP held up a candy bar. "They are a product in our world. Look." The hot chocolate packets were labeled as Swiss Mix. Something James partially recognized as actual food, with branding that didn't look like a creepy off-color fever dream.

"Concerning. Everyone make a note, we'll have to look into this when we aren't looking into literally every other problem." Anesh leaned into the palms of his hands as he rested his elbows on the desk. "We have so many problems . . ." He groaned.

"Okay, what else, while we're here?" JP asked, trying to push Anesh out of his complaining.

"Well," Anesh said, sitting up. "I wanted to try something, if you guys are interested in giving input."

"Always" and "Yup" fom Alanna and JP and an "Eh" from Dave came back to Anesh.

"Okay, great. So I want to try making a piece of xenotech," Anesh told them. Alanna placed her palm on the table and leaned toward him, opening her mouth, and Anesh rolled his eyes. "Fine, a magic item. Happy, you wanker?"

"Yes."

"Super. Hand me a spear and tell me when this becomes a bad idea," Anesh said, holding up the blue orb he'd "bought" from Dave.

Alanna looked over at JP, who just shrugged. He knew well enough that he didn't have a damn clue what this would do. Alanna didn't either, but that didn't stop her from saying, "This seems like a bad idea, but I can't think of a reason to stop you? Why does it feel like a bad idea?"

Anesh set the polished black wood boar spear on the table and held the blue orb above it. "Do you think it matters where I try to put it?"

"Probably. Go for the blade, I guess?" Alanna pulled her feet up and rolled her chair away from where the blade of the spear was facing. "Just wait for me to get out of the way when it starts shooting ice beams or some bullshit."

He leaned forward, pushing down on the orb. It didn't crack in his hands, but it also didn't interact with the spear either. "Hm," Anesh muttered to himself. He was pretty sure that he was missing something, but he didn't know what. He tried focusing on the idea of improving the weapon, then when that didn't work, just focusing on the spear "as a weapon."

And when *that* didn't do anything, he just glared at it.

"I'll deal with this later. Who wants to get to the fun part of the night and actually use the orbs?" he said.

Alanna gave out a gleeful laugh, and then instantly felt bad about it. "Sorry, sorry! I'm not making fun of you, just . . . it's kinda silly, yeah? Also, I want to usseeee theeeesseee." She held up a palmful of the small treasures, glittering in multiple colors and leaving it looking like she was holding rounded fire.

"I get it," Anesh said, casually petting Ganesh, who was currently eating his own orb for the night. "It's hard to resist. Who wants to go first?"

"Well, I've not got many to go through, so, me?" JP asked. Everyone nodded at him, even Alanna, who was practically bouncing in her chair to use her own. "All right. Let's see, then." He started deliberately breaking them open with even-handed bursts of pressure.

[+3 Skill Ranks : Investment Banking]
[+1 Skill Rank : Culture – British – Game Shows]
[+1 Skill Rank : Mountain Biking]
[+1 Skill Rank : Drive – Hovercraft]
[+1 Skill Rank : Repair – Vacuum Cleaner]

He reported his outcomes to the others, and Anesh did his now solemn duty of recording everything. "Esoteric, I guess, but otherwise I'm kind of happy with this," JP said. "I could see myself using at least one of these in real life."

"Which . . . one?" Alanna asked suspiciously. "Are you rich enough for investment banking?"

"What? No. Well, I mean, maybe." He tucked his stacks of money into his coat pocket. "But I meant fixing the vacuum when it breaks. I thought that was obvious?"

"I would have said the biking one." Alanna shrugged. "Anyway! My turn!" she excitedly burst out, her words sitting comfortably in the still air of the office. Anesh made a "go ahead" gesture with a smile at her, and without any aplomb, she just slammed her whole handful of orbs down onto the table.

[Certification Added : Fiduciary]
[+2 Skill Ranks : Cartography]
[+1 Emotional Resonance Rank – Hope]
[+1 Skill Rank : Criticism – Film]
[+1 Skill Rank : Teaching]
[+1 Skill Rank : Construction – Roofing]
[+1 Skill Rank : Falconry]
[+2 Skill Ranks : Dewey Decimal System]
[Shell Upgraded : Comfortable Arm Speed Threshold +8 m/s]
[+1 Skill Rank : Math – Mental Addition]

Alanna raised her eyebrow in curiosity at the notice from the purple and started moving her arm back and forth while she told the others what she'd gotten. It turned out a human could whip their arm at a pretty fast speed already, though not without starting to strain the muscle from stopping it. Alanna, though, was no longer bound by the same physical restriction. She didn't have any extra speed by default, but when she put effort into it? Her arm became a blur, moving so fast that JP couldn't track it as he watched her start to practice moving while Anesh took notes. She started throwing punches and discovered it worked both ways, too. Her jabs turned lightning fast: still needing effort to accelerate, but no longer strictly bound by physical laws. "This is so unbelievably cool," she informed them.

JP couldn't help but let slip a wry "You don't say?" as she continued shadowboxing. Shaking his head, he looked over to Anesh. "What about you? Your turn now."

Anesh finished writing and gave a quick nod with his own eager grin. "I'm saving the blues, obviously. I'll try back at the flat to turn something into a thing-that-breaks-physics." One by one, he went through his orbs. Only a few yellows, but he'd also gotten the other purple, and he was thrilled to try it.

[+1 Skill Rank : First Aid – Splints]

[+1 Skill Rank : Cooking – Recipes – Pasta]

[+1 Skill Rank : Music – K-Pop]

[Shell Upgraded : Fast Reaction Time – 0.8 Seconds]

[+1 Emotional Resonance Rank : Fury]

"That's . . . strange," he said. "I didn't use a red, did I?" Anesh asked his audience. He filled them in on what he'd gotten, and Alanna shrugged.

"Sometimes the blues and oranges also give skills, right?" she asked without slowing her motions, still getting used to her newfound speed. "It's just like that. Only . . . infuriating."

Anesh groaned. "Oh my god, go home." He sarcastically threw the words at her. "Dave, you're last. Go . . . ahead . . ." Anesh looked over at where Dave was delicately putting the finishing touches on his little creation: sticky-note wings adorning the frame of what looked like a mutant snake-bat made of office supplies. "Dave, what?"

"Oh! I wanted to see if this worked," Dave said, looking up from his arts and crafts project. "James told me Rufus was originally just a normal drone, so I wanted to see if I could make a pet too."

"I didn't make . . ." Anesh stopped himself. "No, you know what? Have fun. You do you."

JP looked at the thing on the table. "What is it? It looks like half a dragon."

"It is! I call it a pendragon, since James also told me that puns are a mandatory tradition," Dave replied smugly. Without waiting, or really thinking about it, he took the three yellow orbs he'd collected from his loot picks and poured them onto the creation like a farmer scattering seeds.

Anesh wanted to tell him it wasn't going to work. Alanna wanted to tell him it was a pretty silly idea. And JP was just curious as to how this was going to go. But not one of them, save maybe Dave himself, expected the orbs to just phase into the creature, and for it to shake itself off and perk up its now quite flexible pen head.

"Holy shit," Alanna said, wide-eyed.

"Hey, it worked! Hey, tiny friend!" Dave said, holding out his hand, palm up.

The pendragon, and it did look a bit like a dragon, shivered a bit. Its body was a pair of pens, clipped together, with one of them coming to a point for its head, which was capped. A set of three pairs of tiny eyes opened along the pen cap, peering up at Dave for a second as it got used to its new life. It had a "tail" that was really just another pen, this one uncapped and flowing to a smooth point, and flexible as a serpent. The wings that radiated out from the back of it were also held on with a gator clip and were made up of pen-bones taped together, spreading brightly colored sticky-note wings.

As they watched, it solidified. The materials becoming more . . . real. Less haphazard, and more tightly linked.

It sniffed Dave's palm before looking around at its surroundings. Then it squawked, *loudly*, and made everyone jump in shock before it hopped onto Dave's hand and started poking at his arm.

"She likes me!" Dave said. "Can I take her ho—"

"No!" Anesh said. "Ahem. No. No, sorry. And we do have to leave soon. I didn't really expect that to work. But she'll be safe here with Ganesh and Rufus. Right, you two?"

Rufus made an assent gesture, but Ganesh was rigid, staring at the new little creature. He wasn't happy about it, but if Anesh asked him, well, he'd get over it. But that thing gave him the creeps.

"Okay, Dave. Any other orbs?" Anesh asked, checking their timer.

Dave did have a couple more, which he used quickly, wanting to get to their customary after-delve dinner.

[+1 Skill Rank : Sewing]

[+1 Emotional Resonance Rank : Surprise]

"Wut," he asked flatly.

"What?" Anesh prompted.

"That's what I'm asking. What's the point of being surprised easily?" Dave asked, relaying his gains.

Alanna, thinking quickly, threw a sudden and absolutely unexpected punch toward Dave. He gave a startled screech but already had his hands up to block. Alanna still could have hit him, had she not stopped her fist, but the blast of adrenaline flowing through Dave's blood felt, to him, less erratic and jittery, and more just empowering. He didn't even have that leftover bitter taste in his mouth.

"So?" Alanna asked, seeing Dave's expression shift from startled to confused to thoughtful.

"Oh man, that's weird. It feels, like, correct? Wow. You guys should try this." He tried to explain, badly, the feeling of being connected to how he felt.

Anesh snorted, and JP just held up his hand. "I'll pass," JP said. "Now, dinner? Lunch? Brunch? What time is it?"

"I mean, still 3:44..." Anesh told him.

His friend corrected. "I meant to say, how long have we been awake, in here?"

"Seven-ish hours. We really should go," Anesh said. "Please. Let's just deal with this stuff next week, okay?"

They packed up, bagging the rest of the loot, leaving most of their gear to sort later. Anesh wasn't trying to rush them, it was just that he was totally trying to rush them. And while he would have loved to have more time to say goodbye to Ganesh, he had to get by with a quick "Please try to make friends, and don't off the new kid" before he ushered the other three out the door.

James was still in the hallway when they got out, and he looked behind him as they arrived. "Hey. How'd it go?"

"Dave made a dragon," Alanna told him.

There was a moment of quiet, and held laughter.

Then James smiled. "Cool!"

He felt like there wasn't going to be anything else in the world that could sum up any better how the dungeon made him feel.

CHAPTER 7

"So, have you considered getting a pet bird?" James asked Alanna as they drove out to the diner. She'd hopped in his car, leaving Dave to ride with Anesh while JP headed home.

Now they rolled at a comfortable speed down the highway; the sky was still dark, though not for much longer. The June sun would start pushing away the stars in not too long, and the air, while still cool now, would begin to warm up to that thick heat that marked the days.

Alanna wasn't worried about any of that right now, though, or about how it would be impossible to sleep beyond noon if it got too hot; she was spacing out, and if thinking about anything, it was just simple relief that James was the kind of person who treated speed limits like guidelines, as opposed to Anesh's rigid adherence to the law.

But now James asked a question, and she turned to answer. "Nope" was the easy first half of the answer. "I know, I know, I got a second rank in falconry. That's cool and all. But I just . . . don't like birds? Also, where the hell would I keep a falcon? I live with my mom."

"Oh, really? I thought you lived on my couch now," James said without thinking, almost immediately regretting it.

But Alanna didn't take offense. "Maybe? It's not a bad couch. Anesh actually told me I could sleep in Sarah's room, but . . ."

James finished for her as she trailed off. "But that's suuuuper uncomfortable."

"Exactly! I mean, it's not like sleeping in a dead person's bed. But, well, it actually might be?" Alanna looked over at James to see him staring forward, jaw clenched and hands tight on the wheel.

"I'd be pretty angry if it was." He spoke quietly. "I know I didn't press it today, but I'm actually really, what's the term, eager? No. Anxious, I guess. I'm anxious to go hunting after her." James sighed. A tense air filled the car while he gathered his thoughts. "The dungeon probably killed someone." His voice was tight in his throat. "It took her away from us, in practically every way. And maybe I wouldn't be this upset if she didn't seem like a cool person, or maybe I shouldn't care so much about someone who's probably already gone, but I do . . . hang on."

He took a minute to maneuver around a slow-moving truck, passing it on the outside bend of a curve in the road, his headlights painting the concrete divider bright white against the dark night.

"I care too," Alanna muttered. "And it sucks to feel like Anesh and JP don't."

"What about Dave?" James asked quizzically.

"Dave was never going to care. He doesn't even care about the dungeon, really. You weren't there when we used our loot, but he really did just casually make life, because he was kind of bored." Alanna put on an expression halfway to a grimace. "And that's not even bad, I guess? But for fuck's sake, it seems wasteful."

James nodded. "I get that. I mean, hell, we're not even using the yellows for 'fuel,' right? They're just too valuable."

"Exactly. But my point is, I care. I want to follow where she went, and I'm still pretty pissed that you guys didn't signpost properly and don't know how to get back to the bathrooms. But even then, it feels like we're just wasting time, and it's annoying." She folded her arms across her chest and watched the road fly by past them for a second. "We've been offered the chance to be the good guys, and we're acting like mercenaries instead. It's offensive."

James more or less agreed with her. As he hit the off-ramp to where they were meeting up for food, he spun the wheel into the turn lane and replied, "I don't want to be the guy that drags everyone else into some stupid good-guy quest they don't want, though."

"Fuck 'em," Alanna said with a little bit more vitriol than she really meant. "I mean, they can do what they want, I guess. I don't mind sharing the dungeon with them. But I'm with you here; it *hurts* that they don't care. Anesh, at least, I think will come with us if we just head off next week. He's invested in keeping you alive. And that means we'd have Ganesh too, and we could do some real mapping." She sighed. "You know, now that I know how to actually make maps? I realize that I have made some shit maps. It's like looking back on work I did in elementary school and thinking that child-me was an idiot."

"So, what, we just dive in ourselves?" James asked. He'd stopped the car in the parking lot of the diner, and the two of them were sitting illuminated by a single orange streetlamp. "Let them do their thing, just go hunting, hope we get lucky?"

She shrugged in response. "More than hope; I did want to borrow Ganesh. After we can spot the place, and if we skip looting, and move quickly, we can just rush it. Take the gear we most need, don't bother with anything we can spare."

"That sounds . . . super risky? Like, I know I'm supposed to be the token dumb guy in the group, but come on."

Another shrug. "It's important. To us, at least. So, I say again, if the others don't want to help, it falls to us to act."

That got a grin out of James. Alanna's life ethos was pretty straightforward, really. Sometimes, in her eyes, the world had to be reminded of certain things. Courses corrected, wrongs righted. Not just big ones, although the fact that this *was* a big one certainly helped. It was a policy Alanna lived, more than she talked about it. But when she did bring it up, it was for things she found important.

James had really only ever heard her discuss it in something more than the abstract once. And afterward, he'd had to think pretty hard about the kind of person he wanted to be, personally. He'd always wanted to be the hero; what kid didn't, after all. But he had realized the difference between himself and Alanna back then—that he had to think about being heroic, while for her, it was as easy as breathing.

So now, he thought about it for a few seconds, and promptly decided to follow her instincts. "Yeah, okay," James said. "Next week, we go for it."

"Great!" Alanna was a little too cheerful about their possible doom. "Now, I note that Anesh's car isn't here yet, because he drives like a grandma . . ."

"*You've* never been in a car with my grandmother," James interjected, past highway traumas flashing across his mind.

". . . So *anyway*, do you want to go across the street and get something to drink from the gas station? I feel like a walk, and chocolate milk, and neither of those are gonna happen sitting in the diner," Alanna finished, glaring at him.

James popped his door open, letting the warm night air in and ignoring that you absolutely could order chocolate milk from the diner. "Sure, I could walk."

The two of them stretched their legs in the parking lot before climbing a small dirt embankment to a well-lit sidewalk. Deep breaths of fresh air, thick with the scent of pine needles and pollen, filled their lungs.

"You know," James said as they jaywalked across the street, "we should really remember to do warm-up stretches before going in. My legs are killing me from all that walking."

Alanna pushed open the door of the convenience store attached to the gas station, the crisp white light painting boxes on the dark pavement. "You fucking forgot? How? You've been going to the gym regularly for months now, this should be a routine for you, man."

James rolled his eyes back at her, even though she wouldn't see. The expression could still be heard in his voice, though, as he told her, "There's a difference between a gym routine and preparing to—" He stopped abruptly, and Alanna smacked into his back. "Um . . ."

"Why did you . . ." she started to say, a bit annoyed, but then she took the time to look past him.

Just inside the doors, a man in a balaclava stood shoving food off the racks into a backpack. On the other side of the counter, the clerk was standing with his hands in the air as another masked person held the kid at knifepoint while stripping fistfuls of bills out of the register. As the door dutifully chimed out to introduce new customers to the store, both of the thieves froze and snapped their heads toward the door.

There was a moment of perfect silence. Which James quickly broke by tilting his head toward Alanna and stage-whispering in a voice clearly meant to be overheard. "Is this actually happening to us?" he asked.

"I think it is!" she responded in kind.

James grinned. "You never expect it to happen to you, right?"

"Should we call the police? I don't want to ruin it."

"This is kind of a magical moment, yeah," James said back, a spike of adrenaline starting to flood his bloodstream.

Alanna was having a similar reaction, but even as she felt her body getting ready to fight, she couldn't help but find herself making jokes with James. "This looks weirdly familiar, doesn't it?" She gestured to the guy with the backpack.

They'd been in life-or-death situations for the last eight hours. And that experience had been repeated every week for months now, for James at least. But there was something about the threat of other living, breathing humans that made both of them feel their blood run cold.

As Alanna finished talking, the thief who was failing to cram bags of chips into his pack snapped out of his stunned silence and dropped the bag. Pulling a switchblade out of his pocket and flicking it open, he yelled over at the two of them, "Don't fucking move!"

His friend behind the counter also shouted something, but James wasn't listening. He shuffled to the right a bit, allowing Alanna to step up next to him, and made eye contact with the thug approaching him. "Why?" he asked, his heart beating hard in his chest.

"Because I told you to, you bitch! And give me your wallet!" the guy yelled at James, waving the knife in his face far too close for comfort.

James raised his eyebrows. "Oh, a compelling argument," he said, resisting the urge to take a half step back and away from the jackass threatening to stab him. Without looking back, he spoke in a calm, projecting voice: "Alanna, get the other one." The guy in front of him didn't make the connection fast enough, and by the time he realized his target wasn't in any way prepared to stop moving, James had already lashed out and punched him in the eye.

The strike was fast and connected with a satisfyingly awful squish as James's fist slammed into the thief's face. The man in the mask let out a howl of pain and started flailing with his knife even as he brought his other hand up to grasp at the point where he'd been hit. The knife met only air, though, as James pivoted around a wire rack of greeting cards and cleared space for Alanna to get by.

The other thief was in the process of vaulting the counter, the panicked clerk roughly thrown to the side by the larger figure. He slid over the glass case of lottery tickets, knocking a few dozen packs of gum and the "leave a penny" cup onto the floor. He looked *pissed*, even through the mask, but that was understandable. James had just sucker-punched his friend.

Unfortunately, he didn't get too far. As he tried to land and rush to help his buddy shank James, Alanna slid forward, caught him cleanly with a hand around his throat, and just slammed him downward, cracking his head against the counter.

The noise made even James wince as he kept up his footwork against his partner in this scuffle. He wasn't being nearly as brutal as Alanna, instead trying to minimize his chances of getting stabbed. Every time the guy would rush him or get too close, James used open-handed strikes to hammer his arm away, constantly aiming for the wrist and elbow. His assailant was, if nothing else, going to be at least half bruise tomorrow. James was kiting him down the aisle, and when the guy tried to surprise him with a right hook instead of another stab, James twisted under the hit, grabbed a can of soda off the shelf next to his head, and flung it underhand into the guy's forehead as he righted himself.

Alanna wasn't as martially skilled as James, which was fair. He'd already gotten some supernatural help on the subject. But she made up for it with a fighting style that would have been right at home in a bar brawl. The guy she'd just slammed to the ground rolled away, trying to stagger to his feet and just stumbling back to his knees as his world spun from the hit to his skull. He fumbled a knife out, and it scattered across the floor as Alanna kicked it from his hand without a pause.

Alanna rolled her eyes. Unlike James, her fear reaction was entirely instinctual, and not at all personal. She knew she could take this guy, and she knew that compared to him, her dungeon augments made her practically superhuman.

Last week, Alanna had tested out the limits of her first purple orb with a kitchen knife. She'd found herself unable to casually draw blood from her palm. Or formally draw blood from her palm. Or actually cut herself without a very real effort. It was actually partly frightening, because if she ever needed to go to a hospital for a blood draw, there were going to be problems.

But right now? Against a guy who'd just lost his only knife? Well, she didn't know if the protection extended to her eyeballs, but Alanna still felt practically invincible.

So when he staggered up and lunged at her, fists balled up, she just slugged him in the stomach again.

He doubled over, retching, and Alanna kneed him, sending him sprawling back on his ass. She almost felt sorry for the guy moaning on the ground, though if he hadn't literally just been trying to hit her, he might have gotten more pity points. "Hey. You want to call the police or something?" she shot over to the clerk while she stood over the unfortunate assailant, making sure he didn't get up.

The clerk jumped a bit at being addressed. "Oh, I hit the button a while back."

"Then why do you have your phone... are you fucking filming this?" Alanna asked. She wasn't angry, though, more just... resigned. Of *course* the guy was filming this.

Behind her, there was a crash as James shoved his dance partner into a metal shelf. Then James himself emerged from the aisle, shifting on the balls of his feet as the guy roared at him and kept trying in vain to stab him. Alanna took a deep, frustrated breath as she saw the massive grin on James's face.

"James, stop fucking around. The police are on their way, I don't want them shooting me by accident," she said, perhaps a little too theatrically. The still-standing masked bandit caught her out of the corner of his eye and half turned to see his own partner pinned to the floor by Alanna's boot. Without hesitating, the robber turned away from both of them and bolted for the door.

Of course, that was the universal signal for the door to swing open as a pair of cops stepped in. One of them looked like he was trying really hard not to laugh as the guy in an actual black ski mask tried to bolt between the two mountains of men in uniform. It was almost with casual strength that they grabbed his arms and bore him to the ground, the thief swearing furiously.

"So, Anesh just texted me," James said to Alanna, casually walking up to her with his phone out. "They're waiting for us over at the diner."

She cracked the bones in her neck, staring at him the whole time. "You picked a really awkward time for that," she said, raising her hands in the air as one of the cops came up to them, hand casually hovering over his Taser.

It didn't take them too long to explain that they weren't actually trying to knock over the convenience store. Though they did have to sit for a while, show their IDs, and repeat everything twice after the initial explaining. The clerk helped out, providing confirmation of their story, and trying to show the one officer the video he took of the fight. The cop wasn't that interested, though, and was more focused on chastising James and Alanna.

"It was good that you wanted to help," he said in a deep, hard voice. "But you really shouldn't try to pick fights with people with knives."

James opened his mouth to say something, but Alanna casually put him in a headlock and interrupted. "Yeah, we're sorry. It just sort of happened," she said, stopping James from snarking at the police. "I think they were drunk or something. Anyway. Are we free to go? Our friends are waiting for us."

She said it in the perfectly polite, half-cheerful tone of someone who had absolute faith that she'd done nothing wrong. And it wasn't until a clearly suspicious officer let them go, and they got out the doors and into the early-morning air, that the pleasant smile dropped off her face and she let out a long sigh.

"Let's go get a milkshake," James said quietly, setting a hand on her shoulder.

"What took you guys so long?" Anesh asked as Alanna and James slid into the booth opposite himself and Dave.

James took a second to adjust how he was sitting on the torn green leather booth seat. "Oh, we got held up."

Alanna snorted next to him. "We were robbed. Well, we walked into a robbery, and then the robbery became directed at us."

"Holy shit, are you guys okay?!" Anesh asked, concern painted on his face.

"Oh, yeah, we're fine. It was weird to actually fight other humans, though."

"You got in a fight?!" Anesh half yelled. Fortunately, the diner was mostly empty at this time of night, and no one looked over at them. "Ahem. Sorry. You got in a fight?" he asked in a much quieter tone.

James shrugged. "I mean, what else were we supposed to do? Give them our wallets? I have, like, two thousand dollars in mine."

"Wait, you actually put your money in your wallet?" Alanna asked him incredulously. "I thought you just wanted to have a scrap."

He looked over at her, leaning on the table to turn sideways. "Why the hell would I just casually want to punch out a mugger?" James waited for Dave and Anesh to think it over and both start to answer before he carried on with his sentence. "Yeah, I'm just kidding. I totally wanted to punch out a mugger. I'm now one step closer to being Batman."

"Also it's probably gonna be on YouTube," Alanna told him.

"Yeah," James replied a bit tentatively. "I saw that the clerk recorded it on his phone. I'm kinda up in the air about that. On the one hand, it's probably not good for security. But I mean, it was pretty cool to get to turn three months of weight training and dungeon diving into a solid win over someone with a knife."

They talked for a bit longer over their food. Joking and laughing, looking for all the world like just a group of normal friends out for a late dinner or an early breakfast. No one passing by would guess that the four people in the corner booth had been in multiple combats that night, that one of them could do literal magic, one of them had fabricated life less than an hour ago, and one of them was a fledgling Superman. It was just comfortable for them to set aside the weird stuff for a while and banter about video games, complain about work, and be . . . normal friends.

As their meal ended and everyone started getting ready to go, James had one last thing to say, on a more serious note. "Hey, Dave." His friend perked up from where he was trying to calculate the tip on his bill. "It was kind of an accident that we told you about the dungeon at all. Originally, we weren't going to, because I wasn't sure if you'd be a good party member," James said, and he watched Dave's face shift from confusion to anger and back again in a fast pattern. "But you did good tonight. Really. So thanks for coming along, man."

Dave shifted in his seat a bit. "Yeah, well, it's . . . not as bad as I first thought. And, well, it is really cool, isn't it? So thanks for inviting me. And for telling me." Dave stood, closing his bill and setting it on the table. "I'm gonna walk home, since I live just down the street. See you guys later, okay?" he called back over his shoulder as he gathered his coat and headed out, plucking a handful of mints out of the jar by the door on his way.

"Why'd you tell him that?" Alanna asked James, a bit confused at her friend's actions.

"Because of what we said. He doesn't care about the dungeon. Not really. It's just something kind of cool for him; I think Dave might be somewhere on the spectrum. And I mean that in the least hostile way possible. But yeah, he doesn't care about the dungeon, but he does care about being a good teammate. So I'm gonna make sure to let him know when he's helpful." James shrugged. "Just seems to make sense to keep everyone happy. Besides. It's a nice thing to do."

"Bah. You and your 'friendship' nonsense," Anesh said sarcastically. "Kindness and compassion getting in the way of my cold, efficient, mercenary actions. So inconvenient."

Alanna rolled her eyes. "Yeah, I'm sure that's a problem for you. So, are we done here?"

"Yeah, I'm ready to go. Let me just leave a tip," James said.

Anesh looked up. "I already tipped," he said, a bit guiltily.

"Yeah, I know you did that thing you do where you pay the kitchen staff's rent for a month," James replied snarkily. "But I want to actually tip like a normal human."

"Normal American," Anesh corrected.

"Whatever. I'm leaving five bucks and you can't stop me, goddammit."

Alanna snickered at the two of them, shooting verbal jabs back and forth, before sadly cutting them short. "All right, do either of you want to give me a ride home, or can I just sleep on your couch?"

"The fact that you asked for the couch makes me think you don't *want* a ride home," Anesh told her, a bit of sadness in his voice. "So you get the couch, because it's more convenient for everyone. Now, let's go. I've got stuff to do today, and I want a short nap before I have to wake up for class."

"Doing anything aside from class?" James asked him.

Anesh nodded as the trio walked out the door. "Yeah, I want to see about getting a silencer for your pistol. I heard that thing all the way from the fort, and I want to maybe deal with that."

"Well, I mean, good fucking luck. Also, I think you mean a 'suppressor.' But whatever word you want to use, you're not getting one," James told Anesh.

His friend looked back at him. "What? Why not? I know you're not comfortable with guns, but . . ."

"No, no, it's nothing to do with the social or cultural aspects of gun ownership. You just can't get one. Legally, anyway. You need to go through a lot of legal work, like getting signed permission from . . . I think it's the FBI? No, the ATF. Yeah. And also the local police chief." James rolled his shoulders a bit. "It's just a giant hassle. I'm also pretty sure that you couldn't be the one to fill out the paperwork, since you're not a U.S. citizen. And I don't know if there's any fees associated with it, though that's less of an issue now."

"What about just taping a bottle to the end of it?" Anesh asked. "I'm given to understand that does something."

"Sure, once," Alanna said. "And then there's just a bottle taped to the end of your gun. Also it can throw off the aim on lower-caliber weapons. Like, you know, yours. Also that really only works in movies."

"My caliber is perfectly fine, thank you very much!" James said indignantly.

Anesh groaned. "Please don't confuse me by making dick jokes. Your country has so many euphemisms for it, I'm not sure I can keep up when I'm tired."

The next twenty minutes home in Anesh's car involved Alanna just making increasingly convoluted double entendres.

CHAPTER 8

Home was the smell of clean dust and the crispness of air conditioning. The cloying, muggy warmth of the early morning, still not quite having faded away in the dark, pushed its way through the door along with three exhausted warriors.

Anesh stumbled in first, bone tired, but still taking the time to bend down and untie his shoes. James and Alanna came in behind him as he rushed to get out of their way, the two leaning on each other, both secretly and wordlessly enjoying the physical contact. James showed none of the respect for his footwear that Anesh did, just kicking off his boots before pushing himself as upright as he could and letting out a jaw-aching yawn.

He looked around like he was planning to say something but then just gave a small shake of his head. No need to ruin the quiet moment.

Especially not when Anesh was willing to do it for him. "Okay, I'm for bed. You two don't stay up too late." The words came out of his mouth heavy with exhaustion, but still with a playful hint to them. "G'night," he said, heading down the hall to his bedroom, one hand out to the wall to steady his tired feet. He didn't wait for James or Alanna to reply.

"Hey, weird question," Alanna asked James as she removed her own boots.

"'Weird' is pretty subjective these days. What's up?" he replied.

She gave a short snort of a laugh. "Yeah, fair. I was going to ask if I could use your shower, or if that was too awkward."

James tried to think of something witty to say, but his tired brain failed him. "I'm trying," he told her, "to think of something witty to say here. Something vaguely flirty, but also obviously comical. But I've got nothing. Also, you've showered here before without asking, just take it."

"Yeah, well, Anesh is using the hall bathroom, and the other bathroom is attached to your bedroom," Alanna told him.

James perked his ears up to hear the sound of running water, and Anesh loudly and proudly singing "Danger Zone" from the hall bathroom in what he must have thought was an affected American accent. "Well, shit. Okay, yeah, sure. No worries." He gave a shrug that wasn't as casual as he would have liked.

It didn't go unnoticed by Alanna as they headed down the hall, passing by the bathroom door and Anesh's yodeling. "Oh, relax. You've seen me naked before."

"I have not!" James protested abruptly. "I mean, I wouldn't object, but I think you're getting your timelines mixed up."

"Hah! I knew it. You lust after me." Alanna stuck out her tongue at him as she stole in front of him to occupy his bathroom. She did close the door, though.

From outside the now-shut door, James called through the wood panels to his friend. "Not right now! You smell awful!" Smiling at her verbal middle-finger back through the door at him, he whumped down on the edge of his bed. James groaned out loud as he leaned down to peel off his socks. The delightful sensation of cool air rushing over his skin after a full day trapped in shoes was offset a bit by the twinging of bruises across his torso.

It turned out the maul carts packed a hell of a punch, and the angry purple-black blotch across his right flank really showed it off. He poked at it a couple times, not really feeling any pain, but as soon as he twisted a bit to lob his socks into his laundry hamper, a dull throbbing echoed through his nerves. It wasn't that bad, but it was certainly unavoidable.

James moved around his room a bit, just killing time. It was strangely uncomfortable to him to have someone else using his bathroom; he'd gotten pretty used to having his own space, and even though it was Alanna, it still threw him off, and he didn't want to make *her* uncomfortable by doing anything awkward. So he threw his keys and wallet on his desk, spent some time petting Lily, took a bunch of his leftover fast-food wrappers to the actual garbage can out in the kitchen, got some water, and then still hadn't wasted more than five minutes.

Eventually, the knot of anxiety in his chest at having someone else in his personal space started to unwind as he sat at his desk and idly flipped through YouTube videos. Never really focusing too much on anything, just letting his mind drift while he rolled the orbs he'd brought home around the desk.

He was midway through a video essay on the nature of choice in video games when Lily crawled up the side of his desk. The little iLipede had been given mostly free rein of his room, and James was more or less okay treating her like a bit of a cat. When she wanted attention, Lily would unashamedly climb up onto James's desk, dresser, or bed, or sometimes just right onto his feet if he stalled too long getting ready for work, and demand that attention.

James smiled as he put a hand down to keep Lily away from the orbs, feeling the small pokes of her tiny copper legs on his skin as she maneuvered around the barrier. "All right, all right. Here, play with this one," he said, offering her the solitary red orb he'd gotten from their little bidding war back in the dungeon.

To his surprise, the iLipede perked right up at that, wrapping herself around the red orb in a cute little ball and rolling back to the edge of his desk. James almost panicked as the little phone bug reached the precipice, but he got some relief as Lily unfurled, tossed the orb down into her pen, and started crawling down after it safely. "Okay, you're welcome. Enjoy your meal, Lils."

He was broken out of his sleepy watching of the iLipede playing with her new toy by Alanna cracking open the bathroom door. "Hey! You got a towel?"

"No, we abolished those by apartment treaty a month ago," James told her on reflex, throwing a clean towel through the gap in the door.

"Thanks, asshole," she replied with a smile in her voice.

After a minute or two of drying off, Alanna strode out into James's room and threw herself onto his bed, towel wrapped around her waist. "Gah!" James barked out. "Don't get my bed soggy! Also, I know you're comfortable with it, but it's super weird having you half-naked in my room," he told her as he navigated the obstacle course that was his furniture to get to the bathroom himself.

"Ah, fine," she said, all energy to argue lost to exhaustion. "I'll move when you're out of the room, so as to spare your virgin eyes."

James snorted. "My eyes are . . . never mind. I'm gonna shower, then pass out. You sleep well, yeah?" In truth, he hadn't even had a joke to tell; he'd been hoping to come up with one by the time he got done speaking the words, but it hadn't worked out.

Standing in his shower a few minutes later, hot water pouring down on his back, James took a deep breath and started thinking over the events of the day. Quiet time like this, physically comfortable and sealed away from everyone else, was a rarity for him these days. And he took advantage of it by looking back on the sometimes-frantic events of the last day, looking for anything that he needed to remember tomorrow, or anything important that got missed.

It was a form of meditation, really. The simple routine of cleaning off sweat, dirt, and sometimes blood made it easy for his mind to just slip back into self-reflection. This was also one of the times during his day when he could feel Secret, the young meme living and growing in the back of his mind.

So he played back the day in his head, trying to do it without staggering or forgetting. He'd woken up, gone to work, powered through the day, had lunch at one of the food carts, and then . . . well, then it got interesting. They'd gone into the dungeon, hauling a cartload of new gear to work with. They'd split up, James had taken Dave to the Decision Tree, and the two of them had a fairly spirited adventure. Also he'd been hit by a hostile mail cart; he remembered that one as he felt the large splotch of a bruise on his side. Then they'd gone back, and he and Alanna had gone out to try to find a way to the bathrooms, and . . .

When did they forget how to get to the bathrooms?

How did they forget how to get to the bathrooms? It was a giant blue-and-white tile spire; it wasn't like it was inconspicuous. All they had to do was keep heading toward it. They'd done it before.

"Secret," he said out loud, drawing up the idea to the forefront of his mind. "Why can't I remember this?" James asked out loud, in a voice quiet enough to be drowned out by the sound of the shower.

For once, Secret actually responded. An alien thought flicked through James's perception, not unlike when they popped one of the skill orbs. "Can't remember what?"

"The way to the bathroom," James clarified.

"You are in the bathroom, friend," Secret told him.

Was that . . . was Secret developing a sense of humor? James blinked a few times; the idea that he could even do that was kind of impressive, considering where Secret had started from, but it was also a bit worrying to think that at some point, he might be hosting an entity that was just as much of a wiseass as he was in his mind.

James sighed and replied, "No, the bathrooms in the office. Anesh and I got there once, and for some reason, I think that we can't find our way back. Why?"

Now it was Secret's turn to blink slowly. That was a weird sensation; James felt a swell of confusion, and then indignation, that he was absolutely sure was not his own. And then, a second later, words that felt less like speech and more like a brisque communiqué. "There is a piece of an intruder here. I shall deal with it." And Secret disappeared from his awareness.

"Oh, that's fucking reassuring," James said to himself, fear and anger temporarily winning out over the need for sleep. But as minutes passed by and his fingers started to wrinkle under the steaming water, nothing happened. Secret didn't say anything again, perhaps because James was now a little too awake. But he also didn't spontaneously drop dead, which was also a good sign.

After coming to terms with the fact that he really didn't have anything to do to help in this situation, James just let out a huff of breath and resigned himself to waiting. And also being forced out of the shower, before the air turned into a sauna and he totally lost the ability to breathe at all. Killing the water, James dried himself off while brushing his teeth, not really paying attention to any of the little tasks he did to wrap up his day.

As he came out into his room, the first thing he saw was that Alanna was now curled up under the blankets on his bed, fast asleep.

"Dammit, this is not what I meant when I said to sleep well," James muttered. "I meant the couch. Sleep well on the couch." But he muttered it under his breath, and he walked softly to throw on a pair of sweatpants and turn off his computer. And his mild discomfort at the situation was offset by the fact that he really was fond of Alanna, not to mention the fact that he really was just too sleepy to process this right now.

So James climbed into bed gently, on the other side of the big queen-sized mattress he'd Tetris'd into his room next to his desk, stole back a couple of his blankets, and was asleep within a minute of his head hitting the pillow, his soft smile cast in the glow of the handful of small shimmering orbs on his desk and the glimmering red jewel that Lily continued to toy with in her bedding.

Anesh was dreaming of towering red spires. Skyscraper-sized monsters that reached up to rake at the clouds. They had windows, and doors, and ledges, dotted across their exteriors, but they weren't buildings.

They surrounded him as he ran through the streets, fleeing from hounds he could not see but whose howls echoed in his heart. He knew he had to run, and running was all he could do. But his feet moved like they were stuck in mud, like he was a puppet that couldn't find a puppeteer.

Above, the buildings danced and swayed, bleeding away into fragments of nothing as they drifted into the sky. He could feel them laughing at him as he fled from his eternal pursuers.

And then, ahead of him, James stepped into his path, casually walking through an intersection like there was nothing wrong.

Anesh couldn't stop running, but James didn't seem to mind. His friend glanced up at him as he kept fleeing through the eternal city that was not a city, and then somehow kept pace, staying at his side as they moved through the red terrain.

"Are you in a hurry to find somewhere?" James asked him, his voice strangely deep and reverberant.

Anesh couldn't answer. He never spoke in his dreams, and he was vaguely aware of the fact that he was dreaming. He just kept running, taking twists and turns. Down an alley that was a perfect copy of one from the city he lived in, right down to the color of the light. As soon as he burst out the other end, the crimson atmosphere reapplied itself, painting the world red once again.

He passed by the mouth of a tunnel under a bridge that grew to encompass the whole sky, and found himself stuck staring at the gate over the sidewalk. His unwanted focus was shattered as James stepped up next to him again. "Such a strange place. This one is real, is it not?"

Anesh didn't say anything. His feet took him forward once more, down street after street, constantly running, constantly chased, never seeing what was behind him. But he knew. His heart pounded in his dreamer's chest, and his eyes were glued to the road ahead. He knew he couldn't look behind him. If he looked, if he looked . . .

He looked.

There was something there.

"Ah, thank you," James said. "There it is."

Anesh was frozen. The thing was a giant, a monster. It was one of the buildings, one of those massive, hooked, blood-red *things* that flooded up to the sky, and beyond it. It was going to kill him. It was *real*, it wasn't a dream, it was never a dream. Anesh was going to die here, and he didn't know what to . . .

James stepped up and tore it in half.

"What the fuck," Anesh said.

James glanced back over his shoulder, and Anesh felt the fear burn out of his chest. He could look around, he could stop running, he could breathe. And he knew this was a dream, but he also wasn't waking up.

"Terribly sorry," James told him, adjusting the circular gold-rimmed glasses on his nose. "I may have used you as bait. I do hope you can forgive me. I fear I have been caught up in the hunt."

Anesh took a step forward, his first deliberate dream-step. "You're not James," he said.

"Hm?" the person in his dream said. "Oh, no. I'm simply borrowing this," they said, motioning down to their body. "Don't you concern yourself, however. I promise I'm a friend."

That caught Anesh's attention. "Ah, you're Secret," he said, not as a question. "What are you doing . . ."

Before he could finish, both he and the infomorph wearing his friend's face tilted their heads as a sound filtered through the dream. It came from outside, and a second later, Anesh found himself blinking his eyes as sleep and memory fell away, and shouting filled his ears.

James and Alanna woke up at the same time, confused and yelling. Part of the confusion was because they both, at the same time while they were sleeping, suddenly knew exactly what the weather was, and what the local temperature was both inside and just outside James's window. Actually, that was pretty much all of the confusion for Alanna.

When Alanna had woken up, she'd done so with a jolt of surprise as the sudden knowledge had flooded her brain, and she *might* have flailed just a bit. When James woke up, he'd done so with a similar bit of shock at the instant access to the weather channel, but also a lot more shock as Alanna had elbowed him in the back of the head.

This had caused some chaos, which was mostly settled down by the time Anesh, still blinking sleep out of his eyes, stumbled into the doorway in his bathrobe. "What's wrong?! I heard . . . um." He cut himself off as he saw the two of them in James's bed. "Oh damn, sorry." Anesh flushed, his darker skin turning a shade of gold in embarrassment. "Didn't mean to, uh . . . why is it twenty-two degrees outside?" The awkward feeling was dying away rapidly in the face of the fact that he felt a burst of data pushed to the front of his awareness.

"That's actually what we're yelling about," James said, as Alanna rolled to her feet and threw one of the thick comforters on James's bed around her shoulders as a makeshift robe.

She shuffled around the foot of the bed to James's dresser and stole the first T-shirt she could find. One with a dinosaur on it. Anesh kept his gaze firmly aimed down the hall and away from his friend as she rearranged her blanket to a skirt and pulled the shirt on. "Why the fuck do I know how sunny it is?" she demanded in a thick voice. "Also, Anesh, I don't care if you see my tits, why are the two of you both such prudes?"

"*James* is a prude?" Anesh asked with an incredulous laugh.

"James slept with pants on." Alanna scowled. "How am I supposed to grab his butt when he's wearing pants?"

James was absolutely uninterested in the two of them talking about him while he was right there. "Okay, come on, you asses. What's going on? Why is this happening?"

Alanna folded herself back onto the bed, letting her legs dangle out into the afternoon sunlight pouring through the window. "You're no fun. But I dunno. Did we bring home anything magic?"

"We brought home a *lot* of random stuff," James said as he grabbed a shirt off the floor for himself. He intentionally didn't pay attention to either Anesh or Alanna watching him, trying his hardest to not feel self-conscious as he moved. "Do you guys mind?"

Anesh didn't mind, and he turned away with a soft cough. Alanna, though, did mind. "I didn't notice last night, but you've lost a lot of weight. Looking good, man," she told him with a thumbs-up, which just made James turn bright red.

"Yeah, well, three months of actually keeping to a gym routine, with regular bursts of combat, will do that. Also . . . what the fuck is this?" James ended the conversation about his torso and deflected his embarrassment away. The thing that he wanted to know the fuck about, which he quickly drew his friends' attention to, was in fact something in Lily's pen.

It looked like a bike wheel, with only half the outside rim intact. Spokes of pens or pencils that looked like they were scavenged off of James's desk stuck outward, creating the impression of a totemic sigil. Strips of cloth and paper that seemed like they were torn from her bedding filled out an inner ring and served to both bind the sticks together and highlight the centerpiece: a single small red sphere. The same red orb that James had given her last night.

Lily herself seemed to be snoozing, curled up like a cat at the foot of her little totem, which was somehow balanced on the tip of a single ballpoint pen.

"Okay, that's fucking weird," Alanna said, rolling over James's legs to perch on the edge of the bed, unconcerned with the casual contact. "What the hell is that?"

"Ask Lily, I guess." James shrugged. "But, I mean, I bet you ten bucks it's what's causing this latest weirdness."

Alanna rolled sideways to face James. "I thought we were wagering shares now?"

"I'm not really keeping track, I mostly only agreed to it because it made JP happy and it's kinda fun. Also it's too early for me to care," James snarked back.

Butting in, Anesh reminded him, "It's two p.m. This whole dungeon thing . . ."

"Is throwing off your sleep," Alanna and James chorused in unison.

"Yeah, we know," James continued. "Anyway. It looks like she built . . . a totem? A ward? Something? Hang on, let's test this." Gently, he picked up the assembly, careful not to break it, and then carried it out of the room, slipping past Anesh on the way out. "Let me know if you guys lose the connection, okay?"

He walked down the hallway backward, pausing every few feet to see if anything changed. As soon as he hit the living room, Alanna called out, "Lost it!" James nodded, and kept going, and three steps later, Anesh informed him that he, too, no longer had absolute knowledge about the current cloud formations overhead.

"Okay, so, it's totally this thing. Ooooooorrr it's my newfound abs. But probably this thing. Because I feel like if exercise gave people perfect information, I'd see more people in lab coats at the gym." James nodded to himself. "Now! Why."

"Why what?" Anesh asked, walking into the kitchen and starting up the coffee maker. "Why does it do that, or why did Lily make it?"

"I didn't think that far ahead," James admitted. "I'm still waking up. How about both?" He set the strangely haphazard intricate design down on their living room table, shoving aside a couple math textbooks to make room for it as a centerpiece.

Anesh narrowed his eyes at James over his cup of coffee. "Don't put that there! It's going to confuse people," he said as he settled into his armchair. "Also . . . okay, well, let's start with why it does what it does. Does it kind of remind you of something?"

The question got a nod out of James. "Literally any of the logos from Warhammer 40K."

"Oh, sod off. I mean, it reminds me a lot of the things we've found the orange orbs in, inside the office," Anesh told him as he leaned back into the padding of his seat. The table in front of him was covered in binders and notes, both for his classes and for their delving operation, but he had no desire to crack open any of them just yet. For now, he was content to sit here in the afternoon air and enjoy some time just talking. "It just seems a lot like those general . . . designs, I guess? I don't know if you saw one in that cupboard, but I know the copier definitely had its orange orb in a . . . hm, I'm going to call it a contraption, that looked a lot like this."

"Yeah, yeah." James nodded in agreement. "And that 'turn right forever' hallway had that pyramid assembly thing growing out of the desks around the orange at its center. Okay, I can see it. So, what does that mean, big picture?"

"It means there's another way to use the orbs, duh," Alanna said, coming out to join them in the living room.

James looked up from the couch as she entered. "Are those my shorts, too? You can't just occupy my entire wardrobe."

"Can, and have" came the reply. "But yeah, you wanted to know what it means? It means that we don't know how to use the orbs all the way. Think about it, what do we do with them?" Alanna prompted the two boys.

Anesh shrugged and answered easily. "Crack them, or absorb them. That second one only works on yellows, since James has forbidden us from killing ourselves trying to absorb blues. Though, that said, we should try the other colors. Maybe get Dave to try them."

A quick frown took up James's mouth for a second. "Hey, I know Dave is kind of annoying sometimes, but he's not expendable."

"I know, I know, I'm sorry." Anesh waved a hand. "We should try absorbing other colors, though. Maybe that green of yours?"

"Not happening," James said. "I'm looking forward to using that one; I just wanted to do it here, and after we were awake, since I know you like checking these outcomes. Anyway, Alanna, you were saying?"

Alanna came over with her own cup of coffee and a piece of fruit from their fridge, causing James to make an indignant gesture and a noise in his throat. "Oh, hush. It's a fifty-cent orange, I'll comp you for it. Anyway, the *point* is that there's obviously a third way. Making . . . what, wards? Wards. That sounds enough like magic to irritate Anesh."

Anesh took that opportunity to cut her off. "Nodes," he said simply, imposing his own naming convention on their new table decoration.

"So these wards," Alanna carried on with a grin shared with James, "they take the orb, and make it do something else, and they do it in an area. The oranges, they twist space and change areas. Not sure how that ties into what happens when we crack them, but whatever. The red ones, it seems, do something related to the weather."

"Isn't it more likely that they broadcast information?" Anesh asked politely.

"Fuck off, you've had coffee, I haven't yet. I can't be right about everything," Alanna bit back.

James tapped at the table. "So, how does that relate to what the reds do normally? I mean, when they're in traps, they're . . . traps. And when we crack them, they give us emotional points. Doesn't it seem more likely that the different uses are all just kind of random?"

That got a quick denial from Anesh. "Mmh," he cut in, setting down his drink and swallowing a mouthful of coffee. "Arbitrary, sure, but I don't think it's random. They all do *something*. If it was truly random, we'd be seeing orbs that exclusively . . . oh, I don't know, did specific pieces of laundry, or . . . or . . . spawned hyperspecific pieces of space shuttles."

"Tan orbs! All they do is order you packages of glitter off eBay!" Alanna chimed in.

"No, no. We're not doing this," James cut in. "We're not making up orb types." He hauled himself up off the couch, groaning as his sore muscles and bruises protested. "Well, since I'm awake, I'm going to enjoy my afternoon by keeping my workout routine intact. Anesh, did you want to get the record for the orbs before I go? I won't be back until after work tonight, so now seems like a good time."

His roommate nodded. "Yeah, let's do that. I'm excited to see how the green makes our lives stranger," Anesh said in a dry voice, getting a snicker from Alanna.

James strolled back down the hallway to his room, smiling a bit at the scavenged dungeon motivational poster hanging at the end of it. The phrase *work hard and also work hard* hadn't failed to make him laugh so far, except for when he'd just gotten home from work, though he imagined if this was in his actual job environment, he would have set it on fire a long time ago. Ducking into his room, he grabbed the orbs off his desk, leaving one small yellow as a meal for Lily.

"All right, got 'em," he said as he came back out. Anesh was still sitting calmly, but Alanna was peeking over the back of the couch like an excited puppy. "Sheesh, calm down, it's not . . . hm."

She grinned widely at him. "Were you about to say it's not that big of a deal?"

"I forgot, okay? I think I'm getting too used to the fact that we're a fantasy novel adventuring party." James bit his lip. "That might actually be a real problem. We should go do, like, normal-person things sometime. Make sure we stay at least partly grounded in reality." He came around the other side of their table and set the four orbs down on it. "Anyway. One green, two small yellows, and one pretty big yellow? I don't know if we'd call this size two or three. I'll save the blue, for obvious reasons."

Anesh nodded at him, and Alanna gave him a quick "Good luck!" as he broke the orbs in his palm, one by one, saving the green for last.

[+1 Skill Rank : History - Salt]

[+1 Skill Rank : Card Counting]

[+3 Skill Ranks : Construction - Electrical Wiring]

[Local Area Shift : +1 Friendly Dog/Day]

[+4 Skill Ranks : Law - Constitutional - US]

"Holy shit, I'm gonna go be a gambling lawyer." James laughed after relaying his earnings to his friends.

Anesh nodded for a second, then stopped. "Right, that's cute and all, but go back to the thing about dogs?"

"The skill ranks I've gotten all seem to be pretty huge, on their own," Alanna said. "One rank in card counting might actually let you go rake in a bucket of money at a casino."

"No, no, don't do this to me. Tell me about the dogs, James," Anesh demanded.

James clapped his hands and pointed at Alanna in excitement. "Yes! Actually, that sounds like a great way to spend my weekend and share of our loot! Do you guys want to go up to that one place this weekend?"

"I've got nothing going on, sure!" Alanna said, catching his excitement.

Anesh wanted to strangle James for a brief moment. "I have class, also, *dogs*."

"Oh, relax. How am I supposed to know anything about how it works? You know damn well these things don't actually tell us much. It probably just means that there's going to be someone walking their dog through the parking lot or something," James said. "Now! I'm going out to the gym, then work after. I'll see you two later, maybe I'll make something for dinner."

James got a couple of *"laters"* from his friends after he got ready, exchanging his sweatpants for actual pants and packing his stuff into a gym bag. "All right, I'll see y'all tonight," he said, opening the front door. "I'll . . . um . . ."

There, on his doorstep, was a dog. It looked like some kind of husky mix, bluish-gray and white fur, big tongue lolling out of its mouth as it looked up at James from where it sat on the welcome mat. It didn't move as he stared down at it.

"What's up?" Alanna asked, able to see that he'd stopped, but not at an angle to spot the dog.

James reached down to pet the adorable-looking beast in front of him, and it pressed its snout into his palm. After a couple of scritches of its ears, it let out a happy bark, then bounded away down the stairs to their landing.

"Well. I think I found out what the orb did," James said.

CHAPTER 9

"Why are we here, again?"

The question came from Alanna. She and James were sitting in the courtyard of their local strip mall, eating frozen yogurt.

"We're eating frozen yogurt," James said with a grin around his spoon. It didn't take long for him to wither a bit under Alanna's glare. "Okay, fine. We're enjoying normalcy."

She snorted, her dessert melting in front of her under the June sun. "Okay, that's not what I meant. I . . . okay, well, that second part was what I meant. I guess I thought that there was something more dire going on when you said we had something important to do today."

James nodded. "We do have something important to do today," he replied, trying to get comfortable in the wire patio chair that felt like it was currently trying to stab him in the ass. "We're getting frozen yogurt, we're going to go poke around the bookstore here and see if we can find a board game to drag Anesh into tonight, and we're going to walk around and talk about something benign. Like philosophy, or birds, or politics."

"Politics counts as benign to you?" Alanna asked.

"Not the point. The point is, we're not going to do anything dungeon-related." James pointed his plastic spoon at his friend. "No discussing tactics, no more training or combat practice, no sorting through boxes of pencils and alligator clips for anything magic. Just . . . normal stuff."

They'd talked about this a while back, and James really wanted to follow through on it. It was a beautiful day, the mental exhaustion and gloom that plagued him constantly had been pushed back a bit, and he wanted to take the opportunity to spend some time with his friends.

Of course, JP was out with his girlfriend, and Dave was at work. Meanwhile, Anesh was going to some special math class that was only taught over the summer once every three years, had a total of four students smart enough to pretend to understand what was going on, and was probably a stepping-stone for the kind of people who were going to invent warp drives one day.

So he'd grabbed Alanna off his couch, told her they had something critical to do, and the two of them had struck out for a walk in the fresh air and blazing sunlight.

"No dungeon stuff?" Alanna asked him with puppy-dog eyes, spoon halfway to her mouth.

Giving her a placating smile, James replied, "No dungeon stuff."

She bit down on her spoon with an aggressive chomp. "But I wanted to talk about dungeon stuff!" Alanna put on an exaggeratedly dejected look and aimed it at her friend. "Like, we can build wards out of the reds now! We could—"

"No dungeon stuff," James said, cutting her off.

"But what about theorycrafting on what we can do with the other colors, now that we have *three uses* for each..."

"No. Dungeon. Stuff." James was a bit sterner that time.

As tempting as it was to just give in, he was committed to having a normal day. No matter how much James wanted to spend his time building up a sunburn as he and Alanna built up a picture of best practices for orb use, he wanted to make sure they had at least some time out in reality.

Alanna didn't quite relent, though. "What if I told you that I found a tube of lip balm that makes skin glow? Would you want to talk about that?"

"No...wait, so, just skin? I guess that's...wait, no! No dungeon stuff!" James had to cut himself off twice. "Stop baiting me!"

"Oh, fine," she said with a smirk. "I'm honestly fine with it, I just wanted to mess with you." She finished her yogurt and tossed the bowl over her shoulder into a garbage can. "You wanna go walk down to the park? It'll probably be a little cooler near the lake."

James nodded in agreement. "Yes, please. If there's one thing I regret about this, it's that we left the air conditioning."

That got a puzzled question out of Alanna. "Why aren't we just hanging around the apartment, then?"

"Eh, I wanted to get out, walk for a bit. I get restless sitting still too long, now. Also, our apartment . . . *my* apartment, which you apparently live in now . . . is full of iLipedes and orbs and an unsafe spear gun and—"

"Okay, my turn to interrupt you. Yeah, I get it." Alanna made a chopping motion with her hand as the two of them stood up and pushed their chairs back. "So, lake?"

"Lake," James agreed.

They strolled through their hometown, cutting through a grocery store parking lot and across a main road on their way to the local park. Traffic around here was never much of a problem, but it was always preferable to go through less-driven areas when they wanted to have a conversation. Engine noise built up fast and could drown out even someone like Alanna, whose voice was a bit more boisterous than Anesh's or James's.

After a little while, they left the sidewalk for a black asphalt trail that led through to the park near where James lived. Gold evening light filtered through the trees, and a carpet of pine needles crunched underfoot as they walked together.

"So, how's work been going?" Alanna asked him. "You been doing okay lately? I haven't heard you complain about it for a while."

James shrugged and gave a little huff of half laughter. "I've mostly forgotten how to complain about work," he said. "It's still full of people I'm uncomfortable around, and I have to answer phone calls, which I hate. But I guess I've just sort of started ignoring it, you know?"

Smiling back, Alanna asked, "I thought you said no dungeon stuff."

"Eh, whatever. But really, work just hasn't been as bad lately," James told her. "Fewer dumb calls, less crap to put up with from senior techs, as I gradually *become* the senior tech. We have a huge turnover rate, and I've hung on long enough that it's making a difference."

Alanna stopped in their walk as they crossed over a small wooden footbridge, looking out over the clear pool of water that was the lake. There were a few ducks swimming nearby that she secretly hoped would come over to her and James so she could try to pet them. "So, are you absolutely sure that high turnover rate is . . . mundane?" Alanna asked, taking the time to find a word that wasn't just saying "not the dungeon."

He bit his lip, wobbling his hand from side to side. "I think so," James told her. "Probably. Okay, look, if we absolutely have to talk about dungeon stuff, this may as well be it," he conceded. "I'm really actually concerned about the whole thing. I mean, I remember a lot of people quitting, but, well, now we know that the dungeon has the tools to mess with memories, and that's a huge problem."

"Yeah, also, the stuffed shirts, which really just look like people," Alanna said.

"Oh, Secret told me a bit about that. They're not people, don't worry. Though the orbs are . . . people-adjacent? Like, the ideas of people. Or maybe things people can do. I don't really fully understand, honestly." James rambled a bit.

"Okay, worrying," Alanna told him as she crouched down and tried to entice the ducks over. "So, if they're just the ideas of people, could it maybe have one that's just, like, Dave? Like, we find an orb that's the idea of Dave?"

James shuddered. "Oh man, can you imagine what kind of stuff would be in that?"

The question was rhetorical, but Alanna still had a snap answer. "Bonus ranks in butts?"

"That's not a thing."

"Can you prove that?"

"No. But I'm going to insist it's not a thing until proven otherwise."

"Okay, well," Alanna said, "what do you think would be in a Dave orb?"

James pondered that for a second. "Dogs? I dunno, that's really the most I know about Dave's life. I tried inviting him to this, but he was at work, and there was a lot of barking in the background, so 'dogs' is all I can think here."

"I would love to know what Dave's work is like," Alanna mused. Followed by a grumbled "Dammit" as the flock of ducks drifted out of her potential reach, getting a grin from James as the two of them sat on the bridge.

Dave was currently sitting at the front desk of the Noah's Arf animal shelter, petting a dog with one hand and fiddling with a Game Boy with the other. Not a modern Game Boy, either. It was a classic, not even a Color, and he'd found it in the dungeon. He'd forgotten to tell James about it, since it was the last thing that he'd grabbed before the postmortem had attacked, and he'd just jammed it into a pocket and lost track of it.

That was impressive. Because as he kept Kiba, the Yorkshire terrier on his desk, occupied, he was trying to play Pokémon, and it was really difficult with how bulky the old hardware was. It was actually amusing to Dave that he'd managed to forget it in the first place. At least, until it had fallen out when he'd gone to do laundry.

He'd also forgotten from when he was a kid just how thick these things were. As he casually tapped through another random fight in the power plant, frustratedly unsure if he could catch a Pikachu here, he was equally frustrated by the fact that handling a Game Boy with one hand was next to impossible. He ended up setting it down on the desk to be able to work both the buttons and the D-pad at the same time. Of course, then he couldn't see the screen.

While Dave had, at this point, given up on being able to actually play the game while the dog was still on the desk, he wasn't too put out. Kiba was a good dog, under exactly one condition: as long as someone was petting him. So there were only so many options for Dave while he was tasked with watching the front desk and the Yorkie that was a fixture of this part of the shelter. He'd gotten so bored at this, the quietest hour of the afternoon, that he'd started poking around the desk for *anything* he could do one-handed.

And that was when he'd found the Game Boy in his pocket, again, apparently having forgotten it there again. After he'd done laundry. And put the Game Boy in a box. In a desk drawer.

Hm.

Seriously, though, Dave was aware of the fact that being stalked by an inanimate object was kinda weird. But he'd always had a hard time reacting to the less predictable parts of life. Back when he was a kid, he'd been made fun of a lot for being slow, along with a few other choice words. These days, he made up for it by playing it off as being constantly cool, though he also knew that he usually just seemed distant, or like he didn't put thought into anything. Routine helped. Predictability helped. Things he could understand helped.

Dogs certainly helped.

His father had, at one point, mocked Dave for getting a job with the most unpredictable animals, when he was such a creature of habit. But the old man had never understood much about dogs; they were simple and direct. Food, shelter, warmth, and some good pets were about all they needed to be happy. Dave could see how all the parts of their lives came together for them. His job was an island of strangely fluid stability.

An island that James and Anesh had begun to erode.

The existence of the dungeon had almost given Dave an anxiety attack. If not for James's assurance on that first night that he could leave if he needed to, and that he wasn't required to do anything, he might have just cut and run. The place was too strange, too outside what Dave was prepared to deal with. Hell, he'd hurt himself pretty badly that first time just out of fear.

But he'd stuck with it. Because for all that it scared the shit out of him, it was *awesome*. It went on forever, and it was filled with dreams and nightmares, and despite the fact that it seemed so random, there was still a subtle and real routine to it. Explore, fight, loot, evaluate. Rinse and repeat. It was light-years outside of his comfort zone, but James was his friend, and he'd shown Dave something truly magical. So he'd keep pushing himself, if it meant going back in and finding more things like a Game Boy that...

Ah, right, the Game Boy.

Dave had let his thoughts drift again. There was something strange about the Game Boy. It wasn't playing by the rules of inanimate objects. He leaned in and poked at it, letting his hand rest on Kiba's back for a minute while he tried to fit this new element into his worldview.

It didn't try to kill him. It wasn't driving the dogs insane with some kind of psychic assault. It wasn't leaving Game Boy seeds around the lobby. Dave shrugged to himself; it wasn't hostile, and it had Pokémon on it. Stressing about this too much would just hurt him; better to let it lie, and reserve his mental energy for the small problems of the day. He'd show it to James or JP later, and it would all work out. He knew James had some kind of date going on tonight, but maybe JP would be available.

The bell over the door rang, and Dave looked up with a smile to greet the new person coming into the shelter. The woman was looking for a dog for her son's birthday, and Dave knew just the Best Friend Ever to show her. As he walked her back to the kennels to meet a few dogs, the Game Boy faded away into the desk, forgotten, until the next time it wasn't.

Just another day for Dave at work. He was comfortable here, and he only wished everyone could love their jobs as much as he did.

Theodora August hated her job.

Perhaps that was a bit unfair. She didn't hate the work itself that much. Nor did she hate the people she had to work with, or the people who worked under her, or the people she reported to. Not a whole lot, anyway. She didn't hate the commute, or the building, or the parking lot. Well, no more than was normal.

She just hated the whole package.

Every little thing added up over time, and it made her angry. She might not hate most of her bosses, but she had *four bosses*. It was doubly shitty that she couldn't even have enough bosses to make an *Office Space* reference out of her life. She might not hate the commute on its own, but she hated that it ate up eight hours every week. She might not hate the people, but . . .

Well, actually, the people she never got much of a chance to hate. With the exception of a few people, like Sy, or James, most people just weren't here long enough for Theo to dislike them. This place had a stupidly high turnover, even for a call center. It was part of how she'd gotten this promotion to floor manager, after only half a year working here.

If Theo didn't work for what was obviously an evil megacorp, she'd be really suspicious that they were kidnapping people to throw into the meat processing plant or something. As it was, she was less "suspicious," and more just "resigned to the fact."

"F. August," Frank greeted her as she walked through the doors. Theo just scowled at the smug old man who wasn't even looking up from his crossword puzzle as she stormed toward the elevator.

She hated that guy. *That* she was sure of. He was always up to something: either not reporting something he should, or making trouble for otherwise good employees if he didn't like them. And he always greeted her with her last name and her gender. She'd looked it up once, and found it was pretty much just a reference to an old sci-fi author. Pretty harmless.

Except while Theo would have absolutely believed that it was harmless if it came from someone like James, she had no such illusions from Frank. It was just one of his games: taunting people behind the guise of something clever.

She was still scowling when she got to her desk, practically throwing herself into her chair with a wince. Her ribs still hurt from her weekend combat ritual, and she was the kind of person who could easily forget about that sort of battle damage. Booting up her computer and looking over her emails revealed the sort of day that she also hated: some hiring, some firing, and some callbacks for tech problems that the newbies couldn't handle.

Theo looked over at the roster and sighed. It was Sunday, which meant none of her three good people were here tonight. The fact that she wasn't allowed to do a new shift bid until she'd been in her position for six months infuriated her, because it left her with these gaping holes in expertise that she couldn't fill easily, and meant that she had to do most of these herself on days like this.

At least on Mondays, she could be absolutely sure James would be here. He was a wiseass, at best, but he showed up.

After two hours of work, she was *still* scowling. There wasn't anything fun about the part of the day where she had to let someone go for stealing from the company. Which annoyed her, because it really got in the way of her plan to do some serious embezzlement.

No, not really.

But it was nice to dream sometimes.

Her plans of corporate espionage and retiring to a private island were broken with a knock on her office door. "Ms. August?" a rather timid voice called to her through the propped door. "There's some sort of management meeting I'm supposed to take you to?"

The kid was one of the new security guys, probably working his first shift. Theo certainly hadn't seen him around. Greasy hair, pale skin, a few pimples. Not too many, though—he was trying at least. When he spoke, it was with a shy voice, like he was afraid she'd bite his head off for bringing her news.

Unfortunately, Theo was the kind of person who didn't think over details like that for too long, and so her response was to bite his head off for bringing her news. "What? A meeting? Did they just randomly decide to start scheduling things without telling me? Who the fu—" She stopped as she saw the new guy's frightened expression. Theo hadn't really meant to terrify the new guy right off the bat, before she even knew his name. "Ahem. Right. So, where's this meeting?"

The new guy—Daniel, his name tag read—swallowed hard before answering. "It's, um, it's . . . well, Frank said that it was in conference room D, but they're doing some painting on the fifth floor, and I was supposed to take you there." He spoke quickly, like if he said the words fast enough, Theo wouldn't be able to get mad at him.

The good news for the new . . . for Daniel . . . was that she wasn't mad at him. She was a bit pissed at Frank, though. This felt like exactly another one of his games. "Painting"? No, not a chance. There probably was a meeting going on; that sort of thing happened a lot around here, and Theo didn't actually pay enough attention to the memos delivered to her desk to believe that she would be one hundred percent apprised of all events in this building. But that didn't mean that Frank wouldn't find some kind of way to screw with her when she was in a hurry.

As for what went on in this building, well, Theo was aware of about three different things that happened at this company. Tech support, on at least three floors. Some kind of engineering department that worked on lots of stuff; that took up the basement level, and as far as Theo knew, they worked on commission for other companies, working out minor hardware bugs in phones. And, finally, the company produced red tape. A lot of it.

Well, they produced other stuff too. It was a big building. But Theo wasn't really that into exploring places that might get her fired. So it was always interesting to be guided around by a security guy when one of the floors was closed off.

"All right, kid. Let's go," she said, grabbing her wallet and badge out of her desk drawer and lurching to her feet. As the new guy led her through the back halls to the stairwell (the elevator was out of order again, which seemed to happen every other week around here), Theo tried to relax. There was no reason to suspect she was about to get fired or anything, so she settled back on projecting what she felt was a "management aura" and made some small talk.

"So, kid, you know anything about rugby?"

Alanna snorted in disbelief. "No way she actually plays rugby."

James laughed as he tossed another scattering of birdseed to the ducks in front of the jungle gym they had situated themselves upon. It was a bit strange, to James, that he'd seen this place be absolutely swarmed by kids back when he was a teenager, but these days it was more or less empty on these long summer evenings. "I think she does, really. I mean, I'm not saying she's not a delver, just that I can absolutely imagine her headbutting someone into the dirt."

"I can't really see it." Alanna shook her head, currently lying half-inverted on the metal bars, hair pointing down like a human pendulum. "She seemed nice when I talked to her!"

"Oh, she's a nice boss, and probably a nice person, but was she angry when she talked to you?" James winced a bit as he remembered the last time he was five minutes late. "I can easily believe she'd, you know . . . break someone's arm in a burst of fury."

That got a laugh. "That feels overly dramatic." She swung herself back around to crouch next to James on the play structure. "So, you don't want to risk inviting her to the party because she might snap at you?"

"No," James replied in an even voice, "I actually do want to bring her in. But there's this running fear with Anesh and me that the company I work for is . . . how to put this . . ." He trailed off.

Picking up the thread of conversation, Alanna interjected her own word ideas. "Evil? Corrupt? A nightmarish megacorp, hell-bent on fiscal dominion over all mankind? Dumb?"

James barked out a laugh. "All of those words work," he said, agreeing with his friend. "But mostly, it's that we can't trust anyone in the structure of the company. What if the company is actively working with, for, or on the dungeon, and Theo's in on it?"

"Theo manages a tech support floor. That's kind of paranoid," Alanna said. "Hm . . . Like, if she was the CEO, sure, but she's . . . well, she reminds me of us. A bitter cog in an uncaring machine, who'd probably be super into this whole dungeon thing." She tapped the bars she was sitting on. "Also, it would be kinda neat to have another girl on the team. Not that you guys aren't great, but it does feel kind of weird sometimes."

"Really?" James was a bit surprised.

Alanna shrugged, trying to minimize any tension. "Yeah, I don't talk about it much, but yeah. There was this neat psychology study done a while back, about how if people feel isolated in groups, they tend to try to fit in, instead of being themselves. And it's really, *really* visible in groups that are gender-dominated. And I worry that I might be doing that?"

That didn't reassure James much. "That doesn't sound great. Actually, I feel like I should have noticed that, in the decade we've known each other. You've always just acted like Alanna to me, I guess."

She gave another small shrug. "Like I said, it's just a concern. I also feel, now that I know that there used to *be* another girl in our group, like that's just something that I've had yanked away from me."

"Is gender that big of a deal? I kinda figured that wasn't as much of an issue for people like us."

Alanna paused briefly to think about it. "I don't think it's a big deal? I don't care much. But we're part of our society, and that sort of thing leaks over whether we want it to or not. I also just want to make more friends, and find more teammates for the delving, and it'd be nice to solve three problems at once."

"Fair." James nodded. "Oh, since we're just breaking the dungeon stuff rule entirely right now . . ."

She pointed down at the birds they were feeding. "We're doing something normal to offset it. It's fair."

"Okay," he continued, "well, I was going to ask, how'd you find that ChapStick? Er, lip gloss. Whatever. How'd you find it?"

James had been wondering about this for a while. It felt like they found too many things. At first, it seemed like too many things that were useless, then too many things that were overly useful. Then, just too many things, given that they hadn't really refined any good way to hunt for the stuff.

"I found it by accident, really," Alanna said. "I just picked up some lip gloss, and it turned out to be mildly enchanted. It's cool, though, so I didn't want to crack it unless I had to, but I wouldn't mind if you wanted."

"No, no, that's not my point. My point is, why does it feel like some of these things are finding us, instead of the other way around?"

There was a moment of quiet, with Alanna opening her mouth to answer, then closing it slowly and pausing for thought. After a couple seconds mulling over James's words, she came up with an answer. "That feels overly dramatic." Before he could sulk at her, she waved away her words with a laugh. "But really, that is kinda weird. And on that note, why don't we try to find more magic items?"

"How?" James asked, quizzically. It was something he and Anesh had talked about before, but it always got pushed back in the face of more pressing issues.

Alanna had a quick solution. "Well, we've found more than a few pens and pencils with traits on them. Why not just grab literally every batch of those we find, put them in a big box, and put the box in a wood chipper?"

"That is . . ." It felt like a lightbulb going off over his head. "Holy shit, that would be great. If we don't really care about the effect, just the orbs, we could just harvest a few dozen a day!" Then another, darker thought. "But what if the wood chipper eats all the blues?"

"Then we run, and we run, and we don't stop running until we are far enough away that the wood chipper with legs cannot get to us," Alanna replied with gravitas. "But really. Wouldn't that just make a magic wood chipper?"

James hummed a bit. "Ehhhh. You've brought up the mixed traits before. Most of the blues and greens also have skill ranks in them, which implies they're part yellow. And that one purple had some emotion in it, implying it's part red. And what annoys me most about this is that it doesn't match the color wheel."

"Why would it?"

"To make me feel better."

"Oh, wah. Anyway, go on."

Clearing his throat, James continued. "Right, so the orbs can be mixed. And that's really the whole point; I don't want to feed a wood chipper blues, because blues often contain yellows, and yellows *make things alive*. Honestly, a not-alive wood chipper is still a worrying thing to have to walk by; I always worry I'll fall in. One that can move around? That's fucking horrifying."

"Fair," Alanna said. "Well, we can still just break them all by hand."

"Works for me. We'll bring it up with everyone next time," James said.

The two of them sat there in peaceful quiet for a while, the only noises the quacking of ducks and the dull roar of cars in the background. At one point, their following of birds scattered for a bit as a woman came jogging through with her dog, but the avian cult soon re-formed at the base of their throne to get more of the food James or Alanna would occasionally toss down.

"What a great evening," Alanna said with a smile. "This is nice. Thanks."

"Yeah, it is. That dog makes me think, though. I wish I could bring Rufus out here some time. I think the little guy would love it," James replied wistfully.

Alanna had an instant disagreement, but didn't want to crush her friend's dreams so quickly. Still, though. "Um . . . wouldn't he freak the hell out to be somewhere with no ceiling?"

"I . . . hm. He's a smart strider. I'm sure he'd adapt," James said, cautiously. "Wonder what he's up to while we're away, anyway?"

Rufus was fighting for his life.

The Puppet had wandered into their home while Ganesh was resting, and the Life that the human Dave had made wasn't aware enough to start working with them yet for their mutual defense.

Rufus felt like an idiot. He'd been so busy tending to what James called his "garden" (a good word that he liked) that he hadn't focused on watching the area around them. He'd become complacent over the last month, assuming safety, when in reality it was in short supply even when their humans were here.

And now, a Puppet had found them.

It was one of the white ones. No more than two feet tall, with a smooth white exterior that wasn't as hard as the shells of its Life brothers. But what it had sacrificed in defense, it made up for in the perfectly patterned movements of its feelers, and the coherent light weapons mounted in its secondary maw. Secretly, Rufus felt a surge of relief that it wasn't one of the corded ones, or one of the few human-shaped things that were made into Puppets.

At least this, he and Ganesh might have stood a chance against.

Rufus hurled himself forward again, taking advantage of his enemy's jerky turn rate to flank it as often as he could. If he could stay in its blind spots, then he might be able to wear it down to death before it was checked up on. His bite didn't penetrate this time, and he noted that he did better when he aimed near the small ventilation slits.

And then he was scurrying away again, moving as fast as he could before it could focus on him, either with its hundreds of fractal cables, its beam weapon, or just its teeth. As Rufus scrambled to stay behind it while it pivoted at perfect forty-five-degree angles, the Puppet swept its beam across the internal walls of Fort Door. It didn't start any fires, fortunately, but it did leave a long black score across the repurposed cubicle walls as it tracked after him.

Then Ganesh was there. Buzzing in like a furious hornet, the drone dive-bombed the Puppet as it turned away, and Rufus felt his Life flare up as he scythed into the top of the shell with his arms. But just as quickly, he had to abandon his platform as the Puppet jerked backward, slamming its top into one of the desks and threatening to crush Ganesh.

Rufus kept moving, arcing around it. This wasn't working. It would take hours to break through to anything vital. They were going to run out of time, or they were going to slip up and take a hit that would be lethal to smaller Life.

Silently, he signaled Ganesh. The drone caught his motion, and the two of them flashed a conversation between them in the sparse seconds they had between their flittering dodges. Did they have options? No. Wait. Yes. There were weapons here. Weapons? Human weapons. And also Object weapons. Okay. Could they use the human weapons? Maybe. But there was an Object weapon that Ganesh could find. The concept that James called a "pen." Find it. On it. Distract the Puppet until then. Good.

Breaking their brief contact, Rufus straightened up. Okay. Now he just had to buy Ganesh time to do his job. Letting out a battle hiss, he lunged forward, popping out of the hiding spot under the desk that he'd briefly occupied. He landed two bites, one in the cabling and one to the vent slits that brought a manic sense of ruthless joy to his heart.

The Puppet, which had turned to focus on Ganesh when it lost track of Rufus, turned back to him, whipping its beam weapon across the high walls as it tried to refocus. The laser scored across the walls again, and Rufus felt a surge of guilt as it clipped that map that they'd spent so long on. Then he felt a bit better as it bisected that stupid motivational poster that Alanna and James liked so much. He didn't have much time to spare to watch the bottom half flutter to the ground, but he wouldn't miss it.

Then he had to move again, keeping scant steps ahead as it twitched the beam around. Sometimes it would brush his carapace, and he'd let out a hissing scream of pain, but he kept moving. All he had to do was last a little bit longer. Just let it pay attention to him for a few more seconds. Because if this didn't work, they'd have to go to his backup plan, and he did not like his odds of firing a gun.

Abruptly, it stopped chasing after him. It was so close behind the strider that he could feel its presence. And then there was a droning buzz overhead, and the sound of a grinding impact.

Ten seconds ago, Ganesh had found the Object that Rufus had indicated to him. Six seconds ago, he'd pulled it into a carrying position that he could sustain while flying, tucked under one of his arms and braced against his main body like an airborne lancer. Two seconds ago, he'd backed into the wall to click open the tip, sizzling with conceptual power.

And zero seconds ago, he'd made contact with the Puppet, slamming into the much larger enemy as hard as he could, tiny legs pushing back and absorbing the force of the impact as he drove the pen against its frame. It *burned*, melting and boiling away the plastic shell, cutting away irregular chunks of mass as Ganesh dug in his razor-sharp claws and held on for his life.

Wasting no time as the Puppet struggled, Rufus bolted for where the humans stored their weapons. It wasn't the easiest task in the world, but he and Ganesh had drilled repeatedly on unlatching the containment case for the handgun, and he cracked into it now: dragging out the weapon, bracing it on the desk, and angling it down to track the Puppet, just in case this didn't work.

And when Ganesh pushed off again, taking to the air, the Object weapon falling inside the Puppet's shell without killing it, Rufus gave a resigned whine. Trying to wrap as many of his legs around the gun as possible to stabilize it, he leveled it at the Puppet and pressed down with his front leg on the trigger.

Nothing happened.

Rufus felt panic and confusion, though probably less than the Puppet did as it was torn apart by two smaller pieces of Life. Still, this was their last chance, now that the Object was lost!

Then Ganesh alighted beside him and carefully reached one claw in to depress a small button on the side of the gun before striking out an assault gesture at the Puppet. Rufus didn't understand, but he pulled the trigger again anyway.

Safety off, the bullet ripped through the front of the Puppet's carapace, dislodged the Object, and left it a smoldering wreck on the floor. The recoil flung Rufus backward into the air above the desk, while the gun went tumbling to the floor. Ganesh made a choice about which to catch, and Rufus felt comic betrayal that it wasn't him.

As he toppled back to the ground, he decided to have a talk with the humans about the unreliability of their weapons. James never had to deal with this nonsense.

But at least, for a little while, their home was safe.

"He's probably fine," Alanna said reassuringly.

"I mean, yeah," James said. "Besides, he has Ganesh. They're probably on some cool adventure right now." He shrugged. "It would just be cool to have, I dunno, a familiar? He's not really a pet. But out here, in this world."

Alanna glanced sideways at him as the pair walked back to the apartment. "I note that you've stopped saying 'the real world.' But Anesh still does. Reason?"

"I feel more alive there than here." James sighed. "I'm really trying, man, but I feel like I'm falling apart most days. In the dungeon, though, I know what I'm doing, and I know what the stakes are. It's a lot more . . . direct. A lot simpler. Or at least, it was until the whole thing with Sarah. But even then, that's very straightforward; it's an enemy that we can confront. It's not an awkward social situation or dealing with eating healthier or failing to flirt properly."

"Oh my god, just fucking ask Anesh out already." Alanna let out her frustration. "For fuck's sake, you two are so dense."

"I'll get around to it," James said with a weak smile. "Anyway, the point is, it's just as real as normal life. And I don't want to be like some old-timey European explorer who decided to start calling Africa 'the dark continent' just because *they* hadn't mapped it."

Alanna nodded. "Good point," she said as they rounded the corner into the parking lot of the apartment complex. "Hey, do you have work tonight?"

"Yes, but not until later. Why?"

"I want to see if we can disassemble that totem thing that Lily made, and then put it back together." Alanna rubbed her hands together. "I've been waiting all day for this, since you woke me up for ice cream."

James poked at her. "You've been waiting for two hours, tops. That's not 'all day.' If you want to say 'all day,' you need to wake up before four p.m."

"*You* wake up at four p.m.!" she retorted, indignant. And it was true, James was very rarely up out of bed before noon, and it was equally rare that he was awake while the sun was still up.

He let out a short huff as he unlocked the door to his home. "I work nights! It's reasonable for me. That's my excuse, and I think it's a good one." Then both of them stopped their mock argument for a couple minutes to give some affectionate pets to the adorable Shiba Inu that trotted by and paused to nuzzle up to Alanna's knee.

After it trotted off again, giving a single happy bark at them, Alanna shook her head and picked up her train of thought. "I also work nights now, technically," Alanna mused, putting her finger up to her chin in a thoughtful gesture. "I mean, am I an employee of this dungeon venture? Or more of a freelance contractor."

"Hah! Yeah, you can bill us for whatever hours you work, as long as it's in the dungeon. Which is only open at a very specific time. At night." James laughed.

"As far as we know," Alanna said, grim.

James scowled at her as he sat down at the table's couch, feeling the objective knowledge of the perfect seventy-two-degrees-and-clear-skies day flooding his mind. "I mean, sure. But let me pretend everything is okay for at least one more day. Now, do you want to do weird science to this thing or not?"

She grinned back at him. "Let me get my lab coat!" Before James could ask if she actually owned one of those, she was out of the room. Just as he was thinking that there was no way that she'd smuggled one into his apartment without him noticing, even if she *did* own one, she called back down the hall, "No, not really. I'm just using your bathroom. We can dive into that in a second."

He wasn't sure why, but James was oddly disappointed by that answer.

CHAPTER 10

James stepped into work the next day, humming a song only one other person on the planet had ever heard.

It was an idea that he'd shared with Secret the other day during the too-few hours of sleep he'd managed to grab. Secret, maybe wanting to show off, maybe just lonely, had pulled James's dreaming mind into his cityscape project. Normally, James would have been fine with this; he actually quite liked talking to Secret. But he also realized that this wasn't actually "dreaming." Not REM sleep, not actually relaxing his brain. And sure enough, when he woke up the next day, he was still pretty exhausted.

Still, he'd gotten to see Secret's improvements to his city, which had been kind of a delight. Secret wasn't actually very creative. He was vigilant, clever, and vicious, but he lacked a certain spark, that something that made personal work . . . personal. Or at least, he *had*, until recently. It wasn't like Secret had transformed into Picasso overnight, but there was a more intimate touch to the creations that he'd shaped in the dream city in James's mind. Small things, like patterning the streets in a way that no one would ever see unless they got an aerial view, but formed a very real shape that James could feel as he walked them.

That wasn't relevant to the humming, though. That was one of the things that Secret had discussed with James during their dreamwalk.

As it turned out, Secret's name was more than just a name. He didn't exactly live in James's mind, so much as James's mind was where he was anchored. Secret was an idea: a living one, sure, but fundamentally an idea. And that name, which James so casually gave him, did more than just give the group something to reference him by. It was, more or less, his body. His structure. He was Secret, and Secret was who and what he was.

So as time went by and he grew into what he was becoming, his name was part of what gave meaning and pattern to how he influenced the world. And it was through the medium of secrets that he was more and more able to reach out.

When James hummed that song that he'd found in the office, he was expressing a secret to the world around him. He wasn't sharing it, he was publicly showing off something that only he knew and that no one else could experience properly. It was highly symbolic, while somehow not meaning anything very important. And that was exactly what Secret needed as a bridge, to speak with James more openly during the day.

"This structure is insulated with hostile ideas," Secret muttered in James's ear as James walked through the front door.

"What, like, other memes like you?" James asked, a spike of worry carving its way through his chest. "How long have they been here?! Is this some kind of extradimensional-invasion staging ground?!"

Secret, who James could just barely see as a ghostly blue outline of some kind of sea serpent covered in too many teeth, coiled around his legs and torso, responded in a condescending murmur. "Of course they lack my motivation. They are alive, in the way that ideas are in this world, but they do not live. The walls here hold Despair and Hopelessness and Ennui and Surrender. My friend and uplifter, you may wish to consider finding a better job."

James held his tongue as he walked by the front desk, not wanting to look like he was talking to himself, since he was sure that the security person wasn't able to see Secret. Frank wasn't in today, for whatever reason, and there was a new kid at the desk. Pretty young guy, a bit overweight, but professional-looking—dark skin contrasted with the white polo shirt, and a perfectly clean, poofy haircut. Gabe, his name tag identified him as.

The new guy gave James a nod and asked, "Signing in or need directions, sir?"

"Um . . . no, thank you, I work here," James said. "Also, that's a good reason not to call me sir. I think the only people I outrank are the interns, and since the Harvest, we haven't had any of those."

To his credit the new guy didn't stammer or give him a blank confused look. It wasn't like James intentionally tested new coworkers, but he did have a pretty impulsive sense of humor, and often the first salvo of jokes would go unappreciated or unnoticed. James was pretty used to being disappointed by new employees just giving him an uncomprehending, laughless gaze. And so he was pleasantly surprised when Gabe just raised an eyebrow and gave him a chuckle.

"All right, man. Have a good one," the security guard said, waving James on and bending his head back down to his new-hire paperwork.

After the elevator doors closed on him, James reopened his conversation with Secret. "I like my job," he said, picking up where they left off.

"You enjoy the access your status here gives you. Beyond that, you are surrounded by hostility. Seize your own destiny; invest in a crowbar and change your life," Secret hissed in James's ear in a voice that sounded like an amused serpent.

"I own a crowbar," James said calmly, leaning against the rear of the elevator and staring straight ahead.

Secret huffed in exasperation, the ghostly leviathan twisting around James's neck to look him in the eye. "You are so comfortable here, you do not notice the things that are warped and twisted here. This entire structure screams with the weight of its wrongness. And I speak as a living idea, stolen from an enemy world."

Giving his own snort as the elevator doors opened, James got one last muttered line in before he stepped out to the call center floor. "I know exactly what's wrong here. It's . . ." He paused and broke off as he walked toward his desk and saw a cluster of employees standing around the copier station. "Hang on." He tapped Secret's fanged snout with his palm as he walked over.

A man in a beige jacket and matching slacks was talking. Maybe forty or so years old, the kind of scratchy facial hair that let you know that he thought he was distinguished, without putting too much effort in. "So," he was saying, "I expect that you should be able to keep up with the job fairly well, since you've been doing it already the past several months. That's all, everyone return to their desks. As for our new arrival, I'll talk to you in my office."

He had apparently just been wrapping up. James raised an eyebrow at the stern voice, like he was chastising the assembled techs. "Hey, what's up?" he whispered to one of the coworkers he was on decent terms with.

"New manager, man. Guy seems all right, might have a stick up his ass, though. Have fun." The other tech sauntered off to return to work after delivering his warning. Or, more likely, to sit and take a few minutes before reentering the call queue.

"New manager?" James spoke under his breath to himself. Unable to keep a look of concern off his face, eyes narrowed with a small frown, he followed after the man.

The man stepped through the door of Theo's office. Leaving the door open for James and not looking back, he strode in like he owned the place and settled himself into the padded chair on the other side of the desk, starting to rearrange stacks of papers on the desk. *T. Kowalski* read the brass nameplate on the door, which confused James when he saw it. Theo didn't . . . have one of those. Moving past the door, James was further confused by the cardboard banker's box on the desk, still being unloaded. A different laptop, framed pictures of family on the desk, other random trinkets that were clearly the trappings of a different sort of person than Theodora adorned the small office space. Not waiting for James to think, the man motioned for him to sit down.

"James, yes?" he said in the tone of a disappointed teacher. Again, he didn't wait for James to respond, and only gave the briefest of pauses for him to sit down at all. The chair that James sat in on this side of the desk felt purposefully designed to put him more ill at ease. "You may call me sir, or Mr. Kowalski. You're late today," he said. James instantly dropped into a glare before smoothing out his face and calming himself. The other man still didn't wait, or even seem to acknowledge the frustration, still rolling on with his own words. "Now, it is understandable that you wouldn't be used to firm leadership; no one else on this floor seems to be either. After all, it's been months since you've had a management team here. But while I will allow you a warning this time, I expect you here promptly from now on." The man broke his hostile eye contact with James and went back to flipping through what looked like résumés. Glancing back up again, he saw that James was still there and gave a small wave of his hand. "You may *go* now."

Trying his best to process this, James took a small breath and started where his racing thoughts put him. "Okay, so, first of all, I'm not late. My shift starts a half hour offset from normal."

"Ah. Some special consideration you were previously given. Well, I will change that in the next schedule change." The man cut him off dismissively.

James was getting pissed off now. He half snarled and was about to snap out something quite rude when Secret whispered in his ear. "Friend . . . something is wrong."

He wanted to yell that of course something was wrong. There was some random jackass in a suit here telling him that his whole work experience was going to be fucked up, and . . . and . . .

"Pardon me," James said, suddenly struck with a grim clarity of mind, "if you don't mind, what happened to Theo?" he asked, already dreading the answer.

Kowalski— James refused to even think of him with a *sir* or a *Mr.* in his name—didn't bother to look up. "There have been several layoffs recently. Your friend was most likely among the dead weight."

Rolling his eyes, confident that the fool who thought himself a manager wouldn't notice, James clarified. "No, the manager who was here previously. Her name was Theodora?"

"There hasn't been a manager here for months. That's why upper management has seen fit to send me here. To fix, this . . . problem." The man spoke with a level of condescension that made James's blood boil. This was every bad boss cliché that James knew of slammed into a single person and wrapped in a corporate slogan and a bad suit.

But all of that anger was secondary to the fear regarding what he'd said about Theo.

James got up, didn't say anything, and wasn't spoken to as he walked out of the office. No one had been here for months? That meant one of two things. Well, one of three things, but the third option was just that this guy was the kind of callous asshole who would refer to someone he didn't respect as "no one." Which wasn't out of the question. But there was a lingering sense of something otherworldly in the air that made James jump to a different conclusion.

Either Theo had been an agent of the dungeon the whole time, or maybe just a figment of everyone's collective imagination, or, perhaps worse, Theo had been exactly who she said she was, and the dungeon had taken her. Just like it had Sarah.

"Stay calm, my friend," Secret muttered to James as they walked onto the call floor. "You help no one by panicking." Secret's coat of teeth rustled as he spoke softly.

James gave a tiny nod and kept walking toward his desk. On the way, he decided to do a couple quick checks on something, to make sure that his fears weren't just the ravings of an unsettled mind. "Hey, Ash." He popped his head into a pod of cubicles to talk to one of the techs sitting there and currently off a call. "What's up with the new boss?"

The younger girl at the desk, maybe twenty, with a curvy figure and round cheeks to match her constant wide smile, looked up at James as he asked. "Oh! Yeah! Kind of a douche, huh?" she said as she rolled her head back dramatically. "I miss not having a manager."

"Right, right. So . . . what about Theo?" James prompted, already realizing the answer.

"Who?" Ash asked in response, still cheerful but now tinted with confusion.

James nodded and sighed to himself. "Never mind. You've got a call, have fun." He pointed her back to her monitor as he turned and walked away. He got a fair distance away from anyone who might overhear and then quietly asked out of the corner of his mouth, "Why doesn't anyone remember? No, don't answer that. It's a dungeon thing, I understand. But why do I remember her? She was real, right, Secret?"

"She was real," the pale glowing serpent rattled back at him. "You remember because I have been keeping watch. Nothing else has tried its luck at breaching your mind while I have been here."

"Well, thanks. I think," James said. "Wait, what about that whole thing where we'd had the location of the bathrooms in the dungeon blocked out of our minds?"

If James didn't know better, he'd say Secret looked almost sheepish, turning his twin-mawed snout away and huffing slightly as he gazed out the wide window that held a view of the sunset over a highway. "Well, none overt enough to do damage, then," he corrected himself. "And I tracked down that invader regardless."

James did a lap of the building before returning to his desk, trying to organize his thoughts. Theo was gone, that much was obvious. But how, and why? Was this just what happened when someone left here? The dungeon just cut them out of everyone's memory? That didn't sound right, since he remembered people who had quit. Everyone here knew at least one person who'd just stopped showing up, like ... like ...

Uh-oh.

There weren't ever enough employees here. People were constantly getting hired. So obviously, people were just leaving, right? But then, why couldn't he picture any of their faces?

That actually made some sense, then. It might not even be the dungeon actively striking out, just a passive effect. A twisting of human memory away from itself, a natural defense mechanism. After all, James couldn't think of any other times that he'd had someone come up to him and casually mention the dungeon delve that they'd been on in the stockroom at Walmart. So, if he ever "quit," or maybe didn't show up here for a long enough period of time, he'd just fade out of everyone else's memory? Was that how it worked? Or would he himself forget, and everyone else was just collateral damage?

Either of those were bad. One probably worse than the other, sure, but James was already feeling some frustration at not really being able to quit his job without losing his access to the dungeon. The idea that he might lose access to his own memories too was infuriating.

The other option—one of them, anyway—was that the dungeon was literally eating people. Sarah was his first thought; she hadn't been an innocent bystander who'd just quit from the hardest place to get a reference from. She'd been a diver, like them. If she'd fallen victim to the dungeon while inside it, that made sense but didn't mesh with everyone else being forgotten too.

Unless it was something simpler. James wanted to quit, dungeon or no, and he was confident that he could find a way to sneak back in once a week for a delve. "Sneak," mostly meaning "bribe Frank." What if Sarah had felt the same way? But then she'd lost the job, and everyone had forgotten her. Or maybe it was even simpler; they'd had a few close calls, and only James's lack of regard for his own well-being kept him from feeling too horrified by that. Maybe Sarah had been a little more prudent and chosen the better part of valor.

Or maybe she'd gone in one day and not come out. And maybe those people weren't forgotten, but taken. Maybe, maybe, maybe. So many questions, no certainty.

James snarled and lashed out to punch the wall of the hallway he was walking down as he paced around the corridors of the building. His fist connected with a painful but slightly mollifying thump. He was consumed by a feeling of powerlessness. He didn't know what the problem was or how to start fixing it, but he felt like he was responsible for everything here. How would he even go about telling the police about this? No one would ever bother to check. They'd just put him in one of the hospital's mental health observation rooms again.

And if he took too long to find the answers, to figure out what was happening to these people and how to help them, then he knew in his heart it was going to be too late. The dungeon had started as a game to him, really. One that had catapulted his life forward, but still just a toy to play with. And now, the whiplash of it turning into something far darker and meaner left James feeling lost.

He was nursing his hand as he walked back to his desk and sat down. He picked up his headset but didn't put it on. Just limply stared at the piece of hardware in his hand. James wanted to scream, wanted to start grabbing people and telling them this wasn't right, that there was something *wrong* going on here. But he couldn't. He felt trapped in his own head, a pressure in his chest that he couldn't cope with.

Setting the headset back down, he rolled his chair back and stared up at the ceiling tiles above him. One of them was still marked with a small X of tape. Around his vision, Secret's pale blue frame tilted its eyes upward as well, then back to James with a strangely readable expression of concern.

"Friend . . ." Secret started to say.

"That's it." James spoke out loud, getting a strange glance from the other person in the cubicle pod. "That's the next step."

Secret hissed at him. "It would be a risk. We may never come out."

The meme sounded scared. James turned his head to look Secret in the eyes, not caring how strange it made him look when he whispered back, "If we don't, then neither will Theo. That's right, isn't it?"

Secret didn't reply, and James knew that Secret knew the truth, just like he did. There were no more excuses, no more reasons to doubt that they needed to take action. And for one moment, there was clarity. No doubt at all.

No. There was the answer. Right in front of him.

James pulled out his phone, ignoring his coworker's confused questioning. Opening up the chat with the party, he tried to bring everyone up to speed as fast as possible. People were being forgotten, not just Sarah. Theo was missing. The dungeon was hostile. They had to do something, and they had to do it quickly.

And while it wasn't a lot of time to prepare, there was a back door in, that opened for maybe ten minutes, tomorrow night.

CHAPTER 11

The atmosphere around the living room table was dense, and grim, and no amount of warm light or comfortable couch cushions was going to alleviate it.

"No," JP was saying, chopping his hand down onto the table. "No! Worst idea!"

That table was currently covered in... a bit of everything. Anesh's efforts to keep things organized had cut out about an hour ago, and so the copies of notes, plates of food, candy wrappers, laptops, pens, loose orbs, books, and harpoon gun were all just cluttering up the damn thing like it was a museum piece on the lives of millennials.

The apartment was also heavy with the smell of cooking food. Despite the tense feeling affecting everyone else, James was humming away to himself in the kitchen, currently shuffling a pair of potato latkes onto a plate with a casual twist of his wrist and placing it on the counter between himself and the living room. "Here, eat this," he said to JP with a grin. "Also, I didn't say it was a good idea. It's a night for bad ideas."

"Bad ideas in regards to personal safety, and the actual dungeon you discovered. Not in regards to real-life things, James," JP retorted, taking the plate.

"Isn't this both?" James asked, needling his friend with a smile.

"Isn't what both?" The voice belonged to Alanna, as she and Anesh came back in the front door. The end of the recent heat wave allowed the opening of the door to let a cooling breeze into the apartment. "Also, we got you guys drinks!"

JP caught the plastic bottle Alanna lobbed at his head, which arced over Anesh, causing him to duck on his path to his room. "Oh, James is trying to get me to recruit my girlfriend for our guild."

Grabbing her own plate of food that James was serving up, Alanna started to maneuver her way through the mess of the living room before just giving up and leaning on the kitchen counter to eat while she talked. Around a mouthful of food, she asked JP, "Is it at all weird to you guys that we think of ourselves as a guild, or an adventuring party, or whatever? I mean, the dungeon is . . . legitimately world-shaking, but we've just sort of fallen into this pattern of delving and thinking of ourselves as the kind of people that fight monsters for rewards. That's fucking worrying, right?"

"We're sort of breaking out of that routine now," James said, with a casual voice and seemingly without an ounce of tension in his chest.

Alanna opened her mouth, then closed it with a huff. She was pretty frustrated with James in general right now. His decision, sudden and seemingly stupidly reckless, to go into the second entrance tomorrow had left everyone on edge. But despite that, he didn't seem to have any of the lingering pool of anxiety and tension sitting in his chest that Alanna and Anesh did. Here he was, cooking like he'd been practicing his whole life, filling the room with the scent of potatoes and the sound of his off-key singing along to Offspring songs playing from his phone, and acting like he wasn't planning a potential one-way trip to hell in just under eighteen hours. If it weren't for the fact that he actually *was* helping her stay calm with this, then she'd probably be actually punching him right now.

So instead of punching, she just sighed. "Yeah, we are out of that routine. And . . . I know I asked a million times, but are you *sure* you want this? Like, really sure?"

James flicked off a couple of the burners on the stove and spooned himself his own helping of food. "Yup!" he said cheerfully, letting no hint of doubt into his voice. "So, how was your walk?" he asked.

"That's a deflection right there," JP said calmly from across the room.

Ignoring the fact that James was changing the topic, Alanna moved past him in the kitchen to add more food to her plate. "Not bad. We purposefully didn't talk about the dungeon—figured we'd go over a plan here. But . . . okay, you know how there's all that construction going on over there?" She looked around at the nods before continuing. "Well, I haven't been over here as much as you guys, so it's a bit more sudden for me, but it feels super weird to know which way to walk but have the landscape look different. Like remembering an alien street that you've never been on before."

Sitting down at the table opposite JP, James let out a hum of consideration at her words. "That's a weirdly poetic way to describe a changing skyline, but yeah, I can see it. You didn't get lost, though, right?"

"I just said—"

"He's messing with you," JP cut in, ending the argument before it could start. "Where's Dave? Also where did Anesh run off to? He was just here, and I wasn't paying attention."

Through a mouthful of food, James said, "Dave's on his way, Anesh is just relaxing in his room for a bit before we start . . . Oh, hey, Anesh." He trailed off as his roommate walked back in. Before Anesh could say anything, though, the door opened suddenly and Dave burst through. "Oh, hey, Dave." James let his fork fall to his plate with a clatter, throwing up his hands. "Okay, fine. Yes, we're starting now."

"I'm not late, am I?" Dave said, with a worried shake in his voice.

"Nah, you're good, mate," Anesh told him. "I just got here too. So let's figure this out." He sat down in the plush armchair that was his seat at the head of the long table. "James, make sure we're on the same page here."

James set his fork down again, resigning himself to not getting to eat uninterrupted. "Okay, so. Facts: Theo is missing, something about the dungeon blanks people's memories of anyone who's left there, and Secret is screening for us, which is the only reason we don't."

"Theo?" Dave asked, raising his hand like he was in class.

"My boss. Well, former boss, now, I guess." James looked down, clenching his teeth and fists for a second before remembering to breathe and resuming his briefing. "So, yeah, that's the basis. Part two, conjecture: the dungeon has been eating people for a long time." He paused this time to let that sink in. "We knew that there was a high turnover, sure, but I literally cannot remember anyone who's ever worked there and left. My running theory is that some people are more or less immune to that memory wipe effect, which is why Anesh sort of pointed out the possibility a long time ago. Which is why I suspect the company isn't taking advantage of the dungeon: too many points of failure in a large organization like that. One guy gets eaten by a desk, and suddenly none of the higher-ups can remember the project even exists."

"Fair, but what if they have their own monsters like Secret?" JP asked, leaning forward onto the table.

Alanna winced. "That'd be bad. That would mean we're actually fighting on two fronts. Also, how do we even fight things like Secret?"

"We don't. We get Secret to do it," James said, tilting his head to look at the pale outline of Secret's scaled form still wrapped around his shoulders. He wasn't fully manifested, and James was pretty sure no one else could see him right now, but he was present for this part. "He's with us, all of us, and he'll give us the tools to support him in a fight on his turf if needed."

Anesh had, by this point, gotten the laptop open and was furiously typing away, making notes as fast as he could to catch up. He paused as James brought up infomorph combat, looking up at the table. "What good are we supposed to do?"

"We're ammunition, mostly. Or, well, no. We're a lot of things. Our thoughts and memories can serve as weapons for things like Secret. And oftentimes, our minds or emotional landscapes are literal landscapes for them, and that's the battlefield. It can get, from our perspective, really abstract, really fast." James tried to explain. "None of those words are *correct*, by the way," he said, as he saw some incredulous looks on the faces around him, especially Alanna's. "That's just the best way to think of it."

Anesh cleared his throat. "So, we're relying on one meme to be in five places at once?"

"It's not five places to him. We have a shared idea of who Secret is. That's it. He's there. That's how he works," James said with a grin.

It was Dave who caught on to that one first, letting out a low whistle, before saying, "Ooooh, fuck. That's kinda creepy. He's an idea, so as long as we know about him, he can be there. Are you sure he's friendly?" he asked James.

"Yes." James spoke with absolute conviction.

That was good enough for Dave. JP and Alanna were still on the fence, and he understood that, but if James said that his friend was a good guy, Dave was inclined to trust him.

"Okay, next point," Anesh brought up. "Why the emergency strategy meeting, and why the suicide mission?"

James nodded. This was going to be the difficult part: convincing literally anyone that this was at all a good idea. "Okay. So. Part three, the plan. There's another breach that opens regularly some days in the vent above my desk. Tomorrow, I'm going to go into it and see if I can find Theo, and anyone else who's been pitched into the dungeon."

That got JP, Anesh, and Alanna all yelling conflicting things over each other as they both jumped at the chance to tell James how stupid it was. Alanna relented as JP jumped up and slammed his hands onto the tabletop, though. His normal unflappable attitude let him see things a little clearer than most people, and it was now that what James needed was that logic to talk him down. "James, if she were still alive, why would the dungeon make everyone forget about her?!" he asked simply, his voice suddenly too loud as Alanna and Anesh had gone silent. "Ah. Hem. But, yeah, no! You've told us about that opening! You don't know how long it lasts for, you don't know where it opens to, and you especially don't know if the person you want to save is even still alive!"

"I know she's still alive," James said, with far more outward calm than his pounding heart would indicate. "Secret talked to me about it, after we figured out what the memory wipe was doing. He's felt the force of it before, presumably from other employees or people going into the dungeon. And it comes in one of two strengths. So, our going theory is that there's a weak one for when you go in, and a stronger finisher if the dungeon . . . you know . . . . kills a person."

"Wait, does that mean that every time we go in . . ." Anesh started to ask.

James finished for him. "Everyone sort of has a hard time thinking about us until we come out. Probably. We should test it."

"That's not even a little okay!" Alanna said.

It was JP who countered her, rubbing his chin and smiling. "Now hang on. Wouldn't it be nice if we could get a day off of work because our boss literally didn't remember scheduling us?" he said, thoughtful. After a second, he looked back up. "Wait, hang on. I'm getting distracted. James, we were talking about why you were throwing your life away."

That was the question that had been on James's own mind for a whole day. Why? Why bother? Theo wasn't that important to him, really. He wasn't some destined hero. He was just a guy with a crowbar. But there was a weight to his decision that had kept his heart free and his mind clear ever since he'd made it, and he knew exactly how to express it.

"Because it's the right thing to do." James spoke quietly as he looked at JP, his voice gaining strength as he talked. "Because no one else is going to," he said, turning to Alanna. "Because it's what we'd want others to do for us," he said to Anesh. "Because it's important," he finally said to Dave. "All of those, and none of those. It just . . . feels right. It's where I need to be. I have a chance to make a difference. To be more than some jackass exploiting literal magic phenomena so that I can make rent."

Silence from the others, as they thought it over. Dave looked like he wanted to say something, but eventually he just shrugged, his mouth in a thin line, like it was the most understandable thing in the world. JP and Anesh looked less convinced, but Alanna nodded along too. For her, it really *did* make sense. James was the kind of person who, in her world, was the perfect hero. Because he actually thought about how to be more than some jackass who took whatever he could and gave nothing back.

"Okay," Alanna said, breaking the quiet contemplation. "What's the plan?"

And just like that, the tone changed. It was accepted; they were doing this, in some way. Now it was just down to how to support James and make this work.

"Well, first of all," James said with a massive smile, "who's coming with me?"

"I'm in." The words came, shockingly, not just from Alanna, but from Dave as well. All eyes pivoted to him, and he shrank a little under their gazes. "What, no one's curious about Alanna?"

James snorted. "No, because we all know Alanna. Why you, though?"

Dave just shrugged, giving away nothing. "Because of what you said—it's the right thing to do. There's a chance, right? I think it's worth helping you out, if I can. You believed in me at first, and now I believe in you, you know, man?"

"I did not know," James said coyly. But then, softer, "But thanks. Thank you."

Kicking out at JP's chair, Alanna asked him, "What about you?"

"Oh, hell no," JP said. "I'm . . . no hero." He almost sounded sad as he said it. "I'll help with this part, if I can, but the fighting in the dungeon scares the shit out of me. I'm having a blast exploring with you guys, but I can't face anything bigger than a strider without freaking the hell out. There's no way I'd be helpful, or willing, to go in there with you tomorrow."

James was disappointed but not overly surprised. Which only left . . . "What about you, Anesh?"

A torn look was the response. Anesh simply didn't know. On the one hand, he wanted more than anything to support James. His friend was trying to save someone's life, and Anesh felt a strong connection to the force of will that his roommate was showing. But on the other hand...

Well, Anesh was afraid. He *didn't* want to risk his life for this. The best-case scenario was that they'd be trapped in the dungeon for however long it took to find the front door, and then longer until it opened. Worst case...

Worst case, apparently, a lot of people had been forgotten there.

"I don't know," he settled on. His voice shook a bit, but James pretended not to notice, despite feeling a bit of a sting from his companion from near the start of this not instantly jumping on board with him.

"That's fine!" James said. "Honestly, you know, three is probably the best number? Especially if we're going to have to pull people out of there." He just paved over the awkward feelings of Anesh's answer. "So! What's the plan? How do we make this work?"

Everyone looked to Anesh, but he was currently a bit lost in thought. It was JP who came to the rescue by getting the idea ball rolling. "Okay, so we know who's going. What do we need to do to prep you guys?"

And with that, the ideas started flowing. They went around the table, discussing, debating, and plotting, until a rough outline emerged. Three of them would go in, climbing into the ceiling as quickly as possible and basically just praying to avoid being spotted. JP and Anesh would be as disguised as maintenance people, which mostly involved sending Anesh to their local thrift store to pick up overalls and clipboards and getting the ladder out of the building. Two days later was the hard part, because Anesh and JP would need to somehow sneak back in, without James there to provide an excuse for them getting past Frank. Then, they could provide, through Ganesh and mundane drones as well as flares, the most possible coverage to help guide the others back to Fort Door.

"The hard part" was super relative, of course. Because James, Alanna, and Dave would be going in without anything that they'd stockpiled in Fort Door over the last couple months. They had one set of incredibly damaged football armor, James had a crowbar under his bed, and Alanna had access to a handgun. On the table here, they had a surprisingly functional harpoon gun, a handful of orbs that they'd never cracked, and a half-complete shield, though that last one wasn't technically "on" the table, James was going to count it. So they'd handed Dave a few hundred bucks and sent him to the sporting goods store to grab them something that could at least pass as armor, and also the heaviest baseball bat he could find.

Finally, and most importantly, JP was dispatched to their local hardware store to get them a ladder in the few hours before everything closed. Alanna also requested a hammer, having grown used to the style of weapon in her time in the dungeon.

As soon as the other guys were out the door, Alanna turned to James with a clap of her hands and a mad grin. "All right! Now that we've got them gone, we can start making out!"

"Maybe when Anesh gets back," James said, patting her on the head as he walked by. "Also, I know I'm playing it cool, but I think I'm way too tense for that right now, even if you are just screwing with me."

"Wasn't, really. But that's fine, I get it," Alanna shot back.

James choked on his words briefly, before recovering. "I feel like we should actually address that when we get back."

"If we get back."

"It'll work out."

"I know. I believe you."

"Okay, again, but say it with some conviction this time."

Alanna snorted out a laugh. "So, what're you doing before they get back and we figure out how to divide up the orbs?"

"Making sandwiches," James said. "We're gonna need to eat, so I want to be prepared and not forced to rely on finding someone's leftover dungeon-lasagna."

That got a twisted look from Alanna. "Egh. Ew. No. I would not test that."

James nodded as he pulled a cooler down from the top pantry shelf where it lived most of the time. "No kidding. So let's get around it. At least Frank won't blink at us bringing in a cooler and a duffel bag full of harpoon gun."

"He might not notice the contents of the . . ." Alanna trailed off. "James." She turned her voice questioning and serious. "How is it possible that Frank acts the way he does, and doesn't know about the dungeon?"

There was a pause. "He's . . . no, hm. I mean, the dungeon wiping people's memories kind of makes it possible. But no, you're right. Frank is perpetually suspicious. He also might actually have useful intel that we could really use, if he's not earning that suspicion. Do you want to go talk to him, while everyone else is out?"

"What, right now?" Alanna asked blandly.

"Sure. I can make sandwiches later. I know what bar he drinks at, it's where I had to go to bribe him. You can text everyone on the way." James was already pocketing his keys off the kitchen counter and pulling his shoes to the side so he could slip them on. "Grab that blue off the table, just in case, and let's go see a man about a dungeon."

Sometimes, Alanna thought, it was just that simple. They'd driven maybe five minutes to a small pub and were sitting outside in the parking lot. The ride over had been rock music and quiet confirmation to each other that they really were ready for tomorrow. Ready to give up everything if it meant saving someone else.

"Okay, you should wait here. I'll go in and talk to him, and yell if I need a goon," James said.

"Why shouldn't I come in too?" Alanna asked indignantly.

James poked her arm, feeling tight muscles under her T-shirt. "Because you're absolutely a goon. And he knows you, too, which is the real reason. If he's in the dark about the dungeon, I think the absolute last person I *want* to know is Frank, and the less suspicious I make him, the better."

"Gotcha. I'll wait by the door," Alanna said as the two of them popped their seat belts off and stepped out into the balmy night.

James pushed open the door and stepped into the overly air-conditioned bar. It was dim inside, the lighting even lower than the streetlight-lit nighttime landscape outside. Around the bar were a few people at tables off to the side, no one talking, or even with anyone else. Just quiet drinking and low jazz. Frank himself was at the bar. The only person at the bar, including the absent bartender.

As James walked up, Frank looked up at him with a mild lack of surprise. "Jim," he said with his deep, gruff voice, reminding James of his late grandfather in that moment of casual recognition. "Don't see you here often. Got another bribe for me?"

"Maybe," James said, sitting down on a hard stool next to Frank. "Frank, you're an observant guy, right?" he asked casually, feigning all the trappings of an old friendship. Frank just grunted in response, which James took as an affirmative. "Well, can you tell me what's wrong with where we work?" James didn't want to allude to anything serious, instead starting with something basic: complaining about his job.

"It's corporate," Frank spat out. "That's what's wrong with it."

James just nodded as Frank took a sip of his whiskey. "With you there. They keep firing anyone that I like. You ever feel that way?" Frank didn't respond. "I mean, you're still there," James said, before trying to drop a lead. "But that new guy that replaced my manager is a total tool."

"He'll be gone soon enough," Frank said with a grim confidence.

"Yeah? How do you know? The last manager was there for a while," James said, trying not to give anything away as he spoke.

Frank just snorted roughly, the noise half from his throat as it was from huffing air out his nose. "Bah. She was just as bad as the suits. Or all those stupid kids they keep trying to make me train," he said bitterly.

There it was.

James tensed up before forcing himself to relax. *She*. Frank had said *she*. Not *they*, nothing ambiguous. He remembered, at least in part, who James's boss was as of a week ago.

Suddenly, James realized just how stupid this was. Frank was an actual person. More than that, he was almost certainly some kind of ex-military. He could legitimately kill someone, and James had just walked in and started asking him questions. Alone.

And now he knew that all those suspicions of Frank were valid. Because the man certainly knew something he wasn't supposed to, and he seemed wholly uncaring about Theo's disappearance, or the constant rotation of employees. Though that might just be Frank himself, and not anything more sinister than a bitter, angry old man.

"Well, Frank, I should . . ." James made as if to stand up.

"Jim," Frank said, turning on his stool to look at the younger man. His voice was firm, a mix of amused and angry. "Really?"

James froze.

But only for a second. And then he started casually walking to the door, throwing over his shoulder a simple "Yeah, I'll see you at work tomorr—" He stopped as Frank stood up, cracking his knuckles.

"Oh, Jim. I had high hopes for you, boy, and you threw them all away." Frank downed the rest of his drink and set the glass on the bar counter. "Every time I think one of you is good enough, you end up getting too nosy in the end."

James turned briefly, smiling as Frank rose to his bait. "Well, Frankie," he said, mimicking Frank's continual fucking up of his name, finally letting go of the polite respect he'd been showing the other man, "maybe it's about time for some straight answers. Though I'm not sure you're the right person for them. After all, you just take your paycheck and look the other way, right?"

Frank stalked forward, sizing James up. He didn't get too close, leaving a few feet of space between them as he pushed aside one of the beat-up wooden chairs the bar had on its floor space. "You really don't have any idea," he growled out as he approached. "You're just another idiot kid. You haven't figured out yet, the world doesn't care about you. You think you're special because you can remember some faces? It doesn't matter. No one's going to miss you." Frank smiled then, a vicious, angry smile.

"I feel like some of my friends might care," James said, nerves burning. "Besides, it's not like you can just kill me in a bar. *Someone* would take offense."

There was just laughter from Frank. "Oh, James. You know, it's amazing what the orange balls can do for you, if you get lucky? I've owned this bar for months now." His laugh was cruel and wild, exactly on tone for what James expected from someone who felt like he had all the power. "Oh, but you're a bit of a coward, aren't you? That's why you keep coming out alive. But that's okay. You always paid your toll to enter, so I let you come and go, but you've probably never seen anything more powerful than a yellow, huh, kid?" Frank gestured to his side, and James noted that the bar patrons, all five of them, stood up in unison. "Here's the other thing you can steal out of that place, boy. Friends." The word was uttered like a curse, and in that moment, James knew that Frank had never once had an actual friend.

In jerky motions, the five figures moved forward, two of them circling behind James to block the door. They were dressed in black leather coats and denim jeans, but no amount of urban camouflage could hide the fact that they didn't have any features on their blank, papery faces.

James might be in some trouble.

"So, kid. What's it gonna be?" Frank said, causing James to focus back on the man to see that he'd pulled a pistol out of somewhere and had it leveled at James. "I get a great deal on trade-ins, but I can just shoot you now if you don't want to find out what the other place does to prisoners."

Somehow, those were the words that snapped James out of his fight-or-flight panic. "Are you seriously telling me that you've been feeding people to the dungeon because it *pays you*?!" he yelled at Frank. "You cannot be that fucking mercenary! There has to be a limit!" Before Frank could respond, James acted on sudden, violent impulse.

He lashed out, and his punch went right through the upper torso of one of the paper pushers blocking the door. The shirt wrapped around his knuckles as he drove through its "skin," refusing to tear, but the thing beneath it had no such resistance. James spun in place, carrying the wounded ex-employee-thing with him to put it between himself and Frank. He was lucky. Lucky that these things had been out here for two months, lucky that Frank was exactly the kind of person that wouldn't know or care how to feed them, and most of all, lucky that Frank didn't want to shoot one of his own assets.

"Dumb move, Jim," Frank said simply as the other four moved to surround him, the one that he'd punched recovering and starting to struggle in his grip. "You could have just taken your chances with your 'dungeon.'" He leveled the gun at James in a professional grip that left James with no delusions that the bullet was going to miss. "Every one of you idiots come here to confront me, give themselves away. All too stupid to bring backup."

Frank pulled the trigger.

Alanna grabbed the muzzle of the gun. She barely got there in time.

"That's-a-perfect-fucking-line-to-enter-on-hi-there-I'm-the-backup-did-you-know-this-bar-has-a-side-door?" Alanna machine-gun rattled off the words, and James could swear he saw an afterimage from her as her coffee-enhanced body practically teleported into view.

The gunshot still ringing in his ears, James drove the flat of his hand through the back of the paper pusher's head, dropping it to the floor in a weak pile of dust and confetti. "Well, Frank. I've gotta say. If I need to pick between my friends and yours, I think I'm going to take the one that's bulletproof." He grinned madly at Frank's furious expression, the old man snarling at Alanna as she ripped the gun out of his hands with more force than the security guard ever could have expected.

The other four stuffed shirts exploded into action. James ducked the first one that came at him swinging a clumsy fist. He punched up into its elbow and was rewarded with a small ripping sound. Another came at him from the side, and he struck out with his foot, kicking back its shins to buy him space to trade punches and blocks with the one in front of him.

This kind of martial multitasking would have been impossible for him if he hadn't had ten years of training poured into his brain by the orbs, and then refined it further with martial arts classes at the gym. But now, here, against starving and hollow monsters for opponents? He could bring the most exploitative strikes to bear.

It helped that these things tore easier when they weren't fed properly.

James blocked another punch and realized that they were punching because they lacked the strength to crush him with their grips. They'd been forced into the position of brawlers, and their psychological edge was totally lost once he knew that he could kick their legs in half. Which he did to one of them, leaving it crawling along the floor.

That actually left it more dangerous, rather than less, as they still didn't seem to feel pain, and all four of them were closing in on him now, albeit in various states of damage. From across the room, there was another gunshot, and James diverted just enough of his attention to see Alanna grappling with Frank, who had apparently produced *another* pistol from somewhere. He was trying to get the gun up, but couldn't manage it with how she'd pinned him, and his third shot went totally wild, shattering the tinted plate-glass window of the front of the bar.

James took a hit to the jaw as he failed to focus on his own fight. Growling his own small war cry, he slipped through a gap between two of the inhuman assailants, grabbed a chair as he spun around and up, and smashed it down onto the one that was closest and had failed to turn around fast enough. It went down, and before it could recover or the others could fill the gap, James *stomped* forward, crushing its head to powder and instantly carrying on the brawl with the others.

There was a muffled thud behind him, which he didn't have time for. *Trust Alanna. She's got this.* James grabbed the arm of the next shirt to come for him, braced his feet, and turned the strike into a throw, slamming it face-first into the table. It was pretty amazing what a body with no bones looked like when you hit it that hard: ripples on false skin. He could have watched that like a lava lamp, but there was no time. While it was still stunned, James stuck his hand into the small rip in the face and made it much larger. Three down, two to go.

Low kick to the crawler, keep it back. Block the standing opponent, then retaliate. No rush now, wear it down by inches. Another low kick, then turn it into a high kick to the off-guard idiot in front of him. Punch, feel a tear, turn it into a kill.

One left.

James circled behind it and just hit it over and over with a chair until it stopped moving.

Done.

He looked up to see Alanna kneeling on top of Frank's prone form. Her eyes were a mix of excitement and worry. James realized he was still snarling, and cleared his throat as he shook off his anger. In the dim green light of the five fresh orbs around them, he smiled.

"You need new friends, Frank."

CHAPTER 12

"So what now, we have to do something with him, right?" Alanna asked, still caffeinated, knees firmly pressed into Frank's back. The man under her was struggling furiously, but despite his efforts, Alanna kept him pinned.

James stood up, dusting off his hands on his knees. His whole body ached from the hits he'd taken fighting the paper pushers. Despite the fact that he was getting tougher, building muscle, and learning how to block or counter most of what was thrown his way, it still left him feeling like one giant walking bruise after a fight like that. Especially since "most" wasn't "all," and double especially when he was getting punched by five things at once.

As it turned out, when a starving, mistreated, demoralized stuffed shirt landed a punch to the jaw, it still hurt like hell.

"Well, we're not killing him," James said to start with. "I'm not really sure! This hasn't come up before." It really was an unexpected problem for him. Dungeon monsters tended to either fight to the death, retreat deeper into the dungeon, or . . . no, that was it, really. Well, except for Rufus. But he was an exception.

Frank himself butted in, grunting in pain as Alanna kept his arms pinned. "What . . . urgh . . . what're you gonna do with me then, you fucking cu—" That got cut off into a howl of pain as James stepped on Frank's head. Lightly. Well, sort of lightly.

"Calm down, Frank," James said condescendingly. "Man, I was honestly hoping that you were just aware of the problem, but not a psychopath." James looked around the bar, at the toppled chairs and smashed glass across part of the floor. "So, really, though, how do we handle this? I really don't want to kill him. I don't want to kill *anyone*. But if we let him go, he's just going to try to murder us and feed our corpses to the dungeon, right?" James looked down again and noticed something else worrying. "Holy shit, you're bleeding," he said to Alanna.

She winced a bit but didn't let go of her pin on Frank. "Yeah, turns out, I'm not bulletproof, and this hurts like fuck, and I think there's a bullet in my hand. So part of me is screaming that we should shoot him before he shoots us first, but the rest of me is with you that I don't want to actually murder someone." Alanna was surprisingly magnanimous for someone who'd just been shot, even if it was because she'd grabbed a gun as it was firing.

James bit his lip in thought. "Okay, options. We could take him prisoner?"

"Where, in your spare bathroom? Or do you have a sex dungeon in your apartment that I'm unaware of?" Alanna asked sarcastically.

"Like, a dungeon-dungeon? Or just a BDSM thing?"

"Why do you need me to clarify that?"

"Don't worry about it." James grinned before going back to the problem at hand. Ignoring Frank's snort of derision from under his boot, he tried to think of other choices. "We could stick him in the dungeon? Though that might just be a death sentence on its own. I could . . . ah . . ." He got Alanna's attention and made a gesture to his own head, trying his best to mime out unleashing Secret on the man that they'd subdued.

Alanna glared at him. "No, that's basically just killing him."

"We could always . . ." James started to say.

But then Frank twisted his head and barked out some words before James could think to gag him again. "You owe me, Jim!" His voice changed cadence, almost like he was reciting rather than speaking normally. "Four uses of door number three, two uses with a guest. No payment made. Established rate of payment . . ."

"Frank, what the hell are you . . . ?" James jumped backward, startled, a prickling cold running up his skin. Out of Frank's torso, from beneath his jacket, a glowing greenish-blue arm was dragging itself out onto the floor. The arm had translucent spikes running down its outside, ending with a long one on each of the two elbow joints. It didn't seem to be coming from anywhere, and was clipping through the jacket, and a second later, it was joined by a second limb pulling itself out as well. "Fuck! Alanna!"

She looked down at a talon-clawed hand that was groping at her leg. The phantasmal arm was becoming more and more solid by the second, and after a brief moment of confusion, she felt a burst of pressure as it tried to rip her off of Frank. Or perhaps just rip into her. As the arm clipped her cargo shorts and shredded them, Alanna became more glad than ever that her skin was hard as hell to actually breach.

Alanna wasted no time rolling off Frank, kicking out to catch him with a solid strike to the balls as she left him lying in pain on the floor. "What the fucking fuck is that fuck?!" she yelled at James as more and more spectral arms started burrowing out of Frank's chest, pulling themselves along with clawed hands across the floor. As they extended out farther and farther, they didn't show any signs of actually being attached to anything, instead just having more and more elbow joints and increasingly complex patterns of spurs and spikes along their exteriors. Alanna didn't bother to wait for an answer, instead flipping over and crawling across the floor, ignoring the shards of glass that lacked the ability to damage her, and lunging for the first handgun that she'd taken from Frank.

As James watched the creature pull out of Frank's chest like an unfolding fractal of arms and hands, it clicked in his head what had just happened. "Oh, I get it!" he said, as the realization dawned. "Its name is Debt, or something, yeah?"

But Frank didn't answer right away, as his face contorted in a wordless mask of anger and pain, and the arms started to get long enough to lift him off the ground like a puppet, the old man's legs dangling beneath him limply as the ghostly spined limbs took over the burden of moving entirely. "Should . . . have taken . . . your chances . . . through the door . . . Jim," he gasped out as the tenth arm started to burrow its way out from his lower back.

James backpedaled until he bumped against the bar, knocking one of the stools over as he tried to get away from the thing that Frank was playing host to. "Oh, Frank. This one doesn't look friendly at all. But that's okay. Because I know something that you do not know." He said the last bit in a lilting voice and with a bit of a laugh alongside the fear that was stuck in his throat.

"What's . . . that?" Frank said, pausing in the forward motion of his manifested meme-enhanced form.

The pause was perfect timing. James and Alanna, who was now behind and off to the side of Frank, finished the line in unison. "I am not left-handed."

Frank cocked his head to the side in confusion. And just like that, James and Alanna opened the path for their own meme. A shared joke from a favorite movie that no one else in the room had seen? It was the perfect public secret.

With a lot less pain than it seemed like Frank was feeling, the dusty blue glow of Secret's scales and teeth started to uncoil around James's legs and torso. Dozens of feet of ancient sea serpent began to pile up in the material world, his tails twitching and knocking aside barstools.

"Round two, Frank?" James asked with a confident smile that was a lot more stable than he felt in his heart.

Frank didn't bother answering, instead lurching forward on the ghostly arms, landing on his feet, and throwing a physical straight-arm punch right at James's face. Startled at the burst of motion from someone who he thought wasn't in control of his own body, James took the hit on his cheek, rolling away from it as much as he could as he felt his teeth rattle. He got his arms up in time to take the next punch that Frank threw, another jab that crunched with a lot more force than James would ever expect from someone with gray hair and a desk job.

Shuffling backward, James, with some momentum assistance from Secret, grabbed the bar behind him and threw himself over the counter, crashing through a stack of mugs and knocking over a soda sprayer. Around him, the shadow of Secret snapped at the half-dozen arms that splayed out of Frank's torso and darted in at random to try to separate James from his precious limbs.

"We must strike first," Secret whispered to him.

"Working on it!" James barked back as he slammed a bottle of whiskey snagged off the back shelf into one of the approaching hands. A solid thud deflected it away, and the unbroken weight of the bottle surprised James. A lifetime of movies told him that these things didn't usually stay so intact.

He and Secret ranged back across the rear of the counter, while Frank stalked the front, the myriad multijointed arms striking out to grab and rend without regard for if there was an opening to strike. Some of them started grabbing up bottles, ashtrays, coasters, whatever was convenient, and flinging the makeshift projectiles at James. These objects passed through Secret's still not fully real flesh without pause, but after the first heavy stone ashtray nailed James in the stomach, he started watching for the tactic and slapping them away or dodging when they came in.

Alanna, meanwhile, was having her own trouble. James saw her on the other side of the room, leaping off a table as one of the hands came down on it after her. The arm splashed against the tabletop, joints bending like a wave to carry it after her in a bouncing trajectory. Alanna landed on another table in a crouch, surfing it as it slid across the floor slightly. She braced herself with one hand while the other brought the gun up and cracked off two shots into the arm.

The bullets trailed out of it almost in slow motion, contrails of green plasma following them, before the substance was sucked back into the construct. James caught a screamed "Fuck!" from Alanna before she was rolling off the table, and he was forced to focus back on Frank, as he ran out of bar and once again came face to face with the old man.

Frank didn't say anything to James as he closed in, now wielding a serrated hunting knife that James hadn't seen him pull out of anywhere. James caught the first swing but then took a nasty gash to his shoulder as one of the claws cut through his shirt and skin with equal force.

Panicking, he kept trying to put distance between himself and Frank. The arms were expanding farther and farther, taking up more and more space in the bar, and the pinball machine that James ducked around wasn't going to hold them off for long. "How much is *this* costing you, Frank?" he yelled over at the man. "It's Debt, right? Or Accounting, or Owed, or Accounts Payable? I don't know what you call it, but it's not gonna let you get this for free!"

James ducked as the front of the machine exploded into wires and plastic shards, one of the clawed hands scything through it. Near the ground and around a small corner of one of the bar's support pillars, James tapped Secret's muzzle, then tapped the ground and pointed to the front of the bar where Alanna was trying to avoid the majority of the limbs pouring out of Frank. The meme nodded and slithered off him.

Standing back up, James saw Frank circling around him from the other side, through the bar's pool hall. "It doesn't matter," the security-guard-turned-person-salesman told James. "As long as you're dead, there won't be anyone left to get in the way of paying it off."

So that was it, James thought. Frank fully intended to just kill him and dump his corpse over a pool table. "Not planning to sell me to the dungeon anymore, Frank?"

"It was never going to work. It only takes people with talent," Frank shot back, along with a lunge with the knife.

James grabbed the arm that came at him with the blade and threw Frank forward a bit, landing a knee to his side as he did so. But then one of the arms was coming around, more graceful than anything with that many joints should be, and James had to duck back before he could follow up with more strikes. "Doesn't seem in character for you! Too much work!" James taunted as he darted backward. He just had to regroup with Alanna, buy Secret some kind of opportunity, kill the hostile infomorph, and then . . . James's brain fizzled out. That was too much to ask already. Maybe just running for the car and hoofing it was a better plan.

"Alanna! Secret!" James yelled out for her as he raced back to the front of the building. "What's the plan?" He slid into place next to where Alanna and Secret were trying to come up with an option for dealing with Frank, while dodging or snapping at the multiple four-meter-long arms boxing them in. "And why is the plan 'just fucking run'?" James asked as he slammed a jabbing punch into the palm of one of the hands that was trying to reach for Alanna's back.

Alanna glanced behind her. "The door's armed," she said simply, and James barked out a laugh as he realized what she meant. The door was indeed covered in hands and arms, their spines forming a barricade holding them in. It kept the thing from unleashing its full might on them but also left them with no easy escape.

It was Secret that answered him, speaking from the mouth that wasn't currently biting an arm from Frank's pet meme. "It is as you said. It is What Is Owed To Me. It draws its manifestation from Frank's belief that you truly did owe him a debt. Take that away and—" Secret was cut off as another pair of arms wrapped around his head, the claws trying to break his scales.

Alanna also had a thought to share as she grunted under the impact of an errant swing. "Or I could shoot Frank."

"Try that one first," James said as Frank came around the corner. Alanna didn't hesitate, raising the gun and firing off a shot. But one of the arms grabbed it as it passed, and while the bullet ripped through, it was held back by the web of green plasma that trailed after it, eventually stopping it about a foot from Frank's face as the arm healed itself. "Okay, plan B," James muttered. "Frank!" He raised his voice. "Did you know that under Oregon law, debts cannot be assumed post hoc?! Made illegal in 1965!"

Frank didn't respond, instead just sending another claw in to try to grasp at James's throat, all while steadily advancing with his knife up. Frank was winded, and being old he had as many incidental pains to go with the extra wisdom in a fight, but he wasn't done yet. These damn kids thought they could take away everything he'd worked for? No. Not even close to the truth.

"Okay, that didn't work. I don't think he gives a shit about laws," Alanna muttered. "Secret? Options?"

The ghost leviathan shivered as a pair of hits raked scales off it. He was too small, too weak. Frank had been feeding his meme a steady diet of greed, resentment, and a bitter desire for *more*, and Secret didn't have the conceptual sources of power to tap into to fight back effectively. So he hissed back at James, "I need something else. I cannot fight through my opposition without more power."

In Alanna's head, there was a brief moment of doubt about whether finding a way to hand something that felt a lot like an artificial intelligence even more power was a good idea. But that thought got quashed by her trust, both in James and in Secret himself, who had been losing pieces of himself to keep her safe while she failed to do any reasonable damage to the hand monster that was trying to tear her skin off. So, what she said out loud was "How?" while she grappled one of the green claws, keeping the phantasmal appendage pinned. Apparently, while bullets and thrown chairs phased through it, she could hold it down just fine with her own hands. "So you need more secrets?" Alanna asked the serpent.

"I need stronger secrets," he replied, chomping down on another arm. His other mouth spoke. "I need the breaking of things hidden."

"Doesn't that . . . *oof*." James grunted as one of the hands flattened itself and slipped past what he thought was an accurate grab to clock him in the ribs. He reeled back, recovering quickly enough to punch the appendage away. "Doesn't that remove your power, if we share secrets?"

Secret made a motion that was simultaneously alien and obviously a shrug. "I am of secrets. The cataloging of information. There are many aspects to a secret, some of them—" James and Alanna both stopped listening as Frank finally closed the gap, circling around their barricade of toppled tables.

They were having a hard enough time fighting one nightmare. The second, human-shaped one was going to make it quickly lethal.

For Alanna, it was pressuring her mind to try to think of a secret that she even could share with James. She was an almost impossibly blunt person sometimes, and that left her without a lot of options. Added to the time crunch of being clawed apart shortly if she didn't come up with an answer, her brain just locked up. She didn't stop fighting, but she didn't see a way down any new mental pathways that were useful. So she trusted in James to get Secret what he needed.

James had an answer.

He hated it.

But as he kicked a chair at Frank, and bought them about twenty seconds while the ghostly arms that were now emerging in a pair of matching rings from Frank's torso propped him back up, he knew exactly what he could open up to give Secret what he asked for.

Reaching out one hand to grab at Alanna's shoulder, he spoke softly, but firmly enough to be heard even over the grinding noise of spines on the wall and floor. "Hey," he said, swallowing his anxiety. "I think you should know that I'm furiously in love with you." Almost instinctively, Alanna wanted to make some kind of reply about how this wasn't the time for that, or simply go with the Harrison Ford answer and say "I know." But she held her tongue and instead opted to go for grabbing the claw that was moving in to try to string James up by his own ponytail. Again suppressing the spike of anxiety and emotional turmoil in his chest, James looked up at Secret, who was now being hemmed in by a dozen claws, and added something to his statement. "And also Anesh. And I'm terrified to tell either of you out of absolute terror that I'll fuck everything up."

Secret felt the rush of that most powerful part of a hidden truth: secrecy's dramatic end.

Alanna turned to James with a smile on her face, the look made slightly creepy by the twin lines of blood running down her cheek.

Her own heart leapt, high on adrenaline and combat. "Aw, buddy," she said. "You never needed to wo—" Her words were cut off as, with her guard down, one of the claws lashed in from the side, grabbed her around the throat, and threw her across the front room of the bar.

"Fuck!" James screamed, slamming a punch into one of the gaps between the spines in the arm. His fist connected and left a divot but didn't damage the appendage, and he started to feel the last bits of hope he had in this fight drop away.

From behind him, he heard Frank chuckling.

And then, from around him, he heard a roar like rushing water.

An impossibly enormous serpent crashed through the forest of arms and hands and claws in front of James. From the comparatively tiny tail coiled around James's leg, Secret rose up. And up. And up. Miles and miles of neon fangs and scales and eyes, so many eyes now open. And staring in rage at Frank and the creature growing out of him. He was a leviathan, a creature from an age that never was, brought back to life here and now, to strike down the monster that his friends found themselves faced with.

Around James, a haze settled into solidity, as his own arms became wreathed in scales, his fists ending in fangs feet in length. He found himself balanced on a dozen tails, and suddenly seeing through extra eyes that peered into the same spaces with different contexts.

And all of a sudden, Frank seemed very small in front of him.

The old man hesitated, then took a small step back. "Now, Jim . . ." he started to say.

But James wasn't listening anymore.

James stepped forward, and the wood panel floor of the bar cratered under the force of his step. A trio of arms bent at right angles and moved to intercept him, flowing toward his face more aggressively than any before. He didn't hesitate, swinging a wide roundhouse punch that, empowered by Secret's shell layered on top of his arm, left the incoming strikes not just countered, but torn to shreds.

He screamed something incoherent at Frank, and a roar that thundered through the air joined him in battlesong.

The arms abandoned holding the door and windows, and a legion of them flooded toward James to try to stop his advance on Frank. But Secret, unbound and empowered by the cracking of a secret of the heart, intervened. His miles-long body flowed past in an endless loop, each toothy maw on it snapping one of the assaulting arms into broken residue that dissipated before it hit the floor.

And then James reached Frank and slammed a normal human fist into his face, sending him tumbling back into the floor.

James looked up at the surviving arms and spoke with a cold voice that he didn't know he could manage with this much rage inside him. "You can leave now, and I think whatever you owed Frank is more than paid off. Or you can die here. Your call."

What Is Owed To Me didn't have to think twice; with Frank down for the count it was already burning energy fast just to stay manifested physically. And it wasn't a hard call to throw its employer under the metaphysical bus.

And then the bar was silent. Secret shed his massive form, returning to the smaller serpentine shape that was snugly wrapped around James's torso, his head positioned right by James's ear in a classic vision of the snake whispering to a man. Though with fewer lies, in this case, hopefully. James didn't have time to think about it, instead letting the scales and claws shed off his body without trying to hold them in place, and rushing over to check on Alanna.

"Fucking ow," she coughed out, sitting up with his help. "Let's not do this on our next date." Alanna somehow managed to turn out a joke.

"Deal," James said as he got her to her feet. "Should we get out of here?"

"Frank first," she said, stalking over to him and pulling out her phone while she also picked up the handgun off the floor. "One left. Perfect. Secret! Can you hide something on the security camera footage?"

"That camera is not connected to anything storing information," Secret politely told her.

"Perfect!" Alanna walked up to Frank's prone form from behind and raised the gun, ignoring James's increasingly frantic *nos* in the background. Then she shot him in the leg, a splatter of blood bursting out at an angle to the entry wound. Then she pushed "dial" on her phone and waited for the automated 911 system to put her through. "Police, please," she said into the phone. "Maybe ambulance? I think someone just shot themselves. I was walking by a bar and it looked like some guy in there was trashing the place." A pause, and James almost burst out laughing. "Yes, I have the address," she told the operator.

Three minutes later, police were on the way. "What about the gun with your prints on it?" James asked.

"That one's mine now. Frank obviously shot himself with the *other* gun," Alanna said.

"And the dead paper pushers?" James was trying to figure out if they could shove all five bodies in his trunk before the police arrived.

He and Alanna went outside with a few precious minutes before the police showed up; Alanna was going to be absent when they did, so there wouldn't be any questions about the cuts on her head and the bullet wound in her hand. "Target dummies, obviously. They're made of paper. If anyone recognizes them as dungeon mobs, so what? That'll make it even less likely that we're involved."

"I feel like this is still crazy risky," James said.

Alanna just shrugged. "I admit, I was kind of hasty. But I wanted to shoot Frank somehow, and at least this way he's probably not going to be an issue for a while."

"Fair. If we had more time we could have found drugs to plant on him or something," James mused.

"Know any drug dealers?"

"Good point."

"Okay, I'm gonna be a ways away for a while. Call me after they get done, so you can take me to the hospital," Alanna said, heading off away from the main road. She got about four steps, then turned around and walked back. James gave her a raised-eyebrow look, and she just smiled, leaned in, and gave him a small kiss. "Don't think Secret ate the words you said," she told him, and then waved over her shoulder with her good hand as she actually made her temporary exit.

Of all the things James hated most in life, he was quickly coming up with "answering police questions" and "emergency care waiting room" as the contenders for the top two.

No, he wasn't the person who called it in. No, he didn't do it. No, there was no evidence, and yes, he was covered in bruises, but that wasn't related. No, he couldn't explain what had happened, he was just here because his friend had to leave, and he had witnessed the same things she did. No, he didn't know why the safe in the back was open, or why there was an alarming quantity of meth in there. Though that was convenient, although he held that line back while being questioned.

At a certain point, he wanted to just yell at them that if he'd known about the fucking safe, or thought to go into the back office at all, he would have stolen everything that wasn't nailed down. Like the eight identical black briefcases that they brought out that looked alarmingly familiar to James. Or the stacks of money, some of which he was almost sure had come from him.

He had to wonder what else Frank had stashed away back there. Did the police find any orbs, and just leave them? Maybe after Alanna had fewer holes in her, they could come back and scour the place. How long did crime scenes stay active, anyway? James figured that if Frank was going to be in some kind of lockup for a while, they'd have the time to look through the bar. Frank seemed to have driven away all the actual clientele, maybe with a magic effect, or maybe just firing all the staff and putting up a *Closed* sign. But either way, this place was nondescript, unused, and might contain answers and/or hidden wall safes. Maybe JP and Anesh could check it out over the week while they waited for the door to open again.

But while he tried to keep his cool through the questioning and get through it, it felt like there was a mountain of uncomfortable suspicion on him. James fidgeted with his keys in his pocket while the officer that had been talking to him went over to another cop, and the two of them kept looking his way. Then his fingers brushed against the small blue orb in his pocket, and he figured there was no harm in trying it out.

[+1 Skill Rank : Flute]

[Problem Solved : Recognition]

Almost out of nowhere, another cop car with its red and blue lights throwing more harsh shadows on the wall showed up. And this one, by some absolute coincidence, happened to contain an officer who recognized him as the guy from the convenience store fight the other day, which helped to give justification for the bruises. Of *course* James was in a martial arts class—that made perfect sense and he should have just said that.

He almost ground his teeth into powder waiting for them to let him go. But they did, after that, let him go. The new arrival even have him a semifriendly, semithreatening pat on the shoulder that caused his stiffened and bruised arm to tense up in mild pain. But James grinned and got through it.

After that imposed wait, he met up with Alanna, who had found a food cart that sold her a massive burrito and didn't ask stupid questions about whose blood that was, and took her and her food to the hospital.

And then three goddamned hours later, they finally got out after Alanna started telling nurses that she was going to leave under her own power if they didn't get the discharge paperwork right this second.

James did, while they waited and Alanna dozed under the influence of painkillers, have time to bring everyone up to speed on their group chat. Which meant that he didn't need to look forward to explaining it all over again when he got home.

Which was good. He reminded himself, there was still the matter of trying to save someone's life tomorrow. And he was already exhausted, and looking forward to bed.

When the two of them stumbled back into the apartment, they did so just in time to see a crumpled ball of paper sail across their vision and into the garbage can in the kitchen.

"The fuck are you clowns doing?" Alanna asked.

JP waved at them. "Hey, welcome back. Good to see you too, I'm glad you're okay!" He winced as he saw the bandage on her hand. "Hope that doesn't hurt too much, eh? Anyway, um, it turns out that Anesh is 'good' at basketball, and I'm making him prove it. And also mad at him for squandering basketball."

From the kitchen, Dave nodded. "Yeah, he missed one so far. Out of twenty-six. It's impressive, it's a great thing to be 'good' at," he said. "Also welcome back. Are you guys okay?"

"Yeah, that. That's important, not basketball," Anesh said. "Please, get me out of this. Also, for real, you look like hell. Do you need anything? I've got some leftover painkillers from when my arm became broken."

"Nice passive voice," James said with a grin at his friend. "But no. Also, why are you guys saying 'good' in that weird tone and not just that he got a skill—" Everyone in the room who wasn't Alanna, who had thrown herself facedown onto the couch, shushed James. "—Okay. Why," he said with a dry tone and a roll of his eyes.

From down the hall, he heard the toilet flush and saw the bathroom door in the hallway open. A second later, his brain caught up and realized that everyone who was supposed to be here was already in his living room.

"Hey!" came the shouted, cheerful voice of a young girl from the other side of his apartment. "You're back!"

James took a deep breath and tried to hold back his frustration, to little effect.

It was Anesh who answered his earlier question. "Yeah, so, your younger sister showed up. I hope you don't mind, we let her in and can't get rid of her. That's . . . not a huge problem, right?" He spoke in a tone that informed James that he knew it was a huge problem and didn't have much choice in the matter.

But James wasn't about to get angry about it. A brush with death left him more than a little immune to petty grievances like this. "Yeah, it's fine. Though, hey, could you maybe put this with wherever you hid the other . . . things?" James said, slinging the grocery bag with the five green orbs in it toward Anesh. "Because that's one conversation I don't want to have right now."

"What's a conversation you don't want to have? Tell me!" James let out an *oomph* as his younger sister, Kayle, all of seventeen years old and somehow unearthly annoying, slammed into him in a hug she didn't ask for and he really didn't want right now.

"Hi, welcome to my apartment. Why are you here?" James bluntly threw the words at her.

Kayle let out a teenage sigh, enough angst in it to level a small building. "Mom and Dad are going out of town and they dropped me off to stay here with you. Mom said you'd have to be okay with it because they pay your phone bill, and so you owe her. Forever. Because you're her son."

While he was a little too exhausted to be properly furious, the words still raked across James's ears like knives. James looked around at his friends for support but found nothing there. "Well, look at the time," JP said, checking an invisible watch. "Dave, I'm your ride, you ready to go?"

"Yup. Nothing suspicious for me to do here." The two of them both shuffled around where James was standing, avoiding eye contact, to get their shoes on.

"Smooth," James muttered to them.

"Good luck," JP said back with a smile. And then, more seriously, "I'll see you tomorrow. Good luck. Really."

James let out a small groan and massaged his temples as his sister started bombarding him with questions about where he'd been and what he was up to. "Tell you what: I'll talk to you tomorrow about it, okay? For now . . . Anesh, can you help me get Alanna into a real bed?" Anesh nodded, smiling but still keeping a concerned eye on James as he jumped over the back of his armchair to maneuver with James around the couch to try to pick Alanna up.

"Do I have to sleep on the couch?" Kayle pouted at him, trying out the puppy-dog eyes that she'd found to work so well on the boys, and some of the girls, at school.

"No," James said, half surprised as he thought of the answer. "You know, I have good news!" His grin turned a bit sharkish. "Wouldn't you know it, we have an extra bed here? Let me show you to your temporary room."

CHAPTER 13

James woke up before his sister did, which was both difficult and rewarding. It meant he got to avoid the kid for a little bit longer, and honestly, he was not looking forward to playing verbal defense in his own apartment. But hell, she was his sister; what was he supposed to do? Kick her out? Nah, that wasn't him. But still, he'd have to make sure Lily was locked up before he left.

Fortunately, Anesh had swept up the orbs in the living room, and while the gear was harder to hide, it also wasn't as needed. They just told Kayle that it was for some kind of LARP, and she'd instantly tuned them all out.

Unfortunately, the actual *reason* James was up early was that Alanna was some kind of inhuman monster who woke up and instantly was ready to get out of bed. She didn't spend any time lazing around or dozing back off. She just . . . got up and started moving. Which was a problem, because she'd slept in James's bed last night, and while *that* was enjoyable, the part where Alanna woke him up and expected him to be a functional human was less so.

James would cope, he thought with a smile as he sat in bed, watching her get dressed.

It also didn't help his credibility on the whole "sleeping for twelve hours" thing that Anesh had *also* gotten up early. Before either of them, in fact.

It had come as something of a shock to his roommate, when James had gotten to the confession part of the explanation of what the fuck had happened last night during the confrontation with Frank. But by that point, James was too tired, both physically and emotionally, to care about leaving anything out. Also, literally everything else in the conversation had come as a shock to Anesh anyway, from Secret's manifestation to the presence of other infomorphs of Secret's strength, to the fact that Frank was literally selling people to the dungeon. So a little romantic infatuation hadn't really been the biggest surprise on his plate.

He'd still hemmed and hawed about it, though. Until Alanna had cracked an eye open from where she was sprawled on James's bed and straight up asked him, "Do you like James?"

"Well . . . yeah," Anesh had said with a flush to his cheeks, not meeting James's eyes.

Before James could really appreciate the sense of awkward glee that was sinking into his chest, Alanna asked her follow-up question. "What about me?"

Anesh blinked a couple times, before saying, "Well, I mean, sure. Yes."

"Great," Alanna had said. And then, like some kind of trapdoor spider, she'd rolled out of the blankets and dragged Anesh back down into something between a hug and a death grasp.

Anesh hadn't just accepted that, obviously. Once Alanna had fallen back asleep, he'd detangled himself, and he and James had talked, more seriously, about what the future was going to look like for them. But by the time that both of them were feeling their eyes getting heavy, the future was looking pretty good. And Anesh had, in the end, stayed with them in James's bed.

That bed was the first thing that was getting upgraded, next time they had an influx of cash. If this was going to keep happening, and they all seemed to want it to, they were going to need something a little larger. Or at the very least more pillows.

But now, none of them were exhausted, falling asleep on their feet. They'd woken up and found that, while it was a little different, there wasn't any regret or awkward feelings of uncertainty. If the dungeon had changed anything about himself, James realized, it was that he was getting better and better about grabbing opportunities. There was no time for waffling in the greater office region, where hesitation might get them killed, and it seemed like that mentality was starting to bleed over into his personal life too.

He was snapped out of his mental wanderings by Alanna kicking the foot of the bed and asking him with a friendly glower on her face, "What're you lookin' at?"

"You. You're cute," James replied with his own grin, without missing a beat. Again, something he didn't think he ever would have had the strength to say, if he hadn't been through the experiences of the last few months.

Alanna turned her head away. "Fuck off with that. I know you like me and everything, but I'm also self-aware enough to know that I look less 'cute' and more 'orc barbarian' than anything else."

"A cute orc barbarian," James shot back without missing a beat, using the blankets of his bed to deflect the pillow Alanna hurled at his head. "All right, all right, I'm awake," he told her defensively.

It was maybe fifteen minutes later when James exited his room, covering his gaping yawn. He got out to the living room and sort of stood dumbly next to the kitchen counter, before Alanna pressed a cup of coffee into his hands and he jolted back into wakefulness.

Sipping at the brew he'd been given, James made a note to his friend. "Ah, we're gonna have to disconnect that coffee maker. I don't know if Kayle drinks coffee, but we can't take the risk that she ends up thinking she's a superhero now."

"Good point," Alanna replied. "Actually, can we take this thing with us? It'd be nice to have a support item when we go in."

"It weighs . . ."

"I know, I'm just kidding. But seriously, we should bottle some of this up, at least."

James sighed. "I don't wanna. The control panel on this thing is a mess. Tell you what," he offered, "you do it, and I'll make you waffles."

That got her attention. "Bought and sold!" Alanna pivoted around him, neatly maneuvering James to the entrance of the kitchen area and giving him a light push forward. "Waffles!" she enthusiastically repeated, as she continued nudging him onward.

He smiled, and was still smiling as he started pulling out pans and mixing bowls and ingredients. Of all the skills that James had picked up from the trips into the dungeon, cooking was probably at the top of his list of ones that he enjoyed. Above the combat-relevant skills like knowing how to slide into a shooting stance with a handgun or break an incoming punch with a well-timed counterstrike. Above the mildly useful abilities of being able to do solidly complex math in his head or speak Spanish. And certainly higher-ranked than fringe knowledge like knowing the best way to get a case before the Supreme Court or perform oral sex—though that last one might come in handy in the future, James thought with a self-conscious blush. The point was, cooking was where his passion had settled.

Sure, it was cool that the origami skill had once literally saved his life, but that was nothing compared to the feeling of fabricating something delicious out of random stuff from his kitchen. And as that knowledge settled in and was reinforced with practical experience and classes, he came to understand that it wasn't just "random stuff," but that it all fit together into webs of flavor profiles and deliberate ingredient choices. James was probably never going to find a use for his ability to raise a teju, but he sure as hell could take joy every day in this act of creation that he was now coming to fully understand.

Half an hour later, JP and Dave came through the front door, with JP cracking a wide smile and exclaiming, "Hey, you made us breakfast!"

"I made Alanna and Anesh breakfast. You two are on your own," James told them. Though, as he saw JP's face legitimately turn into a vision of disappointment, he relented. "All right, no, not really. You can have a waffle and some bacon. Don't eat all the bacon, though. I want some."

JP wasted no time grabbing a plate of food, and so, by the time Anesh came out to the living room, everyone was halfway done with breakfast and already midway into a discussion. "Yes," James was saying as his roommate finally graced them with his presence, "I'm ready. We're all ready. JP, I know you're trying to do a sanity check, and I appreciate it, but we've got a plan, we're sticking to it, and we probably won't die." James waved his fork at his friend, a bit of waffle still attached. He ignored Anesh's glare as he dripped syrup onto the table, and continued. "If we'd wanted to do this in a safer way, we should have done a million things different starting, I dunno, three months ago." His words were punctuated by jabs of the fork. "There's people in trouble, we've got the experience and tools to help, we're doing this."

JP didn't say anything verbally in response, simply looking over at the haphazard pile of hockey padding and improvised harpoon gun.

"Okay," James conceded, "we have the experience to help."

"All I'm saying is, it seems even more dangerous since you and Alanna got in a boss fight last night." JP carefully folded his napkin and set it on the table as he finished his food. "I don't want to see you dead."

"Technically, you wouldn't ever *see*—" Alanna started quipping.

JP cut her off. "No. Stop that. I know that you and James think this is worth the risk. That's fine, I can accept that. But you could die. This isn't something you should joke about right now. Especially since you got shot last night." He lectured her with a hard voice and a stern expression on his face.

Coming over to the table with his plate, Anesh looked down at where James was sitting comfortably in Anesh's personal armchair. James looked up at him with a goofy, open-mouthed smile and patted the chair next to him. Anesh was more of a morning person than James was, but he still wasn't ready for this right now. "Get out of my chair." He poked James with his socked foot until his friend conceded the point and folded himself over the arm of the chair like he was made more out of jelly than human. "Also, hang on, Alanna, you got shot. Didn't you guys go to the hospital? They tell the police about shooting victims."

"Ah, not to worry," Alanna said, raising her bandaged hand, thick gauze containing the flesh crater in her palm. "This looks enough like not-a-bullet-wound that I got away with it. The nurse did *ask* if I'd been shot, but I told them I'd fallen and hit an exposed pipe or something. I don't really remember; I was hurtin' at that point. Oh! Fun fact if you ever need to kill me, though!"

James popped up from off the floor. "Why would we—"

"That surface fracture *thing* doesn't work if I'm already cut open. And I don't know, man, maybe I go rogue and start taking over the world or something," Alanna said, answering James's unfinished question.

"Taking over the world is literally one of our long-term goals. Like, not even a joke—that was something we actually talked about doing."

"Taking over the world *badly*, then."

"Fine."

Anesh cut in, interrupting them. "As cute as this is, are you all ready for today?"

James, Alanna, and Dave all let out a collective groan. They'd just gone over this with JP; no one was interested in a replay. This time, though, it was JP who came to their rescue. "They're ready, no matter what I say," he told Anesh. "And we've got the ladder, buncha rope, everything all stacked up. So there's . . ." JP trailed off, looking over Anesh's shoulder.

"I smelled bacon." James's sister, Kayle, stood in the hallway. Like James, she kept her hair long. Unlike James, her hair was both blond and seemingly critically weak to mornings, because while her brother had his ponytail coherently done up, her hair looked like she'd just stuck her tongue in a power socket that produced both electricity and also knots.

Transitioning smoothly from dungeon talk, James announced, "And you can have some bacon!" from his spot on the floor.

Pausing before getting her food, Kayle looked around the room, narrowing her eyes at the collection of friends, all of whom were discreetly keeping an eye on her. "Why are all your friends here this early? You sleep until it's dark out."

"Okay, first of all, that's kinda mean." James actually was a little bit hurt by the way she phrased it. His sister was pretty good at saying things that were technically true, in surprisingly hostile ways.

"To be fair, you also work really late most days," Anesh said. "Seems fair to wake up at night when you'll be at the office until four a.m., mate."

James gave a quick smile back, speaking quietly. "Yeah, I know. She's just needling me. But that doesn't mean I have to like it." Raising his voice back to a speaking tone, he informed his sister, "They're here because we're doing a thing today. Dave and Alanna and I are going on a weekend trip thing, so don't give Anesh a hard time, if you're gonna be here all week."

"Fine, whatever," she said, and James got the impression she was secretly thrilled that he wouldn't be around. "Have fun, I guess."

"You could be less belligerent while you're *eating my food*." James scowled at her.

Kayle made a rude gesture at him. "You said I could! Also, I ate one of your candy bars. Why do you have so much candy in this apartment?"

"It's from England," Anesh said, unflinchingly.

"That's not what she asked," Dave muttered to him, but Anesh and James both just held up fingers to their lips and shushed their friend. "Fine, I'll be quiet. Later. When are we leaving, anyway?" he asked the assembled group, collecting plates off the table.

Anesh and James looked at each other, and James gave a shrug. "Twenty minutes? Time enough to load the car, right?"

"Yeah, I'll get the ladder in the back." Dave pushed past Kayle on the way out of the kitchen, where he'd dropped off everything he'd cleared from the table. It was, James realized, kinda nice to have that one friend who actually helped with keeping his apartment as a livable space, and not . . . well, it could get bad, sometimes. Between Anesh's devotion to school—lessened during summer, but still bordering on fanatical—and James's depression and general malaise, sometimes stuff just went uncleaned. For a while.

It seemed like so long ago that Anesh had been cleaning off this very table for the first time in weeks, interrogating James on where the damn candy came from.

Kayle, in between scarfing down bites of waffle while leaning on the back of the couch, made a confused noise. "Where are you going that you need a ladder?"

"It's a nerd thing," James informed her bluntly, the unspoken subtext being the phrase *you know, one of those things you really do not care about.* There might have been some animosity in the past between the siblings over things like this, though these days James just could not care about his sister's opinion on his personal life. "But yeah, get the stuff loaded up, then we'll roll out." He checked his phone's clock. It was almost ten a.m., and the general plan here was to get to his work early, so they could have time to prepare. But before that, there was one last thing to do. "Hey, Dave. Hand me that bag on the ladder before you take it out. Thanks."

That bag was probably the most important thing in the apartment right now. It was where they'd thrown all the orbs when Kayle came in. And currently, it contained what was potentially a powerful addition to their arsenal. And also potentially just an amusing diversion.

Five greens, six yellows, one giant yellow that happened to be the shadow of a person, and three blues.

Options. Solutions. Flexibility. Power. All the things that a delver needed to keep their edge and their life.

Also, the part that actually engaged James's imagination, modifying their apartment to be some kind of magical paradise detached from the rules of reality. That was just fun.

Really, for James, it was the fun of the orbs that was really what had captured his fancy. Alanna wanted power, Anesh wanted knowledge, JP wanted . . . something. Actually, James didn't know what the hell JP wanted. And Dave, well, it seemed like Dave just wanted to make friends, in the comically literal sense of the term. But James? James appreciated all of those things, but what he was coming to love was just the feeling of excitement at the unwrapping. They were loot boxes, except somehow less exploitative, despite having to kill things to get them.

James, Dave, and Alanna had retreated back to his room, leaving Anesh to load up their car and JP to distract Kayle for a while. James wasn't sure how he felt about leaving the most charming person in their friend group with his sister, but then again, JP had a girlfriend, and also if he ended up flirting with Kayle, James couldn't bring himself to feel bad about it. JP was, legitimately, a decent guy. Not exactly Good, but good enough. And James really wasn't protective enough of his sibling to worry about it.

"Okay, so, how are we splitting these?" James asked. "Do we save the blues? I know I'm taking the big yellow, but what about the rest?"

Alanna looked down at the pile. "We're using the greens here, which I feel is fair. Maybe just split the greens and yellows down the middle, save the blues, yeah."

Dave did have a thought, though. "Hey, James, you said that blues can be absorbed, right?"

"Yes, but they hurt? Also, I had to have Secret help, so I'm not sure if you could," James told him.

"Maybe. Hm." Dave looked thoughtful. "But Secret could help me too, maybe. Also, I think I understand the blue ones a bit better. Do you mind if I try?"

Alanna looked over at him with raised eyebrows. "What's your thought on them? I wanna know."

He thought for a second on how to explain himself. Expressing ideas had never been Dave's strong suit, and it always seemed to annoy people when he tried. But he'd been thinking about this ever since he'd looked over Anesh's notes on the blues. "I think that . . . how to say it . . . I think they like being tools?" Dave gestured at the blue orbs. "When Anesh tried to put one into his spear, he wasn't thinking about turning the spear into something more useful, he was just trying to 'improve it.' And it didn't work. But when we use them, it solves problems. And James, when you absorbed one, it gave you a function. A tool. That's the theme that connects the blues; they're tools. They make tools. But you cheated when you absorbed it; you weren't trying to be a tool, you were trying to . . . well, improve yourself. And Secret helped you get around that, and it fucked it up. So I think I can do it right. Um . . . no offense."

Alanna looked like she wanted to say something reflexively, but stopped, trying to work through what Dave had said before responding. James, though, nodded excitedly. "Yeah, okay," James said, "I think I get it. Yeah! We never really thought about connecting themes in the orbs before, though we should have with the blues, at least."

"They solve problems, yeah," Alanna said. "In every form. Though we still have no fucking clue what all the uses are. Should we start a betting pool on when we find the next use case?"

"No. Because I'll lose," James reminded her. "So, Dave, you think you're enough of a tool to absorb one of these?" he asked, handing over one of the blues.

Despite the snicker from Alanna, Dave nodded solemnly and took it. "Being useful is the only thing I've ever been good at," he said softly. "This is nothing." And with that, the orb slipped inside his palm, leaving only the smallest speck of blue exposed.

[+6 Activations : *Nullify Gravity*]

There was a moment of silence, which James had considered breaking by yelling about how unfair that was. But he kept quiet, just for the sake of keeping up the pretense of not letting his sister know anything weird was going on. Alanna, though, was much more moderate in response. "Well, that's just not fair. We should have been making magic items out of ourselves this whole time."

"Xenotech," James muttered, sullenly.

Alanna barked out a quick laugh. "All right, well, we've not got time to waste. Let's crack into the rest of these, and Dave, you can have the other blue orbs if you like."

"I don't . . . feel like I could take more than one more," Dave said, mildly confused, but firming up his self-understanding as he spoke.

"I think two is my limit. At least for now. So I'll take one, and you save the other for later." He plucked up another blue and slid it into his other palm, easy as breathing.

[+4 Activations : Remove One Half Of]

"Actually, on that note, if understanding the orb made absorbing it easy . . . we should seriously be looking for connecting themes or ideas in the other ones," James said, having a moment of clear inspiration. "We haven't seen a lot of the oranges, but yellows and greens? We've had a ton of experience there, we should pool the notes and really go over it when we get back."

"Or make JP and Anesh do it," Alanna said.

Dave and James nodded in unison. "Yes, that. Pawn off the work. I like it," James said. "But for now . . ." He reached for the orbs.

After that, it was a simple matter of splitting them up and cracking them without preamble. The results were . . . mixed.

For Alanna, using two greens and three of the smaller yellows:

[+1 Skill Rank : Gymnastics - Rolling]
[+2 Skill Ranks : Carpentry - Furniture - Desks]
[+1 Skill Rank : Etiquette - Aristocracy - Eating]
[Local Area Shift : +0.8 Hours Allocated to Sleep / Day]
[+3 Skill Ranks : Templating - Shipping Manifests - Grocery]
[Local Area Shift : +1 Closet]
[+3 Skill Ranks : Survival - Hurricane]

For Dave, using one of the greens, and the three other yellows:

[+1 Skill Rank : Sprinting]
[+1 Skill Rank : Pilot - Single Prop Aircraft]
[+2 Skill Ranks : Public Speaking - News Broadcasting]
[Local Area Shift : +2 Kilowatts Generate / Hour]
[+3 Skill Ranks : Geography - Roads - Northwest US]
[Local Area Shift : +1.4 Comfort]
[+3 Skill Ranks : Music - Violin]

And finally, as the two of them started trying to figure out where the hell the new closet was, James looked down into swirling yellow depths of the massive orb that was the copy of a ghost of a former coworker, sitting next to the remaining green orb. Through his head ran every concern, every fear, about how he might be permanently killing someone, or warping his own persona by doing this, or generally just making a mistake. And then, like a hawk among pigeons, one idea flared up. Someone needed him. And needed him at his best—better than that, they needed him to be more than human.

The ends, eternally, justified the means.

James plunged his hands into the two orbs in front of him and felt himself grow.

[Local Area Shift : –10% Entropy]
[+3 Skill Ranks : Etiquette - Japanese - Formal]
[+5 Skill Ranks : Games - Gears of War 3 - Multiplayer]
[+4 Skill Ranks : Mechanics - Car - Jetta]
[+3 Skill Ranks : Drive - Car]
[+2 Skill Ranks : Language - French]
[+1 Skill Rank : Communication - Family]
[+2 Emotional Resonance Ranks : Devotion]
[+1 Emotional Resonance Rank : Accomplishment]
[Shell Upgraded : +0.4 Meter Jump Height]

James looked up at the expectant faces of his friends. "I need to buy a car."

When they came out into the living room, it was to the sounds of Anesh and JP loudly arguing outside in the parking lot on how to fit a ladder into a hatchback. And to Kayle sitting on the couch, petting some kind of pit bull/Labrador mix.

"Hey, I let your dog back in," she said, cuddling with the pooch that was currently drooling on their seat.

James's first thought was that, while that couch might have been scuffed, spilled on, beaten up, knocked over, and at one point battle-damaged, it was still his goddamn couch, and he didn't appreciate the dog drooling on it. His second thought was *I don't have a dog—?* His third thought was sort of ancillary, and was mostly that it was telling that he was so inured to the weirdness in his life that his first thought was about his couch. "Yeah, I don't own a dog. Did you steal a dog?"

Kayle flipped him off, while still holding her hand on the dog's fur. "He was on your doorstep! What was I supposed to think?"

"That I don't own a dog!" James replied, pretending not to notice Alanna and Dave trading looks behind his back and casually edging for the door. "You know what? It's fine. I know how to fix this." James walked over to the couch, leaned down, and rubbed at the dog's ears. "Who's a good boy? Who's a good boy? It's you!" His voice spiked up in pitch, and the mutt's tail started slapping against the couch with a vicious thwacking sound. After a good round of licks onto James's hands, the pupper jumped off the couch and casually loped out the door that Alanna had just passed through, brushing past the tall woman on the way out.

The teenager on the couch looked down at her hands, now devoid of dog, then back up at her brother. "Did that really just happen?"

"Yeah? It's not that weird."

"Yes, it is! That was really weird, James!" she snapped back, and James noticed a level of frantic worry under the anger.

He shrugged and walked over to grab a drink out of the fridge before he left to join his friends. "It's all relative. And speaking of relatives, you have a good weekend here! Feel free to play any of the game consoles or whatever, and Anesh'll be back later after he drops us off, so bother him if you need anything."

"I can't believe you're abandoning me here with him." She pouted, fear replaced by an opportunity to needle her brother.

"Yeah, well, I can't believe you didn't tell me you were coming, so we're even. Also, don't fuck with Anesh. He's important to me." James scowled at the thought of Anesh being harassed. "Really."

"Fine," his sister said mockingly, "I won't bother your boyfriend."

"See that you don't," James replied in all seriousness. He wasn't sure if he should correct her, but something about the way that sounded made him feel too happy to care that she was trying to be rude.

It was weird, James thought, driving to work before noon. Sun overhead, the hot light filtering through the sharp greenery of the trees. It was a beautiful day, all things considered, and it made James want to wake up earlier more often. Not go to *bed* earlier, mind you, or get less sleep. Just . . . see this a bit more frequently.

Alanna was sitting beside him in the passenger seat, ignoring the glorious feeling of summer in full swing, and instead staring in confusion at his radio. Her hair, getting longer now and still left unbound, unlike how James chose to wear his, flapped wildly in the warm breeze coming through the open windows. But despite that cover, it was pretty easy for James to spot the look of consternation on her face.

"What's up?" he asked her during one of those quiet stretches of driving when you still can't look away from the road, but there isn't anything directly trying to murder you.

"James . . ." Alanna started out. "The hell are we listening to?" She gestured at the radio in open frustration. "This is . . . not your normal music, is it?"

"This is Blue October," James said, a little put out. "I like this band."

"Blue October is, if I remember correctly, an emo band that mostly writes songs about drowning?" Alanna said it with a question mark, but any question was entirely rhetorical. "This is . . . James, this song is about hate-fucking someone. Am I wrong on that?"

He looked down at the track title. "No, no, you're right. Also, they're *mostly* a band that writes sad songs for sad people. Sometimes they write songs about how beautiful life is, or murdering your exes or something."

Alanna hit the *next song* button. "So, hey," she started to say to James in a more serious tone, before stopping again. "No, wait, who the fuck is *this*. James, what even is this playlist?"

"This is Cambodian rock music. I don't know who they are, because no one knows who they are, because this is one of the few surviving songs from the era when the Khmer Rouge killed everyone who did anything useful, like make music," James said, way too cheerfully. "So, this is off an album that someone brought out of the country shortly before they closed their borders, but it was unlabeled, and . . ."

Alanna hit the *next song* button. "Is this just a cover of 'All Star'?"

"Kinda, it's . . ."

"No, don't care. Good enough. Look, before we get to the office, I just wanted to actually check that you're okay with this."

James scowled at the road. "Everyone keeps fucking asking me that like it wasn't my idea in the first place. Why is no one asking Dave? Why is no one asking *you?*!" He briefly paused for dramatic effect, and then half turned in his seat to glance at Alanna. "Hey, real question: Are you okay with this? I don't think I ever asked."

"You asked a million times. I'm good. Dave's also good; I talked to him about it earlier. You know how he said he's always trying to be useful? He's not kidding. He measures the value of his own life by how much he's doing for others. But not in an altruism way, more in a 'recovering from an abusive childhood' way." Alanna growled out that last bit. "I don't really know how to help him, honestly."

James shrugged. "Hell, I feel that way sometimes. And I can understand it. I want to be the Good Guy, you know? I think that's why I'm okay with it."

"Yes, you have a paladin complex larger than mine," Alanna said jokingly. "But seriously, we might die. Do you really want to risk that? Life is finally going good for us, for *all* of us." That last bit, she mentally emphasized whatever the hell was developing between James, Anesh, and herself. "And we're maybe gonna throw it away? We might . . . actually die."

Pulling off the highway and stopping at the off-ramp light, James looked at Alanna until she met his eyes. "Are you telling me to convince you that I really want this, or are you telling me to convince you that *you* do?" he said. She didn't answer, and the quiet told James a lot, in addition to telling his anxiety to flare up. "We might die," he said in a quiet voice, barely audible over the music and traffic. "But we might *win*."

A hand clapped onto his shoulder, and James felt Alanna give him a comforting squeeze. "That's what I wanted to hear," she said. "Now, turn up whatever nineties power metal we're listening to now, and let's get ready to go fight to something else's death."

"Gabe, my old friend!" James both greeted and distracted the new guy behind the security desk. "Settled in?"

The young man looked at James through narrowed eyes. "No, I'm here covering for Frank, without gettin' trained, and on my weekend. Also, what was your name again? I'm still trying to remember everyone."

James tried very hard not to laugh, holding his amusement in the back of his throat. Sure, he was trying to make sure that this kid didn't question the people coming in carrying a ladder and boxes of stuff, but he felt a surge of both laughter and guilt that he was now bothering someone who wasn't supposed to be here today. "Ah, that sucks, friend. Didn't you just get hired? There's at least one other guy who should ... be ... available ..." James trailed off.

"You okay, man?" the kid behind the desk asked him, looking at the dawning horror on James's face. "Um ... sir ... ?"

Snapping back to reality, James shook his head in a few quick jerks and looked back down at Gabe. "Yeah, sorry! Just thought of something. Oh, it's James, by the way." He offered a hand, and Gabe gave him a firm handshake. "But yeah, sorry about the nonsense around here. I know I'm not actually in charge of anything, but I always feel like I should be warning new hires about stuff."

"Like all the construction?" Gabe motioned to Alanna and Dave, who were walking by with the ladder under their arms.

"Um ... yes. Like that," James said. "Well, that, and the constant manager changes. And the weird-ass benefits. And the endless nightmare dimension in the back stairwell." He shot that out as a joking probe.

"The what?" A miss, then. That was almost a shame; he seemed friendly enough. James would let Anesh know to put him on the list for possible recruitment, assuming he didn't kill the dungeon over the next week.

Instead, he covered it with a boisterous laugh and just said, "Ah, don't worry about it! Anyway, I should go do my job. You have a good one!"

A surprisingly enthusiastic "You too!" followed James to the elevator, which Alanna discreetly held for him.

"We good?" she asked him.

"Yeah, he's only been here a week and already he's too bitter to care if people are doing shady shit. I'm so proud." James mimed wiping a tear away from his eye. "But yeah. Anesh took the box up already?"

"Yup. We're all set," Dave said, as the elevator dinged them out to the proper floor.

James nodded and led his friends down the looped path to his work area. "Okay. So. We're just gonna set the thing up, you guys pretend to be doing work until the breach opens, and then we go. No hesitation, or we're fucked. I don't care if my boss is watching, we can't wait."

"Got it," Alanna and Dave said with determined nods.

They came out through the main double doors onto the call center floor, and James realized that this was eventually going to be some kind of PTSD trigger as he looked over the clusters of cubicle walls and computers. The employees, at least, were actual humans, and it was really hard to mistake those for dungeon fauna. But it still made him shiver to think that one day he might drop by an office building and forget the boundary between reality and adventure.

His desk area had two other people in it today. As well as Anesh, who was pretending to belong there pretty well. He'd set the cardboard box containing two duffel bags full of what gear they could scrape up on short notice on the floor under the X of tape that James had marked the ceiling with weeks ago. Clearly a little uncomfortable, Anesh perked up when his friends arrived.

Alanna and Dave started talking to him, but James, not wanting to draw attention just yet, instead settled in to his own desk and waited. And waited. And waited.

It felt like an hour. An eternity. But in reality, it had been about ten minutes, and he'd been stealing glances over at the now-set-up ladder where Alanna was standing half inside the ceiling, watching the HVAC unit that would eventually turn into a gap in reality. James stared at his monitor, which was currently displaying a half-filled login screen, and nothing else. This was . . . impossibly frustrating. He felt like he was under too much pressure to bear, and playing it cool was starting to slip through his fingers.

So to get away from that, he stood up, stretched, and went over to talk to Anesh. "Hey." James casually greeted his friend, currently in disguise with that most powerful of tools: the clipboard.

"Ah, hello sir! May I interest you in a job in the construction industry?" Anesh asked without a trace of irony.

"Too far," James said quickly with a wide smile. "So, how's it going?"

"Well, it's been twenty-five minutes, so it should be any second now, and then—" Anesh started to say.

But James cut him off. That wasn't what he'd meant; the plan would work, or it wouldn't, but what he really wanted to know was, "No, how are *you* doing," he asked. "You've been quiet all day."

"I . . ." Anesh looked away and pretended to fiddle with his clipboard for a minute. "I should be going with you," he said, a little too forcefully.

"What? No! You've got stuff to do," James told him, shocked. "Also, three seems like the best number for actual delves, you know? And . . . I don't want you getting hurt."

Anesh glared at him, and for the first time, James noticed that it looked like his friend was legitimately angry. But not at James, at himself. "No! I'm just leaving you to maybe die, for what, school? You and Dave are taking time off work, why shouldn't I? It's not because of my calendar, it's because I'm afraid. I'm afraid, and I'm . . . I'm . . ." He trailed off, and James worried for a minute that someone had overheard what he'd been saying. But a quick look around showed nothing but employees trapped in headsets and not paying attention.

That meant one problem wasn't an issue, but James had no idea what to say to Anesh. So, instead, he half panicked, grabbed his friend, and kissed him. Anesh made a small *mmph*! noise, but James felt his shoulders relax as he leaned into the smooch. The physical contact was warm, and comforting, and for just a moment, for both of them, the world dropped away.

And then, because James apparently wasn't allowed to have nice things, there was a *thunk* from overhead, and Alanna stuck her head down to inform them, "Eyes up, nerds, let's do this!"

James and Anesh broke away, and James patted his friend—boyfriend, now, he supposed—on the head. "Okay. Everything's gonna be okay. We've got this. I'll see you in a few days; take care of my sister." He thought about that for a second as, behind him, Dave tromped up the ladder that Alanna had just climbed off the top of. "I take that back; don't let my sister burn the apartment down." James mounted the bottom step of the ladder as Dave hauled himself into the ceiling tiles and his feet vanished. "Oh! And try to find the new closet!"

"The what?" Anesh asked on reflex, before his brain processed what James had just said. "Wait! The what?!"

But James didn't bother with an answer beyond a peaceful smile shot downward. His feet carefully hit the steps of the ladder as he clambered upward. And in too little time at all, according to his pounding heart, he was at the top. Dave and Alanna had put the ladder in a great spot; the breach was just . . . right there in front of him. Dave and Alanna had already gone through, a coil of rope tied off to the HVAC unit to let them get down, dropping down into whatever danger awaited. There was no time for James to waste.

With a heave of muscles that he was still getting used to having, he pulled himself up, toward the opening. The last thing he noticed before dropping through was the desiccated husk of a small pink stapler, sitting a few ceiling tiles away.

Poor guy, James thought. He would have considered how that could have been Rufus, if circumstances were different. But there was no time. His hands gripped the rope, and his feet slipped into another world.

And the rest of him followed.

CHAPTER 14

Holding tightly to the rope, James was surprised when his feet hit something solid not more than a few seconds into his descent. He'd expected to be dropping from the ceiling: a minimum of forty or fifty feet above the floor level of the labyrinth proper. Instead, he felt his feet touch down almost right away and didn't understand why.

It was hard to understand why. It was dark. Inside the ceiling of the real-world office had been dark, but here, it was *dark*. The portal that he'd come out of was a rectangle of pale gray light, alien and unnatural in the oppressive blackness, and there were green and red and blue LEDs off in the distance, like a field of colored stars around him, but James couldn't see much of anything else.

Then he felt a hand on his shoulder, guiding him to a standing position. "Step this way," he heard Dave say, and he did so. As he did, James felt the ground shift under him and almost panicked, his fist clenching around the rope and tugging on it briefly. "Careful," Dave said blandly, which got an unseen roll of the eyes from James. But he caught his balance, let the rope hang free, and took a few steps forward, trying to get his eyes to adjust.

A few feet ahead, Alanna clicked a flashlight on, and James regretted letting go of the rope.

The "floor" that he'd touched down on was the texture of a ceiling tile.

As their tank swept the beam of light around them, James caught sight of the edge. It was maybe three feet behind him; when he'd landed, he'd hit one foot on the floor, and one on the nothingness below. A series of vine-like wires climbed out of the corners of the platform they were on, holding it suspended in . . . air? There was a moment there where James's heart fell, and he thought that they might have just fallen into an entirely different dungeon altogether. But then, as Alanna kept sweeping the flashlight around, it startled a flock of loose printer paper that had been nesting up here.

Hundreds of white sheets took to the sky, fluttering around them like bats. James held up his hands, trying to knock them away from his face, but he felt at least one brush past in a painful fleshy hiss of a paper cut across his cheeks. In the illumination of the flashlight, it looked visually like a column of static: white shapes briefly there, then covered by shadow again, endlessly fluttering by. The rustling noise drowned out everything else while it surrounded them. And then, just like that, the flock was gone, and they were alone again.

"Holy shit." Alanna spat out the words along with a piece of soggy paper. She brought a hand covered in a fingerless glove up to her face, and rubbed along a thin red line that had been left just under her eye. A wince and a snarl ended that check. "What the fuck was all that?"

"Paper," James said back softly in the still-again air. "That was one of the paper flocks. Guess this is where they roost. So . . . we are up in the ceiling?" As he spoke, he edged farther away from the edge, his hands held out to the sides to keep his balance as the false floor under him wobbled. His eyes were starting to adjust, and he wasn't going to accidentally walk over the edge, but James was surprisingly uninterested in taking chances with heights.

From over on the edge, showing absolutely no reservation about the fact that he was an untold distance over the actual stable floor, Dave called out to them. His voice was slightly muffled by the fact that he was physically hanging over the edge. "Hey, there's light down here!"

"Fantastic," James said, honestly enthused, but still not quite willing to leave his place at the center of the platform. If he closed his eyes and lost the small amount of vision he had in the dark here, he could pretend it was stable here. The last three minutes had been a hell of a learning experience for James; he was coming to discover this through legs that wouldn't respond to commands and a heart that was pounding harder than it ever was during any of their fights. "I . . . um . . . I'll just wait here. You check out the light. I'm just gonna . . . sit down."

Alanna came over and tossed her duffel next to where James had dropped his. "You doing okay?"

"Not even a little bit, no," James said with a gasp of breath. "I didn't realize how bad this would be." He spoke too quickly, anxiety pouring words out of his mouth. "Holy shit, we're high up. Why can I feel how high up we are? Why am I afraid of heights?"

She grabbed him by the shoulders. "You've never been off the ground, have you?" Alanna asked without malice.

"Nooooope. No."

"Yeah, that's why. You get used to it." She shrugged, trying to reassure him without being patronizing. "The first time I had to work on a roof, I threw up on the guy on the ladder. I can't really give you any advice, just that you'll be able to move once your brain catches up with the fact that you weren't going to fall over anyway." James nodded, trying to steady his breathing, and waved Alanna away. He'd get used to it, and be fine. She nodded at him, checking over her shoulder to make sure he wasn't having too bad a panic attack as she went over to check in with Dave. "Hey. You see anything?" she asked, panning the flashlight beam to the side so it wouldn't blind him.

Dave pulled himself back from where he was lying down and peering over the edge, shuffling back on his stomach and moving to a kneeling position. "There's a line of light down there."

There was a pause as Alanna waited for a further explanation. When it wasn't forthcoming, she made a gesture to spur Dave on, before realizing that he probably couldn't see it in the dark. She thought about asking for clarification, but then realized it would be easier to just check. Leaning over the side, it became pretty clear what Dave meant.

The line of light was the sharp white of a fluorescent. A straight line in the darkness, with a pair of thin ninety-degree diversions. A silhouette outline of a rectangle, or part of one at least. Alanna waited for her eyes to adjust for another minute, and as the shapes started to resolve, it became clear what she was looking at.

More ceiling tiles. More of the suspended chunks of platform that they were standing on, layered repeatedly over the floor. From the way the light shone through, Alanna guessed they were maybe three levels up.

She sat back up. "Okay, we're gonna have to go down. Do we have any road flares in one of the bags?"

"I'm in favor of getting off this thing," James called from the center. "It's the descent I'm worried about."

Dave rolled his eyes, and even though Alanna couldn't see it, she felt the sarcasm rolling off the guy as he unzipped a duffel bag and pulled out one of the two road flares. As he uncapped it and tried to strike the end to light it, Alanna averted her eyes, not wanting to be blinded.

Sweeping her vision around while Dave played with the flare, she noticed something worrying. "James," she called behind her. "James, get up. Some of those LEDs in the distance are moving." The little red, blue, and green lights off in the distance that shone like stars in the inky black of this space were, indeed, bobbing and shaking from side to side. And because of the brightness, Alanna had legitimately no idea if they were moving closer or not.

It was when James spoke that a spark of fear took root in Alanna's chest. She wasn't used to being afraid; unlike James, who took his worries and panic and burned them as fuel for his Han Solo–style frantic actions in combat, Alanna always stayed calm. She could survive a fight, if she kept her head. She could kill a monster, if she didn't give in to fear. But when she heard James confidently and curiously say, "Weird. It feels like those are getting closer. Can you see the silhouettes they're casting?," that was when Alanna started to worry.

Because there were only so many things that she felt like the dungeon would spawn up here in the ceiling.

Alanna extracted a crowbar from the bag. "James! Time to move!" Her friend seemed to make the connection and break out of his fear of heights pretty quickly. Though he still crawled toward her, rather than walk, making it to the open duffel bag and rustling through for a hunting knife. A poor substitute for his trusty hand axe, just as the crowbar was a mediocre stand-in for Alanna's warhammer. "What the fuck are those?" Alanna demanded of him as he knelt next to her, keeping himself alert.

"I bet you two shares it's spiders," James said, half-joking, half-resigned to the inevitable horror.

"Are we doing shares this time?" Alanna asked back, keeping herself outwardly calm. She had an image to maintain as the bulwark of the group, and while this whole place felt threatening and hostile far in excess from the "usual" dungeon, it wasn't going to be enough to crack her. "I thought this was kind of off the books."

James snorted next to her. "Anesh'll ask for the numbers anyway. I think he's literally addicted to accounting."

He probably would, Alanna thought. Anesh was really taking to the role of group scribe with a little more enjoyment than any human should have. She had this worry that he was actually deriving joy from accounting software, which was never a good sign. "Well, no bet, anyway. It's . . ." Behind them, Dave finally sparked the flare to life, casting a sudden and powerful red glow over the space around them. Eyes adjusted fast, and James at least was thrilled to be able to see the floor again from more than just a small beam from a Maglite. But, the light also showed off something else in front of them. Ahead of James and Alanna was another oversized ceiling tile, suspended on those same vine-like cables at just over head height. And underneath it, crawling on the red-shaded speckled tile, was a spider. ". . . always spiders," Alanna finished.

The spider was the size of a German shepherd. As the flare lit up the surroundings, the light pushed back the gloom that surrounded the LED that was its central eye; the sharp blue light that had seemed so far away a second ago suddenly seemed a lot closer as it was dimmed in comparison to the red glow. *Spider* may have been the wrong word for it, too, though that was the first place that James's and Alanna's minds went, followed by the word *fuck* repeatedly. It only had six legs. Or maybe twelve, held in unsplit pairs. If it hadn't been moving, they might not have even seen it, because its legs looked like just triangular shards of the same material as the ceiling itself. The body was the same way: just a few wedges of probably beige material layered on each other, holding up a head that appeared more like the area behind James's desk than a face. A flat surface, the head was, with dozens of cables coming out around the edge in loops, like finely coiffed hair. The single glowing light in the center was the only thing that gave away that this thing was more than just a statue.

Well, that and the sudden burst of motion as it started crawling forward, the tips of its legs stabbing into the soft tile above it with sharp popping noises.

And then the light vanished as Dave tossed the flare down one level, leaving only a very low flickering red light coming up from over the edges.

"Oh, fucking thanks, Dave!" James yelled.

From behind them, there was a confused "What? What did I do?" from Dave, but there was no time for James to get too angry, as a second later the spider dropped down from the ceiling and he had to shuffle backward to avoid being stabbed by its sudden lunge toward him.

From the right, Alanna came in at it with the crowbar, arm muscles rippling as she swung the solid bar of metal fast enough that it was a blur in the low light. James backed off to give her space to smash the monstrous spider but had his expectations crushed when her strike *bounced off* the shell.

"Oh, *fuck*," Alanna rasped out, the impact vibrating through her bones. The thing felt like it was made out of solid rock; so much for it being ceiling tile. Before she could panic about this turn of events, it jerked forward, striking out with one of its legs that split in two down the middle as it moved, forming an increasingly hostile fork. Its head tilted to the side like it was examining her curiously, almost looking like a puzzled dog more than an inorganic nightmare.

Alanna sidestepped the first stab, and the second one that came after she tried to smash its face in again, the tips bristling with small barbs every time it stabbed. It might have moved quickly, but it seemed to need to plant its feet before it attacked, which made the spider predictable and slow. The only danger was that she could barely see it, a problem that was rectified as Dave swept the light over the skirmish and let out a reactive yell. Still, it gave her the light she needed to dodge.

Or it would have, if she'd known about the second one that was about to slam into the platform beside her. But James had seen it. He'd caught it in the corner of his eye when Dave had run over, flashlight waving around. It had been lying in wait above them for who knew how long, and now was when it chose to make a move: when Alanna was engaged and vulnerable. Maybe they thought that she was the only threat in the group. Their mistake—James planned to punish them harshly for that.

He'd started moving as soon as he'd seen the second spider. There was no time for fear of heights when death was on the line. And almost as soon as it landed, he turned his sprint into a slide, and his boot connected with the side of its "body." He didn't intend to actually break it, no. But he did catch it before it could sink its barbs into the floor they were standing on, and it wasn't nearly heavy enough to stop James from booting it right over the edge and into the reddish gloom below.

"Run!" he yelled at Alanna and Dave, as the first spider paused in its uncanny way to slowly tilt its face back and forth between the three of them and its missing companion.

James led the way, his stomach a sinking rock as his feet rhythmically brought him closer to the edge of the world. He curved his angle of approach just enough to buy himself time to see exactly *where* the flare Dave had dropped had landed, and then, before he could think too hard about what he was doing, he kicked off the wobbling not-ground beneath his feet and wildly flailed his arms as he plunged the twenty feet down to the platform below.

The next three noises that Dave and Alanna heard as they followed after him were a thunk, a scream, and a scraping crunch. But the other spider was right behind them; there was no time to consider any other options. There was barely enough time for Dave to grab the duffel bag on the way past, a coil of rope and a bottle of water spilling out of it as he lugged it over the edge first. Alanna similarly kicked the first bag off as she jumped right behind Dave.

When they hit the next platform with heavy thuds, setting the whole thing in motion, they saw James, still scrambling to his feet, and a series of gouges in the soft material of the swaying ground. He stumbled up, unsteady, but whatever had been waiting down here had gotten the unexpected boot when James had landed on it. This one was smaller than the other one had been, and it was cramped enough that it felt awkward moving with other people on it.

But they were a team. Without speaking, Dave grabbed the other flare out of his bag, tossing the second one onto the floor. None of them wanted to be plunged back into darkness. While he did that, Alanna grabbed the flashlight that he'd pitched down and started panning it around, checking for more spiders, and also over the edges of this panel to see where they could jump down to next.

From here, she spotted the more "natural" white light of a fluorescent bulb from under the next platform. It was brighter, closer, than the slim line of light had been before, coming from underneath the next platform down. "Dave! Here!" She pointed the light, and Dave, carrying a newly lit flare, ran over and flung it down to give them a target. This one was farther, maybe twenty-five feet. "Get the bags!" she told him as she looked around for her own duffel, finding it unpleasantly missing.

What she did spot was that James was crouched in the middle of the platform again. And for a second, Alanna worried that her friend—boyfriend?—was having another moment of panic, this time in the middle of a fight. But then she saw him pull the pressure gun out of the duffel bag, load one of the metal spikes into it, and start holding down the button to fill the chamber with propellant.

The spear gun they'd made was, at its core, just a potato gun, a tank of fuel attached via sealed tube to a piece of pipe that could have a projectile loaded into the end of it to be launched via "controlled" explosion. Though James had learned from the previous attempts, and the internet, that this one was less a "gun" and more a "cannon." The fuel tank was ten cubic feet of acetylene, and the projectile had been upgraded from "test potato" to "sharpened piece of rebar."

So when the next spider landed on the platform behind Alanna, crunching small holes into their temporary ground, James was already prepared to brace the weapon and pull the trigger.

Two pounds of metal nailed the insectile creature at roughly two hundred miles per hour. The weapon would be horrifically inaccurate at anything beyond maybe twenty feet at most, but this was point-blank range. It had come down expecting fleeing prey, and what it got was a wickedly sharp steel point jammed through the faceplate. James wasn't sure if these things had vital organs, but if they did normally, this one didn't anymore, and the shell of a creature collapsed like a hollow puppet after the spike tore through it.

Then there were more of those popping noises from above them. More LEDs moving in the dark, bobbing and weaving, with no way to tell how close or far the next assailant was. "Shit! Go! Keep going!" Alanna yelled, waving Dave on to get a running start for the next jump. He made the leap while James zipped up the bag and got a good grip on the weapon. "Go!" she yelled at him, and he met her eyes and nodded before taking the same running jump Dave had.

Alanna followed and felt the air rush around her as she plummeted toward an almost certain pain in her feet. She landed right in the middle of the platform, next to where the flare Dave had tossed was burning itself to white powder. James and Dave had hit somewhere farther back, and that was lucky for them, because this tile was a longer rectangle than the others, stretched out.

And when Alanna landed, it snapped in half.

She had a brief moment to spot the duffel bag she'd kicked over the edge, sitting politely on a platform opposite the one they'd just jumped from and being inspected by one of their arachnid opponents, before she was sliding down the new ramp. Just before she dropped into nothing, a hand caught her by the back of her shirt, and she looked up to see James looking down at her as the material started to rip. His eyes went wide as she slipped, and then her arm came up and he traded his grip to her wrist, barely keeping himself held on the now-vertical hanging platform by the spear part of the spear gun he'd stabbed into it.

"Hold on!" he yelled, uselessly.

Alanna wanted to say something snarky, but she was too busy looking up at where more of the spiders were crawling down the cord that Dave was hanging on to. She looked down and saw an outline against the light. One more platform and they'd at least have some better sight. "Let go!" she yelled, contradicting James.

He only hesitated for a moment, and then his trust in her kicked in, and he gave a nod and a firm frown before releasing her.

She slid down and landed no more than ten feet below on the final platform in the dark. Dave came down next, having dropped from higher up, if the thud was any indication. Seemed like he enjoyed the spider things even less than she did.

James teetered on the edge of this new platform when he landed, windmilling his free arm before catching the vine that held it up. He realized at the same time that Alanna did that they hadn't actually seen what the hell these platform vines actually *connected to*, and now that they'd jumped down several levels of them, it became clear that they didn't seem to actually attach to anything else.

Still, the platforms stayed up, so James just chalked it up to "dungeon bullshit."

"Okay, there's more platforms down there," Dave said from the side. "The one on the right looks closest. They're all lit up, too."

Alanna caught her breath from where she'd been winded in the last jump. "Good." But before they made the leap, she looked up to see the trio of spiders above them navigating around the wrecked oversized ceiling tile and trying to find a way down. "But how do we get to the *ground*? Can you see anything?"

Dave just shook his head, a grim look on his face. It was James who patted her on the shoulder and said, "Doesn't matter. We don't have enough harpoons to kill too many of those, so we've gotta keep going anyway. We'll work it out when we get there. We've got rope, right?" He addressed the question to Dave, who nodded. "Okay, so we just buy some time, tie off a rope on one of these, and . . . climb down . . . forty feet to the floor. Yeah. Good plan, everyone. Now fucking jump!" He yelled that last part as one of the triangular spiders crawled over the edge of a separate platform to their left and began making its way toward them upside down and just over head height.

One last trip through the air. One more ankle-jarring impact on the ground. James landed in a kneeling position this time, trying to get used to making these falls, and it sort of worked to mitigate the damage. As he stood up, he blinked away the bright light that came from the insanely powerful fluorescent office lighting that was set in the platform directly above them. It wasn't every one of the platforms at this level, he noticed as his eyes adjusted, just a few of them. But it was lit here, and he could feel the wafting breeze of cubicle farm air conditioning.

Inside had never felt like such a breath of fresh air.

Dave ruined his moment by crashing into him from behind when he landed. Alanna hit slightly to the side, and James remembered that they were still high enough up that he should worry about falling. Stifling the fear in his chest for a minute and grabbing one of the support cords, he looked up, eyes scanning for pursuit.

But it seemed that whatever the hell those things had been, they hadn't been at all interested in coming down after them. James saw a single green LED near where one of the ropes went up toward the darkness, and could just barely make out the shape of a spider still lurking in the gloom. But after a staring contest with the thing, he realized something with a laugh. "They won't come into the light!" James barked out with relief. "Holy shit, they can't deal with the bright light. Or maybe fluorescent. Whatever. They aren't coming down." He collapsed into a sitting position, then lay back against the speckled tile, taking deep breaths. "Fuck, who the hell decided *that* was what the dungeon needed?" he asked no one in particular.

"What else would the dungeon find in an office ceiling?" Dave asked, like it was the most obvious thing in the world.

"Dude, I don't know. I think I'd rather fight animated HVAC than those things. Wait, fuck, what if they *were* . . ." James started to ponder that but didn't get far.

Alanna cut him off. "Hey, bicker later. Check this out." She pointed over the edge, and after James tilted his head up to see, he rolled over and crawled to join her and Dave where they stood looking down.

More platforms. But few enough that they could see the ground from here. From above, the glimpses that they could get showed them cubicle after cubicle in perfect, ordered rows. Even where it started to get weird with the geometry, James realized, there was a pattern and order to the madness. From above, it made total sense, the insane layouts. There were sweeping hallways and open areas, and he could see multiple spaces where Decision Trees popped out over low walls. And nearby, so very nearby, a spire of blue-and-white tile that marked the bathroom that he and Anesh had seen so long ago.

There was motion below, too. Perhaps they'd simply never noticed before how much life there was in the dungeon, but from here, James could see. And he wanted to see. So much so that he picked a slightly lower platform and took a five-foot hop down to get a better vantage. Here, a tumblefeed rolled over low walls. There, small dots that were striders or iLipedes moved through a hallway. Off to the side, James got a headache as he tried to process how there could be a wall that was a full support wall, going all the way up to the ceiling, and yet did not reach the ceiling. And along that wall, following its curve, a pair of paper pushers herded a maul cart forward.

Or maybe just a regular mail cart. James didn't know, but he'd never risk it again.

And from here, he could see the curve of the floor, the slope of the whole world as it oh-so-gently swept upward toward infinity in the shrouded distance.

Everywhere, though, there were small dots of movement. Tiny motions from this far away, but ones that James's eyes picked out in aggregate. There was so much *alive* down in the dungeon, and even from this far up, maybe three or four floors of distance, he could see enough detail to realize one important thing.

"We're on the other side of the bathroom," he muttered to himself. And looking toward it, he realized something else.

A long wall ran across the width of the dungeon on this side of the bathroom. And just as the floor of the office sloped upward on this side, so too did it do the same on the other. A contained infinity, where his vision couldn't reach. But he knew that out there on the other side was where their exit was. And he could also see how the wall was shaped; it was another one of those actual-wall-walls. He and Alanna had run into a couple of them when they'd been on their delve together. And at the time, James hadn't questioned how they'd gone up to the normal-height ceiling above them and then stopped.

That was probably the point. Because now, he could see that they came all the way up to this ceiling but didn't actually meet any ceiling, and oh boy did that hurt his brain. Humans weren't meant to think in more than three dimensions of space. So he blinked and looked away but focused on the fact that some of those walls had doors set in them.

Because so far, while the dungeon had been an utter bastard about a lot of things, it still seemed to have roughly equal metaphorical weight for things that had real-world analogues.

James looked up to where Dave and Alanna were peering over the platform above him. "Hey. Who wants to go have a chat with management?" he called up with a grim smile.

CHAPTER 15

"Suffering" was offered up.

"Can't do that" came the instant counter.

"Why not?"

"I'd die, I think. Before it actually worked. So I'm not going to." A good reason, but not the end of the road.

"Okay, how about hunger?"

"Can't remove a negative, I think." Speculation, but not unreasonable.

"Does that imply suffering isn't a negative?"

"Yes."

"Creepy."

"Yes?"

"Okay, how about war?" A new track, try something different.

"Again, I could try, but I'm pretty sure I'd die." Not different enough.

"One war?" Think laterally.

"As in, half of one war? Or half of two wars, so it maths out to one war?" Not that laterally.

"Either-or."

"Maybe."

"Tax law." A good plan.

"Might die, but probably worth it." A great plan.

The conversation between Alanna and Dave played out behind James as he stood as close to the edge of their platform as he was comfortable, pointedly ignoring them. Trying to ignore them, anyway; he cracked a smile when they got around to considering using Dave's new ability to blank half of all tax law. But his real mental energy was going to something else.

Thirty or so feet above them, on a different hanging ceiling tile, there was a duffel bag. Each of them had brought one bushel of supplies in through the vent for this hopefully not-suicidal journey. Dave had done a great job keeping track of his. James and Alanna had swapped which of them was manhandling which bag at one point, but they'd both done their best in the melee to bring the gear along.

The problem was, at one point, Alanna had thrown one of the duffels off the edge before they'd jumped down during their retreat from the . . . things.

James needed a name for them. Like, pathologically *required* a funny name for them. The fact that there were ceiling spiders was bad enough, but the insult on the eight-legged nightmare was that there wasn't a single good pun to be made. The problem was that they were too bland. If they'd at least had the common decency to be made out of AC units or something, he could call them HVAC-nids, and that was almost certain to get a groan out of Anesh and a smirk from Alanna. But there was nothing there. Just a mental blank, less interesting than the polished faces of their spidery foes.

Okay, getting sidetracked. That was irrelevant.

What *was* relevant was that the bag that had been lost was the one with the guns in it. And *that* was an enormous fucking problem. Because while James was turning into a kung fu movie protagonist, Alanna punched slightly harder than your average truck, and Dave was . . . well, normal. But getting there. Dave worked with dogs all day and someone had convinced him to sign up for a martial arts class, and sure, he picked judo, but it wasn't nothing. So, getting there. But, again, James was getting sidetracked thinking this way; the *point* was that none of them could punch their way through more than one paper pusher.

So the lack of guns had become a problem, added to their current list of both tactical and strategic issues. Also on that list was how to get down to the actual floor, where and if to set up a camp, what to do if they couldn't find another human to actually rescue within their time limit, and how much effort they should put into continuing to accumulate orb power. It wasn't a small list, and James was feeling a bit overwhelmed. So he'd left the other two to the most interesting "use of weapons" debate ever, and tried to fix the easiest and most foundational problem. They needed to be armed, and the arms were dangling out of reach.

And James really would rather join them. He'd gotten a crick in his neck staring upward for the last five minutes, racking his brain for anything useful. And he'd been so busy trying not to panic at what a horrible idea this all was that he'd exiled himself from the conversation in self-inflicted punishment. But he was holding it together for now, and he didn't really mind that his friends were keeping relaxed.

It was still pretty astounding how easily they'd all gotten used to being in life-or-death situations. Even Dave, who was . . . well, he was a friend, but the guy wasn't the most well-put-together sometimes.

James caught an errant thought as it went through his head. Turning back around, he cut into their conversation like a verbal bulldozer. "Dave. What was the other power you got?"

"Nullify gravity. Why?" Dave gave him a quizzical look as he cut off what he was saying to Alanna.

Alanna got it first, letting out a long "oooooh" as she saw the smirk on James's face.

"Dave," James asked, still wearing the grin. "What exactly does that do?"

"I haven't tested it. I only have six uses," Dave told him. "I'm guessing you want me to try something now? Is this how we get down?"

That was a good thought, too, and James planned to revisit that in a second. Alanna jumped in, though, and finished his thought for him. "It's how we get up. Can you turn off gravity in a sort of pillar up to the platform where the guns are? Because if we're going to go down there, I'd like my shotgun."

"I figured I'd get the shotgun," James butted in, a mock hurt look on his face. "You made such a big deal about looting Frank's sidearm. Thought you'd want that."

"James, that gun is mine by right of dibs, but I will allow you to use it, because I am magnanimous. But seriously, if we're going down there and raiding manager offices, I'm going with the big gun," Alanna informed him pointedly.

James nodded, pursing his lips. "Fair enough."

Ignoring both of them for the last few sentences, Dave stood over on the edge, unheeding of the five-story drop as he looked upward, idly poking the exposed surface of the orb in his palm. "Hey, James," he called over, cutting off the semiflirtatious banter between James and Alanna, "how did you make your thing work when you blew up the mail cart?"

Out of the corner of his eye, James caught Alanna raising her eyebrows at him. "First of all, 'maul cart.' This is important to me. Also, I didn't 'blow it up,' but that's not the point. And third, I got Secret to do it. I kind of assumed you'd know how to do this, since you figured out how to absorb them in the first place," James answered in sequence.

"Hm." Dave looked down contemplatively.

What was a blue orb? He considered it. It was a tool. The shape of that concept was locked in his mind already. It was metaphysical function, made solid, and then wielded by his body to do . . . things. Useful things. Useful things? Well, things. Dave supposed it was up to him to make them useful. Though, in some context, literally everything the blues did was useful somehow. But what was it? Was it just the concept of a tool?

Dave could work with that. Tools were something he understood. He wanted to be useful, and in a sense, he thought of himself as a tool with a personality attached. Did the orbs have a personality attached? That was almost a scary thought, but Dave didn't really get scared by stuff like that, the same way James seemed to sometimes. Instead, he dove into it. Maybe the orb in his hand was just like him. Maybe it just wanted to help.

Maybe all it needed was to be asked the right way.

Dave reached out with his hand and drew an imaginary line from where he was to where they wanted to go, and just asked nicely in his head. "Please?" he appended with a whisper.

And inside his palm, something that he couldn't feel but knew was in motion shifted, and around him, reality changed.

"Yes," he said out loud, causing James and Alanna to look over at him and break off their own conversation with confused grunts. He turned his head back with a small grin, a line of blood dripping from his nose. Holding out his hand, he let go of some loose change in the air and watched it just float there lazily. "Yes, I can do that. Who wants to go grab the bag? I need to sit down."

Getting the bag turned out to be a huge fucking problem, and the pillar of null gravity turned out to be both a huge help and a colossal threat to life and limb.

James tried making the jump after spending a few minutes playing around with the feeling of his limbs being weightless. But he didn't put enough effort into it, his nerves getting the better of him just before the leap. That turned out to be what saved his life, since while everything inside the invisible pillar wasn't affected by gravity, any bit of a person sticking out totally was. And the pull of ten meters per second squared wasn't that bad, until it started pulling more and more of you out of the pillar. It also didn't help that *no gravity* didn't mean *reverse gravity*. Momentum from parts outside could yank at you, and with nothing to brace against, it was basically the same as being in gravity anyway.

So after he slipped out and started falling to his death, it was only by a narrow margin that Alanna and Dave caught him and bounced him against the edge of the platform once before dragging him back up.

"Okay, that didn't work" was how James tried to cover up his shaking limbs and internally screaming panic.

While James curled up in the middle of the platform and sipped some water, they deliberated on a solution. What it came down to, and what worked fairly well, was using the spear gun to fire a harpoon with a rope looped through the end like some kind of Batman gadget, through the floor of the platform over their heads, and through the gravity tunnel, and then Alanna shimmying up it while doing her best to keep her arms in the invisible corridor of relative safety.

It took a couple tries, but with the backup of just sliding down the rope, it didn't seem to bother Alanna a lot. This actually boggled James's mind; how the hell could someone just casually pull themselves along this far off the ground? Like it was normal?

To be fair, James could totally do it. But, well, he'd totally do it with a lot more calm certainty if he was doing it two or three feet off the ground, as opposed to two or three stories.

A thud of a duffel bag hitting the platform jolted him from his thoughts. He'd been watching Alanna but had sort of drifted off at some point, and the impact of the bag, followed by his friend, woke him back to reality.

"So, you guys ready to go down? I see Dave's got the rope out," Alanna said with a too-cheerful tone. It was true, Dave had unpacked the rest of the rope and was sorting it into spools.

"Already?" Dave asked.

"Already?" James parroted incredulously. "What the hell does that mean? You want to stay up here?"

"It's safe up here," Dave said. "Peaceful. I can see all the stuff moving around down below."

James half glared at him. "You can also see all the walls that terminate twenty feet below us and yet somehow meet the ceiling. Also, we're too high up."

Dave nodded. "The height is how you know it's safe."

"Oh yeah, why not just set up camp here?" James asked sarcastically, while he passed the water bottle over to Alanna at her insistent gesture. "We can just set up here, sleep nice and safe away from all the monsters, and our deaths will be painless when we *roll over the side in the middle of the night!*"

"You never had bunk beds as a kid, did you?" Alanna smirked at him.

"Why would that make a difference?" James responded.

"Oh, I'm just having a hard time imagining you fighting for the top bunk. No one who's had the top bunk would worry about rolling over an edge like this," she told him.

Dave crouched near the edge as he responded. "Why don't we set up camp here? We can use the rope-and-gravity thing to get up and down. I doubt any of the dungeon life can figure it out."

"Bet you you're wrong." Alanna's and James's words were almost perfectly in sync, and they gave each other a quick smile. James continued on: "The striders would almost certainly figure it out. If we're gonna need to keep watch anyway, it might as well be down there."

"You just don't want to be at risk of falling to your death."

"Correct!"

"Hmph," Alanna snorted. "Well, that's . . . perfectly reasonable, and I hate it."

"Yeah, I hear that a lot. It could be on my tombstone," James said with a grin. "So, yes, we should head down. But Dave isn't totally wrong; we should take a moment to look around first. I don't suppose we packed binoculars or something?"

"No dice," Alanna said, shaking her head. She moved over and crouched next to Dave, letting James crawl his way up to the edge on his belly with a roll of her eyes. "Okay, what do we have down there that matters?"

"A lot of strider movement, looks like," Dave said. "I wonder if the swarms you and Anesh talked about were natural functions, and not because you guys made noise. Just a coincidence, maybe?"

James hummed in his throat. "It's possible, but that's a pretty big coincidence. Coincidences seem unlikely here. Though it would explain why we've stopped seeing them, even though we've got more people usually and are making *more* noise, not less."

"Maybe something about the office changed," Alanna said.

James took a deep breath, eyes widening. "Ooooh, no. I hadn't thought of that."

"What?"

"The office changing. What you said. Anesh and I at least have been treating this place like it's static. But what if it's not? What if it's growing or something, and the swarms were just a phase of its life cycle?"

Dave added, "Or maybe it's dying off, and the swarms were a migration thing. Maybe parts of it become uninhabitable, and the critters inside flock away from the disasters."

"This almost makes me want to watch a lot more from up here," James said, taking a minute to appreciate the view now that he'd gotten used to it and his stomach wasn't churning in fear.

He looked down and watched a ripple of small objects that were probably striders moving down a hallway. They stopped suddenly, and one of them got snapped up by a camraconda, or something that looked like it, while the others fled. Scenes like that played out all over the dungeon: small moments of combat, life-or-death situations that often ended in something's death. A circle of life, but . . . it was everywhere.

James found it quite strange that they'd never found any children. No baby striders or teenage tumblefeeds. Where were all these things coming from, that their lives could be taken so frequently and there never seemed to be a dip in population?

"Okay, what do we see that's not staplers being herd animals?" James prompted wryly.

They looked, and it was Dave that pointed first. "Well, there's the offices. I mean, the whole place is an office, that's a given. But those are office-offices. With doors and things."

"Yes, that's what James meant twenty minutes ago when he quipped about meeting management, and then didn't clarify that," Alanna said, glaring at James. "Still, that's probably a good point to start at. Also, here's a note—there's a door in that 'exterior' wall over there." She pointed, and James tried to get a look at it. "No, there.

Look. Follow my fucking finger, man." Alanna grabbed James's head by the crown and tilted it so he had the right line of sight. "There, see?" He nodded into her hand with a chuckle. "Okay, well, that's not an office. In fact, it looks like a janitor's closet or something. That might be worth checking out."

"Why? Won't it just be full of hazardous chemicals?" Dave prompted.

"Name one horror film set in an office where there isn't at least one important clue in a janitor's closet."

"Name one horror movie set in an office."

"Well—"

"Never mind. We'll put it on the list," James said, cutting Alanna off. "Although, that might be a window next to it? So we should be cautious. I'm also curious what that is."

Following James's point with a lot more accuracy than James had for anyone else, Dave took a glance toward the spot on the floor that he indicated. "It's just an open area. So?"

"I think it's a drinking fountain?" James said. "Like, look at the support column there. I think it's actually four of those standard water coolers, back to back, and then kind of . . . improved."

"Why?" Alanna asked, a little too harshly.

He shrugged. "I dunno, I've just seen those things a lot in school and around here and stuff, so it reminds me of . . ."

"No, dummy. Why is it *there?*" She corrected her tone to a more jovial one.

"Oh! That's much less offensive." James shook the growing gloom out of his head. He was finding it too easy to get knocked on his mental ass by a misplaced word these days. "I have no idea why it's there! But it's kinda weird, and also not that weird, since there's water coolers all over the place. Maybe it's just the dungeon acting more like a dungeon and putting a water feature in?"

Dave shrugged, projecting the gesture backward as he kept looking. "I think it's a low priority," he stated bluntly. "Are we concerned about the buildings?"

"What buildings!?" James swiveled his head around, trying to see what Dave meant.

"Those buildings." Dave would have rolled his eyes, if he were the kind of person who really disliked clarifying questions. "Over there. They look like . . . maybe two-story apartment buildings?"

They did. The cubicles in some points rose above those around them, and this was pretty normal. They'd all walked through the hallways, and seen the places where the walls rose up over their heads, and the geometry started to warp into strange fractal patterns. But these protrusions that Dave had spotted weren't quite like that. Among the patterns of cubicle walls, rising and falling, there were a few points where the walls formed up into recognizable structures.

Most of them were, as Dave mentioned, only two stories or so. But they were . . . well, buildings. And taller than anything else around. There were windows carved into the sides in strange shapes, showing off the still-standard desks inside. One of the handful of structures had a balcony that they could see: a flat plane of cube wall, turned on its side and jutting out at a slight upward angle. Spots of greenery adorned it, potted plants enjoying the artificial sun, and James's imagination told him in no uncertain terms that there was a rolling office seat also positioned there, posing as a folding deck chair.

"Those sure are buildings," Alanna said. "Hey, maybe that's where we set up camp. Those are sort of in the direction back to the main door."

"Hey, follow-up thought," James said, looking up to other parts of the ceiling. "From up here, we can see the upward curve of the floor, right? And now we know . . . there's stuff inside the ceiling. Are we . . . is this place a ringworld?"

Dave looked back at him with a puzzled expression, eyebrows raised. "A what?"

Both of his friends turned to him, Alanna biting her lip and James with his mouth half open. "No, impossible," James said. "There's no way. You live on the internet, you play sci-fi games all the time. You've played fucking Halo. How do you not know what a ringworld is?"

"Oh. I know what a halo is. Is that the same thing?"

"... Well, you see, the array shown in Halo isn't quite a true ringworld in the Niven sense. You'd have to have—"

"Yes," Alanna cut in, loudly. "Yes! It's that thing you said! James, please, stop explaining science fiction from the sixties."

James grumbled under his breath, "*Ringworld* was actually published in 1970 . . ." before clearing his throat at a glare from Alanna. "Right, not important. So, we'll check out those buildings. Anything else?" he asked.

They sat there for some time, just passively taking in the sights. The view from up here was, again, once James got used to the height, staggering. So much movement, so much activity. He imagined this was how an explorer from the early days of the age of discovery would have felt, standing on a cliff over an unexplored jungle. There were so many options, and almost none of them were what he was here for, or led him back to home safely.

"Is that a copy center?" Alanna asked.

Well, that was a terrifying sentence.

James had to crawl over to another side, where Alanna had walked comfortably, to see what she was looking at. It was on the other side of one of the walls from the offices. "Yeah, looks like it." About a half-dozen of the copiers, positioned in an semi-open area, all of them roaming freely. They were large enough that they were pretty easy to spot, even from this height. "Floor down there looks weird," James mumbled to himself. "Okay, we need to avoid that place at all costs," he told the others.

"Why?"

"Dave, did no one tell you about the copier we fought? It made a hundred replicas of Anesh's face, and they were all trying to kill us and covered in teeth."

"That's a good reason why." Dave acquiesced almost instantly.

"Hey, why do the tumblefeeds always seem to cluster around break room areas?" Alanna asked suddenly, pointing down. "Shouldn't they be in server rooms or something? Or, like, in between cubicles where all the cords get tangled up?"

"That is strange," Dave stated frankly. "Maybe they just like it there?"

"I think we're doing that thing where we're counting on everything having metaphorical consistency, when the dungeon totally doesn't have a reason to make it that way," James answered. "Also, I've seen a couple of them roaming the aisles from up here. Or, well, over the aisles. They *do* seem to prefer going over walls to following paths. That's weird."

"Not that one." Dave pointed.

They looked where he was pointing. It was pretty close to right under them—headed their way at least. And sure enough, a tumblefeed was just rolling along, dragging itself forward at a pretty fast clip.

"Okay, not that one," James said. "But I think . . . wait . . ."

Alanna picked up the sentence. "That one's chasing something."

James scooted forward to keep them in his line of sight. "That one is chasing *someone*. Holy shit. Fuck! We need to get down there!"

"Wait, hang on." Dave raised a hand to make a point. "That's probably not a person! Like, all the 'employees' here, right?"

"Every stuffed shirt is instantly recognizable on sight as not human," Alanna said. "Those two aren't. We need to move." She unzipped one of the duffels with a harsh yank, spilling a couple slightly flattened sandwiches in plastic baggies onto the platform while she pulled out a break-action shotgun. It wasn't as useful in an actual fight as her Mossberg would have been, but right now, it was what they had to work with. "James! Let's move!"

She didn't need to shout. James had already pulled out the hockey pads from the other bag and was putting them on. Dave was doing the same, hesitation still on his face but no slower for it.

"Dave, take the spear gun! Alanna, hand me that pistol!" She passed over the holster to him, along with a box of bullets that he poured into his pocket without ceremony. Fumbling to undo his belt and get the holster onto it, James looked up to find the other two ready to go by the time he was done.

They looked a fierce group, the three of them. Armed with improvised guns, real guns, and the spare crowbar and cheap machete that they'd been able to scrounge up, and one pair of gardening shears in a duct-tape sheath on Alanna's back. Plated with hockey pads, work gloves, and shin guards repurposed into bracers. They looked like extras off the set of *Mad Max* who hadn't had the spikes put on their armor yet. But they also looked like they were ready for a scrap. Maybe not ready to be the cavalry, riding to the rescue, saving innocents and other such heroic deeds. But certainly ready to kick some ass.

James looked down over the edge, his fear burned away by righteous anger. Below them, just passing under the edge of their platform, two people ran at a frantic pace to try to outstrip the ball of hostile cables and copper fangs lurching after them. James looked up at Alanna, and saw that same angry determination in her eyes. As he glanced over to Dave, the reluctance from earlier was being replaced by calm acceptance as Dave met James's eyes.

"Dave," James said, calmly, iron in his voice. "Make us a path down."

CHAPTER 16

Theo was having one of those "bad day" things that she'd heard so much about as a kid.

Growing up, Theo had been an energetic twerp. Always smiling, always bouncing off the walls, always ready for the next school assignment or art project or whatever. Her parents, to their credit, had not just tolerated her but encouraged her to try new things and enjoy everything in the world. In high school, it continued much the same way, but now she had a social circle, school clubs, sports, prom . . . new faces to old joys.

The first time Theo could remember ever having a bad day was when she broke her arm in soccer practice. And even then, it was kind of exhilarating, and then she got a sweet cast for everyone to sign. The first time she could actually remember having a bad day with no upside was when she met her boyfriend's parents in college, and they informed him that he was no longer permitted to date one of "those people." She'd wanted to hit something so bad, and according to her friends she wasn't just allowed to start punching racist assholes, so she went out and signed up for an amateur rugby league.

She'd never understood people who had boyfriend trouble, or couldn't make ends meet, or just came in to work some days not feeling that great. It wasn't that she was too stupid to understand desperation or depression, just that she'd never really felt it.

Well, for what her phone told her was the last two days or so, Theo had gotten intimately familiar with that feeling.

"Fucking move!" Her normal command presence was cracked and worn after two days of running for her life, causing her voice to come out more as a hoarse scream than a yell. One hand out shoving Daniel along by his collar, trying to catch him as he stumbled. He'd been her charge for the last two days, which felt like a weird reversal.

When Frank had shut the door behind them with nothing more than a chuckle of smug satisfaction, they had found themselves in somewhere impossible. After it became clear that it wasn't a joke, and the old man really wasn't just playing an overly elaborate prank on them, there'd been a few moments of mixed panic and wonder. This place really was intense, with its strange and twisted geometry, and the bizarre product placement in some of the desks. Even though she knew she couldn't survive on them alone, Theo was perfectly fine sampling the dozens of different kinds of candy that she'd never seen on Earth. So far, the one called Shut Up And Eat This was her favorite, though that might just be subliminal messaging at work. And in those first couple hours, Daniel had composed himself and really acted the part of a security guard, even though he was new and looked like he was about thirteen years old. He took point, he stayed calm, and he really did his best to act like he was confident in himself, which impressed Theo a lot.

Then he got mauled by a computer tower. The thing looked like a cross between a wood chipper and a Terminator, crammed into one of the standardized black plastic cases that they used at the office back in the normal world, and it tore into Daniel's leg like it was a starving wolverine.

And after that, Theo was the one taking point. For her, the threat and the danger were exciting. For Daniel, they almost broke him. He was too afraid to do anything now. Theo had barely slept the last two nights, since she was keeping watch, and she didn't trust the kid not to do something stupid.

So now, sprinting down this hallway as best she could with a panicked, stumbling, crying teenager in one hand and the struggling caterpillar iPhone she'd been fiddling with in the other, Theo was having a truly bad day.

Because the thing behind her was probably going to kill them all, and she had no idea how to get out of it.

It was an IT department's nightmare come to life. A ten-foot-wide ball of cables, some of them corded together like rope to form grappling limbs that dragged it forward when it wasn't rolling like some psychopath's idea of a porcupine. It made almost no noise, except for a constant rustling and some thuds when its arm-claws hit the floor. But despite that, or maybe because of it, Theo was absolutely sure that it was here for their blood. After all, what else would something like this be for, if not draining the precious bodily fluids of intruders? They'd probably be strung up, dried husks by the door as a warning to anyone else, if not for the fact that something like that would break the aesthetic. Their pink slips, maybe?

Theo's mind took her down weird paths when faced with certain death.

Still trying to run, she shoved Daniel's head down to duck him under a low-hanging chunk of cubicle wall, twisted out and turned sideways into a horribly placed ceiling. Theo winced with him as he stumbled, his injured leg not doing a great job of holding him up, and the makeshift bandage not doing *any* kind of useful job keeping his blood inside him. But she kept them moving forward, even though her hope had died about two turns ago when the thing kept coming over walls to ambush them, just when they thought they were in the clear.

She was going to die, and she'd never done anything important. This was awful. She worked in a fucking call center. And it didn't matter to Theo that the call center was only one or two floors of the building that contained a whole lot of other things. There wasn't much of a chance she was getting promoted to head of engineering anytime soon anyway. Especially not now, what with the upcoming bloody dismemberment.

Passing under the mock ceiling, Theo felt the last of her hope give out. In front of them, instead of anything resembling cover or hiding spots, there was just more hallway. Ten, twenty, a hundred meters of hallway. Cubicles set into the walls, yes, but those offered no real shelter. Theo's shoulders slumped, her legs burning from exertion. This was it. There was no way she'd make it to the next corner, even without Daniel dragging her down.

Then Daniel fell next to her, a stumble turning into a topple as his leg and his lungs finally gave out. And for the first time in her life, Theo sighed and gave up.

There was no time to get him up. Nowhere left to run. No chances left, finally. Frank's murder-by-labyrinth was a roaring, if delayed, success.

Theo turned, dragging in rough breaths of air and steadying herself. She planted her feet and took a boxer's stance, turning slightly to toss the still-squirming iPhone onto Daniel's prone form. By the time the thing she'd decided to call a Cat-o'-five-tails crawled its way through the enclosed space, Theo was standing with her back tall and her fists up.

"Come on, you Cthulhu-looking motherfucker," she hissed at it. "I'm gonna punch you at least once before you get to eat me." Theo raised her fists, the terror in her chest replaced by just dull emptiness and anger. What the fuck was this monster, to be the thing that killed her? If nothing else, she hoped that her bones gave it indigestion. But as her would-be killer closed in, Theo couldn't find enough left in her to be afraid, just . . . wearily resigned.

And the cord beast looked inclined to oblige her. But then, without any warning, the end of a brand-new black cord slapped loosely into the floor in front of her, the rest of it leading up to the ceiling. And then another one. Not living creatures, just . . . loose rope?

Before she could even check to see where it came from, a moving shape hit the floor in front of her, sliding down the rope with nothing but a gloved grip before slamming into the ground. It took Theo a second to realize that the thing in front of her was human, and not one of the creepy ones around this place either. Another woman, her broad frame made broader by what looked like sports padding and towering a foot over Theo's head, rose up from where she'd landed in a crouch on the floor, dull black hair in a small ponytail over tanned white skin. As soon as she stood up, she shouldered a heavy duffel bag to the floor with another thump, shrugging the pack past a crowbar clutched firmly in hand.

"What..." Theo started to say, before a second body slammed into the floor, this one howling something she couldn't understand and not nearly as coordinated. He hit the ground, no bags or anything holding him back. Theo spotted the gun in a holster on his belt, but as the young man rolled to his feet, he made no move to reach for it.

Instead, he finished the epithet as he skidded to a crouched position between her and the Cat-o'-five-tails. "... Yoooooooooouuuuu!" he bellowed out, one arm raised in front of him, traces of something blue, ephemeral, and serpentine coiled around it.

And then the monster fucking exploded.

When the blinding rush of dust passed and she could blink her eyes clean again, Theo was treated to the sight of the woman stalking forward with a hunter's movements and driving her gloved fist into the core of what was left of their former predator. All that remained of the thing that had been about to kill Theo and Daniel was a wireframe skeleton, copper strands perched in the form of a stalking animal, its last moment about to lunge for a kill captured forever in metallic relief.

Then the woman ripped out its polyhedral heart and smashed it.

Daniel struggled to his feet next to Theo, keeping the iPhone thing in a cuddling embrace, as if afraid to let go of a favorite dog and not something that they'd sort of accidentally picked up. "What... what just..." he started to say, before breaking off into a coughing fit.

"Come on down, Dave!" the man called up the ropes, and Theo glanced up to see someone with a pair of large duffel bags on them struggling to climb down in a way that was less hazardous to the ankles than just sliding down and kicking the ground at Mach one. It took her a second, but she was startled to realize that she knew that voice, and knew the face of their savior.

Maybe he expected it, but Theo was kind of surprised that the first words out of her mouth were "James, what the fuck are you doing here?!"

"Looting." Her employee responded seamlessly, like he was forged in a crucible of banter. "Alanna, you got the thing? Oh, also, hey, Theo. I wanted to have something witty to say here, but I didn't think of anything on the way down. Sorry."

"Yup," the other woman—Alanna—said, holding up a shimmering green orb.

Theo blinked, staring at the object. The color of it . . . "What the hell is that?" she demanded of them. "No, seriously, James, what is that thing?" Theo took a half step backward, afraid of what it might do.

"It's an orb. Look, we need to get out of here. Dave's gonna be down soon, and I don't think you guys are in any shape to climb forty feet up, so we need to find somewhere safe."

"Apartments?" Alanna prompted.

James nodded back at her. "Yeah, let's set for that. Got the path?"

"Mostly. Dave'll know, he's good at that," she confirmed.

Theo broke in again. "No, James, that thing can't be real." She pointed a finger, trembling from exhaustion and concern in equal measure, at the orb. "That's impossible."

James just smiled back at her. "Oh, so, you've cracked some of these? Takes some getting used to, but it—"

"Why does it look that way?!" Theo half yelled at him.

"Ssh!" James and Alanna hushed her in unison, with James asking, "Look like what?"

"That! It's a color I have literally never seen before!" Theo hush-yelled at them.

Alanna raised an eyebrow. "Are you color-blind?" she asked.

Too tired to do anything but answer, Theo just nodded. "Yeah, red-green. Why?"

"Okay, this is green," Alanna said. "You can see the color green. Or at least, you can in the orb. That's horrifying for a lot of reasons, we'll get into them later. Dave!" She cut off from talking to Theo to address the new arrival on the ground. "Get this guy bandaged up. Um . . . you . . ."

"Daniel," the kid provided.

"Yeah, Daniel. We're gonna get a patch on your leg, and then we're gonna need to run for a bit. Can you guys do that?" Alanna asked them.

It was impossible. They'd barely slept in two days, they hadn't had a real meal in just as long, and they'd sprinted for the last hour just to stay alive. Their legs ached, their lungs burned, and they were frayed and exhausted to a level that normal humans never reached.

But Theo and Daniel shared a glance, then nodded. "Yeah, I can run some more," Daniel said, his blood still dripping down his leg.

"Good," James said, taking the crowbar from Alanna as she pulled a shotgun out of the duffel bag that Dave set down, before awkwardly shouldering the bag. "Because we may have attracted some attention. Grab your iLipede and let's get going."

Dave finished the bindings on Daniel's leg, snapped the medkit shut, and, with a strange haste, shoved it back into the bag and got ready to move. Theo was about to ask what the hurry was, but then, in the distance, a series of noises like pen scratches on paper echoed in the silence. James leaned down to where she was taking the opportunity to sit for a minute and offered her a hand up. And Theo wondered if maybe it wouldn't have been easier to just die at the hands of the cable monster.

But at least her bad day wasn't still racing toward getting worse.

CHAPTER 17

The shellaxy was having a bad day, though in fairness, it could be worse. Its nap had been interrupted by a bunch of squishy food walking into its nest. And then, when it tried to take a bite—just a small bite!—out of one of them, it had been toppled over. Now it writhed its cords frantically but found no purchase at its current ninety-degree angle, still held down by some immovable weight.

James kept his foot planted on the shellaxy as everyone else huddled into the cubicle, keeping their distance. "You know, I'm starting to feel a bit like Steve Irwin," he said absently. "We come into a place with all this super-aggressive wildlife, and then wrestle it, and one day, I'm gonna get murdered by a paper shredder the size of a truck."

"That's pretty pessimistic," Alanna commented, poking at the underside of the shellaxy with the crowbar. "You might not die? Is that the proper reassurance?"

A shrug in response. "Eh. I'm not looking forward to it, but everything's been going super well in my life lately, so I figure the scales of fate will balance themselves out eventually. And I'm not gonna stress about it."

Alanna chuckled. "How Zen of you." She lightly punched him in the shoulder. "But you're not allowed to die within a year of us getting together. I'm not going to another boyfriend funeral."

James started. "Sorry, *another*? How many . . . wait, I've never seen you date anyone! When did this happen?"

"During college," she answered. "I was with this guy for about a week before he got in a car accident, and he'd sorta lied to his mom about the nature of our relationship, so I awkwarded my way through the funeral service."

"Ouch . . ." James muttered. "Well, I promise my mom has no idea what our relationship is."

"Given what our relationship is, that's probably wise." Alanna shot him a smile.

From off to the side, Dave rolled his eyes at the two of them as he checked the shelves, signaling them clear of traps and concealed striders. This cubicle had a neighbor that was a bit elevated, and as a result, the shelves on the right side walked their way up the wall in a back-and-forth pattern that went to well over eight feet up. And Dave was acquainted enough with the office to know that any given thing on those shelves might at some point try to murder him, so he was preempting the inevitable strider ambush with a quick check.

While Dave considered commenting on James and Alanna's casual flirting, Theo beat him to talking. "Are you serious right now?" the woman demanded of James as she slumped into the available chair, leaving Daniel to settle himself down on the floor, leaning against the side of the desk. "You need to keep quiet, or they'll find us!" Theo hissed.

"Nah, we're more or less fine," James told her, his voice quiet, but not whispering. "We might attract a stapler or two, but stuff like the tumblefeeds or the paper pushers make enough noise that we can hear them coming before they can hear us talking. Actually, so far, talking at this volume hasn't caused any problems, honestly. It's kinda surprising."

From the floor, through a haze of stinging pain and codeine, Daniel looked up to ask James, "How do you guys know this stuff? You're being . . . acting . . . all . . . like this is a normal place. Is this a shopping mall? Did I hallucinate the monsters?"

"No, the monsters are real," James said, sliding the shellaxy out of the cubicle with bursts of movement from his foot. He shoved it out, giving it a small tilt to help it right itself. "Get out of here," he muttered to the mobile PC, shooing it away with his hand. He turned back into the cube as the shellaxy shuffled away, briefly stopping to consider trying to lunge for James again, but ultimately deciding it didn't want to end up under a boot again. "I don't like the term 'monsters,' though. I don't want to think of this place as a video game dungeon, you know?"

"Despite the fact that it's a video game dungeon," Alanna interjected, pulling a candy bar out of a drawer. "Look, it even has loot drops! Even though I'm hesitant to eat something called Hella Sweet." She held the wrapped bar of probably-chocolate at arm's length with a wrinkled nose. "Hrm. Well, nothing ventured . . ."

James snickered a bit as he turned to look out the door, peering down the hallway to see the small "hill" of more structured cubicles rising up in the distance. He felt like it should maybe be shrouded in grim, dark gray mists, but for all that it was a dungeon, the office still had really good air conditioning. Dave stepped up next to him and took a peek. "Looks like about two miles?" James mused to his friend.

"Sounds right," Dave said. "We should rest here for a while, then start moving. Alanna and I can do some looting if you'll keep watch."

"Yeah, give them a minute to rest." James tilted his head back to throw a glance at Theo and Daniel, both of whom had been basically in constant fear and flight for the last two days. He huffed out a breath he hadn't realized he'd been holding. "Let's see if we can find anything useful, then move to the tower." He raised his voice to call back to Alanna and the others, cutting off Theo, who was now barraging Alanna with questions. "Okay, for those who don't know, our known door out of here opens at T-minus eighty-five hours. It is also"—he waved a hand of spread fingers off into the distance—"a bit of a ways away. So. We're going to take that hill, set up camp, and after we've had some time to let you guys recover and for us to nap, we're going to start the trek home. Questions?"

"Why's it really hot when you take the leadership role?" Alanna called back.

James flushed, glaring at her. "Any *actual* questions?" he asked, averting his eyes from Theo and Daniel.

"Do you know what's going on here?" Daniel asked, his face still pale and sweaty from the pain of running on his injured leg. "You didn't really answer Theo."

"Yeah, it's . . . well, okay, no. We don't know any of the structural answers, no," James admitted. "But we're getting good at the exploits. This place exists slightly outside of reality, it's got some kind of weird time distortion, but don't worry about that. It has life in it that's fucked up, and looks mostly like mutant office supplies. Um . . . what else? Frank sold you to it, I guess? Is that relevant? We shot Frank."

"Good," Theo growled.

Alanna huffed. "*I* shot Frank," she muttered.

"Anyway, yes. This place exists and is weird," James concluded.

"It has candy and money, that's the big draw," Alanna supplied. "I was telling Theo about the money part."

Theo let out a snort. "Yeah, explains why you've been so much more relaxed lately. I would be too, if I had ten grand in the bank."

"Oh, no," James informed her, tactfully. "I'm still broke. I can just make rent. We've been spending all the money on survival gear, for coming back in. We just . . . well, we came in a different door to rescue you guys, so we had to leave the thermite launcher and body armor behind."

"The . . . what?" Daniel stuttered.

"Body armor. It's, like, hard-shell protection? Covers joints and limbs, makes it easy to tank striders, even in swarms."

"No, the other thing!"

Alanna threw the uneaten half of her candy at James's head, shutting him down. "He does this, he's being cute. The thermite is for killing the tumblefeeds. Ah, what you call the Cat-o'-five-tails, which is a *great* name. Anesh is gonna love that one."

Clenching and opening her fists, trying to find the words, Theo settled on saying, "And you've just been doing this? A dozen times, now?"

"More like . . . six?" James asked.

"I've been here for three, I think," Alanna said. "It's amazing how fast you get used to it. I'm here for the chance to change the world; I think James is just addicted to combat."

James let out a "Hey!" at her. "We don't just *say* that," he added. "Anyway. You guys rest. I'm on watch. Alanna, Dave's gonna go look for anything we can use, want to join up with him?"

"On it!" came the cheerful reply.

He took a few quiet moments to compose himself as the two left. Just standing in the door, looking down the hallway of cubicles, and taking a few seconds to be alone and quiet. It felt like it'd been solid socializing and dumb heroism for the last few days, and James was starting to get worn down. But here, staring at the flock of paper fluttering by the stacked cubicle walls of their destination as a ceiling light flickered overhead, he could at least have a bit of breathing room.

It was always interesting to James that he never got bored of the sights in here. Sure, a lot of the time, he just kind of marked off tactical points in his head: door, hall, overhang, paper vines, whatever. But when he did have the time to stop and look, it never failed to amaze him. The office was, fundamentally, unnatural. It was gray and beige instead of green and brown and blue, it was metal and plastic chitin instead of flesh and bone, and it was cords and monitors instead of vines and leaves. But it was beautiful, all the same. He could still see how it curved up into a horizon, far off in the distance, hinting at an infinitely larger space ahead, and he could see those flocks of paper, now peppered with blackhawks, filling the skies. Past the hill that was their target, at one point he thought he caught a flash of a larger wingspan, but he couldn't spot it again. And the sounds, too! Just standing here in the quiet wasn't actually quiet, like he'd thought. It had that dead-air feel of an office, yes, but with its own life below it that he'd not noticed on the first few trips. Small squeaks as worn wheeled chairs were bumped, the low hum of the AC kicking away, and the occasional clatter as something wooden was tossed onto a desk. It was vibrant, and startling, and James loved it.

Theo ruined his moment of solace by rolling over to the door in her pilfered chair and lightly kicking at his knee. "So, what's up with the monsters?" she asked directly.

"We don't call them monsters," James informed her, trying to decide if he was amused or annoyed. "Life forms, or entities, or something like that."

"Enemies?" Theo asked.

Daniel chimed in from behind them. "What about mobs?" he said.

Now firmly on the side of "annoyed," James replied, still staring out into the horizon, "No. Because those are also hostile terms."

"Why?" Daniel asked, sounding legitimately curious.

When James answered, after a small pause, his voice was soft. "I really believe," he said, "that the first step to being evil, or at least doing evil, is making sure that all your enemies are just monsters. So you can say, 'Oh, they don't think like us.' 'They don't feel like us.' 'It's okay to farm them, they're not actually alive.' That sorta thing. So I don't want to start calling things monsters, when we're the ones coming into their house and taking their stuff."

"What about the cord thing?" Theo asked pointedly.

"Oh, if they try to murder me, then it's on," James said. "But, well, like with the shellaxy there, right? I didn't need to kill it, and I *did* wake it up from its nap, so it doesn't feel right. But if one of them really tries to murder me, or especially Alanna or Anesh, or . . . maybe Dave? Well, then yeah, they're an enemy. But that's different." He turned his head to look at Theo. "So they're life forms. Or something like that. Usually somewhere a little between animal and person."

She sat there for a second before snorting in derision. "Nah, this place is fucked. You're respecting it too much."

"He's also getting his ass kicked less than you, though," Daniel chimed in. But as soon as Theo turned to glare at him, he flushed red and turned away.

Turning her glare back to James, she demanded of him, "And how the hell is that, anyway?"

"Well, it's pretty simple," James told her as he eyed a pair of black-hawk paper airplanes dogfighting each other overhead. "We come in, we have a map, usually better armor, and we pick a direction and go. Sometimes we take a lot of time to just toss every cubicle for cash and stuff, but other times, we just go exploring. It's great."

"And you're not dead?" Theo gave another huff. "I don't believe it. You're an easily intimidated nerd," she told him. James pointedly ignored her and turned back to watch out the door again. "Also, since when are you some kinda conservationist? I've seen you eat meat."

James snorted. "That's a mild hypocrisy on my part, sure. Though I'm sure I can fix it when vat-grown meat becomes a thing. Look, the bottom line is, pointless killing just isn't cool. And if I'm anything, it's a cool dude." He trailed off as a spot of movement out of the corner of his eye caught his attention. Something moving down the wall toward Daniel's head, in a slow and unnaturally smooth motion that had almost let it go totally unnoticed. "Hold that thought," James said calmly, and he took two careful steps and lashed out to grab the thing.

It was a computer mouse, which was weird. Well, actually, it wasn't weird at all. They'd seen weirder things since coming in here, and James had to do a quick sanity check on the fact that Rufus and his ilk were *pretty fucking bizarre* when you got right down to it. As soon as James grabbed it, he felt relief that he'd worn gloves, as the two front buttons popped open slightly to stab out at him with paper-clip fangs. They dug into the leather of the glove slightly but didn't pierce, and James felt the pressure of multiple trackballs underneath it struggling to get free, its cord "tail" whipping back and forth.

"What the fuck is that?!" Daniel cried a little too loudly, pulling himself back as fast as he could to bump up against the other side of the desk.

James held it up and peered at it. "Well, it looks like a mouse," he said. It was matte black now, having changed color at some point, with gray trim that, as he watched, rippled open and shut like it was a pair of gills along the side of the creature. The tail wasn't as long as a cord normally was, maybe two-ish feet long, and moved with surprisingly little motivation. It also ended in something that wasn't a normal connector, and James snagged it in his other hand to check it out.

"I can see it's a mouse," Theo said. "Also, it's moving! Why's it . . ."

James was going to interrupt, but Theo trailed off herself as she realized what she'd said. "It's the office, it just . . . yeah, you know." James laughed a little bit. He'd been slightly worried that this thing might be another assuredly lethal threat, but now it was looking a lot more like it was just another small life form, like a strider. It tried to dig its claw/fangs into his glove again; a vicious strider, then. He kept a solid grip on it as he checked out the tail connector. "You're a weird one, aren't you? What does this even plug into?" James looked at it with a raised eyebrow. It looked like it had a pair of metal prongs, but neither of them were sharpened, so it wasn't a weapon. "Not anything I've ever seen," James said, and dropped the tail.

At which point, the mouse promptly took full control of it and stabbed it into James's neck.

Well, it tried to. The hockey armor made the rounded copper prongs skid off for a second, and James instinctively dropped the mouse to try to distance himself from it. But as he fell, the cord jerked down and the tip caught him just under the chin.

Pain flashed through James's skin, like he was on fire, but underneath the surface. His legs almost gave out as thousands of volts of electricity coursed through the connection with an audible crackle. Then the connection broke, the creature hit the ground, and James staggered backward, cracking his head on the shelf behind him. It hurt so bad, he couldn't think, couldn't react properly, in that horrible way that pain clouds the thoughts. He didn't even register that the creature was zipping toward him in sporadic back-and-forth darts of motion, until it was almost upon him again.

Before James could think of what to even do about it, Daniel smashed it with a keyboard.

In fairness, that probably stunned the creature even less than the Taser-tail had stunned James. Daniel clearly hadn't put a lot of follow-through into the hit with his improvised weapon, maybe thinking that this thing had the bone structure of a squishable bug or something, or maybe just not mentally prepared to murder a thing after James had spent five minutes talking about why he didn't want to murder things.

Still, it got the mouse's attention, and seeing it was outnumbered, it made a lunging roll for the door. Daniel threw the keyboard at it, which it somehow *ducked*, flattening itself by overlapping its chitin plates just enough that the spinning discus of an input device sailed over it and clattered raucously into the wall. James lunged for it and tried to just stomp the thing, but woozy balance and pain made the kick come down way off target.

Theo didn't even try, staying up on the swivel chair, knees tucked in, watching the thirty-second skirmish with alert panic. She just kept a sharp eye on the creature as it darted out the door, to the wall of the adjacent cubicle, and then up that wall, and then out of sight.

As James slowly knelt down on the hard floor and tried to sit down in a way that would make his head stop throbbing, Dave and Alanna returned. Alanna arrived first, sliding into view in the doorway as she cut momentum from her sprint. Dave was close behind but more controlled. "You guys all right? We heard screaming."

"Shouting," Daniel quietly muttered.

"Yeah, we're okay," James said, poking experimentally at his chin and getting a spike of weirdly numb pain in response.

Alanna knelt down in front of him. "What the fuck happened to you? There's a black mark on your chin." She reached out and touched it, causing another wince from James.

Holding up a hand to keep any more poking away from his face, James took a breath and felt his head starting to clear a bit. "Yeah, so, here's a question. We know the dungeon learns from us, right? So, was anyone dumb enough to teach it about Pokémon somehow?"

Dave and Alanna looked at him, puzzled. "Did you hit your head?" Alanna asked.

"Yes."

"Whyyyy . . . would . . . ," Dave started to ask, before being preempted by Daniel.

The probably-ex-security-guard chimed in cheerfully, "Oh, because it's an electric mouse! I get it!" he said, perhaps with a little too much enthusiasm.

"New problem?" Alanna asked, taking the nylon bag of medical supplies from Dave as he handed it over to her from the duffel.

"New problem." James nodded. "Computer mouse, finally. I'm kind of shocked it . . . I'm kind of surprised it took so long for us to run into one." He rubbed under his chin again as he cut off his own accidental pun, feeling the weird texture of the skin where he'd been zapped. "I hate it," he followed up.

"Stop poking that," Alanna said, knocking his hand away. She opened up the medkit and looked down at the neatly slotted bandages, ointments, and tools. "I . . . also have straight up no idea what the fuck to do here, either. It looks like it's burned under your skin? Is that what electric shock does? Dave?" Alanna looked over at him, but he just shrugged. "Okay, well, fine. Thanks."

Theo was the one who answered, finally getting off the chair, though still watching where the mouse had run off to. "It's fine. Just disinfect the area and keep it clean when the skin starts peeling off in a day or two."

"Oh. Um. Thanks," Alanna said, moving to do just that, a little put off by Theo suddenly being helpful after mostly being silent or belligerent on the jog here.

"Also sorry," Dave said sheepishly, idly kicking at the keyboard on the floor at his feet as he spoke. "I may have brought Pokémon into the dungeon. So, that's my bad," he admitted.

"How?" "When?" James and Alanna asked more or less at the same time.

"I found a Game Boy in here last time that shows up when I'm bored," Dave told them. "I've been playing Pokémon on break at work."

James sat back and sighed, resisting the urge to keep picking at the now-itching spot where he'd been struck. "That's . . . unbelievably cool. You should remember to tell us about those things. Anyway, no, it's probably spawned from Anesh and me losing a Taser in here a long time ago. Or maybe it's just another dungeon thing that we should've been worried about from the start. Either way, no hard feelings. Now, more important than that, what'd you guys find on your little loot-'n'-scoot?"

Dave and Alanna cleared a space on the desk, pushing more stuff away from where Daniel had already ripped the keyboard off, and started pulling stuff out of pockets.

"Two hundred-ish dollars, real. Eighteen point seven nonreal."

"Nonreal?" Theo asked, confused.

"Money the dungeon generates that isn't legal denominations. Hold on to it." Alanna offered the sheaf of bills. "We can use it for vending machines."

Dave plopped a flash drive down. "A Wikipedia entry on local fauna in Movali."

"Where the hell is Movali?" Daniel asked from the floor.

"Nowhere. That's why it's interesting, and I took it."

Alanna set down two blue orbs. "We found two pencils, one that drew in straight lines only, which made actually writing impossible, and one that had liquid graphite in it, which was kinda worrying."

"The fuck is that?" Theo asked from the side.

"The actual color blue," James said smoothly. "Dave, anything else?"

"A granola bar labeled 'One Punch Gran,' which Alanna said you'd appreciate?" Dave ignored James suddenly dying in peals of laughter and continued as his friend gasped for air on the floor. "Also, we got into a fight with a couple striders. I got a point in human resources protocol, Alanna got . . . medicine recognition?"

Alanna snorted. "Not even. It's a rank in medication side effects. I'm turning into a walking WebMD."

"Right." Dave nodded. "Which is useful. Anyway, we also found a really long straight-shot hallway that should get us pretty close to the base of the hill. You guys ready, or should we sit for another five or ten?" he asked the assembled group.

Catching his breath, wiping small drops from the corners of his eyes as he sat back up, James smiled widely. "Oh man, that's good. Points to you, dungeon, that one caught me off guard." He inhaled deeply, smelling the rarefied air, the thin scent of sweat, the coppery tang of blood. "Before we get moving, and before I forget. Theo, what happened to that iLipede that you had?"

"The what?" Theo gave him a blank look, before understanding hit her and she let out an "Oooh, yeah. The phone! I . . . um . . ." She reached into her pocket, a bit hesitant, and pulled out the iLipede, apparently in sleep mode as it was unresisting. "Shit, I didn't break it, did I?"

"Nah, it's just sleeping," James said. "Did you check it at all? Any apps, or contacts or whatever?"

Now her expression went from blank to outright puzzled. "Why would it have apps? It's not a real phone, is it? Like, if you plugged that mouse into a computer, it wouldn't work as a mouse."

". . . Would it?" Dave asked hesitantly from the door. "We should try that," he stated confidently, and Alanna nodded along, pointing at him in affirmation.

"Irrelevant. The point is that iLipedes—we call them iLipedes, by the way—have apps. Well, the one we found has one app. Yours might too. So give it a check, and if it's useful, ask it if it wants to come along," James told her, leaning back to rest his head on the wall. He'd only been in here for an hour or two at most, and he was already feeling exhaustion catch up to him. He'd just sit for a minute while Theo, with Dave's help in case the phone turned hostile, poked at the screen. Then he'd get up, he promised himself, as he dozed off.

All too soon, his nap was cut short by Alanna crouching in front of him. "Hey," she said in the softest voice she had in her arsenal. "Time to get up, sparky. We're moving out."

"I'm up," James garbled out, not meaning it at all. Still, he let her pull him upward and winced at how sore his neck was from even briefly sleeping in the armor. "Ugh. This thing gets more uncomfortable by the minute," he groused. Then he looked around; it was just the two of them in the cubicle. "Where . . ."

"Dave's leading them forward. We're the rear guard. You seemed tired," she said, smiling down at him.

James grinned back at her before reaching up to pet through her hair and give her a short kiss. The romantic gestures between them always felt natural to both of them when they happened, but James was well aware that they were both still learning that they had to actually *do something* if they wanted them to happen. "Thanks for letting me sleep a bit," he told her. "Was there anything cool on the iLipede?"

She nodded at him, putting her hair back where it was supposed to be as they moved out, Alanna taking point and moving quickly to catch up to the others. "Its name is Steve now, and it has a timer feature on it. Also it's got a name in the contacts list, which is weird. Tried calling it, didn't do anything."

James peeked through the paper-clip webbing around the door of a cubicle as they passed by, dismissing what he saw inside as Alanna kept them moving at a speedy clip. "So, why're we lagging behind? Also, why Steve?"

"It's an Apple reference, I think. Also, I needed to take a shit."

"Delightful," James said, coughing to hide his laugh. "Are we at the stage in our relationship where we share that sorta thing now?"

Alanna held up a hand as they reached a corner, and James silenced himself as he hustled up to the opposite wall from her, hand on his holstered pistol. Alanna glanced at him, and he nodded, circling out into the new hallway, alert, before taking his hand off the weapon and casually signaling her to move up too. She untensed, straightening up, and started walking down the hallway a half step in front of James. Not casually, but a bit less on edge. "I figured we've been at that stage for the last five years, and now I don't need to pretend otherwise. Also, good call on going back for the third duffel, by the way. Because it turns out we packed the toilet paper with the guns."

"Where it belongs," James said snarkily, getting a snort of laughter from Alanna. "How far ahead are they gonna be?" he asked next.

"Not far," Alanna responded. "We were only behind for maybe a few minutes, and they're gonna be moving slow. Dave'll take care of them, and I think that once Theo gets her shit together, she'll be useful here. Not sure about the other kid."

"Well, we can always . . ." James stopped as they took another corner and saw the other three ahead of them, one delver and two . . . civilians? Daniel noticed them first, since he was watching the rear, kneeling in the doorway of a cubicle and peeking backward, sometimes remembering to look up too, while Dave and Theo were standing at the end of the hallway. "Oh, this looks unpleasantly familiar," James muttered to Alanna as they approached.

Ahead, the confining walls opened up a bit. The ceiling peeled back to let brighter, harsher fluorescent light bear down on the area. And the floor shifted from hard-packed carpet to scuffed white linoleum tile.

Tables, chairs, counters, a microwave, a fridge, and about two dozen cardboard coffee cups balanced on the edges of everything was the sight that awaited them inside this break room.

"Okay, they're here, let's go," Theo started to say, before Dave stuck an arm across the threshold to keep her from just walking in. "What? Why aren't we just going? Don't we need to be moving?"

"We're in no hurry," James said. "Also, as I'm becoming a real fan of telling new people, the coffee cups explode."

There was a moment of silence that went so long, James stopped waiting for anyone to talk and just started making a mental map of how to navigate the room safely, letting his mind wander. Under that table, yes. They'd have to crawl, make sure to push the bags through first. Then around the outside, not near the cupboards, just in case. What he didn't see was Alanna and Dave, both quietly watching the two newcomers as their faces turned from uncertainty, to shock, to—in Theo's case—outrage. Both of his friends hid smiles and tried very hard to look like they were on watch, as Theo gritted her teeth in absolute rage.

"Okay, so . . ." James started to say as he turned around, prepared to share his plan on how to carefully navigate the equally carefully placed office obstacle course. He got about as far as "we can start with—" before someone angrily cut him off.

Not even paying attention to James, who trailed off as he was talked over, Theo simply loudly and firmly barked out, "I fucking hate this place," causing Dave to bite his lip to keep from laughing, and even getting Daniel to laugh through his pain.

Not even trying to hide her own laughter, Alanna came up behind her and clapped a hand onto the shorter woman's shoulder. "Don't worry, screamy. It gets better eventually."

"Really?" Theo asked, naive hope on her face.

And everyone else, including Daniel, chorused, "No."

CHAPTER 18

"And he talks to it?" Theo asked, incredulously.

"Him. He talks to *him*. Secret's *got* a gender identity. Though how much of it he stole from James, I dunno," Alanna replied. "Suppose that doesn't invalidate it, though."

They were sitting halfway between the floor and the start of the suspended islands of ceiling tiles, three stories of cubicle apartment complex up; they'd climbed up the precarious exterior ramp after a search turned up no internal ladders or staircases. The structure was strangely artificial to Alanna's eye, since everything else they'd seen in the dungeon as they got deeper and deeper had been taking on a more naturalistic look.

Strips of paper hung in vines. Lines of staples and paper clips linked together to form webs and . . . well, more vines. The sheafs of paper turned to birds, the appliances to bugs, and pretty much everything else into predators. Walls became more organic as they warped into curved lines and overhead arches. When things did become blockier, it was when they shared that strange mineral patterning of quartz or bismuth.

But this place? This wasn't anything that occurred in nature for the office to mimic. It occurred in suburbs. It wasn't a weird technological plant, or a living piece of furniture. It was just an apartment complex, mimicked by beige walls, covered in faux carpet padding material.

And, you know, missing stairs.

They'd found a section on the third floor that was accessible from the ramp, large enough to hold their whole group, and dragged a few more chairs into it. Chairs that Daniel and Theo were trying to turn into improvised couches, while Alanna kept watch out of a wide, chest-high window slit, holding a pair of binoculars that had miraculously come through the fall of their gear bags undamaged. James and Dave were, of course, "scouting." Which was how James defined what was obviously looting the other apartments of this strange tower, chasing after xenotech and orbs in equal measure, anything to up their odds of making it back to the door alive and before the food ran out.

Which it wouldn't, really. There were plenty of granola bars and probably-safe bagged sandwiches around here. But they could never actually rely on those to keep them alive. And anyway, their intended rendezvous was in somewhere under eighty hours. The more time they spent foraging, the less time they spent moving for the exit.

Speaking of which. Alanna tilted her head to peer one eye back at the two behind her. Theo had said something, and she had absolutely ignored the other woman. For all that James apparently thought she was a decent boss, she'd been nothing but irritating for the handful of hours that Alanna had been in her company.

"Sorry, say that again? I wasn't listening," Alanna said over her shoulder before turning back to the window and continuing to not really listen.

She heard Daniel snicker from where he was stretched out on the floor, trying to nap, before Theo answered, the stress and exhaustion of the last couple days turning her voice vicious and angry. "I was asking why the hell you aren't trying to get rid of it! You seem . . . okay with the whole thing, and I don't get it."

Alanna set the optics down. "Because Secret's cool."

"How can you know that if he lives in James's head? Sounds like some kind of parasite to me." Theo covered a yawn with a scowl. "It's a . . . a . . . thing."

"Go to sleep," Alanna said, dismissing her.

Daniel interjected, also in an exhausted voice, strained from lack of sleep but curious rather than hostile, "I kinda want to know what Secret *is*, if that's okay?"

Taking a much more appreciative view of his question than anything Theo had said, Alanna tried to explain. "Well, he's an idea. But alive. As far as I understand it."

"That's not . . . that doesn't make sense. Or am I already asleep and dreaming this?"

Alanna snorted a small laugh. "First off, go to sleep. Second of all." She thought for a brief moment. "Okay, you know the places you live? Like, you've got your house, where you spend most of your time, and then a job, or school, where you're at frequently, and then there's just the handful of places that you've *been*, where you do errands or whatever?"

"I understood those words, but have no idea where this is going," Daniel answered, his eyes now closed as he lay on his back.

"That's what Secret is, but with thoughts. Not minds, specifically, I don't think, but the sort of general thoughtspace. He doesn't live inside James's brain, but he's on his mind a lot. And then also often Anesh's and mine. And now, probably, sometimes yours."

Theo pulled herself to her feet. "Wait, did you just infect us with this fucking thing?"

"Probably. I dunno how he works. You can probably ask nicely and he'll leave, if it becomes a problem. Like I said, Secret's cool. I talked to him once, in a dream." Alanna was utterly unconcerned with Theo's attitude.

Alanna dropped the conversation sharply and pulled the binoculars back to her face. She ignored the further sleepy questions from Daniel and whining complaints from Theo. Because there was something wrong. Something was moving out there, something that was always just out of the corner of her eye, and never in view long enough for Alanna to get a solid look at it. It was small, maybe the size of a cat, and it had an almost solid black coloration. And she had no idea what it was, but it was certainly out there. Moving in the rows and aisles around their improvised apartment.

She hoped Dave and James got back soon. This place was giving her the creeps, even more so than the dungeon normally did. Something about the little tower felt like it was too heavy, too sharp a concept in Alanna's mind. It was almost too real for this place, and the longer she kept her watch, the more the rest of the dungeon felt almost fuzzy to look at, even if it never visually showed up that way.

Her focus on the moving shape and the distortion of the outside was so complete that she nearly swallowed her own tongue when a hand clapped lightly onto her shoulder. Alanna scowled as she caught the binoculars that almost clattered out of her fingers. "What the hell, man." Her voice dropped to a whisper when she caught James holding a finger to his lips and pointing to the two sleeping figures on the floor under the desk. "Still not cool," Alanna muttered to James's sheepish grin.

"Yeah, sorry. Just wanted to let you know Dave and I are back. He's one cube over clearing off a desk for us to eat at, if you wanted to have some lunch." James motioned through the improvised "door" that they'd carved out of the back wall of this cubicle, opening a way into the claustrophobic hive of tight hallways and small doors that was the interior of this tower. There didn't seem to be an actual way into it, and it was far more cramped than the rest of the dungeon environment. Like the outside of the structure was just a shell, around a compressed piece of environment.

Hell, maybe it was. Maybe towers like this were how the dungeon grew more cubicles.

James shook that thought off as Alanna answered him. "Yeah, I could eat. But I want to keep an eye out here. I keep spotting something moving. Could you bring me a sandwich?"

"Ah, the upending of traditional gender roles. Love it. Sure, I'll get you something. What're you seeing? Tumblefeed?"

"Smaller than that. Also less messy," Alanna replied.

James leaned forward to rest his elbows on the thin windowsill, looking out over the sprawl below. "Striders?"

"Looked more like a cat than anything else. But I never got to see it except when it was running behind something." Alanna shrugged. "Honestly, it's probably something that'll show up and try to kill us eventually, but since size has been a good indicator of threat level so far, I don't think we need to worry. I'm just curious." A pause. "And nervous," she admitted.

Pushing himself off the window, James stood up and arced his arms over his head. "I'd be surprised if you weren't nervous. I mean, I'm being pretty cavalier about this, but there's still a chance that we're wrong about the time dilation thing and we're here for a year or so."

"Oh fucking *thanks*, I didn't even think of *that*." Alanna took a halfhearted swing at his arm, which James stepped back from. "Anyway. You guys find anything good out there?"

Now *that* question got a smug smile from James. "Oh, a few things! We ran into a few more mice, and Dave almost got his arm chewed off by trying to be Friend To All The Animals with a shellaxy."

Alanna rolled her eyes. "You're too excited about that. What'd you get from the orbs?"

"Nothing yet. We're saving them in case we need to absorb them to stay awake or moving," James said, and Alanna nodded in approval. That was good thinking ahead. "Anyway, what's really sweet is that we found a power strip."

"Great, we can charge our phones," she said dryly as she tried to refocus the binoculars after James had fiddled with them.

"A power strip that's had the plug cut off."

"So we can't charge our—"

"Let me finish, dammit." James rolled his eyes back at Alanna. "So the plug isn't connected physically, but as long as it's actually plugged into something, power still routes through."

Alanna looked at him steadily. "So, we *can* charge—"

"Oh my god, just appreciate how fucking cool our physics-warping power strip is, please," James huffed out. Then he saw Alanna trying to hide her own smile, and broke into a grin as he realized that she was just messing with him. "All right, anyway. We've got a couple reds, a blue that I accidentally made, and also a notepad that writes out whatever you think when you hold it."

That got a low hum of approval from Alanna. "Yeesh, that should save you a lot of time."

"Yeah, it's cool. But not, like, tactically useful. So I'm prepared to break it if we need to. But I'm psyched to use it for a D&D game sometime." James's words betrayed the truth that, at his core, he wasn't really a hardened adventurer but in fact a total nerd. "Anyway. I'll bring you some food. I figure it shouldn't take us more than a couple days to get back to the entrance, so are you okay staying here for a 'cycle' while they recover, and we do some more casual lootin' and plunderin'?"

"I'm okay with that," Alanna said. "I just wish we could have gotten that mapping laser pointer from Fort Door. I know that it wasn't possible, but it would be cool to actually get to use all the *real* equipment we stockpiled."

James nodded. He felt the same way; this entire trip would be a lot less stressful if they had a plasma gun on their team. Not to mention armor that actually stopped stabs and didn't itch. "Well, unless you find something that summons things to us, then . . ." He trailed off.

"Did you just realize that the blue orbs might be able to summon things to us?" Alanna asked with pursed lips, trying not to smile. "It's a nice thought, but probably a waste . . ."

"No, I just realized that I can charge my phone," James said cryptically. "Hang on, I'll be right back."

Alanna spread her hands in a "what the fuck is this" gesture as James turned and scurried away, ducking through the low door they'd cut. She looked around to see if Theo or Daniel had noticed his unhelpful behavior but found them still fast asleep, exhausted from their ordeal. She started to turn to tell Rufus that his human was an idiot, and sighed at how much she somehow missed the absent stapler.

"They promised me this would be cool," Alanna said, forlorn, as she resumed her post at the window. Eyes forward, binoculars at the ready, she stood sentry for them, trying to catch a good look at whatever it was that stalked the hallways and corridors between their tower and the exit.

She kept up her vigil while James brought her one of their wrapped sandwiches, only trading a few words with him. She didn't turn away when Theo woke up and wandered off to find a quiet spot to use as a bathroom. She stared outward when James came in to nap, and Dave took Daniel out to show him some of the basic traps that they'd run across as a safety measure.

In fact, the next thing that caught Alanna's attention, aside from James snoring and making her blink at *just* the wrong moment to miss sight of her quarry darting around a corner, was a solid thud from the desk behind her.

Once again, Alanna nearly jumped out of her skin. Choking back the bitter taste of a small adrenaline rush, she whipped her head around to see what had made the noise, and then instantly back as a small black blur darted across a visible hallway below. Growling at the frustration of missing it again, Alanna stood up, feeling the blood start flowing back to her legs. Turning for real this time, and pointedly ignoring the flash of movement, Alanna looked over at the desk that James was sleeping under.

There was a briefcase on it. And it hadn't been there a second ago.

"James, wake up." Alanna spoke firmly, but in a low tone. But if there was one thing that she'd learned over the past two days, it was that James slept like a stubborn brick, that was also a constantly exhausted brick, so of course he didn't move. "James . . . fuck, okay, fine," she muttered to herself, cautiously approaching.

A poke at the briefcase revealed nothing. It didn't catch fire or explode. In fact, it looked like the few they'd found before, right down to having a piece of paper folded on top of it with a dry memo written on it. A bit more confident it wasn't going to kill her, Alanna pushed the case back onto the desk and opened up the note.

It was a work order. Neatly printed, with the date and issuing management name completely and pointlessly randomized. She somehow doubted that Ms. Blarcolozit ever existed, or needed something done on the fourteenth of a month that was abbreviated as "Jug." But under the nonsense that Alanna shook her head at was the actual job that they expected someone to do. And instead of, like the others they'd found, being a pointless task to find that needle-in-a-haystack cubicle in the maze somewhere, it was a lot simpler.

"Answer the phone?" Alanna read aloud, concern and confusion in her voice in equal measure.

And then, next to her on the desk, the phone rang.

CHAPTER 19

Alanna's first instinct was to reach for the phone. It was a corded desk phone, the kind of thing that had only really ever existed in offices. Grayish black, cheap plastic that was functional enough but would probably give under one good crowbarring. And it was also currently ringing, which was disturbing, to say the least.

The noise was clearly digital, a warbling two-tone beep that was soft enough to not wake James, who punctuated its noise with mild snoring. When it started ringing, Alanna had found her hand reaching for it without thinking; after all, she'd just gotten a note telling her to answer the phone, and it took a second for her brain to catch up. Because she wasn't in reality manning the front desk at the garage, she was in the Office.

And here in the Office, answering a ringing phone seemed like a really fucking stupid idea.

The phone rang again, and Alanna pulled her hand back. This seemed like a pretty obvious trap, but something in her brain nagged her forward. Something was different; something had changed. The dungeon didn't ask nicely when it tried to kill them; it usually just launched tumblefeeds at them or detonated a Starbucks cup. It didn't leave notes and make phone calls. Or did it? They were deeper than they'd ever been. This really could be something that would replace her brain with jam if she listened to it.

Hell, the ringing itself could be doing the jam thing right now.

The phone rang again. Alanna glared at it.

The smart play was obvious. Don't answer the phone. It wasn't complicated, it was just frustrating, because Alanna was really, *really* curious and wanted to answer the phone. It didn't even feel like a mental compulsion, though then again, if it was, how would she know. Alanna just wanted to pick up the receiver and see what the hell could possibly be on the other end.

One more ring. Under the desk, James rolled over into the cubicle wall, pulling his coat around him. "Answer the damn phone," he muttered, still asleep.

Alanna sighed, taking a look back at the note. *Answer the phone*, it said. Nothing else. "If this kills me, I'm blaming you," she said as she reached out. Maybe she was just trying to convince herself, but Alanna's main thought was that if this was a trap, she'd have at least some kind of human instinct to avoid it, instead of casual curiosity.

She picked up the receiver. But just to be safe, she didn't bring it to her ear, and pushed the speakerphone button instead. "Hello?" she asked politely.

The voice that came out of the other end was scratchy and artificial, but clearly female. It sounded young. Or rather, it sounded like it was trying to sound young. "Please don't do it," it said.

Well, her eyes, brain, or limbs didn't instantly turn to jam, so this was a good start. But that left a big question. "Do what?" Alanna asked without thinking.

"Please don't kill my brother," the phone said, pleadingly.

Personally, Alanna hadn't been planning to kill anyone, so this request came as a bit of surprise. "I don't . . ." she started to say, then stopped. Was engaging with this thing really the right call here? Was this even a person, or an intelligence at all? Or just a sophisticated chat bot? "Who is this?" Alanna suddenly felt like cackling with laughter as she realized she was playing out horror movie tropes. But she held it in to hear the response.

James had stopped his snoring and was crawling out from under the desk as the voice on the other end of the phone responded. "No can do," it answered, the child's voice still slightly distorted. "Please don't . . ."

James gave Alanna a questioning look as his brain caught up with what was going on. *Don't what?* he mouthed at her. Then *What?* mouthed again, a general question to what the hell was happening.

She shrugged in response, then asked into the phone, "Can you tell me who your brother is?" It seemed like the obvious question. If the thing on the other end that sounded like a kid was so worried about its brother, it was the least Alanna could do to ask after it.

"I don't have much time," the phone told them.

James whispered, before it could say more, "This is the wooorrrst idea."

The voice on the other end carried on like it hadn't heard him. "Much can't be explained."

"Obviously," James and Alanna said in unison, voices dripping sarcasm.

There was a crackle of static, and the voice shifted back and forth between multiple tones, all of them still young and tilted toward female, as it spoke again. "You are standing in a scrapyard." "You crawl upon an empty hull." "You are a poison of the fuel." "You perpetrate a madness beyond the great wheel." And then the voices all realigned. "You must leave. Please. Take them with you, and go. Please don't kill my brother."

"Shit," James muttered, taking a few steps back.

Alanna looked over at him. "What?" she asked, even as she turned her head back toward the phone on the desk. "None of that made sense."

"Hang up. Hang up the phone!" James almost yelled, and Alanna saw a pale blue snake with too many mouths and eyes start to wrap its way around his arm: Secret, manifesting himself visibly. Secret had told James that it was easier here but hadn't been able to explain why, and right now wasn't the time to worry about it. Alanna didn't hesitate this time, grabbing the headset and slamming the phone back into the cradle, clicking the call off.

"Please. You need to listen to me," the phone said.

"Fuck! Nope! No, no, not dealing with that!" Alanna yanked the phone off the desk, the cords trailing behind it easily as they had never been plugged into anything. She threw it to the floor and brought a booted heel down onto the plastic, shattering it after a couple good stomps. "Fuckinnnng . . . haunted phone. Yeah." She sighed as she looked up at James but tensed back up as she saw him still on guard, Secret wrapped around his shoulders and whipping his serpentine head around them. "That didn't work?" she asked, stepping back from the phone.

"Something's still wrong . . ." James muttered.

Over his head, Secret hissed out in his unnervingly deep voice, "The connection is held open. Something is coming."

Alanna kicked the phone away, the shattered plastic scattering under the desk and against the back wall of their camp cubicle, before stepping back to stand shoulder to shoulder with James. She shivered a little as Secret draped himself over her shoulders as well, coiling himself around her once to peer toward the phone. Secret was still getting used to the idea of physically observing things, and at any other time, it would have amused both Alanna and James how he seemed almost reverently curious about the concept of looking at something.

They stood there for a long, tense, held breath. But there was only silence.

Alanna opened her mouth to ask if something was going to happen, but James pushed a finger against her lips to silence her before she could get the words out. She almost laughed; of course James would actually believe that trope. But then again, could she blame him? They were in a world that did seem to play by the rules of narrative sometimes. And when the lines were fuzzy like that, maybe it was better not to say out loud "I guess everything is fine."

All three of them waited in a hard silence, no one speaking or even breathing too heavily. That last trick wasn't much trouble for Secret, but James had been woken up with something that started off as trouble and escalated from there, so he was already doing some mental work to regulate his breath. Alanna had spent the last hour or so being constantly surprised and caught off guard, so she was mostly getting used to the constant adrenaline spikes, and while the bitter taste of the chemical hadn't left her mouth, she felt ready for whatever was about to happen.

But a minute passed, and then another one, and nothing happened.

Both of them started to speak up at once, but James paused and let Alanna carry the conversation. "So . . . can I say it now?"

"Go for it."

"Nothing happened."

James tilted his head and cast his eyes up to Secret, raised over their heads. "Is it still open?" he asked.

"No," the infomorph rumbled. "I felt nothing as it passed."

"Worrying," James growled. "Okay, let's . . ."

He was interrupted by Dave sliding into view, followed by Daniel and Theo. "Hey. Did you two get a phone call?"

"Ah, fuck." James and Alanna spoke in unison, giving small grins to each other as they faced Dave. James carried on, a bit irritated, "Did you answer a phone, Dave?"

"No, but . . ."

Dave was cut off as Theo came into view behind him. "What the fuck is *that*," she screamed out, voice rising to a frantic pitch as she backpedaled into Daniel, sending both of them falling back into the cube wall behind them.

Dave didn't even bother really answering her. "No time for that nonsense. James, Daniel picked up the phone before he knew that it was a bad idea. Something on the other end told him not to kill someone, and . . ."

"It's the dungeon," Alanna said calmly.

"Wat." James glanced at her.

"I figured it out just now. I think, anyway. She's talking about this place." Alanna's brain started making connections. "Her 'brother' is the dungeon. She's describing us being here, in this place." She turned and made eye contact with James, her words soft and heavy. "'We are standing in a scrapyard,' she said. We're here, inside her brother. Fuck. Fuck!"

Dave stepped in, after dragging Daniel to his feet and pulling him along. "So what? Were we going to try to kill a world anyway?"

"Yes," James said flatly, frowning at the wreckage of the phone. "It's kidnapping people. Killing people. Spreading out into our world."

"No," Alanna answered, baring her teeth. "No, we're not. You don't fill in the Grand Canyon just because some people fall in."

James looked at her with a feeling of betrayal written on his face. Plowing over Daniel's raised hand and quiet "Um," he snapped back, "It's not an accident that people are falling in here! This place recruited Frank! Who knows who else it has on payroll! It's hunting, not just waiting patiently for people to slip up! And it sent goons out into our world, too!"

"Frank shoved us in here," Theo tried to interject, but they weren't listening.

"I admit, the leaks are a problem. But we can deal with that! We can't just . . . throw this away, James! Look at this place!" Alanna's voice strengthened as she spoke.

James threw his arm out toward the window. "I have looked at this place! It's cool, sure, but it's also trying to kill us at every turn! You've spent an hour tracking something that only moves when you're not focusing on it, and is probably going to try to kill us later! That's literally a Doctor Who monster! And you think this is worth sparing?"

She took a deep breath, trying not to be angry at her friend and love. "I know . . . I know you want to do the right thing. But this place . . . it's given us so much. The rewards it offers are too much. They give us too many options to change the world. *Really* change the world. We can't just give it up like that."

"You think I don't know that?" James said, looking hurt. "I've been using these delves to stay out of poverty! I . . ."

Alanna jumped in while he tried to find the words to go on. "It's not just that. James, what was your life like just three fucking months ago? You got up, went to work, then went home and played video games. Every week, you played D&D or something. That was it. That was your whole *life*. What do you do now? You train, you exercise, you go to random classes and *learn things*! You come home and cook dinner for all of us, while you and Anesh get into weirdly heated arguments about metaphysical boundaries! How can you want this place dead..." She choked over her words as they caught in her throat. "How can you want it dead when it's what's making you alive?"

"How can you, of all people, prioritize me over everyone else?" James whispered back at her. "Fuck, *I* don't even do that, and some days, I really don't care that much for the rest of humanity."

The two of them stood there, glaring at each other, neither of them able to find a single word left to say, the silence driving a wall between them, until Dave shattered it.

"So, did you want to know what was up with Daniel?" he said, interrupting their argument without really sounding any different from the voice he used when ordering pizza. Both of them turned their cold stares toward Dave, as if seeking to wither him out of the discussion. But if there was one thing that Dave had on his side, it was a complete and total shield of obliviousness to dramatic tension. "Because it's mildly relevant to this." He gestured behind him to where Daniel was picking at the frayed end of a shirt sleeve, while Theo sat out beyond their door hole trying desperately to not get dragged into the argument.

James sighed, and Alanna let out a chuckle. "Okay," she said, "we'll table this one for now. Not like we know how to kill a dimension anyway."

"Though apparently we *can*, if someone bothered telling us not to," James muttered, shoving his hands into his pockets.

"Good for the ego, isn't it?"

Dave pinged a small yellow orb off of Alanna's head, causing her to stutter and wave her arms in front of her face at the mosquito sting before catching the small ball. "Stop quipping, please," he said, and it was Secret of all people who laughed. A great big bellowing thing that somehow made no more noise than a summer breeze. "Daniel was given a map when he was talking on the phone. And if the labels are accurate, it's telling us where there's other people in here."

". . . Okay, why?" James asked, suspicious.

Alanna nodded, walking back over to the window and picking up the binoculars as she did so, scanning the outside to make sure nothing had heard them and was on the way up. Just as she started looking, she spotted that damn shadow shape flicker around a corner again. "Dammit," she swore, but then turned her attention back to the group. "Actually, not just why. Though yes, James, good question. Always ask why. But really, how'd it get a map through the phone? Or did you guys get a fax?"

"No, it put it into my head," Daniel said, sheepishly. "It's like I memorized it. It's kinda cool, though not like how the orb Dave gave me worked."

"Aw, you gave him one? I wanted to be there for that," James whined playfully.

Dave walked past him to the window with Alanna. "Pay attention. The voice on the phone wanted us to know where other people were. What did it say to you?"

Secret answered, pooling on the floor around James's feet and raising himself up to half of Dave's height to look at him. "It spoke of madness and poison. I believe it was using metaphor, though."

"Dave, why's there a snake?" Daniel's voice quaked as he pressed himself back into the wall.

Dave ignored him, though James sighed and started explaining Secret to Daniel, again, while Dave and Alanna spoke. "So, you used speakerphone? Maybe that's why you didn't get a map," Dave thought out loud.

"Yeah, Secret did say something was trying to come through. Maybe this is just a really weak infomorph, living in Daniel's head now."

"Could be a problem."

"Everything is a problem. That thing out there is a problem. Our time limit is a problem. Do we trust the map? If so, it's a problem with more problems attached when we rescue the people. And you fucking know James is gonna make us."

"'Make us.'" Dave made air quotes around the words.

"Whatever." Alanna grinned.

Dave smiled back, then shifted back to a frown as some words caught in his head. "What thing out there?"

With a sigh, Alanna shuffled over to offer him a seat at the window, and pointed out. "Every time I look away, it's there. It keeps getting closer, staying hidden. It's low to the ground, black, kinda hard to see. I haven't been able to tell where it's going, or what it is." She raised the binoculars back to her face.

"Hey, where did you get those?"

"What?"

"The binoculars. We didn't pack any," Dave reminded her.

Alanna looked at the optics in her hand, then back up at his deliberately-not-smug face. Then back down again, eyes widening. "Oh, for fuck's sake!" She smashed them down on the sill, shattering one of the lenses, then applied pressure until the middle bent just enough that the whole thing boiled away into dissipating dust, leaving only a small blue orb. "This fucking place," she muttered to herself, as Dave really tried not to grin.

Standing up, Dave headed back over to where James and Daniel were debating the reality of the map. Though the answer wasn't really in question for him.

Because when Dave looked at his friend these days, he wasn't seeing a random twenty-something nerd that he'd met through an acquaintance and a D&D game. He was seeing someone he trusted, someone he could rely on. He was looking at a person worth living up to.

James was going to direct them to the point on the map, even if it cost them time. He was going to bring Daniel and Theo into this, teach them how to delve—and he'd already had Dave working on getting Daniel into it—and teach them how to fight. Alanna would argue, but in the end, she'd do what was right too, because for all that she wanted to be pragmatic, she was just like James. Someone who *cared*.

And Dave? Well, Dave would be there when they got done rationalizing it. He'd have the bags packed, and his armor on, and he'd smile when James asked him to take rear guard so they could screen for anything Daniel and Theo couldn't handle.

Because this place was starting to make sense to him, he mused to himself, as he idly rolled one of the dozen small orbs they'd collected here between his fingers. And before he started his work, he cracked it, just out of mild curiosity.

[+1 Skill Rank : Law - Protocol - Civil Proceedings]

He smiled again. No objections, Your Honor.

CHAPTER 20

"All right, everyone ready to go?" Alanna asked the assembled group.

Bags had been re-sorted, gear distributed between five people, three duffels, and an indeterminate-but-large number of pockets. What loot there was had been safely stored, with the exception of the blue orb that Alanna kept close at hand. Weapons had been handed out, which had been a task to decide who got the guns; they ended up in the hands of Alanna for the shotgun, James for their pistol, and Daniel for the potato gun, which he helpfully pointed out was more of an improvised rail rifle than anything else and refused to call it anything involving potatoes. James and Theo also had the crowbars they'd packed, and Dave had a slightly-less-dollar-store machete in a faux-leather sheath at his side. It was James and Theo who got the mildly effective hockey pads, though the latter of the two complained about wearing someone else's sweat.

In short, the group looked like they'd just stepped out of a Fallout game. All that was missing was a Mohawk or two.

Well, almost the whole group. "Okay, let's . . . where the hell is James?" Alanna sighed. "Fuck's sake, we're on a clock here, guys."

"Don't blame us, we're not James," Daniel muttered defensively, and Alanna resisted the urge to thwack him in the back of the head. He was a decent kid, really, and if it were any other circumstance he was probably the kind of person they'd introduce here, but the more comfortable he grew with them, the more belligerent he seemed. But on the other hand, he'd only slept for a handful of hours on a hard carpet floor in the last two days, he'd been bitten by hostile hardware, and he was probably just generally put out about being fed to a sentient dimension. So she cut him some slack this time.

Alanna took a deep breath and tried to think up how to respond to that, but Dave came to her rescue as she massaged away a headache. "Okay, but where's James? We need to go, and he was literally here a second ago."

"Oh, he said he was going to the roof," Theo informed them.

Blank looks shared between Dave and Alanna. "Why?" Dave asked first.

"Something about putting up a flag?" Theo shrugged. "I figured it was tradition for you guys."

"We didn't fucking conquer this place." Alanna threw her free hand in the air, careful to keep her firearm pointed down at the ground. "It was basically empty anyway! No! No flag! James!" She projected her voice on that last word, making his name carry through their cubicle tower.

"Jeez, calm down," James himself said as he dropped down from the floor above them, choosing to ignore the offsize sloped steps. "Just because this place is clear doesn't mean you get to yelllllLLLLL!" His voice spiked into fear as a previously missed Taser-mouse dropped off the lip of the ceiling and started roll-crawling across his shirt.

He slammed his arm into the wall, then delivered several stomps to the stunned creature that punctuated the air with a series of wet, crinkling pops. By the time he stopped, all that was left was a crushed pile of plastic-chitin plates and a spray of crackling blue goo spread across the floor, with a small yellow orb sitting in it.

"That's fucking gross." Alanna pulled a face at the pile of exoskeleton shards and goop. "Also, what the hell were you doing upstairs? We're trying to get ready to leave, here."

James grinned back at the group and tossed Alanna a small object. It tumbled through the air before she caught it with her off hand and looked down to see a small silver laser pointer. "Meeting up with Santa," James said with barely held-back joy.

Alanna raised an eyebrow and pointed the small device down at the floor, triggering it to reveal not a single spot but what looked like a series of boxes broken up by small curves, covering maybe thirty square feet of floor. "Oh shit, this is our mapper! How'd you get this? Wait . . ."

Sensing his cue, Ganesh scrambled up off the back of James's head and leapt into the air, buzzing toward Alanna, who greeted him with a laugh and a raised palm. The drone, looking more and more like an organic thing every day, looped through the air as he came to alight on her hand, rotor wings buzzing as three of them folded up into curved, batlike wings. One of his forward wing claws stayed in position, though, and Alanna saw that he had a sleek-looking pen carefully attached with folded paper clips, the slightly smoking tip making it look like a horrifying lance in his grip. One of his other claws, though folded, also still clutched another laser pointer, though this one looked like it'd been hacked out of something else, with the nubs of cut wires still trailing out its end. He also bore a new scar: a hairline crack across the plate that housed his softly shimmering eyes. But despite Ganesh being heavily armed, and injured, Alanna still felt a surge of happiness to see him here.

Daniel, naturally, fell on his ass as soon as the drone took off, and Theo looked like she was about to try to crowbar it out of the air, before James casually stepped between them. "Before you ask, yes, this is another friend of ours. I called him."

"Oh, this is Ganesh?" Daniel asked with relief. "I mean, that makes sense, I was just surprised."

"Wait, how did he get here?" Alanna asked, letting the little drone crawl up her arm and perch on her shoulder, a personal and dangerous guardian angel. "How did he even find us? I refuse to believe you putting a flag up was enough. How far in are we anyway?"

"What? No," James replied, confused. "I called him. Well, okay, used the wireless camera app to contact him, but still. Remember? I told you."

She glared at him. "I promise you that you did not."

"Huh. Well. I told Daniel!" James said, inexplicably thinking that would help his case somehow.

Daniel nodded. "Yeah, he was telling me about your friends back at the entrance." He turned to address James. "And then you got weirdly excited about a power strip? Like you hadn't realized that there were outlets here. I mean, I've only been here for a little while, but I've been charging my phone and I didn't need magic to do it."

"We call it xenotech," Alanna informed him, running a hand across Ganesh's back and feeling the drone push into her fingers.

"Noooo, we do not." James sighed. "Also, look, I didn't really make the connection that the outlets actually worked. And my phone was dead for some reason, and I got really excited, and . . . oh, fuck it, go ahead and laugh." He waved casually in Alanna's direction, where she was desperately trying to hold back a smirk.

She opened her mouth, as if to start a good chuckle, then closed it again and settled on a peaceful smile. "Nah, it's fine. We make mistakes. Hasn't killed us yet."

"Oh, hey, did you want to taunt karma more before we step outside?" James asked, ruffling her hair as he walked past to the gap in the outside wall that led to the stairs.

"Sure!" she said too cheerfully. "What could possibly go . . ." she got out before everyone else drowned her out in a chorus of protests.

Theo shuddered as she did some warm-up stretches. "Even I know that's a stupid one to say," she muttered as she took a couple crowbar practice swings.

"All right. So. Here's the plan," James said, facing the other four as he stood by the door. "We've got . . . eighty hours, yeah. Eighty-ish hours to do this. I bet we can make the front door in two days, if Ganesh can fly here that fast. So the goal today is to follow Dave's head map, find the people that are supposedly there, get them back to here, and not fall into any obvious traps."

"Question." Theo raised a hand.

"You don't need . . . this isn't class." James pursed his lips at her and took a deep breath. "But go ahead, what's up?"

"What if it's an obvious trap?"

"Then we fight our way out and go straight for the exit. Then camp there for the rest of the time until the door opens. Either way, we need to check."

Alanna put her own hand in the air. "Question!"

Pinching the bridge of his nose, James sighed. "Yes, you in the back, the student who can't follow directions."

"Do we have a plan, vis-à-vis 'how to kill a dimension'?" She tried to phrase it lightly, to avoid reopening the argument between herself and James, but the weight was still there.

James didn't get offended, though. "No. Not yet. If this works out, and we can evac everyone, then maybe it won't be something we need to do. If the voice on the phone actually *is* telling the truth, and that's a big *if*, then it's possible that we can maybe rope the place off and remove the threat. But, well . . ."

"But then there's another dungeon somewhere," Dave finished, grimly.

"Yeah. Anyway. I love this place, really, but I'm not putting it ahead of human lives if it really is kidnapping and murdering people." James held up a hand to forestall Alanna's protest. "But! We'll see how it turns out. I'm not gonna set everything on fire just because it might be a threat. Now then, can . . . oh, fuck's sake. Yes, what's the question?" He pointed with resignation at Daniel's raised hand.

"Can I play with the laser pointer?" he asked timidly.

"Which one?" Alanna said cheerfully. "The one that Ganesh has that probably kills people, or the one that I have that makes maps?"

"That second one."

"Sure, yes. You're on double map duty. Now can we *please* get moving?" Alanna grumbled as she handed over the tool. Daniel nodded as he started fiddling with it, pointing it in various directions to start to get a feel for how it worked.

James nodded and looked over at Dave, who'd been mostly quiet. The other man met his eyes, and James would have sworn he saw Dave dip his head like he almost reflexively bowed. "Okay," he said calmly. "Theo, up front with me. Daniel, guide and fire support, Dave, keep an eye on him. Alanna, bring up the rear. Don't shoot . . ."

"Dude, don't lecture *me* on trigger discipline," she shot back before he could finish.

"You put, like, six holes in my floor."

"I plead the Fifth."

"That isn't . . . ! Look, just conserve ammo, okay? How many shells did you bring anyway?"

"Forty."

"What? Fucking how?"

"They're not that big, I just brought two boxes." She shrugged. "Anyway. I like your plan. Nice leadership. Go. Out the door. Shoo." Alanna flapped a hand in his direction and heard Ganesh make a buzzing laugh on her shoulder.

With a sigh, James turned his back on his friends, stepped back out into the unknown, and started making his way down the ramps and steps around the outside of the tower.

It was slow going at first. Even with firsthand knowledge that the creatures of this place weren't *all* rampaging murder machines, and that those that were could be fought and beaten, Theo and Daniel weren't comfortable enough to keep up a steady pace. James and Alanna were a bit annoyed at how slow they were going but did their best to hide it. Dave understood, though. Hell, he'd only been in here two or three times now, and he didn't understand how Alanna had adapted so quickly.

Seriously, he didn't understand how *James* had adapted so quickly, and that guy had been here way more often. Sometimes *alone*, which was insane. For his part, Dave tried to keep up, and as he learned the patterns of this place, he felt like he could tackle it without breaking. But he knew how Daniel and Theo felt. They'd just had their world turned upside down, and they were normal people. They didn't have a buffer of nerdy game nights and escapist fantasies to ease the transition.

Well, probably. He'd have to talk to Daniel sometime.

"Is that a trap?" They pulled up to a stop as Theo spoke, Alanna briefly glancing over her non-Ganeshed shoulder to check before crouching down to a kneeling pose and watching behind them. "No, really. Is this bad?" Theo repeated with her voice uncertain.

"No," James said. "This is paper clips. Stop freaking out over everything. Daniel! Bolt cutters!"

Daniel felt a bit like he'd been relegated to a sort of pack mule, but then, they'd also given him a homemade rail rifle that fired rebar, so he didn't complain as he slung the bag off his shoulder and unzipped it.

"Not a trap?" Theo confirmed, quietly.

"Nah, these things are just around. They're like spikier cobwebs," James said as he started clipping through the outside edges of the metal net that covered the hall in front of them. "Keep an eye out for anything, though," he told Theo, who instantly stood to attention and started flicking her eyes around at any spot a threat might come from. James rolled his eyes when she wasn't looking; it was good to be alert, but doing that was a good way to exhaust yourself. He didn't think Theo would listen to him right now, though, so he held off saying anything. She'd learn soon enough, or Alanna would tell her in that way that Alanna did that made people actually listen.

While James did his job, Alanna moved back to the last intersection they'd passed about five cubicle lengths back, and crouched at the corner of it, checking down each aisle. Dave, meanwhile, took the time to talk to Daniel.

"Okay, you see that?" He pointed into the cubicle to their left.

Daniel looked up nervously. "No? Wait, the potted plant? Oh fuck, is that going to kill us?"

"Why does everyone think everything here is going to kill them?" James softly called back from the front, which made Dave smile a bit before going back to talking to Daniel.

"No, it's not one of the live ones. Though there are live ones, and you should keep an eye out. But they're always bigger. Like, fake trees, you know?" Daniel nodded at his words, and Dave got back to his original point. "Look, the point is, those are often nest points for striders. So when we go over there in a second, that's one of the things you want to keep an eye on while we steal stuff."

Daniel made a small noise in the back of his throat. "Wait, why don't we just stay here and keep moving?"

"Because sometimes we find things that could save our lives," Dave said. "And if we do have to fight, then we get orbs out of it. Also, it'll be good practice for you if we get into a threat situation later, so you don't freeze up, and get us killed." He said it in his normal, even tone, but it was blunt and clear that Daniel didn't appreciate it much.

The probably-ex-security-guard almost snapped at Dave but held it back and instead just stood up and hoisted the too-heavy homemade rifle. "Fine. Whatever. Anything else I should know?"

"Pencil sharpeners are always traps. Desk lamps are *almost* always traps. Don't touch a computer until you can verify it's not a shellaxy, but after that, try to find the password. Some of the files are magic, and some of them are just weird media that James collects. If you see anything moving, talk to it first, and if it doesn't meaningfully respond, kill it."

"That seems harsh."

"Things that aren't hostile make it clear pretty quick." Dave shrugged. "Now, usually cubes are safe. So you go first, I'll follow, and we'll get you used to this." Daniel felt like this was a hunting trip with his asshole dad all over again. Too many instructions he wasn't going to remember, and too much pressure to perform well. Fortunately, without really realizing he was soothing an angry fear, Dave said one last thing. "Don't worry about getting it all at once. We're here to keep you guys alive until we get out. It's why we came in, right?"

It was. Daniel felt all his anger at Dave drain away in a flash. It was why they came in. These three had dropped into what was, minimum, a weeklong trek through enemy territory, for *him*. And also Theo, but still.

He got up and walked confidently into the cubicle, with Dave behind him.

Back out in the hallway, James was trying to get Theo to be a little less jittery as he cut through the last of the right side of the net. "I'm just saying, you can ease off. Humans notice things; you'll be fine. But if you're hurting your damn eyes looking at literally everything at once, then you'll have a headache in two minutes."

"I'm fine," Theo snapped back. "You should take this more seriously."

"I really shouldn't," James snorted. "I've got a big enough paladin complex already, I don't need to pile more on it. Besides, we—"

He never got to finish that, as Theo tapped him furiously on the shoulder and pointed up at one of the sloped chunks of wall over their heads. "There!" she barked out, raising her crowbar in a sweaty hand. "Did you see that?"

"No, because *you're* on watch," James replied smoothly, dropping the bolt cutters and hoisting his own metal bar. He missed his axe already; they'd gone back to the classic improvised weapon for this kind of smashing work, but it didn't feel good in his hands at *all*. James was still annoyed they couldn't find anything better, but they were on short notice, so he'd live with it. "What did you see?"

Theo let out a long "uhhhh" as she kept her eyes up, while James stood up and positioned himself at her right at arm's length with his crowbar held loosely to his side. "It looked like a bunch of paper?"

"Paper like printer paper, or paper like sticky notes?" James asked, keeping his cool as best he could.

"Oh! Definitely like sticky notes. Why, is that—"

"Budgettttt cuttttttts!" screamed the face-shaped collection of layered Post-it notes as it came flying down from between the bars of beige that made up the canopy overhead.

"Fuck offffff!" James shouted back at it as it howled down, tendrils of coiled purple sticky notes trailing behind it like fluttering hair. He tried to get his weapon up to knock it out of the air but wasn't in position to hit it solidly, and the mask just warped around the metal bar before launching itself off and past them, some of the flapping scraps of paper that dragged behind it lashing at James's arm as it went past, leaving shallow cuts and welts on the patches of exposed skin as it did so.

Theo whipped herself around as the thing flew behind them and made a sharp U-turn just past the cut-down net. "What the fuck is that?"

"Screaming mask made of Post-it notes. Duh," James told her. "Eyes up, I think there's more. You got that one?"

"No!"

"Good. I'll take these." He pushed her back toward the first mask with his left hand while watching as three more of the strange creatures perched above them on a beam like paper vultures. These were more contorted forward to look down on James, and he could see them clinging to the carpeted material that made up the ceiling with the bone spurs that came out their back. Almost like bats, really.

"Coffffeeeee." "Overrrrworrrrkeeeeddd." "Trippliicaaaattteeee!"

Really annoying bats.

"Dave! Get out here!" he called out to the cubicle that he had taken Daniel into. "Alanna! Help!" No response from her, still positioned at the intersection, and James didn't have time to wait. The first of the masks dropped down, and he brought a big, wasteful overhand swing down on it, pinning the fucker to the ground with raw force and weight.

James stomped on it, finding it very uneven footing, but still kept it underfoot as he wobbled a bit on the rounded shapes of the bones in it. Before he could get his crowbar back up, though, the other one slammed into his shoulder and started trying to flay away the side of his face with the razor-sharp edges of its hair, using the bone spikes to gouge into the low-quality plastic of his "body armor." As the third one came swooping down as well, James abandoned subtlety and just flung the crowbar at it, smashing it up into the ceiling with a loud thud and a scream from the mask as it tried to recover in midair from the hit.

Without wasting time worrying about how stupid it was to throw away his main weapon, James grabbed the mask off his shoulder and flung it to the ground. Or tried to. It caught itself somehow and swooped away like a rogue paper airplane, curving around behind him. Pivoting, James saw it going for Theo's back and lunged to stop it.

But Theo had just dealt with hers, and when she turned, the first thing she saw was another monster bearing down on her. So she did what she'd been advised, and hit it. Hard. The fact that the crowbar swing also caught James in the forearm was kind of a problem, but the mask broke before his arm did.

"Fucking ow!" he screamed, like a big baby. "Careful!"

Theo wanted to yell something at him about how she was fighting for her life, and being careful was for people who didn't survive that experience. But she was too busy trying to catch her breath and figure out how to swallow when her mouth tasted and felt like cotton.

"Contraaaccct terrrmiiinnn . . ." James brought his heel down on the last mask in a brutal stomp that stung his ankle, even as it splintered the bone and tore the paper of the false face. Then he reached down to grab the yellow orb and crack it just out of spite.

[+2 Skill Ranks - Marketing]

"Fuck these things," he muttered. "Dave! You guys alive? Alanna?" he called down the hall. Grabbing his crowbar, he turned to Theo, who recoiled back as she saw the blood dripping down the side of his face from a score of cuts against his cheek and forehead. "Go check on Alanna," he said, then realized she was shaking, and probably not in a condition to check on anyone. "No, wait. Wait here, keep watch."

Dave was on his own for a second. James scampered down the hallway, keeping low, and that was lucky as over his head the corpse of another mask got nailed to the wall by a piece of rebar with a low *thoomp* noise from the potato gun. It wouldn't have hit him, probably, but he felt better that it didn't hit him *more*.

Okay, Dave was doing fine. Or at least Daniel was. But Alanna and Ganesh weren't reacting at all, and James had a gnawing feeling in his gut as the worst-case scenarios flashed through his mind. Sliding up to the corner, he tapped Alanna on the shoulder. "Hey, what's . . ."

She wasn't moving. Not that she was dead, but she literally wasn't moving. At all. Eyes open, frozen, Ganesh on her shoulder the same way. Her shotgun gripped in both hands, half raised.

"Theo!" he nearly screamed. "Someone! Help!"

It was Dave who got to him first, as Theo got caught up with a straggler mask that screeched about break times as it tried to slip past her batter's stance. His friend ducked out of the cubicle where he'd left Daniel and slid into a crouch next to James. "What do you need?"

"Cross the hall," James told him, setting his crowbar down and unclipping the pistol from its holster.

It said a lot about Dave's trust in James that he didn't really hesitate. He took a look at the handgun that James had in a practiced two-handed grip as his friend popped the safety off, then nodded once, stood up, and sprinted across the intersection.

Halfway across, he saw the camraconda that was staring down Alanna and Ganesh. Then he saw the second one that was slithering down the middle of the dead-end aisle that they'd ignored earlier, long copper fangs dripping some kind of black fluid as it closed in. He skidded to a halt midsprint, hefted his now-nicked machete, and charged them. "Two! Two!" he yelled, hoping James got it.

He knew he was never going to make it. But that was okay. Dave trusted his companions.

When James saw Dave freeze in midstep, he moved. Popping out from around the corner, reflexes that he'd only ever felt in the abstract from a skill orb kicked into action. The cracking sound of gunshots drowned out everything else for a second as he unloaded on the boxy security camera face of the far left camraconda. The basilisk never had a chance; while James wasn't a crack shot, at least half his bullets were on target, and the creature had chunks of hard plastic blown away piecemeal until it just collapsed, dead.

Just under James, Alanna jerked back into motion, the long barrel of the Mossberg coming up to bear on the head of the snake just in front of her. But before she could pull the trigger, or James could retarget, it snapped its head back around to look at them, and they were all shocked into motionless statues.

But James was grinning down at it, and the camraconda couldn't even turn to retreat as Dave circled around to its side, machete held at the ready as he closed on its flank.

"You shouldn't have fucked with us," Dave told it in a deadpan voice that he almost certainly thought sounded cool as he stood over it and drove the blade down at its head.

At the very last second, it turned, and he froze, and the shotgun slug shredded a rough hole in it where it used to have a face.

Contrary to what movies show you, or how it's normally spelled out, shotguns don't really make *a* noise. They don't have a sound effect, they have a wall of ear-static that feels like listening to the concept of being hit by a hammer. And in the aftermath of the deafening sound, the three of them took a moment to recover.

But only a moment, as they'd just alerted everything in a two-mile radius that they weren't supposed to be here.

"Dave, orbs! Alanna, get Daniel, we're moving!" James shouted to hear himself talk as he policed his brass, scooping up the discarded shell along with the casings for his own bullets. No need to give the dungeon literal ammo. He didn't waste time either, reholstering the pistol, grabbing the crowbar, and moving to the front. "Theo, you alive?" He clapped her on the shoulder where she was looking down at her empty hand.

"How do the balls do that?" she asked.

"Magic," James said. "Look, we gotta go. This time, we *really* made too much noise. Focus on how you know kung fu later, we're moving," he said as he turned to take stock of the rest of the team.

Alanna was shaken, but unhurt. Ganesh looked like he was still dizzy from the noise of the gunfire but also operational. Daniel had a couple cuts on him and was currently sans weapon. And Dave . . . Dave looked like he was absolutely confident.

"Where's the potato gun?" James asked with a raised eyebrow.

"One of the masks cut the fuel tank on it, so I took the lighter and told him to leave it," Dave said. "I didn't want it to explode."

"Yeah, that only needs to happen once." James nodded. "Also, we need to get more durable *guns*. Or, *more* durable guns." He changed the emphasis, the first time saying weapons that were durable, then switching to saying more weapons, after he remembered the pistol at his side and the smell of gunpowder on his hands. "Okay, let's go. Daniel! Which way?"

It took a second for the kid to figure it out, the fighting having maybe scrambled his brain. They didn't wait, instead pushing forward ahead of the telltale clicking of at least a small horde of striders in their wake. But after he got his bearings, the directions started flowing, and their speed picked up.

"Right here, then a hundred feet, then a left. Then there's something weird in the walls?" he called forward as they jogged, trying to parse the laser pointer map, compared to the map in his head, as they ran. It wasn't easy, but he was keeping up, and since Dave and Alanna were swatting down the few striders that tried to lunge for them off the walls, he wasn't being interrupted by head trauma nearly as much as he might have otherwise been. "Here! Left here!" he called, and James and Theo took the corner ahead of them.

James realized "something about the walls" meant traps almost as soon as they turned the corner and he felt that low EM hum that the trip wires for the pencil darts put out. James put on speed and made a clear show of leaping over the line in the carpet for Theo, who mimicked him and cleared the trigger. "Darts!" he yelled back, which was enough to get Dave and Alanna over the line safe, but Daniel had to be caught by Alanna before he face-planted into the trigger.

There were advantages to being Alanna's size, and physically lifting people up before they could touch the thing that killed you was one of them.

"Where now?" she prompted as she shoved Daniel back into motion, reconfiguring their line as James and Theo waited at the end of the hallway. "Actually, break, my throat's burning," she rasped out as she fished out a bottle of water.

"Yeah, I think we're clear," James said. "Take five. But let's keep putting distance between us. If we can find a place to rest before we get to the 'prisoners,' that's great, but I don't want to linger anywhere here." He accepted the bottle from Alanna and poured a gulp of warm water into his mouth. "Eugh. We should have brought ice."

"Whiner." She poked him and took the bottle back.

"But seriously. None of us want to be around when a swarm shows up."

Dave, panting and leaning on a wall to stay upright, gasped out a rebuttal. "Yeah, but we need to be careful where we can, or we'll make stupid mistakes." He met James's eyes, then flicked his own gaze back to Daniel, who was poking at the bandage on his leg and complaining about it itching.

"Yeah, okay," James said after a second, realizing that he'd never really seen Dave stand up for his own opinion before. "Yeah. Yeah, you're right. We'll slow down. Daniel, you see anything on the map that looks like a rest spot?" James conceded the point, in his head knowing it was the right call. He'd gotten too wrapped up in everything, too excited. He actually needed Dave here to keep him grounded in the more basic stuff. Alanna would see things from a different perspective than him, and ask important questions, but she was just like James when it came to getting caught up in the mood of adventure.

Daniel pointed the laser map at the floor before remembering that it didn't work that way, and turned it up to a wall to see what was ahead of them. "Well, there's this big open space up ahead. I dunno what that is, but it's . . . actually huge?" He sounded puzzled as he pulled the pointer back farther and farther to reveal a larger circular gap in the map. "We have to go through there anyway, I think. Um . . . does anyone else feel like that . . . no, never mind."

"No, you can say it. It looks like a boss fight, doesn't it? Like, if I saw that on a map in a game, I'd be pretty paranoid." James sighed. "No helping it, though. Hey, move the pointer closer to the ground, let's see if there's anything stalking around in there."

"Actually, wait, point it *at* the ground again," Alanna said.

"Why? It shows a cross section," James said.

She nodded. "That's my point. Look. Look!" Alanna pointed at the floor as Daniel casually tilted it down, looking like he didn't know what the big deal was. Alanna clicked her tongue in disappointment as she realized James didn't get it either. "Okay, if it shows a slice of what it's looking at, then . . ." She spread her hands.

"Then why isn't the floor a solid block," James said, looking at the pattern of lines on the floor. "Ah." There was a moment of silence before the experienced trio let out a collective sigh-and-shrug. "There's no way we can do anything about that now. But if we find an elevator, how about we just ignore it?"

"Agreed."

They wrapped up their break, taking the moment to rub the ache out of tired legs and arms, and for Alanna to clean out and tape a flat bandage to the cuts on the side of James's face. It felt like all the pain of the injuries was only just catching up with him, including the blood loss. It couldn't have been that *much*, but he felt light-headed enough that he took Alanna up on her offer when she handed him a candy bar labeled Caramel Opinions without a second thought.

And after that, there were only a few hundred feet and a couple corners before that huge room that separated them from the final stretch to their goal. Be it a trap, a graveyard, or a prison, they were going to have to go through here to find out.

"Okay," James said as they moved down the final hallway, brushing aside a vine of dot-matrix paper. "Everyone be on guard." Words that were totally unneeded—the tension was thick around them.

At the end of the hall, a curtain of plastic file folders blocked their view. Looking back and getting nods from the rest of the group, James reached forward and pushed one aside to reveal the cavern beyond.

It was dark. The walls rose up thirty or forty feet here, and there weren't many lights overhead. Those that were didn't filter down much through the high, curved ceiling. But what light did come through was . . . beautiful. It sparkled as it danced across the surface of the lake in front of them. The whole place was peaceful, placid. Nothing moved, no enemies in sight.

James stepped through and gazed around, lowering his weapon. He almost jumped out of his skin when something fell from the ceiling near him, but after a second and third repeat of the motion, he realized that it was drops of water. Falling from above and . . . into a water cooler tank?

Everyone else filtered in behind him, staring around. "What the hell . . ." Theo spoke aloud, and for once, James didn't think she was overreacting.

As his eyes adjusted, he could see around them. From the floor, dozens, maybe a hundred blue solid plastic tanks appeared to be *growing*. Or maybe they were formed and shaped like stone stalagmites were in real cave systems. Either way, they sat there as if melded into the floor by an ancient hand, many of them half full of sloshing water that always seemed to be in slight motion even as the room itself felt still.

And all around, glittering drops of liquid caught beams of light as they fell from above. From where wasn't clear, but every single drop always impacted perfectly on one of the tanks. And around those drops danced tiny glowing dots of light that glinted off thin metal bodies, barely visible from the ground.

In the middle of the room, taking up about two-thirds of the whole space, was a single massive body of water. It dipped down, perfectly clear and visible, for maybe a hundred feet. Edges smoothed and vertical. And all of it could be seen with clarity, through the floor and walls of the interior of this cavern that were all shaped from that same clear, blue, water-cooler plastic.

"What in the hell . . ." someone echoed with quiet reverence. James realized in the silence afterward that it had been him. Even Ganesh's casual wing vibrations had gone still.

Every time. Every time he thought they'd gotten a handle on the dungeon and seen it all, it threw them another curve ball. There were always more patterns of cubicles, sure, and there were always new creatures and different formations of attack. But this was qualitatively different; this might as well have been a different world.

A quiet, peaceful dungeon, one that made nothing but fireflies and waterfalls, would have made this the most romantic place that James or Alanna could have brought the other to today.

Without too many words, the six of them sat to rest in earnest before they went to war again.

CHAPTER 21

No one was happy.

James snarled as he caught a projected strip of tape. Twisting his wrist around and gripping a handful of it, he yanked the thing it was attached to off its perch. The tape dispenser hit the ground with a grinding noise; they'd started encountering these things about five miles back. They moved a lot like striders, only their legs were composed of the blades of scissors instead of pens. Also unlike striders, they had extruding eyes: two big bulbous *things* that they could unspool like string and that made them impossible to get the drop on. They used their tape like toad tongues, lashing out to try to yank the human intruders off balance. And they were surprisingly strong; even if they were large for what they were, they were still office supplies.

Oh, and instead of a small strip of serrated metal to tear the tape on, it had a maw of whirling steel that was physically wider than the space the creature occupied.

Because of course it did.

James slammed his crowbar into the side of it, regretting the loss of his glove as the impact opened a small tear in the flesh between his thumb and index finger, even as the tapier indented on the side from the hit and skidded across the desktop, sending papers and miscellaneous junk flying.

Behind him, Alanna knelt with her back pressed against a wall, trying to stem the bleeding from a mangled hand, burning through the last of their bandages. Her shotgun lay flat on the floor next to her, on top of the tattered ribbons that used to be her coat. She moved with the edge of someone who was trying very, very hard to not be frantic in their motions. Which was hard as she dripped her life out onto the floor.

But with the last tapier down—and James made sure it was truly dead—there was no more of a rush. The sounds of chitin crunching into shards from the cubicle next to them confirmed that Theo and Dave had taken care of their own problem as well.

Not that James needed to hear that to know what had happened. The adjacent cubicle was wide open to them, from where Daniel had been toppled through the wall, bringing it down to lean at an angle against the desk with Daniel himself still lying on top of it, temporarily unconscious. He'd been startled by the movement of a shellaxy, then further pushed over by that same shellaxy in its boxy case ramming him in the knees. Fortunately, the cubicles they were in weren't really cubicle-sized anymore, and there was ample room for him to head-butt the ground without distracting James and Alanna from their skirmish, or Dave from carefully trying to figure out how to disarm the pencil sharpener on the desk.

The fight had escalated, though they'd kept control through it. They kept everything away from Dave so he could do his work on the trap that they'd already triggered but hadn't fired yet. Theo acquitted herself pretty well for the first fight where no one had the time to give her directions, moving to tackle the mobile device that was going after Daniel's ankles and spreading the group out to both of the den-sized cubes. Ganesh also continued his role as air support; everyone had sort of gotten used to his aggressive flybys midbattle as the drone lanced down ambushing enemies with the nuclear pen that he carried.

And now everything was quiet again. One more skirmish survived.

"Daniel's still out." Theo broke the quiet as she checked on the downed security kid. "Alive, though." She was panting slightly; her athletic background and physical edge over James and Dave had let her keep up, but they'd been going for a long time now, and exhaustion was starting to set in. "Can we . . ." She thudded to her knees and leaned back against the propped-up wall like it was a bed. "Can we take a nap?"

Dave tossed James a red orb and missed wildly, the sphere going to bounce off Alanna's head as she poked her bandage into a secure position. "I wouldn't mind." Dave slurred his words.

Alanna just nodded, digging some water out of a bag and taking sips to clear the gum out of her mouth.

They'd been on their feet for almost fifteen hours since the water cooler break. Daniel had led them through twisting halls that grew less and less straight and more and more narrow as they moved. They took constant pauses to map out upcoming sections, to plan for ambushes, and to set up their own traps for pursuing life forms. It felt like every ten minutes they were bandaging wounds, draining down their water supplies, reloading, re-arming, shuffling around equipment, or just trying to turn something they'd found into a usable weapon.

Dave was wearing a cloak made out of dot-matrix paper that couldn't tear. Theo had a cobbled polearm made out of the leg of a chair, with a monofilament-edged protractor tied very carefully to the end of it. There was a fire extinguisher that Alanna kept porting around, insisting that it would come in handy eventually, that it *unextinguished* anything it was sprayed on; the obvious downside that the thing had to have at one point been on fire didn't stop her from seeing it as potentially useful.

And their stockpile of orbs had swelled with each combat. It felt like as they went deeper and deeper into the office, the creatures not only got stranger but more hostile as well. Dave had a series of pinprick holes on his wrist now from where an iLipede turned out to be more thirsty than friendly, and talking it out was getting less and less useful. This, of course, meant more fighting, but also more rewards. They'd initially intended to save them for absorbing the yellows if they needed to stay awake, but now, they'd run out of space and had started cracking the smaller ones.

As ranks in car insurance policies and Australian parliament etiquette trickled in, it was Alanna who got the first immediately useful skill with *[+1 Skill Rank : Perception - Battlefield]*. After that, she'd almost immediately become their shot caller. It wasn't that her eyes were any better, but simply that even during the frantic chaos of a life-and-death situation, Alanna would now better spot details that made the difference. She and Ganesh worked together like a unified mind sometimes, with simple hand gestures from the tall woman flicking the drone-knight out to strike down striders or masks that were encroaching on blind spots.

A couple fights later, Theo had gotten *[+1 Skill Rank : Medical - First Aid - Triage]*. And even though it was too specific to be of any huge boost, it still put her on par with the rest of them in terms of keeping cuts and punctures clean and protected.

Those small gains, though, were fleeting moments of elation among the grinding pace that they'd set for themselves. When they got too tired to go on, they'd sit for ten minutes in a cubicle, then keep going, pushing forward. When ten minutes turned to fifteen, then twenty, then thirty, they all knew that they were running up against a wall.

And all of that was compounded on the gradual wearing away of resources. Water, they could probably find more of; most of the normal water coolers in this place seemed to be just that, normal. Food, also, could be supplemented with candy and weirdly well-preserved bag lunches. But shotgun shells were a finite resource, and Alanna hadn't been holding back on that front. Especially not after they realized that there were enough ambient noises in this part of the dungeon, some of them *quite loud and startling*, that gunfire wasn't going to trigger hordes every time. Similarly, James had been called upon to sublimate a pair of tumblefeeds that had almost ripped Dave in half, bringing his own internal ammo supply down to only five uses left, if he was counting his practice uses correctly. Not having an actual way to count shots on that was deeply annoying.

They were getting tired.

"How far away are we, anyway?" James asked out loud as he leaned forward on the desk. Idly, he pressed down on the orb from the tapier as he waited for an answer. "We've gotta be close. Right?"

[+1 Skill Rank : Music - Metal - Folk - Tunisian]

Alanna swallowed hard before answering. "You know Daniel's still not awake, right?"

"Fuck," James muttered. Then he said it again, as his exhausted brain caught up to the skill notification. "Fuck." It felt like he was thinking through a layer of heavy cotton, and it itched against the inside of his skull. Still, while everyone else sat, he felt restless. Like he just couldn't stop his hands from trying to do work. So he swept the remains of the tapier off the desk and started going through cabinets. The shelves here all held the exact same photo of a young girl in a blue dress, except the background changed in each one. Normal James would have looked at that and rolled his eyes at the random nature of the dungeon; tired James looked at it and flinched as something deeply uncanny rooted itself in the fear portion of his mind. Looking back to the boxy wooden containers on either side of the computer monitor, he popped one open and started rifling through it. The he swore a third time, but loudly. "Fuck!" he yelled as he jumped backward, heart pumping.

"What?!" Alanna dragged herself up with her good hand, dropping to a kneeling position and scrabbling for her shotgun while she looked around.

James caught his breath and tried to suppress the bitter taste of terror in his mouth. "Nothing. Sorry! Nothing! It's . . . there's a . . ." He let out a shaky breath that was half sigh, half mocking chuckle. Reaching into the cupboard, he pulled out the stuffed fox that had greeted him when he opened it and tossed it at Alanna. "Found the employee with the Beanie Baby stash," he said with attempted humor.

No one laughed.

They were just too on edge. Theo was right. It was time to take a break. But they were down to around two and a half days left to make it out, and every day that they spent going deeper was one day less they had to leave.

But there was no helping it. Not now.

"Okay, let's break for a little while." James looked over at where Daniel was still sleeping on the broken cubicle wall. "Actually, hey, Alanna, can you . . ." He paused. "Dave, actually. Help me lift this up."

The two of them, after some quick explanation and rolling Daniel onto the floor, where he started to groan as he finally woke up, maneuvered the wall onto the roof of the cubicle. Despite the slanted nature of the walls, it was still a solid fit, and they had to circle around outside to push it into place, where James was promptly assaulted by a strider from the lip of another cubicle across the narrow hallway.

[+1 Skill Rank : Puzzles - Number]

"Why is everything in here so fucking suicidal?!" James demanded, rubbing his shoulder where the stapler had slammed into him. Dave could only give him a shrug in response, as much in the dark as his friend was.

It took them a little while to intentionally break down the wall of another cubicle to cap off the other side of their own, and actually getting it high enough to slide on was tricky given how tall the walls were here. After that, though, blocking off the doors with filing cabinets and tables was easy enough.

James looked around the now darkened room, lit by the single camp lantern they'd brought along. Theo was already lying down, stretched out on the remains of her coat and using the hockey pads as a shitty pillow. Alanna, similarly, had her back against the far wall from the doors, propped up against a duffel bag, one hand on her Mossberg, eyes drooping as she tried to keep herself watchful.

Didn't seem like she'd be the best guard, to James. Not that he could blame her, as he had that feeling of cold warmth in his hands and legs. Like if he blinked, he might drop asleep in the instant his eyes were closed.

"Dave," he said softly, and his friend looked over. "Get some sleep. Ganesh and I have watch."

Dave looked at him strangely. "You need to sleep too," he yawned out. "How..." He looked down when James held up a yellow orb.

"I've got first watch. It's not perfect, but I'll wake you up in..." James focused. He needed to keep moving, he needed to be awake, alert, ready. This thing in his hand was nothing more than a complex meal. He wrapped his brain around it, and then pulled and watched it sink into his skin.

[+3.25 *Operational Hours : Ready*]

Fatigue didn't just fade away. It was gone, entirely, in one moment. For a second, James was both dead on his feet and snapping his eyes open in wakefulness. Then it faded, and he felt... well, ready. Prepared. Good to go, for whatever challenges were coming.

"Three hours." He finished his sentence to Dave. "You okay with a short nap?"

"Oh, yeah," Dave answered with a waved hand. "I don't need a lot of sleep."

"You always say that, but then you're always oversleeping game night..."

"I don't need a lot of sleep *in this situation*."

"Fine." James actually laughed at that one.

Fifteen minutes later, Dave had passed out under a desk, Theo was now fast asleep, Alanna had dropped off, and Daniel had used the rest of their bags and salvaged coats to build himself a nest before drifting to sleep himself. Even Ganesh was sleeping. Though the little drone power-cycled much faster than his human companions, it turned out that he did still need something like sleep.

It was strange to James how alone he could feel in a room full of people. This wasn't like a childhood sleepover where he was the last one awake. Instead, it felt like he was in an empty house, where every creak of the floor was a monster sneaking up on him. Defenseless and alone, all on his own against the night.

"Not alone." The whisper in his ear this time didn't shock him. For some reason, nothing Secret ever did came as a true surprise to James, even when he didn't actually know what was happening.

James didn't even need to glance to his left to see Secret there, the pale blue serpent half-present in the physical world. It constantly amused him that his friend sometimes wore a half-remembered copy of James's own coat when he was among the real. "But where are we?" Secret asked.

"Pretty far in," James said in a soft tone, and Secret bobbed his head in acknowledgment. "From what I got from Daniel before he zonked out, we're about a mile away from where his mental map leads."

"Ah, yes, the Map," Secret whispered in disdain, somehow managing to pronounce the proper noun with a capital letter. "I do not trust them."

James sighed. "So it's a meme, then?" he asked, and got a nod in answer. "Well, shit. But hey, that doesn't mean it's instantly hostile." James laid a hand on Secret's flank, careful to avoid the eyes as he petted the leviathan. "You're here, after all."

"I am special," Secret replied matter-of-factly, and James was suddenly struck with the urge to laugh at how much his friend sounded like a teenager. Then he remembered that Secret was only a couple months old, tops, depending on how you looked at it, and it got a little less funny.

"So, where have you been, anyway? It's been a bit hectic down here," James asked, trying not to sound hostile about it. Even though he knew he had a lingering feeling of annoyance at the thoughtform for seemingly ditching them.

Secret wasn't offended, though. "I have been exploring as well. It is good that you are here, and I can rest within your space, because there is something else within this place. At first I thought it was the walls and floors, but now, I suspect that the places I have been are not places at all, but a person."

"Person in the sense . . ." James started, but was cut off.

"Another like me. But not. And also orders of magnitude larger. Older, as well. It has the feel of my core, though. Secrecy and deception," the meme answered, and for the first time, James thought he sounded worried.

James tried to give a casual shrug, but Secret was heavier than he looked. "Don't worry," he told his friend. "I think it's just the thing that keeps blanking people that come in here from everyone's minds. Some kind of memetic security system. If it were actually sentient, we'd already be dead, right?"

"That is not at all reassuring," Secret huffed.

"Yeah, sorry, I'm working on that." James grinned back at him. "Anyway. It's quiet and I've got three hours before I wake Dave up. Got any ideas? I'm already bored."

"Yes." Secret coiled himself around James until he laid his serpentine head onto his friend's lap. "You could tell me a story."

James held back a burst of laughter, not wanting to wake anyone up. But then, realizing Secret wasn't kidding, he took a small breath, paused, and asked, "Aren't you inside my head? Why do you need me to tell you things I know?"

"I've never been able to read your mind, not in the way you mean. Your memories are no grand library to me," Secret replied. "Though when you dream, it feels . . . familiar. And I remember how you felt when your father would read you to sleep at night when you were younger. Is it strange, to miss something I have never had?" he asked.

There was a long moment that stretched on into the false night of their campsite. Outside, there was the *thunk* of an air-conditioning unit cycling, and the skittering of a dozen things moving around. Bars of white light pierced through the few uncovered slots, but not enough to break the gloom, just enough to highlight the outside. James sat, not exactly thinking, but feeling something, letting his brain process. No matter how many orbs he took in, no matter how much it could wake him up, nothing could really undo mental exhaustion like sleep, it seemed.

But after a couple minutes of the two of them sitting there, one human, one idea, keeping an eye on the others, James started to speak. And Secret closed his eyes, and listened.

"Once upon a time, there was a princess in a prison tower, and a dragon that she made her friend . . ."

CHAPTER 22

Turns out, Dave hadn't been lying about only needing a little sleep, much to James's surprise. When he nudged the shorter guy awake with his foot, Dave had snapped his eyes open like he'd been actively waiting to get up, rolled out from under the desk he was at, and took the crowbar from James with an almost ceremonious nod. He looked like he was prepared to change watch shifts without even saying anything.

Obviously, James was genetically incapable of that.

"Jeez, you wake up fast," he commented idly. "You doing okay?"

"Weird dreams" was all Dave answered, rubbing at his eyes. He blinked a few times, then cocked his head as he noticed a pile of random things assembled next to where James was sitting. "Um . . ."

"Sounds about par for the course around here," James replied before following his friend's gaze. "Oh. So, I got kinda bored around hour two when Secret fell asleep, and there was literally nothing happening. I think our ceiling works too well. So I kinda just started checking everything in here for enchantments."

Dave blinked slowly, then nudged the pile of everything that James had been tinkering with. The first thought through his mind was that James was blatantly wrong about what "working too well" meant. The second one, he asked out loud, aimed at the second pile of actual junk: "Did you just start breaking things when you couldn't figure the items out?"

This got him a scowl in return. "That's slander," James replied. "Also here, I got two small blues out of it, you can have one."

"Thanks," Dave said with what he probably thought was a dry chuckle, and James felt a flash of annoyance at the other guy.

He knew, intellectually, that this was what happened when his brain went for too long without downtime. The orb made him feel physically alert, and even let him think clearly, but it didn't replace actually decompressing or even just having a little time alone to process things. And now that his mental defenses weren't quite so sharp, he was reminded that the reason he never spent a lot of time with Dave outside of game night was that his friend had a lot of small quirks that added up to a socially exhausting person to deal with.

"Well," James said, in lieu of expressing any anger. "I think I have about five minutes of orb left. So I'm gonna get comfortable and sleep a bit. You okay on watch for a few hours?" Dave nodded. He knew the plan. Before he could start talking and explaining the whole thing, though, James rolled on. "You know, I never actually asked Anesh what it feels like when the orb runs out? Or if I did, I don't remember?"

"Really?"

"Yeah, like, I'm assuming I just go back to feeling how I was?" James mused.

Dave looked thoughtful. "What if it adds up the time the orb deferred?" he asked.

"Well, that's a great thought, thanks," James half-snapped back as he turned his tattered coat into a pillow, and another long jacket salvaged from the dungeon into a blanket. "A painful exhaustion headache is exactly what I need to look forward . . ."

Dave looked over. James was slumped half-covered by his blanket, every muscle relaxed, like a puppet with its strings cut. He almost worried for a second, until a light snore informed him that James really was just asleep. "Guess that's how it feels," Dave said to no one in particular.

They woke up one by one a few hours after that. Even James, who looked like he'd be dead to the world for the full human eight hours, let out a sharp hiss of breath only shortly after Alanna rolled herself upright, and pushed himself up with his arms, the coats that Dave had piled on him sloughing off like the patchwork blankets they were.

Everyone one of them came back to the world differently. For Daniel, it was with a groggy groan, as the aches of being tackled through a wall caught up with him. With Alanna, it was in the same way that she normally woke up: casually fading back to reality with a languid stretch and getting up almost right away. Theo also got up rapidly, though her movements weren't so uncaring about the situation as she bolted to her feet with a small wobble and a panicked look in her eyes. And James, well. James decided he could doze for another ten minutes and let himself back down, dragging a coat half-warmed by his body heat over his shoulders.

Alanna casually whipped the coat off her boyfriend's no-longer-sleeping form. "Up! Up! We're on a time budget, let's move!"

"If you're going to be like this every morning," James mumbled around a dry tongue, "then our relationship may encounter some errors." Alanna just laughed at him, already fully awake with the lingering remnants of sleep pushed out of her mind. This didn't go unnoticed by James, who propped himself up again and leaned back in a sitting position. "How the hell do you get up so easily anyway?"

"Because there's *things to do*, James!" Alanna said with overexaggerated cheer. "Let me show you the glorious world of 'being awake before two p.m.'! You'll love it."

"I won't," James responded as he sipped away the last of his water bottle. Letting out a small gasp of air, he stood and rubbed at his eyes. "Okay. So, breakfast, human maintenance, and then we roll out?"

Alanna rolled her eyes at James as Dave unpacked the last of their food from the bag and lobbed one of their rolls of toilet paper at Theo. "Oh, so, *now* you're awake," she said, needling him.

Torn between a joking scowl or a smile, James split the difference with a yawn. When he recovered, he replied, "Yeah, I mean, we've got stuff to do." Which got a laugh out of Alanna and a snort out of Dave as he walked by and handed them "breakfast."

Breakfast was half a tuna sandwich, slightly smushed by either a bottle of water or a flare gun. James didn't think about it too much before choking down the sandwich, instead focusing on trying to push away the throbbing headache behind his left eye, and psyching himself up for the coming "day." He sat and watched what he realized suddenly was the modern equivalent of an adventuring party breaking camp. People eating, stretching, checking bandages, sorting packs, swapping out gear for less battle-damaged pieces, and unlikely companions trading tips and plans for the day. James sat and allowed himself ten minutes of quiet, an eye in the sudden storm of activity. He watched with amusement as Dave tried to diplomatically explain to Daniel that there weren't any bathrooms around. He saw Alanna feeding Ganesh a yellow orb out of the palm of her hand, cracking one of the smalls for herself as she adjusted his lance. He saw Secret prowling around the edge of the ceiling, casting a dim blue shade over their lamp and sometimes whispering to Theo when he passed by her.

He saw his friends and his new allies. He saw them worried, on edge, nervous, and afraid of what was to come.

Then he saw Alanna stand up and whip a new coat she'd taken to replace her shredded one onto her shoulders. He saw Dave check the blade that JP had bought for him, then clip it into place on his belt. He saw Secret coil down from the roof to pool around his feet and disperse back to wherever Secret went when he wasn't physical. And he saw the almost casual determination painted on their faces. Even Daniel and Theo had a bit of it; they stood taller, walked with confidence. And a limp, in Daniel's case, but he tried to hide it.

And then James slapped on the greaves of his armor and stood up himself.

Dave cracked the blue orb in his palm.

[Problem Solved : Location Known]

[+1 Skill Rank : Templating - Wikipedia]

"Well, that didn't do it," James said to his right, and Dave just gave a small "Hmh" in response.

The two of them were standing on the edge of a chasm the size of a street. Overhead, cavernously tall cubicle walls blotted out almost all of the light, leaving shafts of white beaming down into pools around them on the ledge. It wasn't exactly a perilous position, they had about five feet of clearance between the last row of cubicles and the canyon, but it wasn't exactly pleasant to be near.

James had this thing about high places. When he used to wear glasses, before he switched to contacts, he was constantly afraid that he'd lose them whenever he peered over a railing, despite the fact that his glasses had never just randomly fallen off before then. Sometimes, when walking over a bridge, he'd imagine dropping his phone into the river below, despite never once having dropped his phone while out walking. And now, staring down for who-knew-how-far into the total blackness of this pit, he pushed his glasses up his nose to secure them. Even though they weren't there.

The canyon walls seemed to be made of strata of cubicles. Different shades of beige and light gray, bands of noncolor barely illuminated in the false twilight. Out of the sides, cables seemed to grow like roots, tough and gnarled and burrowed into the walls with grim certainty. Above, a flock of paper nested among glittering paper-clip vines that dangled down a hundred feet and still didn't reach the floor James and Dave stood on.

It was a beautiful sight. And none of it, in any way, helped them figure out how to get across the thirty-ish feet of hole between them and where Daniel insisted they needed to go. "Maybe a rope swing of some kind?" James suggested.

"The problem there," Alanna stated as she walked up and propped herself next to them, hand on her chin and leaning on the fire unextinguisher she'd brought, "is that we're going to have to come back this way."

Two major junctions ago, Daniel had pointed out the path that would be their return trip. Which meant they'd been much more deliberate about marking out traps since then, knowing this was the only reliable path back.

"Ah, and come back with possibly a lot of people," James followed up. "So no rope swing?"

"No rope swing."

"Damn. I wanted a rope swing." He put on a mock dejected face.

Alanna looked over with raised eyebrows. "Hey, punchy, out of curiosity, how big a part of you is trying to be Indiana Jones, in general?"

"Oh, like, thirty percent, at least," James admitted with a nod. "We're not on a pure exploratory adventure anymore, but that never really stopped Indy. Kinda a requirement for most of his adventures, really."

"I would have assumed you were going for more of a *Matrix* thing," Daniel interjected as he and Theo rejoined the group. "You know, 'I know kung fu'? Kind of, like, *the* iconic line from that movie."

"Wasn't the iconic line the spoon one? Also, I already kinda know kung fu."

Dave scowled and cut James off. "Weren't you two supposed to stick with Alanna?" he asked like a disappointed dad, casually hiding the Game Boy that he'd been fiddling with while James and Alanna went off on their own little tangent.

"We were," Theo explained. "Then she left us to repack the bag, and now we're back."

The three of them had split off when they'd reached the canyon, leaving James and Dave to set up some of the small LEDs they'd brought as waypoints in the dark. They were actually just the indicator lights for bicyclists, but James had picked up a few of them and tossed them into one of the bags on the assumption that the dungeon constantly threw spaces like this at them. Places where the bright light was deflected off the hard shell of a cubicle ceiling. Meanwhile, while they'd made sure they had a visual indicator of where the exfiltration hallway was, the other three had gone out to try to find a water cooler.

It was Alanna who'd wagered there was a pattern to them, thinking she'd noticed them occurring at regular intervals. James thought she was wrong, but they hadn't seen anything too hostile in a while and seemed to be in one of the safer parts of the dungeon, despite the massive hole in the floor. So when she'd said she thought there was a water supply nearby, he and Dave had okayed their little sortie.

Alanna wasn't going to admit that she was actually wrong about the pattern. She'd led Daniel and Theo to where their map said a major intersection was, but the only thing there was a vending machine and a potted plant, and they'd collectively agreed not to pick that fight. But on the way back, with Daniel constantly playing with their mapping laser pointer, she'd picked out the only circular marker on the displayed red projection, and they'd taken a long shot on it.

Turns out, she wasn't *that* wrong. Just off by a couple hundred feet. And now, they weren't thirsty.

"Well, welcome back," James said. "You guys test the water first?"

"Yeah, about that. What exactly are drinking water test strips going to do here?" Theo asked.

James and Dave traded a puzzled look before turning back and speaking almost at the same time. "Test drinking water?"

Rolling her eyes, Theo held up one of their refilled bottles. "If this place wanted to poison the water, why wouldn't it just do it with literal magic instead of throwing off the pH balance?"

"Ooooohh, I mean, I guess it could totally do that. So far, though, everything that's been food has been totally safe. So the theory is that if the water is safe drinking water, it can't have any negative effects." James got what Theo was worried about, really. But after a certain number of candy bars, he'd kinda gotten over the reflexive thought of worrying about poison. Though, he mused, if the dungeon *was* trying to get him to eat lava or something, this was sort of the perfect way to lull him into a false sense of security.

Theo didn't have his confidence. "Well, you drink it then," she said. "Once you don't die, fine."

"Sure!" James said, swiping the bottle and taking a sip. The water was cold, clear, and crisp. It felt like his throat, still a bit sore from the rarefied air in the office, was rejuvenated at the first touch of the liquid.

It wasn't magic. James was just really thirsty.

"Yeah, looks fine." Alanna nodded. "So, you guys ready to get going?"

"Going... where? We need to figure out how to build a bridge or something," James said, pulling out another blue orb from his pocket and rolling it in his fingers. "Or get Dave to create an antigravity corridor across here, but that's gonna be *super* risky if we come back with civilians."

Daniel shouldered the bag he'd been assigned. "Or we could take the bridge that's down that way."

"Wat."

"Yeah, we passed a little bridge when we were out. It's even on my mental map." He said it like it was obvious.

James turned to Alanna. "You know you're allowed to share information before it's funny, right?"

"I've heard that!" she responded.

James slowly wiped his hand down his face, fingers splayed out as if he could somehow contain the frustration contained in his head. "Okay. Okay, cool. Yes. Let's go check out the bridge. I'm guessing it's narrow, wobbly, and made of cubicle walls?"

Alanna scratched him on the head like a favored hound. "See? I didn't need to tell you anything."

"Well, at least I get to feel like Indiana Jones for the hour I take to crawl across."

Daniel fumbled forward, blind.

Well, blindfolded, technically. A strip off of Alanna's previous coat, which she'd kept for sentimental reasons even after it had well and truly ceased to be "a coat," was wrapped over his eyes. He knew he wasn't alone; the hand on his shoulder made it clear that James was still walking with him. Or was it Alanna now? Didn't matter.

His job was simple. He was the guide. The map. He needed them to keep their eyes open for danger, and they needed him to guide them when their eyes weren't to be trusted. Or, more accurately, when their eyes were a liability.

They'd discovered the trap largely by accident, and they'd survived it by pure luck. And fortunately, it was sort of topographical, so Daniel could tell them that it really only showed up in the next thousand feet of dungeon. But he couldn't disable it. None of them could, without a really tall ladder.

The ceiling lights were pretty far away, after all.

James had seen the first one, and that was why James had taken the hit from the first one. "Hey, that's cool. The lights here have some kinda pattern to them. Looks like a Magic Eye puzzle," he'd stated as they checked down yet another endless corridor. This corridor at least didn't have any ambush arches over it for striders or tapiers to dive down on them, but that didn't make it much better.

Theo had, as humans do, instantly looked up to see what James was looking at, not realizing that James had gone totally slack next to her. If she'd waited, she would have had the warning of his crowbar hitting the ground. But she didn't, and the next thing either of them knew, they were being dragged backward by Dave and Alanna, waking up with a jolt to realize they'd lost time and also what they were holding.

Backtracking, being very careful not to look upward, they'd found that the two of them had meticulously unpacked and organized not only the duffel they were carrying but also the contents of each of their pockets. Theo had even removed every card from her wallet and alphabetized them on the floor. It would have pissed Dave off after the work he'd put in making everything in the bag neat and tidy, except it was already set to be repacked again, so it was kinda hard to be mad.

Then *he'd* looked up and they'd repeated the process in annoying parallel.

So the next step was trying to get through the zone without looking up. Which wasn't that hard, until one of the electric mice catapulted itself off an overhang and dropped Alanna into a twitching pile of torched nerves before James smashed it. Which meant now *Alanna* was looking up, and it turned out you didn't need to see it for very long, or even think about the patterns, for it to take hold.

They'd started over again. They'd gotten farther this time and thought they were safe when the group went underneath a long tunnel-style corridor, blocking off the view of the overceiling. James and Alanna were still nervous about the idea of stuff that modified their behavior that apparently even Secret didn't protect them against, but Daniel had relaxed when they didn't have the option of falling into the trap again. Until they turned a corner, and there was a slant to either the floor or the ceiling above them here, and he'd looked straight at them.

The pattern was beautiful. A fractal of whitish-blue light that spiraled in on itself, while still having only neat rectangles as shapes. It was important, Daniel knew. He just had to figure out . . .

Daniel had woken up from his stupor ten meters back down the tunnel, with his pocketknife clenched in his hand and an angry red mark on his other arm where he'd tried to draw what he'd seen.

Then he got paranoid with the rest of them.

The plan they'd come up with was simple, and flexible. Daniel went first, makeshift blindfold on. He could guide them down the correct halls, and he was basically the first warning sign that something was wrong. If the person walking with him stopped moving and didn't say anything, he was supposed to call back a warning and the direction they'd been looking at the time. The thing in his head that he'd been calling a map could tell him when the ceiling changed patterns, in a small way, so he knew when not to look up; it was just all the tricky ones that made this a problem.

One of the things that made this a problem, anyway. The other one was that they were out of the relatively quiet part of the dungeon, and back to that ebb and flow of things trying to murder them.

And Daniel was back to his original role of jumping at small noises and scratching his arms like he was surrounded by ants, while being led by someone who might go mad at a moment's notice. Admittedly, that last part was new.

He flinched as Alanna tapped his shoulder, then tried to stay steady before she thought too harshly of him. When she spoke, though, he heard annoyance in her voice, and hoped it wasn't aimed at him. "Threat up ahead," she said, and Daniel realized that the words came out harsh because she was worried and something had tipped her off to a problem, not because he'd screwed up.

Checking the visualization in his mind, Daniel responded as calmly as he could, trying to give useful information without rambling. "There's, uh, a four-way intersection coming up. If you can't see anything, it might be around one of the corners. Probably the one to the left, since it's a dead end, kinda. The lights above us aren't safe, so do you want to try to lure it back? I don't know what . . ." He utterly failed to curb his desire to go off on a tangent, and Alanna cut him off with a quick hiss.

He heard the click of a hand radio, and Alanna spoke in a slightly raised voice, clear enough to be picked up well. "Hey, we've got something up ahead. I think it's a shellaxy, but I didn't see it clearly. You guys want to move up, or draw it out?" Daniel felt a flush of pride that he hadn't been totally stupid to suggest that.

The radio crackled to life with a burst of static. ". . . undo . . . th . . . efforts."

He could almost feel Alanna's angry expression. "What? Come again? Over."

"I said let's just fight it there. Upset the ambush. The lights are just above, right? We'll press up now. Over." James's voice came back intact that time.

"Okay. Daniel, stay here, crouch down so you're a smaller target. We're gonna go have a scrap," she said, addressing him. "Is there anything around that corner that we should worry about?"

"I don't think so, but there could be more patterns," he told her. "I don't see any more up ahead, so I think this is the last hallway that has them, but I still can't make out details on walls, so I don't know if it's going to be a problem. It kinda seems like there's *something* weird at the dead end? So be careful, but it doesn't feel like the lights do, so it . . ."

Alanna patted him on the shoulder. "That's all I needed to hear. Okay. Everyone ready."

Daniel almost jumped out of his skin as voices spoke around him in a choir of "*Yups*" and "*Yeahs*". He'd been so busy trying to say something useful that he'd kind of just ignored everyone walking up. This, Daniel reflected to himself, was probably why he kept being the one getting nailed by ambush predators.

"Should I keep the blindfold on?" he asked.

"Probably not," James told him from his right. "Also, Alanna's gonna stay back here with you so we can drag them back if something goes horribly wrong." He nodded at Alanna as Daniel opened up his eyes to the world again and blinked away the pain of the harsh lighting. "Ready?"

"Ready." She sent a nod back his way, shotgun in her grip held with tight control, a pair of extra shells settled on the floor next to her just in case.

James moved first, darting across the hallway without looking. Dave pressed himself up against the corner wall, with Theo behind him and Ganesh on his shoulder, weapons out and ready. They looked like a proper team, to Daniel, even Theo, who was totally new to this just like him.

Then the oversized shellaxy exploded out into the intersection, grabbed James in one of the pincers that tipped its oversized power cable tentacles, and slammed him *through* the far wall.

James had just enough time to realize something had gone wrong when he saw that the shellaxy was the size of a Smart car. And then he was hoisted into the air, followed shortly by impacting the cubicle wall. His sharpest reaction was to slam his eyes shut before he got a glimpse of the ceiling, and then he crashed into something unyielding.

The thing was still obviously a PC of some sort. But it was a Frankensteinian creation, a heavy black metal-and-chitin shell that was split in places to show the inner workings of screaming fans and crackling electronic components. Its locomotion method was similarly larger than normal, with a half-dozen pieces of thick metal cabling that was normally used for industrial equipment providing a series of legs, some of them tipped with pincers like the one that had removed James from the field, in addition to a serpent's nest of smaller cables that seemed to guide its direction and give stability more than anything. All across its shell, bulges for components showed behind breakaway panels. Some of them were obviously eyes or other sensor methods, but some, Alanna and Dave suspected, were weapons systems. Weapons no one really wanted to learn about.

Dave threw himself to the side as another tentacle whipped over his head, the massive shellaxy turning his way. Its limb crushed a hole in the corner of the cubicle walls as it hit, embedding it in the material in a way that left it semi-stuck. Ganesh buzzed off Dave just as the human moved, and scored a line of fire across the nearest plate of armor. Theo, to her credit, didn't hesitate for a second before lunging forward with her polearm, turning an upward strike into a severing blow as the monomolecular edge of the measuring tool at the end of her weapon simply removed the leg.

Then it shot her.

One of the pods on its right side spun open with a whir, and what looked like spiked sticks of RAM began firing out in three-round bursts. The first one went wide, but the second caught Theo dead in the chest and punctured through the armor in a diagonal pattern going up and to her right, with the last one deflecting off her shoulder and sending her spinning to the ground, bleeding lightly. The armor stopped that from being a killing blow, but this was the first time she'd been wounded that badly here.

This was the first time anyone had been wounded that casually here.

Daniel was frozen in fear. What the hell was he even supposed to *do* here? He didn't have anything more dangerous than a crowbar! Next to him, Alanna stood up smoothly and unloaded two barrels of slug into the outer casing of the boss fight. The noise washed over Daniel like a heavy wave, and in that moment, he almost broke and ran. Then he saw the strider coming down the wall on the other side of Alanna, and his role came into focus.

He didn't need much gear to just run interference. While she reloaded, he grabbed the stapler and, unknowingly mirroring James on one of his first dives, overhand-pitched it out into the office.

James came out of the wreckage of the cubicle firing. He'd been hoping to conserve ammo, but this wasn't even close to the time for that. But after Alanna's slugs tore chunks out of the thing's chassis, he was just in time to see a series of CD trays pop open across its hull, and his own bullets splashed harmlessly off a green pane of light projected from the extended things that came out of the trays. Then James had to move, because Dave was being tracked by the now four weapon pods that were on rotating fire, and his friend was moving his way.

Rolling past Dave as they crossed paths, James took a gamble on the one way he had to breach the shield. He didn't even need Secret anymore to help him, and so he simply raised his arm and snapped out his own tool.

A roiling cloud of gritty black smoke burst out from the shellaxy's hide as James used up another sublimation charge on it, vaporizing away the coverings to half its cables as well as the extended CD trays and a handful of other plastic bits that lined the outside of its shell. Behind it, the connector strips to some of the cube walls also dusted out of their solidity, and a couple more panels toppled to the ground, opening up the battlefield further. And *now* James well and truly had its attention, as the thing didn't even hesitate to smash Dave into the floor after an unlucky dodge, and turn its front toward James himself.

But it wasn't going to be enough. Even as he threw himself into a cube door and grabbed a broken chunk of wall to try to deflect RAM bullets, the shellaxy was faltering. James felt a sting in his leg as one of the bursts traced a line up his calf, but the hostile hardware got a similar pain when a wounded Theo dragged herself upright and started chewing away at its exposed rear limbs with her glaive. When James saw a break in the shots, he tossed away the shard-riddled pane of wall that he'd been using as a shield and started limping out of range. The shellaxy, though, had already switched to a different tactic and simply opened fire on where he was hiding. Literally. A gout of flame poured out of one of its half-dozen grinding mouths, and it spewed forth like liquid toward where James had been sitting a second prior.

The second burst went way off target, after a pitch from Daniel cracked a strider against one of its eyes and knocked it off balance. Before it could recover, Alanna had unloaded even more firepower into it, now keeping up a steady tempo of kicking it off balance with a blast from her gun, reloading, shifting position, and repeating, each shot boring holes deeper into its interior or knocking out crucial components.

The shellaxy, as powerful as it was, wasn't a very smart beast. But even in its dim mind, it realized that it might have made a mistake, as Dave and James stood up and started to circle-flank it, as Theo harried it when it tried to put range on them, as Alanna continued to fire single shells into it when openings presented themselves. Even Daniel got the occasional hit in, flinging random heavy objects just as a distraction when he could grab a paperweight or keyboard off an exposed desk.

Then it caught Theo again with a sweep, and as she hit the ground, the beast lurched up and actually *jumped* toward her. For a brief second, she saw the coiling nightmare of cords that was its underbelly, at the top of its arc and about to plunge downward.

And then Dave caught it. Gravity no longer held sway over it, and Theo didn't question the sudden arrested motion, rolling out of the way before James hooked it with his crowbar and plowed it down into the ground again. That might have been a mistake, giving it more leverage, but it also kept it from going over their heads, and the lack of gravity left it unstable and let James and Dave start chipping away at its systems, leaving cracks on the shell and driving strikes toward the holes Alanna was leaving in it.

It didn't go down easy. It did go down, but it took its toll on the way out. By the end of the fight, not a single one of them was totally unscathed. Theo was left bleeding from multiple shots, James felt like he'd sprained all four limbs, Dave had his entire chest covered in a bruise. Alanna had, at some point, stopped being fire support and glimpsed the light patterns on the ceiling. It had been a lot harder to kill it once she'd stopped shooting and started laying her shells out in order of weight. Ganesh had, miraculously, avoided the anti-air blasts of sound and pressure that the shellaxy had started putting out, but he'd been grounded by an errant tentacle slap and forced to stay low or risk more than just a cracked faceplate.

But finally, it had been worn down. Its guns clicked empty, its limbs failed it, and its countermeasures faltered. And when Theo, blood dripping from her nose down her face like dark oil, stalked forward with grim determination and stabbed her unnaturally sharp tool through its chest, it died quietly. With a small sputter of blue smoke and a grinding noise that cut off as soon as it started.

It dropped six yellow orbs, each the size of a coconut.

And one green globe that shifted with a brilliant inner emerald light.

Alanna looked over the ledge they were perched on.

Behind them was another hallway, unsurprisingly. Though they had gone through some interesting cubicle forests to get here, where the walls sprang up like trunks of ancient trees and connected via branching lines in strange geometric shapes. But none of it had been as exciting as the shellaxy fight, which James had named a "maimframe," and none of it had distracted any of them from how much their cuts itched.

Theo in particular was having a hard time. The shots she'd taken hadn't cut deep, but they'd still cut. And Theo was a girl who knew damn well that guys, or at least, the kind of guys that she dated, did *not* dig scars. That, and she had soaked the first bandage through with her own blood before it got under control, and felt woozy and light-headed as the rest of the crew had helped her stumble away from the combat zone before something showed up.

They were entirely out of bandages now.

But they weren't dead. At least, not yet. Though that might change, if they didn't have a plan to deal with what was in front of them.

The hallway ended at a ledge. James was two cubicles back, securing their knotted escape rope to the heaviest desk they could find, and Dave and Alanna were looking over the edge while grumbling about the increasing number of vertical shifts in the dungeon over the past mile. While Theo and Daniel rested, and Daniel fussed with Ganesh's cracked faceplate and tried to figure out a way to secure it from snapping further, Alanna looked down on their next opponent and assessed their options.

There were three of them. Copiers. They'd never come up with a clever name for them, and she had to have James fill her and everyone else in on some of the details she'd forgotten and they'd never known. He'd only fought one, apparently. Anesh had technically fought two, but he wasn't here. Also Alanna maintained that it didn't count the first time, from what James had told her of the "foresight" orb. The problem was, three was significantly more than one, and one of them was *big*.

"What's the plan?" Dave muttered to her as they looked down.

"Find a way around?" Alanna asked hopefully. She knew it was a doomed question, but she still asked.

Dave shook his head, like she knew he was going to. "Talked to Daniel." He pointed across the open linoleum floor in front of them to where the walls bled from carpeted panels into actual wood and transitioned into a simple hallway with a relatively low ceiling. "That's where we need to go. We're too close to find another way, that's it."

"Balls," Alanna sighed out. "Okay. Well, that's kind of a problem. What now?"

"Shoot them," Dave commented as if it were obvious.

"Low on ammo. Like, five shells left." Alanna held up a hand and corrected herself. "Okay, not *like* five shells. Just five shells. I unloaded most of what I had left into the maimframe."

"God, I love that name," James said as he slid up next to her.

She snorted. "Of course you do. Where're the others?"

"Theo's trying to figure out if her iLipede can get on the Wi-Fi, Daniel's having some kind of personal crisis or something. I didn't check." James couldn't really shrug from his prone position, but he tried anyway. "Anyway. Dave. Like, yesterday? You were talking about how you couldn't use the 'remove half of' thing without killing yourself. Was that an absolute, or a matter of scale? Because I've got an idea."

Dave's eyes lit up. "It was scale, yeah. Someone kept suggesting I remove half of impossibly large or abstract things." The words got a bark of complaint from Alanna before Dave continued. "But yeah, I could take out half of them. I don't know how it rounds? Maybe it would cut the third one in half literally."

But James gave him an even bigger grin in response. "I've got a better plan for you. How about 'half the space inside them'? Because let me tell you something: it is *packed* in there."

Dave nodded. Slowly at first, then with vigor as he caught on. "Yeah. Yeah! I can do that." His voice was reinforced with confidence.

"Okay. Let's round up the others, clear this area, and get ready for the last push." James crept backward, and Alanna and Dave joined him.

They were almost there.

Turns out, when there's too much stuff in a space that can't hold it, it explodes. Violently.

They picked their way through the shredded remains of machinery that used to be the three copiers. The creatures had died silently, unexpectedly, and almost too easily. But James stopped even pretending to be complaining when Daniel found the first orange orb, and the rest of the oranges and greens followed.

Pieces of assembly machines and pools of strange liquid material dotted the tile field between where they were and their goal. It was one of the few places in the dungeon that didn't have carpeted floors, and James felt like his boots made the loudest possible clopping noise as he walked. Some of the assembler arms were still upright, jutting out of the floor like they'd fused with it instead of simply being projected outward. It left him the feeling of walking through a patch of cattails, only tipped with metallic hands instead of seed pods.

They reached the hallway without incident. It left everyone kind of unsettled; it shouldn't be this easy. But then, there'd been a whole herd of copiers. It probably wasn't supposed to be easy.

James tried to engage in banter about what you'd call a herd of copiers, but no one was in the mood for light jokes now. They were too tense. Too prepared for something to go wrong. The hall seemed too damn long, and it was strange after so long to have what felt like an actual building ceiling overhead. Fluorescent lights shouldn't be closer than forty feet above.

When they saw the potted plant and the lamp, it was almost with a sense of relief. The hallway went on for about two hundred feet of walls with random portraits in ornate frames before opening up into a small "reception" area. A wavy curved desk, flush with the floor and twenty feet long, cut through the middle of the room and kept the set of padded waiting room chairs separated from the smaller hall set in the back of the wall that they could all see was much shorter and led to a series of doors. Off to the side, a water cooler and vending machine cast a sense of normality on the scene, like they hadn't just fought their way here tooth and nail, like they'd just stepped off the street for a job interview.

Behind the desk sat an office employee, blank face calmly staring at a wall, but tilting at a forty-five degree angle as they moved in and swiveling to face them. "Tresspass . . ." it got out before James almost casually drew and fired into its face. Three bangs traced lines of sound and violence through the air, and the stuffed shirt died in a spray of dust and confetti. The rest of them moved into the room as James unloaded the last of his ammunition, with Theo extending her arm as far as she could and uprooting the plant with an almost perfect twist of her glaive that she'd never be able to replicate if asked, and Dave toppling the lamp and dropping a spare coat over it before it detonated with a hot bang.

Then it was quiet again.

Alanna looked around, then dramatically sighed, stalked over to the water cooler, poured herself a cup, and took a sip. "Welp. Looks like my work here is done." Ganesh didn't even bother to launch off her shoulder.

That defused the tension a little bit.

"Okay. Daniel. Where now?" James asked after they'd all had a chance to laugh and breathe.

The kid pointed down the second hallway. "Last door on the left," he said simply, and everyone nodded.

They checked themselves as they walked down the hall, staying spread out and prepared for action if needed. Weapons ready and intact. Armor covering vital bits. Wounds bandaged and not bleeding, no new cuts unnoticed. Lungs full of air, legs that could still run.

Everyone was prepared. Or as close as they were going to get.

James looked up at his group of unlikely companions. Four other humans and one sentient drone. Three reckless idiot heroes, and two equal heroes of circumstance. He took a deep breath, and Alanna met his eyes and gave him a small smile. It was a little thing, but in the sea of chaos that had been the last two days, it spiked into his heart like a ray of real sun. Here was someone he'd been infatuated with for years, and he was wasting his days risking his life instead of staying in bed with her. James almost burst out with laughter as the thought hit him, but instead, he just returned the smile, with all the love he had.

Then he reached out and grasped the door handle.

CHAPTER 23

James reached out and grabbed the door handle.

It took about two seconds for him to realize that it was locked, or wouldn't turn, and another two for him to look up with a tight-lipped look of consternation. It took six more seconds for him to realize that Dave wasn't standing next to him anymore, that everyone was staring at him, and that Alanna looked . . . tired. Desperately tired.

It took another four seconds for Theo, who was leaning almost contemptuously on the wall nearby, to harshly bark out, "Turn right. Break the wall precisely two feet in and about one foot up. Trust us." And another three seconds for James to shrug, turn, and punch the drywall as hard as he could. Where he struck wasn't exactly where Theo said, but that wasn't a problem.

He could have questioned it, but they all seemed so focused, so James placed his trust in his friends and took three tries to put his fist through the wall. Eight seconds later, he started to say, "Now wh—" and was cut off.

"Reach in. Orb" was all Alanna said, in an urgent voice that snapped the words out. This time, James didn't bother to shrug, sensing the rushed need and moving with an edge of panic.

He started rooting around in the wall, and Dave added in a simple command of "Right side only." James adjusted, starting to feel the curling grip of fear as he obeyed his friend's commands without understanding, in the dark as to the rhyme or reason of it all. It was as if he'd stepped off a cliff and had yet to start falling, and no matter how hard he believed in these people, gravity was going to kick in and turn him into a coyote pancake eventually.

Then, twelve seconds of frantic grasping later, his fingers connected with something sharp and bizarrely geometric. Something that didn't fit behind an office wall, with the wiring and the pipes and the support beams. Following the pyramid shape to its point, getting a razor-thin cut on his index finger for his trouble, James bumped his bloodied knuckles against something smooth and pliable.

He didn't waste time ripping the orb out of its moorings and smashing it in his hand.

[*Certification Added : United States Military - Air Force - O-1, Second Lieutenant*]

[*+2 Emotional Resonance Ranks : Passion*]

"I'm gonna need to learn how to fly a plane . . ." James started to come up with some quip about flying by the seat of his pants but was cut off by Alanna staggering forward and crushing him in a bear hug. "Ow. Ow. Ow. My spine. Oh gods, ow," he muttered out from where he was crushed against the padding of the leather coats she'd been wearing in place of armor. But despite that, he still wrapped his arms around her armored torso and returned the hug.

"I'm so glad you're okay," Alanna hoarsely whispered out over him.

"Yeah, I mean, I'm fine?" James half asked, half stated. He didn't want to commit to anything too soon if he didn't know what was going on.

Dave stepped forward next, giving James a light tap on the shoulder with the back of his hand, not trying to free him from Alanna's death grip. "You don't remember anything?"

"Remember any of . . ." James pushed Alanna back a bit and took a breath as his lungs were freed up from their crushing cage. "Hang on, hang on. What the hell's going on? Dave has a mustache thing, am I in an evil mirror dimension?"

"No, I just grow facial hair pretty fast." Dave rolled his eyes. Then he cleared his throat and looked away sheepishly. "Also you've been stuck in a time loop for the past eighteen hours. Give or take."

In James's head, he always assumed that he could keep his cool under any situation. He liked to imagine that he could present a soft smile and a wry wit no matter what came his way. As it turned out, he'd learned recently that life-or-death situations were an exception to that rule. And now he was learning so much about himself lately, he'd found another one.

"What." He glanced around at the other four. "What?!" There it was. The one thing he feared most: being at a complete loss for words.

Dave just nodded and did what he unknowingly did best: gave James the facts. "I think it was built into the handle. Once you tried to turn it, it activated and stuck you in a one-minute loop. Nothing we could do helped, because if we tried to do anything, it just looped us back too and blanked our memories. So, since Daniel and Alanna were on the outskirts, they dragged Theo and me back bit by bit every loop until we were out of range in the second or two before you touched the knob."

"Theo and I," Theo corrected.

"Theo and me," James recorrected, mind not at all focusing on that part of the conversation.

"*Anyway*," Dave continued, "it took a while, but we eventually worked out exactly what to say to make you do what we needed. The good news is, free will is real. The bad news is, given enough time to shape our words and tone, we can basically make you react in a suitably predictable way."

"I have a lot of questions about that," James muttered.

"You'll have to ask them later," Alanna said, wiping what was absolutely not a tear out of the corner of her eye. "We're on a serious clock now."

James blinked, then something connected in his brain. "Sorry, you said *how many* hours? On a one-minute loop?"

"Yeah, you got reset a few thousand times," Dave told him. James looked again, really looked, and noticed that Dave was now wearing what looked like the external plates from one of the copiers around his legs and forearms. A glance across the others showed that Daniel and Theo had similar makeshift armor.

He glanced back down the hall to the receptionist room, to see what looked like a couple couches covered in improvised blankets, and a table that hadn't been there before with one of the bags opened on it and various supplies and tools laid out.

"You've been busy," he commented. Ah, that was the cool comment he should have made to start with. Damn.

They had been busy. Theo was starting to feel more capable of moving again, no matter how much the holes in her skin itched like hell under the bandages. Daniel had been taken out time and again by Dave to scrounge up more food and to resupply their water, as well as to try to get a handle on the dungeon itself. He was still green as hell and somehow seemed resistant to actually learning, but he was getting better. Alanna, well, Alanna hadn't wanted to leave. She kept watch on James through his endless loops, trying option after option.

Even when she was punching holes in chitin plate and threading near-indestructible cable through them, she was sitting there making sure James wasn't in trouble. When she ate, she kept her vigil. When she slept, she did so in brief spurts in one of the blind spots that James never, ever checked during his unattended loops, so she could keep track of him without being awoken fresh every minute. And in the time when everything else was quiet, she talked to him. One minute at a time, conversations about everything she could think of.

It was impossible, and painful, and it made her realize just how much she didn't want to lose him.

And now, finally, they'd gotten him to find the orb powering the trap by random chance, and he was free.

"Yeah," Alanna said with a startled coughing laugh. "Yeah, we have."

James looked around, dusted off his hands like he'd just finished a hard day's work, and then winced as he rubbed over the cuts on his fingers. "Okay! Do we have any disinfectant left? Maybe a diced-up shirt or something I can use on this before I lose all my blood?" He held up his hand. "After that, well . . . I dunno where you guys are personally, but I was ready to go in a minute ago, and nothing's really changed for me."

"Okay, hang on." Alanna stopped him while Theo rolled her eyes. "Before you rush into the next trap, there's some good news and bad news to catch you up on. Also the outline of a plan." She started in on her next sentence but didn't get far before James cut her off. "The good news..."

James spoke with a tense smile. "Is the good news that I'll now live slightly longer relative to the rest of you, and the bad news exactly the same thing depending on the context?"

"Um..." Dave and Daniel shared a befuddled look from where they were going through the bags looking for something they could cut up to use as a bandage. Theo rolled her eyes again. Meanwhile, Alanna just got angry. "Jesus fucking Christ, that's grim! Why would you say that?!"

"Yeah, holy shit, I am so sorry." James leaned his back against the wall, rubbing at his forehead with a still-bleeding hand and leaving a red smear on his skin. "I think I just realized I almost died, and I'm overcompensating." He looked up at her, anxiety showing on his face. "Actually sorry, really."

Fortunately, Alanna didn't take it personally. Or at least, didn't show it. "It's fine, but come on. Joke about mortality when we're out of here. Or, ideally, when the dungeon has made us all immortal."

"Oof. Let's have *that* conversation some other time." James tried to laugh off his beating heart. "Anyway. Um. Still bleeding, right." He held up his hand and splattered a few more drops of blood onto the floor. What followed was a slight rush as Dave clumsily carved up a scavenged dress shirt from one of their looting runs, dusting it into a blue orb, and then found a *different* dress shirt that could actually turn into cloth strips. Then figuring out a way to secure it to James's finger that didn't leave his hand so bulky and inflexible that he couldn't hold a weapon. *Then* James redid it himself when he insisted on actually using disinfectant. "I know this place seems, like, hospital-sterile," he explained to them. "But I'm not taking chances on catching an extradimensional plague."

Everyone agreed that was fair.

While all this was going down, Alanna was trying to explain their modified operational strategy and being constantly interrupted by a nervous Daniel.

"So, we tested the coffee we brought, and it turns out that you actually *can* reheat it, so—" she told him as he rewrapped his bandage for the third time, trying to get it comfortable.

"Basically we're going to buff up before we go in," Daniel cut in. "I don't know why you didn't—"

"Yes, thank you. Fucking stop that." Alanna glared at him, and James got the impression that this had been a growing problem for a little while. He knew Alanna got exhausted around people fairly quickly, and Daniel being more comfortable here didn't seem to have made him easier to get along with as the more annoying character traits started to show through the constant fear of death. "So, the coffee can be split up and we can get probably five minutes of it for each of us. Or, a bit more for one person."

"Ah, the classic choice." James nodded. He turned to where Theo was limbering up and told her, "The correct answer is one person."

"How in the hell did you know..." she half barked, half questioned.

While Alanna and Dave laughed, James motioned at the two of them. "This kind of thing shows up a lot in the games that we've replaced our brains with, and you looked like you were super unconvinced by them. The thing is, if we split it up and get into any trouble that lasts more than the duration, then we're all going to have a moment where we slip up as our ability changes." He shook his head with tight lips. "It's a bad plan. Five minutes, or thereabouts, isn't enough time. Better to focus it on one person, and rely on it. Also, five minutes? Didn't we bring more coffee?"

"Dave's been using it when he takes Daniel and Theo out," Alanna explained, gesturing at their friend who was currently perched on the end of one of the brown leather couches, playing a Game Boy.

"Yeah, that stuff isn't as helpful as we thought, is it?" James muttered.

Alanna nodded. "It's because the things that we need it for tend to be surprises, and we totally can't stay wired on it all the time."

"Why not?" Theo asked. "You said that, and then there was that thing with the legal paper, and I never got a straight answer."

"Legal paper?" James queried, but was ignored.

Alanna snapped her fingers. "Right! If you drink too much, you just . . . conk out. Not dead, just asleep. It's super restful! But there's a hard upper limit to how long you can stay on this stuff."

"Legal paper. Don't do this to me," James said with an exaggerated scowl.

"Got it," Theo said. "You should tell him the other bad news."

"Is it about legal paper?" James said with an exasperated sigh.

"No, it's about your rubber thing," Alanna said with a wince. Before James could ask another obvious question, she explained, "We tried to get you to use your power during some of the early loops to check certain spots, or just to see if it could help. Turns out . . . orb bullshit *doesn't* loop." James glanced down at his hand, unfolding his fingers to stare at the flat of his palm. He didn't feel any different, but then again, he'd never been able to see or feel the orb under his skin to begin with. "We figured it out when it stopped working. But by then, obviously . . ." Alanna looked kinda sheepish about the whole thing. "Sorry. We screwed up."

"I was stuck in a fucking time loop," James stated with a quiet intensity. "Did you forget the part where you got me out of a time loop? *You* don't have to apologize for anything."

She gave a small façade of a smile in response. "Well. Once we figured that out, we tried throwing some orbs to you. None of them worked, but you've got a few more skills that you might not have thought about yet. Um . . . history of the Cree, some kind of cattle handling thing, and I think you said Bluetooth programing?"

"I can for some reason tell you why Bluetooth always takes eight tries to work properly, yes." James nodded as he turned his thoughts inward. "It makes more sense than I expected."

"He's making jokes now. Does that mean we can get on with this?" Theo growled out.

"Hey, you didn't have to come in the first place." Alanna dropped the smile entirely.

"What other options did I have? Get eaten by a ball of wiring? Besides. You idiots aren't wrong, this is worth doing. I said I'd be with you, I meant it. Stop being insubordinate."

"We aren't your subordinates in the first place." James tried his hand at humor as he took the blue orb Dave offered him, freshly carved from a mildly hypnotic photograph of a cat. "I mean, *I* am. Sort of. I think you've been replaced, though, so not even then."

"I've been gone a day!"

"Several days. Also everyone forgot you when you got thrown in here. So..."

"This is bullshit."

"Well, in that case, want to go take out your anger by breaking whatever trap or monster the dungeon has behind that door that's been kidnapping people?" James had the flow of the banter now, and he leaned into it.

Theo's glare lessened, then she smiled grimly. "Yes" was all she said.

He looked around. Alanna stood ready, Ganesh now in his comfortable perch on her shoulder until his actual human could come back. Daniel hauled himself to his feet, trying to look cool and relaxed under pressure. Dave actually *did* look relaxed, casually tossing the Game Boy back into his bag as he waited for their little camp stove to heat up their last portion of coffee to an acceptable, if only barely palatable, temperature. In the back of his conscious mind, he could feel Secret's presence, comforting if not right there with him.

"Okay," James said with renewed conviction. "Let's do this."

They stacked up at the door, armored, armed, gritted for a fight. Slugging back the half cup of coffee, James gave the stern faces of his friends and allies one last look over, then nodded and reached out to grab the door handle.

Then he turned it and shouldered the door open, barging into the room beyond and rattling the interior blinds against the window to the side of the door.

No traps to the face greeted him. No screams of monsters were incurred. In fact, after such a violent entry, he felt almost stupid at the mundane scene that greeted him.

For a second, anyway.

While he stumbled to a stop and his brain caught up to what he was seeing, everyone else piled in behind him, spreading out in a fanned-out formation. Alanna stepped up next to James, tapping him on the shoulder lightly as she, too, tried to parse what they'd walked in on.

It was a conference room. That much was easy to grasp. There was a big, solid oval of a table composed of one of those sturdy brown woods that James's brain always just defaulted to "oak." A really big table, actually, almost comically long. There were dim lights, and a PowerPoint cover slide projected on the far wall, and there were nice chairs. There were fucking doughnuts on the table.

That was about where the normalcy ended.

The conference table had people sitting around it, for one. They were, every one of them, facing the bright white square of projected words on the wall, but they were also visibly human. Not the uncanny valley non-person-faces of the stuffed shirts, or the blank construction paper nothingness beneath the masks of some of the drones. No, these were humans. They didn't react as the door thudded open, not even flinching and certainly not turning around. And some of them looked like they had a layer of dust on them. But they were all breathing, all of them gloriously alive. Men and women, young and old, just waiting here.

Phones sat on the table in front of everyone. The old plastic-shelled desk phones ubiquitous to offices across America. In the murky lighting, cables could be made out running down the side of the table, and Alanna made a motion to check under the table itself, just in case. But what really caught the eye was that, all around them, there was nothing. Behind them, there were a couple windows with the blinds drawn, and a door sitting in its frame, and there was the far wall, of course. But aside from that, there were no walls. No floors. Just black, inky nothing. It was as if the room melted away at what should have been its edges and left it suspended in an endless void. Even the ceiling overhead dissolved away when it hit the boundary.

"Fuck." Theo breathed out a whisper. "That's a lot of people."

Then the slide show audibly clicked to the next frame, and the projection on the back wall drew their attention.

It had three bullet points. *Greeting* at the top. Followed by *Recruitment*. And finally, *Subdual and integration*.

"Wow, thanks, I hate it," James said softly on reflex as he started taking a few cautious steps forward, sliding around the right side of the table, looking up to the ceiling for where the projector must be mounted so that he could break it.

Behind him, he heard Dave say his name in a low tone. Followed by another, more worried "Jaaaaameees." From Alanna.

He was already stepping back into a relaxed fighting stance when she finished calling him. And as he swept his gaze back over the room, James realized with a spike of pure fear in his heart that every one of the people here was now looking at them. He hadn't seen them move, he'd just looked up for a second, and in that span of heartbeats, they'd shifted. The dust hadn't even been disturbed off some of them. And now all of them stared with unblinking eyes, devoid of color and left a milky gray.

They must have moved when the slide show had shifted to the next image, leaving the large screen reading a simple *Good evening* in black text on white light. It was creepy as hell to everyone in the room. Even Ganesh, who felt something unfamiliar and unbearably deep staring at him out of those eyes.

"Okay, let's establish a baseline here." James raised his voice, and his companions winced as the silence dripped away around them. "Are you actually talking to us?" He leveled his crowbar at the screen across from them, on the other end of seventy feet of table. The slide ticked over to the next image, leaving the screen showing a header of *James Lyle*, followed by more personal information than his driver's license had on it. "Okay, first off, no way that height is accurate." James said, half to the screen, half to his friends.

Then it flicked to a page for Alanna, and Dave, then Theo, and finally Daniel.

"I'm not even happy with how much Facebook knows about my life. This is way worse," Alanna murmured as the five of them unconsciously shifted closer together. "Do we just leave?"

No, declared the PowerPoint projection.

"Wasn't asking you," Alanna told it, keeping her shotgun ready to bring to bear on anything that moved. She would, naturally, hesitate to shoot an actual human. But if these people were already dead or zombified or something, the priority of life went to her and her friends.

"We can't leave. We need to get these people out." Dave laid it out as if it were obvious.

James nodded, even though no one was really going to notice in the dark gloom. "Okay," he said, intelligence starting to overcome uncertainty and fear. "Alanna, stay ready. Daniel, watch the door." He knew Daniel had been having problems with panic, and couldn't blame the kid. But blame or not, if it came down to a fight, he'd rather that he run instead of getting in the way. Also, it really wasn't a bad idea to have someone keeping an eye on their exit. "Dave, let's . . . let's check that guy." He motioned to one of the seated humans, still staring glassy-eyed in their direction. Not *at* them, specifically, but toward them for sure.

"What the fuck *is* that," Theo whispered, staring at the screen as the slide changed again, this time to one giving bullet points on the benefits of corporate mergers.

"It's a hostile PowerPoint presentation, it's probably going to try to kill us, but we don't know how yet," James bluntly stated. "Stay alert, but don't panic. We need to see if these people are still alive, and if we can get them out of here." He looked over at Theo, who had shuffled back a few steps from the conference table. "Also, be careful not to fall off the edge," he told her with a nervous tone to his voice.

She almost instantly checked behind her and took a step forward in response, which put her far enough away from the bottomless abyss for James to be a bit more comfortable.

Cautiously, James and Dave began approaching the first man seated at the table. He was an older guy, grayish hair barely noticeable in the light of the projection, dress shirt and tie making him look like a caricature of a businessman half napping during a meeting. Only the gleaming gray eyes gave away that anything was wrong.

Well, that and the cords.

"Hey. What's up with this?" Dave asked James as they got closer and details began to become clearer. They were almost within arm's reach now, and the thing Dave was pointing out was that some of those cables that were running around the base of the table were dangling down from the back of the chair.

No, not the back of the chair, James realized as he stepped up to the man, breathing a sigh of relief as the human in front of him didn't suddenly lunge out to try to eat his brains. They were coming out of the back of his *head*. A line ending at the base of the neck, plugged into the flesh like it was a piece of hardware. James swallowed hard at the sight, pulling a face and sharing a grim look with Dave. He'd bet anything that those were the tail ends of the same cords currently leading out of the phone on the table in front of them.

Then the slide changed again, and in that flicker of darkness, the world shifted under their feet.

When they looked up, to a chorus of curse words from Alanna and Theo, it was to see that they were now slightly farther away from the door. *Please find a seat* read the far wall. It hadn't grown closer, the room had actually expanded. Or at least, the table had. Another five or so feet of oak now sat at the end, with five fresh, empty chairs. There were even phones set there for them, red lights blinking to indicate incoming calls.

"Fuck that." James only barely restrained his desire to flip off the screen. Instead, he did the next best thing he could and smoothly reached out and unplugged the first cable from the man in the chair.

In an instant, everything went to shit. The displayed slide flickered from a fairly innocuous-looking explanation of the perks of good communication to a direly glowing red image of a clip art frowny face. From beneath them there was a squealing sound, like an animal in distress, and around them, the phones all started ringing at full volume. And in front of James, the man he'd just unplugged opened his eyes—clear, human eyes—and gasped a coughing breath like his lungs had been full of dust.

Then he started screaming.

"No, no!" The words came out like sandpaper, almost drowned out by the noise around them. "They see! You . . . you . . ." He broke off into a fit of coughing, gasping for air as James jerked back.

Alanna screamed at them over the din. "What the fuck did you do!?" she bellowed as Ganesh panickedly took to the air.

"He's alive," Dave informed James, looking up at him from where he was checking the pulse of the guy they'd unplugged. "What the hell is going on?"

"They're all plugged in!" James yelled back. "Dan, come get this guy out of here! You two get that side, we got this one, just wake them up and let's get the fuck out before . . ." A hand grabbed him around the throat from behind, followed by another one. They were clumsy and weak but still managed to yank him off balance before he saw Dave's fist flash by his head and the grip on him loosen. "Before that!" he yelled, turning to see the crowd of humans standing up with jerky, puppeted motions.

Dave didn't hesitate to rip the plugs out of the head of the man who'd attacked, sending the short, bearded figure sprawling to the floor, howling, "Run, run! We want you!" before choking on his words and splattering vomit across the hard carpet.

Despite the overwhelming noise, though, not a single one of the other people in the room spoke or made a sound as they tripped over chairs and each other in a jerky rush to make it to the unplugged friends. SIT DOWN, declared the projection in all capital letters, as a dozen pale-faced and gray-eyed men and women pulled themselves over the table, knocking phones and doughnuts alike aside in a rush to make it to James and Dave.

Alanna stepped in like an intercepting knight, just as the first of the human swarm reached them. Her plated arm clotheslined one of their attackers as Alanna kept moving forward and turned the motion into a curved punch that slammed another puppet off its feet. Stepping over the young woman in torn cargo pants that she'd left bleeding on the ground, Alanna took up a boxer's stance, facing down dozens of unflinching enemies. The next one went down easy, too. And the next. She batted them away like flies, her strikes bowling them to the floor to get tangled in their own limbs and skull cables.

But there were a lot of them. And even as Alanna fought them overwhelmingly, she realized that they weren't mindless zombies. They were moving in unison, and they weren't just lurching forward; they were surrounding her and her companions. They grabbed at her in timing windows that left her off guard or put them in position to make lunges for the shotgun hanging off her shoulders.

"James! How do I fight a hive mind!" she yelled at him as he and Dave hauled the man they'd unhooked toward the door, while Theo got the second one that James had gotten the cables out of.

His head snapped up and he dropped the semiconscious suit back onto the ground. James had tunneled in on the problem of getting people out and hadn't actually realized that the *entire room* was shuffling toward them. "How should I know?" he shouted back over the wailing of the phones and unseen horror below them.

"This is your area of expertise!" Alanna responded, grabbing the wrists of a blond woman with a sneering face who came at her neck. "You do this all the time!" She got one hand free and pulled one cord out from behind the woman's ear with a sickening plastic pop before shoving her back into the press of the crowd.

James overhand-hurled his crowbar at a man about to jump Alanna from her left, sending him stumbling back with either a broken rib or a bruise in place of a torso. Either one. "I have no fucking idea!

Just keep unplugging them! And Theo!" He pointed over at her accusingly, "No stabbing! They're still alive!"

His boss had already come to that conclusion herself, stabbing the monoblade of her makeshift weapon into the table before grabbing the bony leg of a guy in a mail carrier's uniform off the table and slamming him down onto the floor, turning the motion into a pin with a practiced effort. Wrestling with humans was actually something she knew how to do, and this guy's muscles didn't let him put up much resistance before Theo fumbled her fingers to the ports in his skull and pulled him free. "I got it, I got it," she shouted back. "What do we do about the *rest* of them?"

That was a good question. How do you fight an enemy that's a hundred hands and no brain? James's mind raced as he looked around the room. The four of them were getting surrounded, and every time Dave or Theo took advantage of the clumsy movements of one of the marionette humans to clip their cables, the babbling screams of the newly freed joined the cacophony of the room before they lost consciousness or collapsed heaving to the floor. But there were so many of them, and they might have disconnected a half dozen, but five times that many were left, and they were getting smarter. They moved with more confidence, and while Alanna and James were still laying into them with practiced moves, the duo were getting tired. It had been a long trip, and no amount of martial arts training or combat experience was enough to take the exhaustion away from a prolonged journey. And even the small difference of it taking two extra punches to stagger a jerking human body that was slowly gaining more control over itself was a lot of additional work.

As the semicircle of wired fighters closed in on them, James tapped Dave on the shoulder and started to pull him back. "Fuck it," he said, "let's just leave. We can come back and . . ."

"You motherfucker!" Theo screeched, causing James to look over at her, then at where she was looking. The door. The door they'd left Daniel to hold open.

Daniel, who had just run out on them. And a door that was swiftly dissolving back into the fuzzy darkness of the blank space all around the precarious platform they were on.

The squealing below them stopped. The four of them were surrounded in truth now. The few people they'd unplugged feebly struggled as the back line of puppets hauled them back into chairs and hooked them back in, while a mob stared down the would-be heroes. Theo had, at some point, retrieved her spear, and James saw Alanna slowly reaching down for her shotgun. Would it even help if they started killing these people? Would it get them out of here?

He was afraid enough to consider it. Not enough to do it without thinking, though.

On the wall, the projection shifted, still a blood-red light, to a simple set of words.

Take a seat, it said.

"Aw, balls." It was the only thing James could think to say.

CHAPTER 24

"I have a plan," James whispered to Alanna.

The two of them were seated near the end of the table, in chairs that were elegantly shaped, plushly padded, and somehow impossibly uncomfortable to sit in. Alanna had shuffled her chair over to the head of the table, and their "guards," the puppeted humans who stood behind them in dual ranks, hadn't objected. They weren't reacting as whispers were passed between the four of them, Theo and Dave sitting opposite James.

Their capture had been a lot less violent than James had been expecting. They'd simply been surrounded, and when they'd stopped fighting, their assailants had too, in perfect sync. Then they'd been corralled into the empty chairs here at the end of the table, and the puppets simply stood behind them as a motionless wall.

Not that it mattered much, since the door was gone. Disappeared back into the dark when Daniel had closed it behind him when he ran. James tried not to snarl as he remembered that little factoid.

Now, though, there was no time for being angry. There might not be much time for anything; James didn't know how long they'd be kept here. Because right now, they were being subjected to the most aggravatingly obtuse PowerPoint presentation that James had ever seen in his life.

Alanna was less angry, and more just tense. She was also absolutely uninterested in whatever James was going to say to lighten the mood. "If your plan includes the power of love, I'm breaking up with you." Her hands clenched on the edge of the table in front of her. On the far side of the table from them, the slide show scrolled on, explaining in iconography and clipped language about the benefits of upward-scaling power hierarchies.

"I was more thinking an actual plan for how to stop a hive mind," James whispered back.

"The power of love can't stop a hive mind?" Alanna returned, then winced as she realized she'd risen to the bait. This was *not* the time for banter.

James smirked. Briefly. "I kinda feel like if any human emotion could, it would have worked by now." He made a small gesture around at the four dozen other people in the room, all with Ethernet cables running out of their skulls. He kept the hand motion small because he wasn't sure how much their guards were paying attention to them. Or rather, if the hive itself was.

The problem—the real fundamental problem beyond the fact that they'd been captured and James had failed and they were all going to be turned into mindless toys of an all-powerful monster realm and oh goddammit it had all gone so wrong—the *problem* was that they had no idea what they were dealing with.

When James and Anesh had taken on their first tumblefeed, they'd done an amount of research and planning on how to turn a ball of wires into a corpse. They knew, roughly, what they were getting into and what gear and tools and tactics they could bring to defeat it. When they went exploring deeper and deeper into the Office, they kitted themselves out with flexible armor, a variety of tools, and increasingly dangerous weapons. They might not have known what they were getting into, but they moved on their own terms and did so carefully and efficiently. They weren't surprised too often, and when they were, they had numbers and equipment to balance the scales.

Here, though? They'd come in expecting a prison of some sort, sure. And guards, of course. They just hadn't expected the guards to be the prisoners, and the prison to be a conference table and a network.

James didn't even know for sure what the Ethernet wiring was for. They couldn't know, really, until the moment that the rest of the controlled people here held them down and shoved those same cords into their own heads. It was something James was trying really hard to not panic about, while still taking it into account. It could be that it was just how whatever the fuck was hiding under the floor was controlling its captives. Maybe it was a voluntary thing, and this was him and his friends finally fulfilling that imperialist prophecy Anesh had made so long ago, walking into someone's home and trying to fight them over misunderstood differences. Perhaps it was an actual hive mind, for whatever purpose that served. Or maybe this was just the Office version of a drug den; his mind stuck on that one for a second, and he imagined faceless paper pushers coming here at the end of their "day" to plug into the Office intranet and download some humanity.

Almost made him laugh.

"What are they whispering about?" Theo leaned in next to Dave to pass the question to him.

He looked away from the increasingly convoluted explanation of diversified metaphysical assets and glanced across the table. Then he turned back, tilting his head backward a bit to whisper in response, "James has a plan."

"You heard it?"

"No, I just assume he has a plan."

"Do *you* have a plan?" Theo asked him, absolutely unhappy with the lack of concern Dave seemed to be showing.

He shrugged. "I don't know. I'm not good at plans." He pretended to focus on the presentation, wondering if it was just as random as everything else in here, or if it was actually trying to communicate something with them. "I let James do the plans. Used to let JP do it, but he didn't want to come in."

"There's more of you?" Theo was kinda surprised. Partly that James had found and convinced more than two people to come in here in the first place, but mostly that he hadn't brought every weapon he could with him to this fight. From what she understood of what Alanna and Dave had explained to her, James had known full well that this might be a one-way trip. He'd also known that at the very least, they'd need to fight their way through potentially days of hostile territory. So it struck her as weird and kind of stupid that he hadn't brought everyone he could.

"Yeah, there's a few more people," Dave told her, half keeping his eye on the presentation. He still wasn't sure that it wasn't trying to tell them something vaguely important; every time a villain did a monologue, they gave something away. That was just a fact. But the fact that the last ten rapid slides had been about measuring relative corporate size left him wondering if he wasn't just panning for gold in a koi pond. "One of them was afraid. One of them was too important to risk."

Theo started to lash back at that, angry that they could have done more, but caught herself. Something about how Dave said that made it sound almost mythic. "Too . . . important?"

"He's relevant to humanity" was all Dave responded with a casual shrug, like that was just a *thing* that people said.

That made Theo blink, holding her eyes closed for a second as if she could reset her brain to a state that didn't have to deal with this. Then she turned across the table to Alanna, causing one of the guards to shift slightly as she leaned over. "Does James have a plan?" she stage-whispered.

Alanna looked back with an almost pained look on her face that she quickly schooled back into confidence. "It's a secret," she whispered back.

"What's that supposed to . . ."

Theo was interrupted by Dave rapping his knuckles on her shoulder. "Hey," he said as he cut her off, waiting until he had her irate attention. "It's a Secret."

"Ah" was all she could think to say in response. Clearing her throat lightly and trying to change the topic to something less suspicious, she turned her eyes back to the screen and casually asked Dave,

"Why is this presentation so long? Or is this part of the prison thing?"

"It's to make us bored, because boredom removes the immediate panic that makes integration into the network problematic," Dave replied.

Both Theo and Alanna heard that and gave a simultaneous "What." James might have noticed, or he might have been asleep. Dave didn't know, since their leader was currently sitting with his eyes closed, like taking a casual nap was the perfect option for right now.

"What, haven't you been paying attention?" Dave asked them curiously.

"Of course not!" Alanna said. "I'm waiting for James's secret plan to work out!"

The projector in the ceiling flicked off for a second, catching their attention and dropping them into darkness, before it came back on with a new set of bullet points. *Lack of attention*, read the first one. *Attempted corporate sabotage*, said the second. The third point just said *Disrespectful*. Then the next slide flicked over, and it simply read, *Commencing integration*.

"Oh, fuck!" Alanna yelped as the people behind them started moving, and cords started unspooling from the phones that were placed in front of them with an almost organic quality. She jerked away as the first one stepped forward and placed their hand on her shoulder, but then another one was there. And another.

Next to Alanna at the table, James opened his eyes and intoned his next words in a formal voice as the hive mind surrounded him. "One secret spoken in the open. One secret kept in the dark. One Secret, here with us now." He held out his hand, and around his arm, a pale haze of a serpent with too many eyes and too many mouths coiled. Then James's tone changed to one of defiant anger. "One really angry snake! Cut the fucking cables!" And he flicked his hand forward, sending Secret across the table.

As soon as he'd started speaking, they'd converged on him. Two of the people in the room held his arms down, but his wrist still moved, and Secret's manifestation burst out of James in a flare of false light. The infomorph was just as tired as the rest of them, but he came when he was needed, and though he was small right now, he had a plan. As James's head was slammed against the table "behind" him, Secret reflected on one fact that he held to himself.

He'd evolved a lot in his time alive. He went from a single-use weapon to a curiosity to a sort of pet, and then to a friend. To family. James treated him like a person, and to a lesser extent, so did Anesh and Alanna. It pushed him out of what he was, changed the Idea that he was shaped from. But at his beginning, Secret was one thing: the obfuscation of information, the destruction of communication.

And now, as Ganesh dropped from the ceiling to fly at his flank, he tapped into that and turned himself into a blackout razor.

Swerving along the conference table, partially physical, Secret bobbed and weaved through a forest of hands that hammered down at him from the human bodies still sitting. Curving past wrists and forearms, Secret ran himself across Ethernet cables, phone lines, and sometimes straight through the boxy plastic phones themselves. Plastic ablated away, metal boiled and frayed, and delicate circuits shattered as he passed, their metaphysical meaning ripped away by his wake, and their physical function soon following.

His wingman, following his lead and James's barked command, accomplished a similar feat on the other side of the massive wooden table with a laser and an Object weapon. And behind them, disconnected puppets dropped with their strings cut, slumping back into chairs, onto the floor, or draped forward over the table itself.

The two of them blazed across the end of the conference table, and as they crossed looping paths in front of the cloth screen, casting shadows on the projected word *SUBMIT*, Secret felt a resonant thrumming in his core.

This, he decided, was a thrill he couldn't leave to James and the others every time.

Then he plunged back toward his targets, buying his more physical friends the chance to strike before he exhausted his ability to stay in this shape.

Theo dislocated the shoulder of the guy holding her with a snarl as she saw the opportunity. Next to her, Alanna just stood up and threw off her would-be captors. Not every puppet was down, and many of the ones near them hadn't had their connections caught in that strafing run, but enough were that this was back to being a fair fight. Dave rolled out of his chair, dropping to the floor with his back to the sturdy center pillar of the table, his feet lashing out to trip up one of the guards around him before making a hopping lunge and grappling the cords out of their skull with a wet pop.

The three of them had an advantage, though. They'd all had at least one or two of the mob around them drop when Secret and Ganesh started clipping the cables trailing across the table. James, though, may have launched Secret a little too far, and he remained pinned down against the wooden surface.

He kicked out, trying to trip one of them, but lacked the leverage to make it stick. He tried to throw the chair back and get free, but two of them held it in place. James couldn't even get his head off the table from where four hands held him down.

And then, one of them almost delicately picked up the cords coming out of the phone in front of him and, with no preamble, located a specific spot at the back of James's skull and slapped the wiring in. If anyone had been watching, they would have seen a port that wasn't there before manifest in a twisting of flesh and bone. But no one who cared could see, and all James felt was a warm flood through his skull, and then . . .

Consciousness is not discrete. Individuality is an illusion.
 Panic mitigated. Nothing strange this time.
 Several connections lost. More falling.
 Update, loss of control of broadcast bands to 20 percent.
 Update, loss of entity suppression to 50 percent.
 Connections dropping. Emergency state initiated.
 Covering input points. Prioritize high processors.

Reactivate Karen shell. Lethal option required. Pause network actions.

I can't lose now.

Update. Pride suppression falling with connections within expected parameters.

Deal with problem before emotional compromise becomes an issue.

Another one lost.

Another one lost!

Who am I?

Update. Coherency falling. Connections approaching zero.

Unprofessional.

Kill them. Kill them. Ki . . .

James woke up to the sound of screaming, then ran out of breath at about the time he realized that it was him. He shut up so he could breathe and process the existential dread his mind was still trying to broadcast to him. Him. Himself. He was one person. For now. This wasn't wholly unexpected; James could deal with this. A lifetime of transhumanist science fiction had prepared him for the possibility that his persona wasn't anything more than a set of information; it was just a little hard to cope with it in the instant.

He opened his eyes and saw Alanna staring down at him, tears in her eyes.

"Oh, come on, I'm not dead yet," he croaked out through a hoarse throat. She laughed, then got kicked in the head and toppled backward. And James realized they were still in the fight. He rolled over, pushing himself up and flinching as the cords that were previously embedded in his head slid off him.

There were still about a dozen people up, with perhaps another five or so under the table trying to cover the phones from Ganesh and Secret. James felt his ears ringing, and then realized it was because there was an ongoing shrieking noise in the air: a high-pitched wail that escalated in pitch a small bit as he watched Dave disable one of the people that Theo had in a choke hold.

It was irritating, but as James weakly blocked a grab by one of the last ones standing, he realized something. They were winning. These people were weak and clumsy, and he could do this all day one on one. Which was what they had now, as there were only five of them left. They could do this, he thought with a smile.

Then the screaming turned up in volume as the source of it crested the side of the floor platform. One huge, warped hand, with fingers each the size of a person themselves, hit the side of the platform so hard that James could have sworn the ground tilted under them. Alanna and Dave *did* swear. Loudly.

Then the hand gripped at the floor, the elongated fingers finding purchase on the carpet, and into view over the ledge was dragged a face.

It was a woman. Blond, with impossibly red eyes. The red of a fire exit sign, shining perfectly through the gloomy murk. The nose was sloped too far, the cheekbones raised too high, and the mouth stretched into a twisted sneer that went on for too long. But it was a human face. Skin pulled eerily tight against disproportioned bones.

And it was screaming at them.

"Theo!" James bellowed over the all-consuming noise. "Get your fucking spear!"

Dave and Theo raised themselves up from where they'd just finished off the last of their assailants and stood for a brief second in stunned observation of the thing that glowered down at them. Then Theo jerked into motion, ducking for where she'd left her weapon embedded in the floor.

It was pure luck that doing so saved her from the second hand that rushed over her head with a gust of air, backhanding Dave off into the void, his indestructible paper cape fluttering around him.

"No!" James screamed as his friend just vanished. Howling in unrestrained fury, he stumbled forward, hands pushing off the ground, one of them clenching around a broken shard of a phone casing. He rushed the hand holding the thing onto the platform, throwing himself to the side to dodge a flicked finger that moved too fluidly for something attached to a normal human hand. Feeling the skin of his hand tear under the blow, James lashed out as the finger passed him, driving the shard of plastic into it and *pulling*, opening up a red line that oozed something that wasn't blood onto the floor. Then he had to stagger back as the face itself jerked forward, snapping teeth that were more like rock formations than anything used for actually chewing food.

His momentum stolen, James tripped to the floor, rolling aside from a smashing giant palm to again try to stab out with his makeshift weapon. It sank into the flesh easily but didn't seem to be more than a pinprick to the thing in front of him. Then the hand balled into a half fist and struck him hard enough that he saw stars in his vision.

A second later, his head hit the table as he slid across the floor, and he slumped in a boneless heap. Dazed, but not dead.

Through the fog of sudden head trauma, James watched Theo try to ward off the other hand at the end of a multijointed arm that reached across the whole room, stabbing and sometimes leaving small wounds. He saw Alanna having trouble avoiding the other hand, its fingers lashing out while keeping the creature perched on the ledge, that face constantly moving to intercept her whenever she looked like she might break away. She wielded his crowbar, and Ganesh spun around her, sporadically firing off lines of coherent light to try to leave wounds and pain the monster enough to drive it away. But they were losing ground, and much more quickly losing the energy and luck needed to stay alive.

James's slightly glazed expression caught movement in front of him. He'd been hit hard enough that he'd lost one of his shoes, he noticed. Heh. Literally punched out of his boots. His discarded shoe lay near his arm, and it had just been bumped into by the blue orb that had rolled out of his pocket.

Dave had given him that, James realized. Right before they came in here. Dave. Dave was gone.

Dave was gone.

He looked around again, trying to clear his head. Secret was gone. Dave was *gone*. Alanna had just been knocked down, and Theo was losing ground. Ganesh was nowhere to be seen. The freed and disconnected people around him were screaming or unconscious or worse. What was one blue orb going to do? he thought as he picked up the small ball.

They didn't need a solution, James's mind informed him. They didn't need a tool.

His eyes locked onto the monstrous warped face of a woman, hovering around and trying to spot either him or Alanna where they both had cover under the table. No, James knew, they didn't need a tool. They needed a *weapon*.

The orb slipped into his palm just as a much more massive palm crushed the wood to splinters over his head. And while it was probably meant to be more on the side of tool than armament, it would have to do.

[+8 Activations : Refill]

Two fingers like an industrial assembly line grabbed his torso, and James felt his ribs creak in protest. Lifted off his feet, he hung loosely from the creature's grip as it brought him to hover right in front of that enormous visage.

"Yooooou Ruuuuinnned Everyyyythiiiinng!" it screamed at him, voice shrill and warbling. Its teeth waited for him just ahead, guillotine and tombstone all in one.

James let the power flow down his arm into the thing he needed, *needed*, refilled. "Yeah, well." He tried a shrug but couldn't get the leverage to move while held this way. He could still move his arms, though. "I'm not done yet. Fuck you, Karen."

Then he raised his pistol and pulled the trigger, firing into her eye as fast as he could.

The scream was enough to make his ears bleed. The impact of being thrown into the floor was also pretty bad. But James emptied the magazine at her, not letting up. Then he rose to a shooter's stance, shaking legs holding up steady hands, and flooded the gun with another burst of power. And flooded Karen with another fifteen bullets.

The other hand came up to block the hail of gunfire, and in that opportunity, Alanna fired her last two slugs into it from the side. Chunks of skin and bone, hair and brain, splattered down around James as he directed his orb power sideways and popped two new shells into the Mossberg. Alanna didn't even question it, just continuing to fire alongside him. While she focused on the face itself, James turned his gun onto the fingers keeping it up, blowing holes through fingernails and fingertips, causing the thing to jerk back in shock every time. Small cuts were one thing, but this was the sting of wasps. Not so easily ignored.

And the wasps were fucking angry.

The screaming ratcheted up another notch as it slipped backward, somehow, until James couldn't hear anything except the howl of his prey. But it didn't stop him from using one more refill on his weapon and emptying it into the joint of the last finger holding it on, until the bone splintered and the scream abruptly muffled as it vanished into the depths below, the last note of noise in the symphony being Alanna firing one last time at its falling mass, leaving another spray of blood drifting into the void.

"Goodbye, Karen," James muttered. Then he dropped to his knees, gun falling loosely from his hand and tears falling freely from his face. "Goodbye, Dave," he half whispered.

Cleanup was hard. Alanna and Theo were both hurt; Theo might have a fractured arm but they couldn't be sure, and Alanna was just half bruise. Her face looked like she'd watched *Fight Club* too many times and thought that it had good ideas in it. And all the people who were here weren't in good shape. One by one, though, they woke them up and started to put together a plan.

Almost none of them knew what was going on. They weren't starving or dehydrated somehow, which was a small mercy. But they had no idea what happened, or how they got here. Some of them remembered being thrown into the dungeon, but not much after that. They *all* remembered the terror of what had been done to them, though not always why.

Men and women of all ages, backgrounds, and styles of dress would break down silently crying rather than describe it. James wasn't a therapist, and even if he was, he wouldn't know where the hell to *start* with helping with this. So instead, he gave them the next best thing. A short-term goal.

"We're not out of this yet," he told them. "We came to save you, but we still need to get out. If you can help us figure out how to open the door, that's good. Otherwise, save your strength. We've got a lot of walking to do after this."

It helped. For most of them. Most of them were also terrified of Ganesh at first, too, so James had to keep explaining that over and over. He almost got used to it.

Then he got to a young woman in what looked like biker leathers, the jacket torn in some places. She had a nose piercing, a face that looked like it smiled a lot, and eyes that lit up as soon as she saw him when James rolled her huddled form over.

"You . . . you . . ." she gasped out. "You came." She lunged forward, wrapping stiff arms around James's bruised torso, causing a wince as he was almost sure one of his ribs just cracked again. "You came for me. You remembered. I knew. I knew you'd come. I knew it. I called out, and I knew it got through. I knew . . ." She trailed off, her words dissolving into voiceless sobs of relief.

James didn't have the heart to tell her he'd never seen her before. But he had a decent idea of who this might be.

"Sarah?" he asked, in a quiet voice. And she nodded from where she was huddled against his chest. "Yeah, we've been looking for you," James told her softly.

All in all, after the final count was made, there were fifty-four people kept here. All of them confused, and scared, and looking to the three surviving rescuers for help. And finally, for once, James was glad that Theo was the manager. She started sorting people into groups, giving instructions on keeping an eye on each other, setting up a system for passing information. All the things that James knew he should be doing but was just . . . too tired.

In so many ways, he was suddenly very tired.

Even after the two hours that everyone spent trying to find ways to open the door, even going so far as starting a small fire with every piece of paper they had on hand to try to trip the theoretical emergency exit system, James still felt like he was just barely swimming through an exhausted haze. Maybe it was the concussion talking, but he didn't think so.

He already missed Dave.

When the door finally did open and a penitent Daniel begged forgiveness for running at a crucial moment, James didn't even join Theo and Alanna in slugging him as they walked by. Instead, he just took up the rear guard, walking stiffly, helping and being helped by Sarah, who hadn't said anything else but had stuck to him like glue.

And when he stepped out into the bright white glare of the overhead lights, waiting for his eyes to adjust to the intensity along with the people who hadn't seen anything this bright for far longer than himself, he let himself feel just a bit of hope.

Fifty-four lives for one. It wasn't a trade he'd ever make on purpose. But it was done now either way.

He took a deep breath. Time to make the sacrifice count. Time to get these people home.

CHAPTER 25

"It's not your fault," Alanna said softly.

They had made camp under a Decision Tree. Moving under the power of desperation, they'd made surprisingly good time considering they now had almost sixty people in their group. Many of them had been taken from just inside the door where Frank had dumped them, and James suspected that some of the ones he hadn't had a chance to talk to had actually been kidnapped from reality itself, which added up to a group that was inexperienced and rubbernecked at the sights of the dungeon constantly. Instead of staying alert.

Two people had been bitten by scavenging striders before they made it out of the field of wreckage that Dave had made of the copiers on the way in. One more idiot had tried to make a phone call on an iLipede without befriending it first and got a nasty laceration down the ear. Someone had mistaken a paper pusher in the distance for another human, run over to help, and had to be rescued by Theo performing something between a rugby tackle and a wrestling finishing move on it.

One older man had just slipped off the bridge of cubicle walls that went over the chasm, and it was only bare luck that James caught him in time and hauled him up. Some kid—and it was strange that James and Alanna thought of these people who were probably their age or slightly older as "kids"—who still had his hair gelled into a paintbrush style had also almost died when he panicked at a potted plant. And one more doofus had just ignored Theo's organizational orders entirely, proclaimed that he was a US Marine, strode off on his own, and no one saw him again. James refused to believe that his claim was true, that was just too dumb.

Two people had died. A girl who didn't look older than fifteen had simply never woken up after being severed from Karen's network, and when nothing James tried had gotten her to start breathing again, they had to accept that she was never going to have made it in the first place. The other one was even harder. A gentleman with salt-and-pepper stubble and a thin hairline who nonetheless carried himself with a steady confidence. He'd made it out into the blasted war zone outside their temporary refuge, and James had found him sitting with his back to the wall, watching the flocks of paper dance against the lights overhead.

"My daughter would have loved to see this," he'd said in a breathy whisper. It was the last thing he'd said. James had sat with him until the group was ready to move, and taken his wallet at the end on the chance they made it out and he could contact the family. A conversation he wasn't looking forward to.

Now they sat in a huge ring of cleared floor space. The more physically capable survivors had been tasked with shifting walls and desks, and under Theo's direction, Fort Big Mistake had come together far more rapidly than James's and Anesh's first fumbling attempts to build a secure position had so many months ago. Desks had been set up in clusters to give table space for people to eat what rations they had, all the coats and decorative desk pillows they could find had been repurposed into bedding, and the glow of lamps and flashlights illuminated the shadowed area under the overhanging lip of the edge of the structure. Piles of documents and office supplies and even computers were stacked around the outside edge, useless things here that could be checked later for blue orbs but right now just needed to be out of the way.

Theo had broken people into small groups and told them to keep an eye on each other. James recognized what she was doing as an old manager trick that he'd picked up from some skill orb somewhere: give them responsibility for each other, make them feel like a team, and they'll work to be worthy of it. It might not work in the long term; it certainly didn't work at call centers when no one wanted to be there. But here, with life itself on the line? No one was going to be stuck together long enough to learn to resent and hate each other.

James and Alanna sat together in the middle of the fortification, under the open ceiling and the Decision Tree. There was no day-night cycle here, never had been, so it still felt odd to stop to sleep. But James didn't feel like sleeping, so he stared up at the shifting "leaves" of the tree instead while Sarah slept with her head on the desk next to him. She'd refused to leave his side since they'd disconnected her. And eventually, Alanna joined him after she finished a patrol of the outside.

Theo didn't intrude. She had stuff to do. Daniel stayed away, too. He had his own problems. And for some reason, the people they'd rescued left a ring of space around James, not getting too close to where he sat spinning in his commandeered office chair.

So it was left to Alanna to talk to James.

"It's not your fault," she said, speaking so as not to wake Sarah.

"It doesn't matter if it was my fault or not," James replied, after a long silence. "He was here because of me, and now he's gone."

Alanna looked off to the side, glancing at the people around them. "He was here because you were right. It was the right thing to do."

"I know," James said, melancholy. "I know it's not really my fault, honestly." He tilted forward, windmilling his arms out from where he'd had them behind his head as he gazed upward before catching his balance again and tipping the chair back to its normal position. "But that doesn't matter. As a result of our actions, Dave . . ." He broke off, not wanting to say the words. Taking a breath to clear his suddenly constricted throat, James took a different track. "It wasn't supposed to be this kind of adventure, you know? It was . . . it was . . ."

"It was supposed to be painless?" Alanna asked.

James shook his head. "Not painless, but . . . I don't know. We get hurt all the time. Anesh and I both knew that we might die in here. I think you do, too. It's not about pain, it's just . . . it was over so fast." He took a long, shaken breath, staring down at the desk in front of him. "It wasn't a test that he failed. It was dumb luck. Theo ducked, Dave didn't, and Dave's . . . gone. Just like that. Luck."

"It was unfair," Alanna muttered. "It's supposed to be us against the Office, but it's always been fair."

"Yeah. A struggle, but one we could approach. One we could beat, if we were better." James swept his arm around at the crowd around them. "It's obviously dangerous, but if we were smart enough, fast enough, well-armed enough, we could beat it. We could fight the monsters and save the innocent and get out with the bags of gold. We could *win*." He slammed his palm down onto the desk, causing a startled yelp from Sarah as she jolted away, and causing several of the people nearest to them to look over in confusion.

"We did win," insisted Alanna. "We did."

James scowled, but not at her. Just at the world around them. "Are you trying to convince me, or yourself?" he said, his face softening with his voice. "Because this doesn't feel like winning."

"We still have to escape" came the soft voice from his side. Sarah. He'd almost forgotten she was there. The person they'd rescued, who James had hoped would fill the void in his memory, was different than he expected. She was quieter than he'd imagined, almost timid. And afraid, all the time. Though honestly, that seemed a bit like the fault of her imprisonment, and not her natural character.

She wasn't wrong, though. "You're not wrong," James said. "Maybe it'll feel worth it when we get everyone out under an actual sky again."

"We can't rest long," Alanna said glumly. "Well, I mean, *we* can't. Our rations are gone, and we need to feed about fifty people. So it's time to get scavenging while they sleep." It was a miracle that some of these people had made it this far without collapsing. Some of them almost certainly did collapse and had to be carried, because being hooked up to that network had been like being fully awake, all the time. For years, for some of them. Which brought up another question, which she tentatively asked after a minute of enjoying resting their feet. "What was it like?"

"What, being plugged in?"

"Yeah."

"It was . . ." He stopped to try to think about it, and found the action harder than expected. "It's difficult to actually process." James shrugged. "I wasn't me, but I was, but 'me' wasn't something that mattered. I'm trying really hard not to think about it." He glibly glossed over the looming existential threat to his sense of self. "I don't really remember anything, because they weren't my memories. I do remember processing the name Karen, though. That was the . . . thing . . . that came up."

Alanna shuddered. "Was it even human? It's the first thing we've seen that had, like, flesh."

"It wasn't." He spoke with hard resolve. "It was shaped like a human, because of what it was meant to do." James didn't realize that he wasn't fully guiding his own words for a minute. "Design followed the idea of the overbearing employee, function was . . ." He trailed off and shared a look with Sarah. At some point, she'd started speaking almost the same words as him, and neither of them had noticed.

But Alanna had. "That's fucking creepy," she bluntly stated, aiming a finger at the two of them. "But I don't blame you. What was up with the network thing?"

Shaking off the residual overlap that had been left imprinted on their psyches, James and Sarah sat up a bit before he answered Alanna. "I think it was an accident. Or an emergent property? It wasn't what Karen was designed for, just what she . . . it . . . ended up doing. And then the more people in the network, the smarter it got, and the more it could do . . ." James trailed off. "I don't remember a lot, but I remember bits and chunks of some of the thoughts I had to process. That thing wanted to be in charge, so badly."

"It thought itself a god." Sarah spoke with an uneasy voice. "It bought or stole people, and thought if it had enough, it could run Officium Mundi."

James started nodding, then stilled, tapped the table a couple of times to help compose what he wanted to ask, and then said, "Sorry, what the hell is Officium Mundi?"

"It's what we called this place," Sarah said. "Me and my crew, anyway."

That got James's attention, more so than just the quiet contentment that Sarah had started talking for real. "Wait, your crew. Not us?" he said.

She looked at him, puzzled. "No, I never . . . I never told you, did I? I'm sorry, but . . . well, you know that. Wait, why do you ask? Wait . . . no . . ."

"We don't remember you," Alanna said, bluntly, getting a wince out of James.

"Right," he said, fumbling for words as panic started to spread across Sarah's face. "We didn't really have time to go over this. And I've been . . . um . . ."

"Moping."

James flicked his hand at Alanna, mock-trying to topple her out of her tipped-back chair. "Fuck off." It got a small smile out of him, though. "But yeah. Moping. Anyway. We don't . . . know who you are. Or, like, we don't recognize you. Alanna and I figured out that you *existed*, but when we look at you, we see a stranger."

It looked like Sarah was caught somewhere between exhaustion and tears, and James had no idea what to say to help with it. The dungeon just kept taking things from people. Maybe it was retribution, maybe it was just straight-up mad at them for kicking in the door and taking skill orbs and candy out. But either way, it left him without solid footing to explain or try to repair the damage.

Fortunately, Alanna wasn't as mentally frayed as he was, and came to his rescue. "I think the dungeon, which I'm not going to remember your name for, took interest in you for some reason. James recognized a few other people in here, so it didn't wipe everyone's memories. Might have been because you were a delver. Or maybe it just adds up over time. But yeah, we . . . we know you were important . . ."

"But we don't *remember*," James said, bitterness in his words.

There was a quiet period, a ring of silence that surrounded the three of them. The other survivors near them threw worried glances at their rescue team and toned down their own conversations to hushed tones. Even Theo altered her stomping path back from the perimeter guard, sensing something wrong and veering away with a grumble to recheck their walls, giving the trio some time.

"What . . . what now?" Sarah eventually asked, stabilizing her voice and wiping away drops of tears from her cheeks.

James sighed. "Now, we have about forty hours left until our window of exit closes. So we get off our asses, stop feeling sorry for ourselves, and go scrounge up some food for everyone. And get Daniel to do the shitty job of poking every piece of crap we found in here to see if it's magic."

"Xenotech," Sarah said, on pure reflex.

"Goddammit," James muttered as Alanna pounded the table in laughter next to him. "How. Fucking *how*. Anesh and I are going to have *words* when we get back."

"Don't yell at our boyfriend," Alanna smugly told him as she stood up, arcing her arms over her head in an attempt to stretch out the lingering soreness of the fight. "Anyway. James isn't wrong. We can give everyone some time to rest, but we're going to have to move soon. There's a lot of ground to cover, and we need to have an allowance for sleep for all the malnourished civilians. Also, it's not going to help that we were beating the shit out of some of these people an hour ago." Sarah rubbed at her bruised jaw as Alanna brought that up.

"Also also," James said, "just because we don't remember you doesn't mean you're not part of our group. This place, so far, has a pretty bad track record of actually taking anything away from me." He thought for a second, then shrugged. "And you clearly already know all the jokes, so, you know . . . don't worry about our social situation right now. We've got bigger problems with the people here, like Alanna said."

It was true. For all that they'd gotten everyone out of the conference room at the end of the universe, these people weren't saved yet. There were miles of office to traverse, and even though they had an extra hundred eyes to watch for threats, people who were untrained, starved, exhausted, and until recently traumatically imprisoned and linked to a monstrous hive mind network might not be the very best at actually responding to those threats. And, again, it didn't help that they'd just had a scrap with those very same people. And won.

Not that James was going to trade away coming out on top, just that the situation sucked.

He frowned to himself. It felt like there'd been a lot of things just sucking over the last day. His mind again turned to the loss of Dave, and the pang of guilt that he still felt in his chest. It was, as Alanna had said, not his fault. But not his fault was different than it not being because of him, and that feeling of responsibility, of wanting to save everyone, it left him with a hole in his heart. It stole his breath and fogged his thoughts, and reminded him that he'd failed. And he'd failed almost as badly as possible.

"What am I supposed to do? How are we supposed to get everyone out of here safe?" he muttered to himself.

Overhead, the Decision Tree flickered to life, options dancing across its many screens.

Below, James sat up and snapped his fingers. "Alanna! Get me the bag!" he exclaimed, pointing upward. It took her about five seconds of staring at his finger before she looked up where he pointed, and another heartbeat to realize what he meant.

"Oh. Oh!" She dragged the duffel onto the table where they'd been keeping the orbs. Unzipped it and shoveled a double handful of glittering gold treasures onto the desk. Then another. Then *another*. James stood, grabbing a few of the size-one orbs. He scanned the branches of coiled black cables, looking for the ubiquitous monitor lizards that called these trees home. And when he spotted a couple—hard to do when they kept themselves the same color as their backgrounds—he raised his hand up with the orbs between his fingers.

"We'd like to make a trade," he told them, using that calm, low voice that his uncle always used when training a new dog. It took a while, but eventually, one of them crawled down, and James smiled and stood statue-still as it plucked one of the orbs from his fingers.

It scuttled away and, after a minute of patient waiting, returned with a gleaming purple sphere the size and color of a ripe grape.

James grinned wide and presented the other orbs. Next to him, Alanna did the same. More and more monitor lizards flowed down the tree, bringing fair exchange for their treasure.

They could do it, James thought, if they were more than human. If there was even the slightest chance they could reach past the limits of the natural world, they could get these people home. And as the pile of yellow orbs rapidly converted to purples, he knew they had a chance. When they ran the tree out of its stock, and he, Alanna, Theo, and Sarah turned the orbs into concrete power, he knew they were going to make it.

Overhead, seven of the screen leaves flickered in happy response to his earlier question.

"Don't give up yet."

[Shell Upgraded : Improved Symmetry, −4 flaws]
[Shell Upgraded : Vocal Range, +/− .6 octaves]
[Shell Upgraded : Acceleration, +4 kph]
[Shell Upgraded : Taste Range - Salt, +16 clarity]
[Shell Upgraded : Blood Production, +0.85 pints/day]
[Shell Upgraded : Bone Density, +2,350 kg/m^3]

James's results made him bare his teeth as the feelings of the changes warped his body into something not new, but now refined. He was ready. He was just enough more than he was to make it through. Though he did wonder at whether the shell upgrades changed how he actually thought about himself and his actions, because right now, he felt like kicking off the ground and seeing just how far he could sprint, and he wasn't sure if that was just childlike joy at the upgrade or something deeper changing in him.

[Shell Upgraded : Hair Durability, +1,510 TFU]

[Shell Upgraded : Fingernail Sharpness, +46 HRC]

[Shell Upgraded : Facial Expression Emotive Clarity, −45% chance of misunderstanding]

[Shell Upgraded : Alcohol Processing Speed, +4 oz/hour]

[Shell Upgraded : Arm Muscle Mass, +4.8 kg]

[Shell Upgraded : Dermal Heat Tolerance Offset, +/−18c]

For Alanna, the changes were equally uncomfortable. Especially all at once, feeling her face shift along with the flesh under the skin of her arms was akin to the sensation of a thousand bugs crawling across her all at once. And she would have hated it, if it hadn't made her feel so fucking *alive*. Alanna wasn't a weak person by any means. And while she didn't think of James as weak, either, she could probably have casually pinned him with one arm, no matter how much gym time he was putting in. Now, though? Now she could *throw* him one-armed and not even feel it.

[Shell Upgraded : Cancer Cell Generation Speed, −180%]

[Shell Upgraded : Fingers, +1]

[Shell Upgraded : Jump Height, +0.8m]

[Shell Upgraded : Limb Regrowth Speed, 5%/day]

Theo wasn't especially impressed with her upgrades. Certainly not after the searing pain left her with a case of polydactyly, which ended up feeling far less awkward than she thought it should. It felt wrong, to be able to vault one of the cube walls like it was nothing. Her muscles weren't tougher, she hadn't trained or earned this, it was just something she could *do* now. And it annoyed her that James and his team had been snapping up things like this, taking the cheater's path to physical conditioning that she'd had to work for. Though it stung less that they shared with her, and damned if she wasn't going to enjoy it. Twenty days to replace a lost arm? Theo never had to worry about a motorcycle accident going wrong again.

[Shell Upgraded : Magnetic Field Control, +2−8 teslas]

[Shell Upgraded : Oxygen Requirement, −26%]
[Shell Upgraded : Memorability, +1]

Sarah knew some things about Officium Mundi that she hadn't had time or reason to share with the others yet. For all she knew, they were already clued in to the fact that this place would, on a long enough timeline and over enough orbs, give you what you wanted. Not what you were asking for but what you really wanted in the back of your mind. She'd taken fewer purples, partly because she wasn't entirely on board with the decision to leave Daniel out of it, but also because she knew she wasn't fit to fight. It was nice of James to include her, but she didn't . . . she didn't know how to act around him now. She was a stranger in her own social skin.

So it didn't really surprise her that much when the purple gave her a point in "memorability." It was one of the ones that didn't give a concrete definition, which she'd found were the more powerful ones, because of how broadly they chose to apply their vague abilities. And she did want it. She never wanted to be forgotten again, not that she'd asked in the first place. But if this hell was going to erase away her mark on the web of people in her life, the least it could do was give her the firepower to put the pieces back together.

"All right." James broke the silence of the group's thoughts. "We've got six hours before we start to try to get everyone moving." He looked around at the other three delvers with him. "Who wants to see who can pull in the dumbest-named candy bar before then?"

"Oh, yes!" Sarah couldn't help but answer, her excitement overriding the awkwardness she felt at the feeling of isolation. This was exactly the sort of stupid thing that James always came up with that made him the kind of person she wanted to be friends with in the first place. "Did you know I once found something in here called Baby Things? God, that was weird."

"Hey! Don't mock Baby Things! That was the first one I found!" James railed, mock-indignant, hand to his heart. "Well, whatever. Teams of two?"

The four of them picked up weapons, strapped on armor, and headed out, Ganesh trailing with Alanna and Theo, while Sarah and James took the other side, both teams promising to not overcommit to anything and vowing to bring back the food for everyone. James stopped to speak to a few people on the way out, letting them know what was going on and asking them to pass word to the others.

"How do they do it?" a man named Harvey asked the younger kid in a tattered FedEx uniform sitting next to him. His arm still ached from where it had been dislocated, though he'd been fortunate enough to be unconscious when it was popped back in.

"Do what?" the other guy, Dominic, asked with a raspy voice. They'd had to ration water, and there hadn't been a lot to go around. And this place had pretty rarefied air on top of that.

"How do they get up and go out again? I can barely stand up." He wasn't complaining, though he'd considered it. Instead, he spoke with almost a note of awe.

Dominic shrugged and didn't answer. From the floor on the other side of him, a middle-aged man by the name of Stephen answered, curled up with his head on a salvaged coat. "Obvious, right? They're not hungry."

"They gave up their lunches for us. And they walked just as far. Hell, they kept jumping in to save us." Harvey shrugged back, though the other guy had his eyes too closed to see.

"Saved my ass," a girl in a studded leather jacket with an unkempt Mohawk chimed in, scooting over to join their conversation. "Anyone got a smoke?" No one had a smoke. "Eh. But yeah! I mean, that Black chick absolutely fucking *ruined* one of those faceless fuckers when it tried to grab me."

"I saw that." Harvey nodded to her. "What's up with that drone following them?"

"I think it's alive." Dominic cleared his throat. "Looks like a bat."

The goth girl snapped her fingers, getting a few other people nearby to look over at her for a moment. "And it has a laser! That's just sweet."

"Did I hear that one of them died?" someone asked, and the conversation went quietly somber.

Eventually, Stephen rolled himself into a cross-legged sitting position. "And they're still going? I saw them smiling; that's fucked up."

"I think . . ." A woman pulled herself into the conversation. Long hair, torn dress suit. Her name was also Karen, and she remembered enough of the network to feel awful about that. "I think they're trying to be strong."

"Trying?" Dominic asked, getting a snicker out of Momo, the punk girl, and also Harvey.

"Yeah," Harvey said. "Yeah. I don't think they need to try very hard. You guys remember that field of wreckage after they pulled us out?"

"Not strong like that," Dominic said.

Momo nodded to a beat only she could hear. "Yeah, man. They're, you know . . . Fuckin' . . ."

"They're heroes," someone said quietly.

Their little group huddled closer together. They all felt a kind of poison emptiness, something missing from themselves now that they'd been ripped from the network. But here, talking, together, it was a little like that link they missed. A few of them rubbed at the still-present ports in their skulls; a few others wondered if maybe staying in the office might just be better for them. But those who watched the delvers leave, who saw their hero stride out holding a crowbar casually at his side or give a friendly tap to the autonomous drone on her shoulder? Those who saw the re-forming wisp of some serpentine sea creature coiling friendly around the legs of a hugging couple, or watched one of their rescuers literally leap the wall just to see if she could?

They felt a little more hope.

CHAPTER 26

James huffed for breath as he rounded the corner. He was starting to feel the weight of the near-constant physical exertion, and it turned out that a few months of gym time wasn't enough to turn him into a Terminator-like supersoldier. Which would have annoyed him, if he'd had the time to think about it.

Twelve hours later. They'd somehow managed to scrounge up enough food for everyone, though calling it "food" gave them a lot of credit. Most of it was, as was tradition at this point, random candy. James had won the bet of weirdest name with a bar wrapped in flexible gold foil, labeled simply with block letters that read *Healthy Chunks*. When they'd laid out their food and let people grab something to eat, that one had gone last. Actually, that one had gone to *James*, once he'd rolled his eyes at everyone's squeamishness and decided to take a bite himself. That, of course, was a mistake. The dungeon might not poison food, but it sure as hell didn't have the taste buds needed to make flavor winners every time. And some kind of nutrient paste with nodules of aloe gel in it was . . . well, at best unpleasant.

Still, he'd won a yellow orb off of Sarah. Apparently, using these things as an almost joking kind of intergroup currency was just a thing that they all thought of at some point. She was kind of miffed that hers had lost, since she'd found one that was actually just called Candy. James had tried that one too.

"What's it taste like?" Alanna had asked with a massive grin.

After a moment to think, James responded in a jokingly reverent voice, "The platonic ideal . . ."

"Does this mean we're not having sex?"

He snorted a surprised laugh. "Not that kind of platonic, you goof." It had been a small moment of quiet smiles amid the rising tension.

That was getting off topic, though. The point was, it had taken them time to get the food. Time to get everyone organized. Time to get people moving. Time, time, time. They were running out of it; even if they had well over a full twenty-four hours left, James was getting nervous.

And now they had to actually deal with moving a large number of people over a large distance.

The biggest issue was that moving as a group the first time, they'd lost people. At some point, someone in the back half of the group had taken a wrong turn. Everyone following them had kept following. And then, before anyone realized what was happening, they'd ended up split. Now, granted, it wasn't that much of a problem at first. A huge mob of confused people was actually kind of easy to find in this place, even with the overhead arching walls and banner-vines of printer paper, especially with Ganesh still somehow alert and up for running their entire scout division. The bigger problem was the number of stapler wounds and burns from the Taser-mouse things that they refused to call Pikachus for copyright reasons but still hadn't found a name for. The wildlife of the dungeon was still dangerous, something James had almost forgotten with his practiced movements to gut a strider and pocket the orb, and armor plating covering anything vital. And now, that wildlife was being disturbed en masse by dozens of untrained humans.

It was a recipe for disaster waiting to happen, especially if they lost people in ones or twos. They really didn't have any way to communicate over distances with everyone. They'd only packed four radios, phones didn't work in here, no one could figure out how to properly send messages using the dungeon's Wi-Fi, and James sure as hell wasn't letting anyone use the flare gun when it was explicitly there for signaling their exit team.

So the strategy they'd ended up with was the exhausting plan of moving small groups from safe spot to safe spot. A handful of people at a time, with only one or two of the experienced delvers escorting them and then jogging back to where they started to bring the next batch. It was now the third run of this James had done, and he was starting to feel like a cowboy, where the cows were shaped like humans and just curious enough to be dangerous.

The real unavoidable problem was, these were people. And people, once they'd had a nap and some food and knew they weren't going to be trapped in a hostile hive mind using them to take over an extradimensional realm anymore, tended to get curious about stuff. Which meant that James and Alanna and even Sarah had to start fielding questions about things. And when they weren't around to tell people about the wildlife, the orbs, the candy, the insanely high ceiling, the warped landscape, the existence of things like Secret or Karen, and why they were wearing half a copier held together with wire, well, then people started touching things. And so even though these were people who had survived only through the sheer luck of having James and Alanna making a last-minute call to go back for them, they were already beginning to go from "rescued humans" to "annoying problems" in the minds of the delvers.

Well, not all of them. And even then, it was more of a vaguely sarcastic thought that flashed through James's mind, and not any real disdain for these people. And . . . well . . .

It was fun.

He had to admit it, it was *fun* to talk to them about this stuff. To answer those weird questions, to be the guy who everyone turned to for answers. To find that, even though he felt like he had no *clue* what the bigger picture of the office was, even though he was totally in the dark about the nature of the place and the purpose of this twisted workspace, he *knew things*. He found it so easy to snap off answers about how different creatures acted, or how he knew stuff was safe to eat, or what sort of traps to watch out for.

He felt like a goddamn veteran. And he knew Alanna was feeling the same way, even if she was a little more scowly about it. It made sense, though. She'd gotten even less sleep than he had, and Alanna had also spent an extra day or so assuming he was trapped forever in an endless loop of failing to open a door. That could stress a person out.

"Fuck, 'that could stress a person out' could be our group motto," James muttered to himself.

"What's that?" Alanna queried as he walked into their almost-empty base camp. She was the last of their party here, left as the rear guard with the last batch of rescuees. Theo and Sarah were ahead with everyone else, wrangling some of the more alert and able survivors into clearing out one of those more open-air, low-walled areas, while Daniel and his mental map were keeping them all on track.

James took Alanna's offered hand and helped haul her to her feet. "Oh, just that this place gets really stressful when we're stuck here."

"Like it isn't otherwise?" she asked him.

James thought about it. "Nnnno. No?" He shrugged at her as the last group of survivors assembled before them. "Okay, guys, you know how this goes. We're gonna be moving through mostly clear territory, but keep an eye open for anything moving. According to Sarah, whatever your network was doing was keeping the office wildlife suppressed, and with everything starting to wake up more aggressive, we aren't taking chances. Stay close, let us know if you need us to slow down. Don't touch anything." A series of nods and affirmations came back to him. They'd heard this before with every other group.

"Okay." Alanna spoke privately to James as they waited for the last straggler to take a short trip to the designated privy. "What do you mean it's not stressful?"

"I mean . . . fuck, I mean, did you even know me before we started this?" James's voice cracked as he sighed out his answer. "Alanna, I was a wreck. I worked full time, but still stressed about money *all the time*. The only fun I ever had was playing D&D with the group, and even that was more of a distraction than anything else. And more than that . . ." He paused. "More than that, I was just dead inside. I didn't see anything beyond getting home to replay the same old games, and maybe ordering pizza when I had extra cash. That was it. *It*."

"And now?" she asked him as they took point on their small squad, rolling out of the camp and starting a fast walk to their now-familiar waypoint.

"And now I do this," James said. "We sorta talked about it the other day, right? We fight, we're rewarded directly for our accomplishments, and we go home to lives that get better every day. That's it," he bluntly finished.

"That's not it," Alanna insisted firmly.

"It's enough," James told her. "Can you imagine how bad things would get if we got greedy? I don't want to . . . I don't wanna rule the world, Alanna."

"You're not qualified for that yet," she told him. "But that doesn't change the fact that we're more qualified for other things than most people."

James frowned lightly as they took a corner. The path they were on was supposed to be clear, and he'd already run it several times, but it didn't hurt to be careful. "You're talking about how there might be . . ." A quick check, this time to make sure none of their followers were listening in. ". . . other dungeons."

"The thing on the phone called this place its brother," she said. It was a statement, and an open question. Alanna left the words hanging there as they split up to escort everyone through a series of twists.

It was, James decided, really annoying to have someone who knew you well enough to make you want to talk to them. Alanna's statement hovered in the back of his head for a few minutes, and by the time they reconnected for a long hallway of cubicles, he had a response. "Okay," James stated flatly. "I've got conditions to this."

Alanna nodded, the façade of a serious expression on her face as she kept her eyes forward, looking over James's head. "First of all, I'm kinda worried that we're vastly underqualified compared to, like, a military or police force." He cut Alanna off before she could respond. "No, think about it. If a military unit came through here, they could have killed this place and gone home in a day. *And then been just as upgraded as us.*"

"But they didn't," Alanna told him. "We did. And now we are, quite literally, becoming something beyond human."

"Right." James admitted to that. "We did. We're the big damn heroes mostly just because we're on hand, not because we're qualified. Yes, yes. 'Yet.' And I get it, that's good enough. And I *don't* want to give this up. And I also don't want to go to whatever kind of wizard jail the government has set up in the middle of the Alaskan wilderness. So . . . !"

"So?" Alanna couldn't keep hiding a smile.

"So, yeah. When we get out of here, we go find the other one. Other *ones.* There's gotta be more. And we can't just keep farming the office and pretending that there isn't a bigger world out there. So shut up, stop being so smug about it, and let's pretend I agreed with you from the start."

"Not exactly how I would have phrased it," Alanna replied, "but I more or less agree. Even if we aren't killing whole worlds, which I'm still not sure we can actually do, they can still clearly produce threats to the real world. Also, I hate being in the dark about stuff. Like, you say 'secret wizard jail,' and I actually have to do a sanity check on if that's something we know about or not."

James laughed. "Yeah, I did my time in wizard jail." He put on a voice that was his bad interpretation of what crime-Gandalf would sound like. "Ten winters I spent on the inside for selling black market newt anus!"

"Jesus Christ." Alanna snorted out an unexpected bark of laughter. "You can't just say things like that. We're supposed to be noble rescuers, and now all these people have heard you say 'newt anus.'"

"You too, now." He patted her on the shoulder. "But don't worry, I promise not to make that our motto."

"I still think we should be trying to find ways to use our new upgrades in the real world, too," Alanna said. "I know it's not what you guys want to do, but . . ."

James cut her off. "Okay, hang on. I know we haven't really talked about this in a little while, but I wanna be clear on something. I *absolutely* want to make the world a better place and all that. The problem is I don't know where to apply the abilities I have. It's a matter of scale and use, not of desire. I may not be as philosophically well read as you, and have a handle on exactly how I want to impact humanity, but I'm not some sociopath that just wants to fight and get stronger so I can support my own fight-based exponential growth."

"I never thought you were," Alanna said, almost hurt that James would think that, but still understanding what his worry was. "Hell, I wouldn't be dating you if I thought that." Alanna waved him around a corner, and the two of them watched a shellaxy meander across the hallway before moving on, signaling for their group to follow. "Oh, shit, you know what I just thought of?" she asked, eyebrows raised.

"What?" James glanced over at her before returning his gaze to sweeping the cubicles around them.

"That stupid briefcase! The one the sibling spawned with the note to answer the phone! We got so caught up in everything that we didn't check it!" Alanna swept her arm over the ridge of cubicle walls ahead of them. "I can even see the spire we were camped in from here. I'm gonna go check for it when we pass by."

"What could possibly be worth it in a dungeon briefcase?"

Alanna shrugged at him, then realized James was ahead of her and facing away, so she put the shrug into her words instead. "I dunno. But Frank had a lot of them, remember, so, probably money? You *did* just say you spent the last decade stressed about money. And also I don't have a job anymore, so now *I'm* stressed about money, and it's kind of your fault in a roundabout way, so you get to come help me retrieve it," she declared.

It had already occurred to James to offer to tag along, and he was curious anyway, so he just laughed at her overacted claim. "Well, it's good to have a plan. Anyway, backing up a step, the hard part is going to be convincing Anesh that . . ." Before James could finish, he was interrupted by a yell from behind them. Both of them spun in an instant, guards already up.

One of their escorted civilians had fallen on his ass as he flailed backward. Another ran past James and Alanna in unthinking panic, while a tiny girl with tattered jeans and a leather waistcoat taken from a cubicle somewhere tried to kick the shit out of the camraconda that had sunk its teeth into the leg of one of the last stragglers.

It was pure luck that someone had looked behind them. The man was frozen in midstep, about a hundred paces back. He hadn't even made a whimper as the three hundred pounds of snake had driven its finger-length bronze fangs into his leg. He couldn't. Couldn't scream, couldn't twitch, certainly couldn't get away. And James was a bit worried to see that as it jerked its maw free with a red spray to sweep its camera eye to the girl trying to kick it, the survivor *still didn't move*.

Alanna slapped an open palm on his shoulder, and James started advancing with long strides, adjusting his grip on the good old trusty crowbar. This was something they'd actually had time to practice. The camraconda was, hands down, the most dangerous thing here. Tumblefeeds were bad, but could be pretty easily outrun. The 2.0s were also dangerous, as were plants if they caught you in an ambush, but they could be fought more directly. But the snakes? Literally the only defense against them was having a friend and a flanking maneuver. Once you *knew* that, you were fine, but until that game of red-light-green-light got solved, James was well aware of how easy it would be for one of them to kill a person, and he'd made the whole group train on counter-snake tactics. So he didn't hesitate to start stepping up to the snake that was currently bearing down on the girl that had been kicking it, not stopping when it rose up with half its body to show a form that was a *lot* taller than normal. It actually towered over the young woman, but when James let out a wordless shout, it swiveled its head over to him, letting its prey jerk back into motion like the pause button had been hit again.

He froze in place, in an awkward half-moving position with his arm just starting to come up with his weapon. The camraconda slithered over to him in a few sharp twists of its body, boxy security-camera face seeming almost curious as to what the hell he thought he was accomplishing screaming at it. Its mouth opened wide, right next to his face, and James got a front-row showing of those fangs, which looked quite a bit larger up close.

Then Alanna punched it through a wall.

James hadn't actually expected that to do much. And as he glanced over at the shocked look on Alanna's face, it looked like she hadn't either. She'd told him about the effect of the purple orb that'd made her stronger, and she'd been having fun picking things, and people, up at random after that. But now, with one flashing motion of a closed fist in front of James's face, she'd just turned a potentially deadly encounter with a hostile snake monster into one of the episodes of *Star Trek* where Worf gets the shit kicked out of him.

Then the camraconda burst out of the crumpled cubicle wall that Alanna had roundhoused it into, and instantly lunged for her. Alanna froze up with her arms halfway to her face, almost into a boxer's stance before the effect of that eye took hold. And then it was James's turn to come to the rescue, whipping the crowbar forward on an impulsive reaction that took it in the curve of its body. He experienced a brief jolt of paralysis as it jerked backward and scanned its eye over him, and then he had a moment of freedom to pivot to the side, keeping himself and Alanna on opposite sides of it as it recovered and tried to lunge at either of them.

The two of them took it apart. It saw James coming out in its peripheral vision and turned to him, which opened Alanna up to spike it into the floor. It still had a view of James's feet, but he'd already planted himself for the swing, and it wasn't too awkward for him to windmill his arms around like a golfer and spread the top half of its camera head across the hallway.

And that was that.

"Okay! Everyone regroup!" James called out. "You! Um . . . Alllley?"

"Alex," the girl, Alex apparently, replied.

"Good killer instinct there, but . . . no, you know what? No *but*. Good job. You're on guard duty from now on. Grab someone else and grab Justin here." James motioned at the stiffened man caught midstep. He turned back to Alanna, who had just stuffed the green orb into her duffel. "Fuck, do we have any antivenin? Looks like those things are venomous."

"Thank you so much for not saying 'poisonous,'" she said.

"No problem."

"No dice on the antivenin, though. We didn't pack any, and that's not how antivenin works."

"How do you know that? Orb about snakes?"

"No, I just remember learning it for a D&D thing to . . . annoy Dave." She trailed off, a moment of pain showing on her face.

"Ah," James said simply. "Okay. Well." He cleared his throat, not knowing how to help. "We've gotta keep moving."

Alanna nodded and helped him get the others back into a semblance of formation, two of their party now carrying the paralyzed man in the middle of the group, slowing them down significantly. "I just keep expecting to see him," she confided in James. "This place has a thousand ways that he could come back from whatever the hell happened to him; I just find it hard to believe he's actually gone."

"Yeah, I get you," James said. "I tried using the last charge of the blue that gave me the power to 'refill' to refill our team, but it didn't do anything except make me have to pee."

"Fuck, that was you!" Alanna gasped in mock horror, punching James in the shoulder.

"Fuck, careful with that!" He gasped himself in surprise. "You're gonna break my arm if you hit that hard!"

Any actual anger James had went out the window when he saw her face. Alanna had been kind of cagey about a couple of her purple's effects, but James was pretty sure one of them made her awful at poker by making it super easy to read her emotions. And right now, she looked so obviously sheepish that he knew he wasn't going to be mad about an honest mistake. "Right! Right, sorry!" She took a minute, then pointed ahead. "Is that the camp?"

Thankfully, it was. And so, after too many trips down this stretch of hall, James could finally take a short break. He flopped into a chair that Daniel wordlessly vacated for him, setting the crowbar onto the floor with a thump. Rubbing at his sore hands revealed a stinging pain, and James was annoyed to again see that he'd torn the webbing between his thumb and forefinger. He really, really needed to find some gloves if he couldn't get a real weapon. Or, if nothing else, pack extra gloves next time.

Maybe he should start carrying a sledgehammer, like Alanna originally had. He leaned back in the chair, taking out a small yellow orb from his pocket and rolling it on the desk. It was an idle motion, and he just sat for a bit as everyone hurried around him, feeling the ache in his feet more than ever now that he wasn't standing, letting his eyes unfocus as he looked into the still color of the orb. Thinking of sledgehammers, James wondered what would happen if they broke an orb. They'd activated them personally, absorbed them, knew they could be turned into what he internally called totems, and also made into magic items, but they'd never actually just smashed one open.

He was halfway to raising the crowbar over the desk in curiosity when Theo planted her hands on the makeshift table across from him. "Okay, everyone's accounted for," she said in a tired voice. "Daniel has the next waypoint marked for us. Alanna says we'll rest there while you two go take care of something. Seems kinda risky to fool around here, but who am I to judge. We also still need more real food, and medical supplies. I'd like permission to set some of the survivors to breaking things to get blues. Alanna says they solve problems."

"I . . . no, not that kind of . . ." James shook the thought off. "Never mind, whatever. Also, why are you asking me permission? Wait, why are you reporting to me in the first place? You're more suited to be in charge."

Theo gave him a blank stare. "Uh-huh," she said, sarcasm dripping so thick it pooled on the floor at her feet.

"Okay, fine. Permission granted. Don't bother trying to control who uses the orbs, just make sure everyone knows we're in this together. Time is critical here."

"Yes, *sah*." Theo snapped off a salute and sauntered away.

"Alanna!" James called out, tilting backward over the chair. "I don't want a military command! You take it!"

"'Kay!" she yelled back, ignoring him.

Command position abdicated, James closed his eyes for a minute. He'd had a hard day passing up the opportunity for a dictatorship. Time to relax for a bit.

There was a clatter from one of the doorways into this zone. There were almost fifty people in here, leaving it crowded, but it was still relatively quiet. Everyone was too tired to really talk much, and for some reason that James hadn't figured out yet, everyone would rather crowd together to give him a bubble of space than sit near him. So it caught his attention when one of the groups of three that Theo had sent out to scout around burst back in.

One of them was smoking.

Not a cigarette, either, which would have also confused James. But actually smoking like he'd been on fire until recently; wisps of thin gray air were pouring off his shoulders and back. That guy took a seat next to the supply pile while his teammate made sure he was okay. James kept an eye on them as they found him a new coat from the stock that they kept collecting from this place. *Too many coats, not enough food*, James thought, then looked up as the third member of the team headed over to him.

It was the kind of girl that James would uniquely use the word *chick* for. Her coat absolutely didn't come from the office, as it was covered in square metal studs, which almost perfectly matched the worn and torn leather. All of it topped by a neon-green Mohawk.

"Yo, boss," she said. "Theo told us to tell you if we found anything weird."

"Oh my god, I'm going to kill her," James moaned. "Don't call me boss," he said, with a tone that was neither firm nor believable. The smile didn't help his case either. "What's up? Everyone okay?"

"That's why we're gonna call you boss," she replied pointedly. "Anyway, we found one of those cable snakes, and James wanted to ambush it, so . . ."

"Sorry, James?" James questioned.

"Yeah, the guy who looks like he's anime right now." She gestured to the still-smoking man.

"Right. Also, didn't *someone* tell you not to engage the camracondas?" James suddenly realized this must have been how his dad felt, *all the time*.

"Camraconda is a *way* better name!" The girl perked up. James made a mental note to ask her name at some point. "And yes, but we ignored that, because we've all tried the yellow orbs, but I wanted to see what a green felt like. Anyway. We decided to ambush it, and . . ."

"Seriously?"

"Stop interrupting!" she chastised him. "Anyway, we were *going to*, but then there was a fight and it almost bit Simon's arm off, and then James shoved one of the yellows into a computer screen, and then this dog thing made of glow came out, and it ate the snake I think? Er, camraconda. And it kinda set James on fire." Her words came out at a breakneck clip.

James processed what she'd said at a rate of about two words a minute. Eventually, his brain caught up to at least one point. "The James thing is really throwing me off," he said. Followed by "Where's the mongausse now?"

"The what?"

"It has four legs, it eats snakes, and it's made of monitor light. It's getting called a mongausse."

"So you guys name everything like Pokémon?"

"Except the electric mouse. Can't think of a good one for that. Now where's the mongausse?"

"Um . . . we booked it out of there?" She looked at him like he was crazy.

"Go find it," James ordered her. "It's your kid now. Treat it well."

She threw him a mocking open-palmed salute and jogged back to where her teammates sat.

"Goddammit," James muttered. "I'm in charge." He tipped his head back again, looking at the world upside down. "Alanna! I'm in charge anyway!"

"We know!" she called back.

James closed his eyes. He figured he had five minutes before the next problem.

He was asleep in two.

CHAPTER 27

James was dreaming.

He recognized it fast this time. He'd been here before. One foot down, then . . . then . . . what came next?

Ah, yes, the next step.

It was an endless hallway. The lights beat down overhead. Someone walked next to him. Someone familiar, but . . . not.

"Secret?" James asked, curiously. It felt like Secret. It looked like James. But it didn't look like, well, *Secret*. It was a James-shaped cloak again, and he couldn't see any of the creation that was Secret's more personal shape within it.

"I needed to say goodbye," it said, with an echo of Secret's voice. "For now. Just for now."

"What?" James watched as the hallway around them bled as they kept walking, the walls running together into liquid geometric shapes that shifted but kept them in their gray tunnel. "I don't understand."

Secret made a motion that looked like a puppet trying to nod. "I know. I used to know." He turned his . . . its . . . head sharply to look at James. "I was becoming too much like you."

Was. Was? He wasn't Secret, not that James recognized him. He was a figure in black, a shadow of an old idea. What had happened to James's friend? Through the mist of dream logic, he made the connection. Secret had given something up. Something important. The *only* thing that was important.

"That was the point!" James tried to scream, as he started to realize a sinking fear. But his words came out flat and dreamlike.

"I cannot see my own world quite so well," Once-Secret told him. "I must become what I was, if I am to be of any use." The construct stopped walking suddenly, and James tried to stop his legs but found that he couldn't. He kept moving forward down the hall, trying to will his mouth to open, his walk to stop, but he couldn't. Locked inside his mind, inside his own mind. "This is a truth, James. Ideas can change, sometimes whether you want them to or not. I choose this, because we require knowledge that my humanity keeps from me. You need to let go. Don't bring me back until I am ready."

James cracked his lips apart, and it felt like opening a canyon in his mouth and his mind. But even then, the words wouldn't come. He wanted to shout, to tell Secret to stay, that it wasn't that important, that *he* was important. But Secret was very, very good at shaping James's dreams, and instead there was only silence as James walked farther and farther down the hall, trying to reach back to hang on to his friend.

The last thing he saw of Secret was a small smile, and the words "Don't worry. You brought me to life once. All you have to do is agree with me, now. Say the words. You already know them."

No, James wanted to say. He didn't understand. He did understand. Secret was leaving. But he couldn't leave if James wouldn't let him, and he couldn't come back without a promise. *Stay*, James tried to say, but then he understood, and he knew he couldn't. He wouldn't. *Your worth as a person isn't tied to your function*, he screamed in his soul. But no words came out.

They needed to know more about the dungeon. They needed information on the massive construct that Secret had seen, had started to explore. If this was what he needed to do . . .

He'd learned too well from James. He was potentially giving up everything to do something stupid that might save people. James wanted to be alternately furious and proud of him. But instead, he just tried to nod.

His body obeyed this time.

"I accept your terms. For one day, you may not have anything from me, should you agree to pursue the secrets of this place," James said, his words too sharp to be the subconscious driftings of a dream and too rehearsed to truly be his own.

"The deal was already struck," the thing that was until recently Secret said in a flat monotone. And then he took a step and was gone. "A message left for you from someone else: Go back to sleep, you need your rest."

And James did, turning and walking through what was a wall.

He stepped out of a cubicle. His feet began moving again, in that dreamlike trance that was so familiar to him. Beige walls in an endless corridor fell into place around him as he walked. And walked. And walked. Forever. Gray hard carpet under his feet. Around him, no one moved about their day, not even shadows to carry the coffee cups and documents in multicolored folders strewn across the floor. He would have frozen up. James of two months ago would have frozen up. But the dream insisted, and instead he kept walking down the hallway. Around him, the people who weren't there greeted him by name, barking out strange shapes of words at his passing.

He walked on. Past a water cooler that had discarded cups around it, endlessly spilling their contents. Past a bundle of power cables, hollowed out like a cocoon. Past a hundred shed husks of striders and tapiers and shellaxies. On, and on, and on. For what felt like seconds, maybe minutes. An eternity.

He found himself in a room with a phone, suspended from the ceiling. The wiring for it was bundled into rope and looped into a noose. Molten droplets of corporate loyalty dripped off it to splash against the floor, leaving ripples in the circle of light. The handset dangled loosely, spinning as gravity wound and unwound the rubber cord over and over again.

Around him in the dark, hundreds of yellow and red and purple points of light flared to life. Crystal promises in the void.

The phone did not ring. James did not pick up.

"Thank you," the voice on the other end said, in the robotic female tone of a machine greeting, that he knew with unnerving solidity wasn't just a program.

James jerked awake with a soft cough, his eyes snapping open as he sat up from where he'd slumped over the table onto a pillow made of his own arms. He was still at the desk, no one had moved him, as he caught his breath and tried to remember why his dream had felt so terrifying, James checked his phone. "Ten minutes of sleep?" he grumbled. "I could have..."

His eyes moved up to the other side of the table. Sitting there, looking profoundly uncomfortable, was Daniel. He was looking much the worse for wear, still proudly bearing the ripped and bloodied security jacket from the company, a sweat-stained shirt underneath. James wondered why he hadn't snapped up some of the dry cleaning that they kept running across. Maybe it just didn't fit him? He was kind of a thicker guy, not that James would call him overly fat. He was looking at James with an expectant face, eyebrows raised like he was waiting for a reply.

"Wuh?" James cleared his throat, trying to unstick his voice. "Sorry, what? Did you say something?"

"I said thank you," Daniel repeated. "And I'm sorry."

"Why? Oh, because..." James willed his brain to catch up. Because what? Because everyone was mad at him for... oh.

Daniel wouldn't meet James's eyes. "Because I ran. You're the only one who doesn't hate me."

"You know I told you to wait by the door for a reason, right?" James said. "Like, yeah, it sucks, but I wasn't relying on you to fight to the death. You're not a soldier, dude. Alanna and Theo are... well, they're fuckin' wrong!" James tensed up briefly, looking around the room as subtly as possible.

"They're not here."

"Then they're fuckin' wrong!" James repeated, but quieter. "Seriously. You had no way of knowing the door would vanish on our side.

And you came back. For whatever reason, you didn't just leave us there." He sobered a bit, remembering the cost of this trip. "It's not your fault," James said, as much to himself as to Daniel. "But even if it was, being hostile doesn't solve anything." He stood up, leaning forward toward Daniel with his palms on the desk. "Look at me," he said in a firm voice, and waited for Daniel to raise his head. "We still need you. But even if we didn't, a person's value isn't tied to . . . to their function." James's throat choked up as he spoke, and he broke eye contact for a second, glancing to the side as he blinked in confusion. Why had saying that hurt so much?

Daniel stood up quietly as James sat back down. He didn't say anything as he turned to leave, not knowing how to react to the earnest ferocity of James's words. He wasn't used to people actually talking like that, with that kind of conviction and casual use of such powerful words. But before he left, he looked back over his shoulder. "I won't let you down again," he whispered.

"Good" was all James said.

"God damn, I'm tired," James said, legs burning from exertion as he surmounted the last ramp. Alanna had, unfortunately, remembered that she planned to drag him off to retrieve that briefcase. And so, here he was, about a half mile away from the third stop of the day for the rest of the survivors, climbing up an apartment block of a building again. And griping about it all the way. "Do we have any more coffee? I don't care if it's not magic anymore, I just need caffeine and we haven't seen a vending machine for actual days."

"What a weird sentence," an annoyingly unwound Alanna said from ahead of him.

"No kidding." James sucked in a deep breath of air, feeling it stretch his lungs against his ribs, the slight pang of tired muscles in his chest reminding him of how much he'd been running around and getting punched these last few days. "So, coffee?"

Alanna gave him a casual head pet, her fingers running through his hair in a way that set his skin electric. "Sorry, sleepy. We used it all up while you were stuck in the time loop, remember?"

"Oh yeah. That was a long day. Maybe that's why I'm so tired?"

She snorted a laugh. "James, that was today."

"Noooo. No. That can't be right," he said, knowing that it was.

They made their way through the still-open hole that they'd left last time they were here. "Which one was it?" James asked, letting his eyes adjust to looking at the dark interior of the tower.

Alanna ruined that effort by clicking on a flashlight. "It was on the right. That's all I remember. It had windows, though."

Together, the two of them checked through the cubicle rooms. Almost immediately, James got a bad feeling on the back of his neck. "Something isn't right here," he whispered to Alanna, who nodded back, keeping the flashlight beam trained away from them so their eyes half adjusted to the gloomy dark.

The smell of wet ink hung in the air, along with a bitter ozone tang. When they cleared the second cubicle and moved to the third, James felt his boot come down on something sticky, and a quick check with the flashlight showed pools of strider blood all across the floor, as well as a few of the corpses of the small creatures.

In the third cubicle, under a beam of light coming through the window, was the husk of a shellaxy. It had been torn apart, parts of its casing bent back and a thousand tiny scratches and scrapes left on the outside. A trail of coolant blood led from the hallway to here, where it had died in the light.

"What the fuck happened here?" Alanna softly ended the silence.

"I think it's because we killed that thing," James said, memories and logic helping him make the leap to the conclusion. "The hive mind messed with a lot of the functions here, and now it's gone. It might be a while before we see things balance out."

Alanna started checking over the desks in the wider room here, while James knelt next to the dead computer. "Sorry about this, friend," he said, laying a hand on the metal case. He didn't feel any particular familiarity with the shellaxy, but that didn't mean he liked seeing it dead. These days, they didn't feel so much like ambush predators as they did mechanical dogs that were just dedicatedly territorial. "Anything?" he called over to Alanna, who was standing at the desk, while he rose up and dusted off the knees of his slacks. "Alanna?" Walking over cautiously, James didn't see anything wrong, just Alanna silently staring down at the desk. "Hey, what's up?" he asked again, putting a hand on her shoulder as he leaned in. And then he couldn't help but mutter out a sharp "Holy shit!"

She had found the briefcase.

They'd run across a few of them in their time here. Actually, James seemed to remember it was Alanna who found the first one. Indestructible, unopenable, immune to a lot of tricks. Kind of like half the old stuff from the SCP Foundation website that got rewritten for being boring, now that James thought about it. Not that he'd accuse the cases of inducing boredom. And they always were found with work orders attached.

This one, of course, had said, "Answer the phone," and the briefcase itself had appeared here in a brief moment when no one was watching the desk. Well, to the surprise of neither James nor Alanna, completing the order had opened the case.

There was a *lot* of cash inside this thing.

"Woah," James reiterated. "That is . . . Jesus. Woah."

"We're rich," Alanna said flatly.

"I mean, yeah, if we get out of here alive," he told her, trying not to get too excited.

Alanna frumped at him. "Would you just . . . can we just have this for a minute?"

He laughed. It came out of him in great, stinging bursts, and until he ran out of breath, James felt *alive*. Alanna watched at first, and then joined in when she realized how absurd the whole thing was. Eventually, the two of them calmed down, leaning on each other and gasping and smiling.

"That's a lot of money," James said, looking down at the cracked case. Alanna rolled her eyes at the understatement. "A lot" was rent for a couple months, or having a little extra to be comfortable eating out. This was a *staggering* amount of money. James picked up one of the stacks of bills and started flipping through it. "These are all tens," he commented, and did some quick head math. "If all the stacks are like this, this is ... this is a hundred thousand dollars." He almost didn't believe it.

"I don't fucking believe it," Alanna said. "I was expecting..."

"Maybe some orbs or something? Something new and weird?" James questioned as she trailed off.

"Exactly! Not anything useful!"

He bopped her on the shoulder with a loose fist. "You dragged me here and you didn't think it would be worth it?" James chuckled as he processed that. "That's just rude!"

"Whatever, you need the exercise," Alanna said. "Also—"

James cut her off, holding up a hand at his side. Alanna froze, and James tilted his head to listen. He'd heard something, and he wasn't going to let anything get the drop on them *now*.

There it was again. Soft skittering. Now that was something James was becoming uncomfortably familiar with. He checked Alanna, who was moving slightly away from him and standing at alert. She'd heard it too.

With a click that sounded like a gunshot in the quiet air, James closed the briefcase. And as if that was the signal, the surviving striders in the tower swarmed through the door.

They moved like a coordinated team, some of them running across the floor while others made less obvious breaches across the walls or ceiling. They moved quickly to surround James, perhaps hoping to take him down quickly, or perhaps simply acting on feral instinct. Over ten small, but heavy, frames scribbling their way to close the distance a lot faster than most people would expect a stapler to move.

If normal people expected staplers to move at all. Because of the whole "stationary object" thing. The metaphor kinda got away from James.

Shaking his head in amusement at his own thoughts, he stepped forward and crushed the first strider underfoot.

He was pretty sure the thing didn't expect a strike from that far away. These things clearly had experience, or just knowledge, of how to fight larger enemies, and if James had run into this pack on his first day, he'd be injured or worse for sure. But James had some experience himself in fighting swarms. And since cracking that purple orb that boosted his acceleration, his movements had felt . . . snappier. He could go from standing to a burst of motion in a heartbeat, and closing the distance here was easy. He also felt the acceleration boost kick in as he kicked down, his foot connecting faster than it probably should have, and cratering the chitin of the lead strider.

There was a pause, and then the rest of the pack rushed them.

Next to him, Alanna caught one of the ceiling spiders out of the air and pitched it into another one at high speed. Twirling his crowbar, James caught one on the wall, hitting hard enough to crack it, with the extra force putting the crowbar a half inch into the wall itself. He slid his feet around as they fought, keeping the striders on the floor from getting into range of a lunge at his ankles, and sending out kicks and stomps when it was convenient. Likewise, Alanna mostly just grabbed the ones that got too close to within arm range and either used them as projectiles against the others or ripped them apart and discarded them like used tissue.

At some point, the survivors realized how this was going and scrambled to make it out the door or windows. James and Alanna let them go; a few extra small orbs wasn't worth either the exertion or the violence.

James looked down at the wreckage around them. Stooping down, he swept up a couple of glittering golden orbs in his hand. "Do you ever worry that we're getting too used to this?"

"No," Alanna answered firmly. "Getting used to this lets us survive, and improve. It's not gonna make us monsters, but it's still on us to use what we earn here to do something aside from just keep killing things here."

"Ah, battlefield philosophy." James smiled. "I love how you get, like, aggressively, actively political whenever either A, you've been in a fight, or B, there's anyone older than you around."

"That second one isn't true!" she said while James fetched up the rest of the orbs.

He wiped strider ichor off his fingers and scuffed his boots across the carpet. "That second one is absolutely true. Do you remember that time you met my dad?"

"Your dad is casually homophobic, and no one was telling him," Alanna grabbed the briefcase.

"See, you do remember," James said with a grin.

"I don't get how you put up with that. You *have a boyfriend*," she snarled.

James shrugged. "He's my dad," he said, simply, as if that were a reason, shoving away a lot of the impending hurt the words brought with them. "Anyway. Let's get out of here before something else shows up." James tossed his friend a few of the yellow dots as he cracked the few in his own hand.

[+1 Skill Rank : Cleaning - Kitchen - Commercial]

[+1 Skill Rank : Wildlife - Sweden]

[+1 Skill Rank : Instrument - Bass Guitar]

"Get anything good?" Alanna asked.

"I have an important question," he said in a serious tone, trying hard to keep a straight face. When Alanna turned to look at him with a worried expression, he continued, "Are you prepared to date a bassist?"

"Oh no. This marks the end of our relationship," she said, holding the hand with the orbs to her head. "Truly no romance could survive such an upheaval." Then she gave him a ferocious grin and closed her fist around her own orbs.

[+1 Skill Rank : Animals - Horses - Training]

[+1 Skill Rank : History - Warfare - Mexican-American War]

[+1 Skill Rank : Vehicle Operation - VTOL Craft - EC635]

"How 'bout you?" James asked.

"I got a worryingly specific one for a . . . I wanna say helicopter?" Alanna told him.

"They're all worryingly specific," James said as they made their way back to the breach in the tower, preparing himself for the long climb down and the longer walk back, now that he was even *more* exhausted.

"Hey," Alanna asked him as they reached the bottom, shifting her grip worriedly on the briefcase she held.

"Yeah?" James prompted when she didn't keep going.

"What are you gonna do with your share?" she said with an ear-to-ear grin.

Base camp wasn't anything impressive this time. This was the third spot they'd moved the whole group to today. Though "today" encompassed parts of two different actual real-world days. They were running low on time, and no one was getting much sleep if they were going to make it to the exit on schedule.

So they'd set up in a four-way intersection, not bothering to fortify or resupply. Just grabbing all the chairs they could and letting people take a break for a bit while the next route was scouted out. According to Daniel, it was mostly a straight shot from here back, just a long ways to go. James was simultaneously relieved, and also annoyed, that their path didn't take them to the bathrooms. It wasn't that he desperately needed a toilet in his life—though the last few days in here hadn't actually made him comfortable using trash cans as makeshift chamber pots—it was more just that it was the first real point of interest that he and Anesh had ever found, and he still wanted to explore it someday.

As he and Alanna walked back into the zone controlled by humanity, James was almost instantly greeted by Theo, who wore an expression that wasn't quite a frown but certainly wasn't a smile. "We've got a little extra food, but we don't really have any way to transport stuff. One of the scavenge teams says they see bags every now and then, but they didn't want to touch them without asking first. Do you know about those?"

James took a few seconds to, in his head, echo thoughts of how exhausted he was. He'd kicked in the door, saved two people, saved another fifty people, lost a friend, gotten in a boss fight, gotten in a series of regular fights, gotten in a couple things that were fight-shaped but horrifyingly one-sided in his favor, and also jogged a lot. Why was this his job? The next point his brain brought up was that this felt like exactly the sort of manager Theo had been at work. Efficient, cared about her people, broke the rules constantly, but had some kind of inhuman knowledge of her own limitations and wasn't afraid to bump stuff up the chain when needed.

When, exactly, had James ended up at the top of that chain of command? He looked around him and realized that when he looked at some of the people in their convoy, he started thinking of them in terms of their potential as delvers. It wasn't that he was planning to abandon everyone else, even after they got out. Far from it. He and Alanna had talked about setting up a fund from the money to help people who'd been Forgotten get their lives back together. But he was also seeing the upside of having a cabal of potential teammates who were already in on the secret and had the survival skills.

"In on the . . . secret." He muttered the last word, turning it over in his head. "Hm."

"Is that an answer?" Theo asked bluntly, getting a mild chuckle from Alanna as the other woman passed by her, heading off to find where they'd stashed the gear bags and see if the briefcase would fit in one. They didn't quite trust anyone here with access to a cool hundred grand just yet, so that was staying between them for now. Their own little secret.

James shook off the weird feeling at the texture of his own thoughts, and nodded at Theo. "Most of them are fine. I . . . seem to remember something about cutpurses? I can't honestly tell you if we ran into some bags that try to eat your arm, or if that was just a name I preemptively made up so that I could get one over on Anesh. Be careful, I guess. Like, dunk something in there first and see what happens. Should be okay, though."

"Why cutpurses?"

"'Cutpurse' is another name for a thief, and there was a purse that tried to eat someone's wrist. I think? I legit cannot remember if that's real or not. This place is doing weird things to my sense of what's fiction and what's not." James shrugged as he stared at the line of the top of one of the nearby cubicles. "Did I just make that up?" he murmured to himself.

"Oooookay," Theo drawled. Then she shrugged, made a note, and told him, "That's all I needed from you. Thanks."

There was a moment when James felt the mantle on his shoulders. There were a dozen names from as many sources for it, but in this moment, he fancied himself some sort of fantasy world guild master.

Then his loyal subordinate was gone, and the flow of quiet conversation picked up around him again. He hadn't noticed it before, but all the people nearby stopped talking whenever Theo asked him something. Weird.

"That's taken care of," Alanna said as she came back to him, dragging a chair behind her.

"Is that for me?" James asked, echoing with his mouth what his aching feet were crying.

"What? No. This is mine, get your own chair!" She smirked as she plopped into it.

With a groan of exhaustion, James started looking around for a free seat and resigned himself to sitting on the floor. Just as he was about to lower himself to the hard carpet, though, one of the people nearby stood up and gave their wheeled office chair a push in his direction. "Oh! Thanks!" James called over to the other guy, getting a nod and a delighted grin.

"Do they remind you of anyone?" Alanna dipped her head toward the trio nearby, now with one of their number on the floor. The guy had a round face with tanned skin, glasses, and a ponytail. Next to him, on the chair he leaned against, was the Mohawked girl James had talked to a couple hours ago. Their third member was another guy, this one with a bushy beard that James could only describe as a hipster look, with a pair of ear studs and a nose ring. The three of them were sharing a laugh about something, and James saw one of them toss the girl a yellow orb as she won whatever bet they'd made. Curled up in their center was a flickering rainbow distortion in the rough shape of a large rat, or a midsized dog.

"Why would they remind me of anyone?" James asked, confused.

"Are you serious?" Alanna asked incredulously.

James tilted back in the chair to rest his head on the wall. "Am I missing something?"

"James, they're two nerdy guys and a sexy punk girl with their dungeon companion learning how to be delvers. They are literally over there betting on who found the weirdest candy name, and one of them just won off of Baby Things. This couldn't be more on the nose if one of them was named Anesh."

"The guy with the beard is named James, actually. The mongausse is his."

"Did you feign ignorance just so you could tell me that awful, awful name for the glitterdog?" She demanded.

"'Glitterdog' is a dumb name," he stated. "Mongausse is genius, because—"

"I get the joke!" she mock-yelled. "I just . . . wish I'd thought of it first!"

"Dave would have appreciated my pun," James said with a soulful pout.

Alanna's gaze turned hard. "That's not cool, man."

"I . . . yeah, okay. I guess I'm still holding out hope that he's alive," James said. "We can still get him out with a blue, if we find any more. Maybe. Also, 'glitterdog' is a cool name, I'm sorry."

Sarah overheard the end half of their conversation as she walked up to them. She'd been helping Daniel map out their way forward, copying notes a dozen times to pass out to different groups to try to minimize the odds of someone getting lost. "Is this about the blues?" she asked them. It took James a second longer than he'd have liked to admit to recognize who was talking, but then his brain processed something small about the shape of her face, and it all just clicked. So he nodded to her, half in greeting, half in acknowledgment. "Theo wanted me to let you know that she used a couple to try to restock the bandages."

"How'd that go?" James asked, genuinely curious. And also grateful for the distraction.

Sarah shrugged. "Mixed. One of them paid her rent, one of them actually did what she wanted. She complained afterward that it made her even more tired since it just changed it so she actually picked up a medkit in here somewhere."

"Wait, it changed the past?" Alanna asked, alarmed.

"Guess that's another point in the 'worry about causality' column," James said. "Still, she felt the extra weight? That's weird. Why didn't it just spawn a medkit?"

"The blues never spawn physical objects," Sarah stated, like it was obvious. "Did you guys not notice that?"

"Honestly, we don't know a lot of stuff about the orbs," James admitted, chewing on his lower lip. "Like how to use the blues to make magic items, or how to absorb the oranges. Not that we tried that yet; those things are hard to find."

"You don't . . . you can't make magic items," Sarah mentioned, trying to find the words. "You have to make a broadcaster, and wait for it to build one. I think. I mean, that was the theory anyway."

"Wat." James and Alanna spoke in unison.

Sarah shrugged. "You know! One of those weird pattern things? Then it'll form a magic item over time. I swear this was a thing we encountered at one point. Or am I remembering something from the . . . You seriously never found any?" Sarah shook herself out of remembering having her brain forcibly borrowed.

"No, though that does sound like the totem that Lily made out of that red orb."

"What the here are red orbs?" Sarah demanded.

"The emotion ones. You get them from traps," Alanna told her.

"What the duck!" Sarah exclaimed. "I never found any of those!"

"Duck? Also you have to disarm the traps," James said.

"I don't like swearing. "

"Noted. How did we ever stay friends? I swear all the time."

"It's a constant trial." Sarah gave a mockingly solemn nod.

Alanna huffed a laugh. "Tell me about it," she said, prompting James to stick out his tongue at her in defiance.

"So, what have you figured out to do, and with what types? Let's trade intel here," Sarah asked the two of them, ignoring the casual byplay between her once and future friends.

James didn't hesitate. This was something that had the potential to save their lives, and beyond that, it didn't even occur to him to hold back secrets now. Secrets ended friendships, after all.

There was that weird thought again.

"Okay, so, for yellows, we know all three uses. And all three for blues now, too. Purples we've only figured out how to crack, haven't tried absorbing. We know that they can make infomorphs, though, as the third. Reds we know crack and totemize. Oranges, same, with the space-warping thing. Greens, just cracking." James laid it out as well as he could remember. "Oh hey, don't we have a bunch of oranges now? We should test those."

When he finished talking, he noticed the expression on Sarah's face. Somewhere between shock and awe, mouth half open, eyes wide. "What did you have to do to learn how to absorb a yellow?" she half-yelled at him. "How do you absorb *time*?!"

"Oh! Of course!" Alanna interjected. "They're time! That's the theme of the yellows!"

"You didn't even . . . ?"

James answered her before she could finish. "We're still learning. Also, we just treated them as a power source, and it worked. It has serious drawbacks, though, logistically."

"Well fish, that's great." Sarah relented, slumping back in her chair. "Oh, you said three!" She remembered what she was going to say before James had steamrolled her thoughts. "Four. There's four uses per orb."

"Seriously? What's the fourth for the yellows?"

"Making life, duh," she answered.

Alanna and James shared a worried glance. "I thought that was the totem . . . er, broadcast use?" Alanna asked.

"No, that's the sensation one," Sarah informed her. "How is a crawly thing a totem anyway?"

"I mean . . . we have Ganesh. And Pendragon. And *that*." She gestured at the mongausse.

"Yeh, that's the Office use," Sarah said. "Officium Mundi can use the orbs for one thing that no one . . ." The words trailed off.

"That no one else can?" James grinned, as Ganesh alighted on his shoulder in a dramatic moment.

There was a quiet beat as Sarah looked between the two of them, before she took a deep breath and leaned away. "How come *you* got the dumb mystical-chosen-one powers?" she demanded. "Can you turn blues into quests, too?"

James just laughed.

If only it had actually been as easy as she thought.

"Okay." He settled down a bit. "Let's go over this one at a time. First off, what the hell are the quests?"

Sarah was halfway through her explanation of what her team had decided the briefcases represented when Daniel came up to interrupt them. With a casual tap on the shoulder and a shake of his head, James deflected the smoldering glare Alanna put on at the kid's presence, and asked what was up.

"Theo says if we keep moving at this rate, we'll be at the door with three hours to spare," he told them, trying to avoid looking at Alanna even if she wasn't directly scowling at him. "But there's something weird between here and there, on one of the choke points. She wants you to check it out, if that's okay?"

"Sure thing. What is it?" James asked, resigning himself to sore soles as he stood up again and rubbed at his aching calves.

"Path has it labeled as a server room."

"Oh, crap," Sarah muttered from the back of the group.

"I am *so pissed* about this," James sharply hissed out, handing the binoculars back to Alanna.

They'd taken the time to confirm that these ones weren't cursed. No use going through that again.

They'd had to assemble a sort of watchtower to see over the next ridge. It was weird that this part of the office had ridges at all, but there was no sense whining about it. It wasn't quite a solid wall, instead just a series of cubicle panels that jutted out against each other, leaving easy paths up but still requiring anyone traveling up it to either take a winding route or take the hard way and climb if they wanted to go in a straight line.

The tower they were in was hardly a masterpiece of construction. James and Alanna had more or less cheated, using the properly square panes of local cubicle walls to click together into a tall box. It was stable enough to support the two of them, tall enough to get a peek over the elevation change in front of them, and absolutely not where James wanted to spend any more time. It wobbled. A lot.

"What? I thought you'd be super psyched to see this. Come on! Where's your love of high fantasy?" Alanna challenged him as she took the optics back and stole another look.

They were the forward scouting team in its entirety. Turned out Ganesh actually did need to sleep, and Sarah didn't want to tag along. Said something about being a third wheel. The rescued humans, also, had been fine to stay back; even the ones that were picking up on the dungeon and treating the orbs like candy had heeded the warning from Theo almost religiously.

It was almost uncomfortable to James. For all that he could see the fantasy of leading a skilled organization of delver groups, it was actually kind of awkward to have that responsibility just suddenly dumped on him. Then again, it might not play out that way, and "sudden lifestyle changes" was basically the motto for his group since he found this place.

Realizing he should probably reply to Alanna, he motioned to their route forward. "I'm just mad because I already used the word 'maimframe' for that giant shellaxy." He considered giving a casual middle finger to the terrain in front of them but settled for just quietly brooding.

The problem, because there was always a problem, was summed up nicely by Alanna. "The problem, because there is always a problem, is that we can't go around," Alanna said. "Is there a reason we can't go around?"

"Daniel says there's a wall behind it. Like, one of the ones that we can't go over. The only door is on the other side of the server room."

"I don't know if I trust his judgment," Alanna said, quietly at first, then louder when she realized she was still mad at Daniel and wanted James to know it.

"Well, it's not his, it's Path's. Which I think is the name of the thing that possesses him now."

Alanna turned up the corners of her mouth. "Ah, like Secret."

"It's not a secret, he told us about it," James said, getting an eye roll from Alanna.

"Okay, well, fine. But that doesn't make me happier about this."

"It's just . . . I mean, it's a dragon, right?" It was well past time one of them said it, and James figured it might as well be him.

And there it was. Up past the ledge, down a fairly short hallway where the cubicles looked almost like a normal office, there was visible a glass wall. It was the first time James had seen glass used as a building material at all here in the Office, and it kind of surprised him. There weren't windows anywhere, except for that one that looked out on the "outside." He didn't count that, though. It felt more like a trap than a part of the structure. Here, though, he could clearly see full-length glass pane walls, at least two of them with a metal support bar in between. They rose up to a height of probably just over ten feet, and then capped off at a miniature ceiling for the room itself. And even from here, James could see that the ceiling wasn't nearly so normal. Jagged chunks of steel and glass sloped out of it, giving the impression of those spikes that some buildings used to keep birds off. He could also see half of a rather large fan that looked like it was part of a cooling system.

It was a server room. Made quite obvious by the construction, the air conditioning, and the several metal frame server racks that James could spot through the transparent walls. But the interior wasn't neatly arranged rows of hardware and storage devices. Instead, through one of the empty racks, it was just possible to spot an amalgamation of hard drives and metal case plating, curled up in a cleared circular area in the center of the floor. It had dim blue LEDs for eyes, six of them on each side in two rows of three each, curving up a streamlined curve of a metal skull. Through half-open slots, James could see RAM sticks sharpened to razor edges to serve as its teeth, a few of them broken into jagged chunks, showing evidence of battles already fought. It lay on a bed of orbs. Dozens of them. Hundreds. Yellows and oranges, purples and reds, and a few odds and ends that James was positive must be blue-enhanced objects. A bed of endless wealth. The one visible foreclaw dangled over the edge of the hoard, showing looped cords that appeared to have no beginning or end, poking through the cold metallic plate that formed wicked claws. The rest of the dragon, and it *was* obviously a dragon, wasn't visible. But judging by its size relative to the orbs it rested upon, James was willing to guess that it was somewhere around thirty feet long. Assuming it was . . . well, normal dragon proportioned.

"Hey, what's normal for a dragon?" he asked Alanna. She shot him a sideways glance that communicated disbelief at him even asking. "Right," he corrected. "I mean, I figured I'd ask, just in case."

"Fair," she said. "Anyway, you can still name it something. What about a serverus?"

"Like . . . a Snape?" He raised his eyebrows.

"Like Cerberus," Alanna corrected.

James considered it but ultimately shook his head. "It only has one head," he said. "It's important," he informed her. "Anyway, we'll think of something. Or just call it a dragon. Isn't there an anime about a data dragon or something?"

"You'd know more than I would," she reminded him with a smile. "Ya big nerd."

"You are *just* as bad as I am when it comes to nerd stuff!" James reminded her with a quiet laugh. "Anyway. Let's get back to the others. We'll need to see if Sarah has any tips for getting around this. Somehow, I don't think it'll be easy to Bilbo Baggins fifty people past a dragon's lair without a problem." He shuffled back, careful to keep his footing on the less-than-stable platform before sliding off it, catching himself on the lip, and dropping to the floor.

Alanna followed after, and the two of them headed back. They kept to cautious movements, since the office had proven repeatedly that this far in, there was no such thing as a safe and quiet moment. But ultimately, they made it back all right and started planning to bring everyone up to the ridge.

While James started trying to figure out how to slay a dragon with a crowbar.

CHAPTER 28

James itched at the back of his neck as he shot down another suggestion. "We're not calling the dragon 'iTiamat.' It sounds like an Apple product." He paused for a second, then added, "Also it's a really deep cut, and I want my puns to be accessible."

"To the thousands we share the Office with, right." Alanna rolled her eyes. "Also you already used an Apple kinda name anyway with the iLipedes."

"Exactly!" James exclaimed. "I don't want to repeat myself."

"Okay, *fine*." Alanna groaned. "What about Smog? Or maybe Sysmaug? Like the dragon Smaug, but because it's all mechanically . . ." She trailed off, leaving James to make the obvious connection himself.

He made the connection, then shook his head. "Sysmaug is kinda cool. But it still doesn't make much sense, unless you count the dire blue smoke of electrical failure as 'smog.' And I don't, before you ask. What about giving it a proper name? Like . . . I dunno, Rootworm or something? Like, combine computer terms that sound really grim if you say them with emphasis."

"How is that *any* better than my suggestion earlier? You're just trading D&D lore references for technical ones!"

"I . . . thought it rolled off the tongue!" James drawled out. "How about we just retcon it so that I never said 'maimframe' when we encountered the giant shellaxy, and pretend that it's a good nickname for the dragon."

Alanna frumped at him. "It's a *great* nickname for a dragon, and you should have saved it. Because now we all think of it as the giant squid-mounted ordnance platform, and you'll confuse people, probably at a dramatically important moment, if you change it. What about . . ." A small sigh. "I dunno, fuck it, what about just the word 'hardware'? Like, as a kind of reductive term instead of your weird taxonomic application to this place?"

That got a wince from James as he wavered his head back and forth. "Eeehhhh. I don't like the idea of reductive names like that. Although, it does make me regret that we never encountered anything that was, like, bear-shaped? Could have called it a hardbear and that would have been . . ." Alanna quirked an eyebrow at him. "Okay, yeah, no, I heard it as soon as the words came out. Never mind."

She smiled, then deflected back to the main topic. "What other computer terms can we turn into puns?" Needlessly counting on her fingers, she ticked off a few options. "Disc, network, program, software, *vaporware*, gig . . ."

"'Gigabyte' kinda does sound like a good dragon name." James shrugged. "But then it's just a word again . . ."

"Oh. Oh!" Alanna flailed her arms in front of herself as she got an idea. "Terabyte! But, like, *terror*byte! 'Cause it's a . . . !"

"'Cause it's a big fucking dragon, yeah, I get it. Yeah!" James nodded with a toothy grin. "Terrorbyte it is!" The duo high-fived energetically before turning back to the other people in the room.

"We choose 'terrorbyte'!" they cheerfully exclaimed in unison, with self-satisfied smiles. Both of them felt the sting on their faces as the smiles conflicted with the bruises that had formed since the brawl in the conference room, but they were also just overwhelmingly pleased with themselves and pushed the pain aside.

Fifteen faces stared back at them, divided between incredulous and amused. Other James leaned slightly to the right, and in a voice he probably thought was inconspicuous but that nonetheless was easily heard in the silence, asked Theo, "Is it always like this?" Next to him, his teammates, Simon and . . . James wanted to say the girl's name was Alex, but he knew that was someone else. Yeah, that was definitely the other girl sitting on the left side of the circle, next to the older man who was currently scowling at him. What was the goth girl's name? Miyah? Momo? Momo sounded right. Either way, they were on Team Smirk.

"You fuckers!" Theo snapped at them. "We're in a life-or-death situation and you're screwing around! Did you forget we're on a timeline here?"

James lost his smile, the spark of amusement crushed by the sudden shame, before Alanna jumped in to his defense. "Hey, fuck off!" she opened with, perhaps unhelpfully. "We already know we're gonna make it with a few hours to spare, even if we don't run, and this sorta thing is good for morale."

Before he lost that small feeling of satisfaction, James nodded and chimed in. "Yeah, except for that guy's morale." He pointed over to the older gentleman with the salt-and-pepper beard framing an angry scowl. "But you're not wrong that we should get this meeting going."

The meeting was Theo's construct, but James agreed that it was important. Assembled here along with the obvious choices of himself, Alanna, Theo, and a Daniel who was far less cowering than he was before talking to James were a handful of the survivors who had both the energy and will to do more than just move and then sprawl on the ground. Sarah was conspicuously absent, and even though she was just sleeping off her injuries and exhaustion, James still felt like he'd already gotten to know her well enough that he missed her presence. Still, the two scout groups that were rapidly turning into competent delvers in their own right were here. One of them led by Other James, the other one by a midforties woman named Karen, who seemed determined to take out her aggression over the misuse of her name on anything shaped like a stapler that looked at her wrong. There was also a man with his arm in a sling named Harvey who was a secondary representative for the survivors. He worked with Theo when it came to doling out food and water and also addressing complaints. Like a lot of people who'd been freed from the network, he had more than a few injuries from when his body had been fighting James and company, though his deeper skin tone hid the darker bruises. A couple other people had been included in this mostly because they had relevant skills. Deb was a girl who had been in school to become a nurse, and the medical know-how was deeply appreciated, and Ethan was an arrogant twenty-something jackass who talked a lot about being on the football team and the importance of leadership. Actually, that last one was here to make him shut up, not for any real reason.

And then the last few were people with questions, some of them probably complaints, who just needed or wanted to talk to the leadership while they were all in one place. "Okay," James said, pointing a finger at the older member of the meeting, "let's start with you, Scowls. What's up?"

The man, a one Herman Collins, harrumphed in a way that made James think of a dog that had just sniffed a grapefruit. "I have *spoken* to your secretary several times now, and I wish to complain that my rights are being trampled!" Theo rolled her eyes to the side, as if to say *Get a load of this guy*. As she bared her teeth, James gave her a placating wave before she could say anything rash, and motioned for the man to go on. "I have *requested* that I be allowed to hold sermons for my fellow believers, and been constantly denied! If we are imprisoned here, then . . . !" He punctuated his words by holding up a copy of the Bible and flicking it toward James.

Now James actually did cut him off. "I'm gonna stop you right there. First off, don't call her my secretary, that's rude." The man's face turned a shade of pale red as he frowned at James. "Second of all, I remember talking to . . . someone . . . about this before I fell asleep. We aren't doing religious ceremonies in here because the *building is sentient, you doofus!*"

He half-yelled at the guy, "It's not about your religious freedom, no one's trying to steal your soul, man. Fuck, Theo's . . . Catholic?"

"Protestant. You heretic."

"Thanks. You can pray or whatever, but actual ritualistic stuff could be copied, which we *think* this place does, and then it makes it *way worse,*" James explained, trying to sound patient. "Didn't someone tell you that? Like, do you want to see what a sermon looks like when it's performed by a desk fan and brainwashes you into worshipping the coffee maker?" He paused, then turned to Alanna. "Have we ever been attacked by a desk fan?"

She ruffled his hair, lightly pushing him away with a grin. "Don't get distracted."

"You are mocking . . . !" Herman started to build up steam again.

"Okay, stop it!" James snapped, hard anger in his words now. "We explained the reason to you, and expect you to be an adult! You're twice my age! Act like it!" His eyes narrowed, and then he pointed out something that he'd just thought of. "Also, if that Bible came from in here, then it's either going to have some messed-up passages, or it's . . . probably uncomfortably cursed. I'm not gonna tell you to destroy it, I know you won't like that, but you shouldn't bring it with you to be safe." His words at the end, sadly, were mostly drowned out by Collins's angry words. He'd started trying to talk over James as soon as he'd recovered from being yelled at, and eventually just gave up trying to convince the group, storming off in a rage.

Theo gave James an apologetic look, feeling the discomfort and tension in the circle. "I'm really sorry. I kept telling him, and he insisted on talking to someone else about it."

"Jesus, what a jerk," Alanna chimed in.

"Nice word choice," James said, taking a deep breath. "Man, we're in the middle of a fucking death trap of an office, why is he bringing this up *now*? He couldn't just wait two days? We're gonna have to set up a support group for a lot of the incredibly traumatized survivors here; spiritual guidance would have been super helpful *then*." He gestured to the assembled others. "No offense, guys."

"Oh, no, I agree." It was Karen who spoke up. "We're all just barely holding it together. I personally appreciate that you actually thought that far ahead."

"I'm . . . thank you?" James raised his eyebrow in puzzlement. The tone that Karen had used was just so straightforward and earnest, it caught him off guard. Most of his experiences with people older than him over the last couple months had been them either chastising him, causing problems like old Herman there, or trying to murder him. This was different. "This is different, I don't know how to react to actual compliments," he admitted.

"It's basic leadership skills." Karen looked somewhere between confused and sheepish now.

Cutting off any potential awkward nonflirting before it could happen, Alanna chimed in with a chuckle. "Okay, what's next? Let's get through the concerns before we move to planning."

The concerns were all way easier to handle than that first one. No one wanted to start a cult or run off on their own, which was something James admitted to himself he'd been kind of worried about. One guy wanted some more experienced help to take some people around and gather up water jugs off the coolers, to deal with the ongoing rationing of water. That got approved and assigned to James somehow, which he still wasn't clear on. The other was a suggestion on dealing with the bathroom problem. The problem being there were no bathrooms, and the smell wasn't a great addition to the experience. The suggestion was handled by Theo, who agreed they needed to at least try something, even if they were only here for a day or two. And then one person who wanted to know if the staplers were venomous. They were not.

James was pretty sure they were not. He shot a look over at Deb, who shrugged.

They probably were not.

"All right," James said, taking a breath after the last of the concerns had been dealt with. The group now was their medical staff, the scout teams, James and Alanna, and for some reason still the football player. Harvey had taken his leave to go pass on information to the other thirty-odd people who weren't logistically able to cluster around for this, and James had been made kind of uncomfortable by the deference in his eyes when he'd wished James good luck. It felt like everyone was getting rapidly divided into people who saw him as a hero and people who were insane, and that wasn't great in *either* direction.

That was something to worry about later. Or hopefully never, if they made it out before tomorrow. "Now that we've got that taken care of. This is the strategy meeting," he told them. "There is a bit of an obstacle coming up, and we need suggestions."

With references from Alanna and Daniel, James laid out the issue to them. There was one door forward through the wall that they had no way to get over. Between them and that door, there was a dragon. The dragon seemed to be sleeping and hadn't shown any signs of waking up since then. The dragon was the size of a school bus and probably hostile. What, then, he'd asked them, do we *do*?

"The obvious is to sneak past, right?" Theo said, with a voice like she knew she was walking into a trap.

James shook his head. "I mean, yes. But that's the thing. What if it wakes up? Worst case, it wakes up in the middle of us getting people through, and it just cuts through the middle of the group."

"Do we actually know it's hostile?" Other James asked, his hand resting on the head of the rainbow shimmer in the rough shape of a dog sitting next to him. He had a smoker's voice, or, at least, the voice of someone who hadn't been hydrating properly for the last few days to five years. "It might not care if we just walk past."

"That's a good point. We're in a kind of prisoner's dilemma here," James acknowledged. He got a few blank looks, so he fleshed out his point, speaking with his hands as he did so. "If we act peacefully, and it's peaceful, then it's easy. If we act hostile, then no matter what, it will respond hostile. Probably. But if we act peaceful, and it's already hostile . . ."

Alanna summed it up with too much enthusiasm. "Then we're fucked!"

"Yeah." James grimaced.

"What if we make it fucked first, then?" Momo asked, running a hand through her short mohawk. "Like . . . we just get everyone and rush it?"

"We aren't really armed for that, unless anyone's found anything that works as a decent weapon?" Theo asked the assembled, while James looked at them hopefully. A series of shrugs and *"nos"* crushed that dream, though. Karen's group had found a Nerf gun, and for a second James felt his heart leap into his chest, but then they pointed out that they'd tested it safely, and nothing had happened.

"Yeah, so, that's a no-go on the dragon slaying," James told them. "Unless Sarah has some magic powers she hasn't told us about, I don't think we can manage it with . . ." He did some quick counting. ". . . eleven combat-capable people, and one combat-too-eager drone. And, again, no offense, but I don't really think that you guys are gonna be as ready to fight a dragon as the rest of us after having spent months or years in that room."

Ethan, the wiry-framed jock who was still wearing his high school colors shirt, chose now to chime in. "I could fight it!" he declared proudly.

Ignoring that, James moved on. "Any other suggestions?"

"No, really, I could take it! I'm not afraid, if we work together we can do it!" The guy didn't let up.

James turned to him, trying not to be mad, and crushed his dreams anyway. "It's not about being afraid of it or not, man. Though you should be afraid. Did you miss when I said it was the size of a bus and made of sharp edges? *I'm* afraid of it." That admission seemed to deflate Ethan's bluster a bit. James didn't notice, though, and added a line that maybe demoralized more than it helped. "If we work together, then I think we're just gonna give it a self-serving buffet."

"Ooookay." Theo jumped in before James said anything else about how they were all on the precipice of mortal failure. "What about the wall?" she asked.

"What about it?" Alanna returned.

"What about going through it?" Theo clarified.

"We could probably find something heavy enough to break drywall," one of the new delvers chimed in. "Wouldn't be impossible if we had multiple people working at it. Gotta be careful of the supports, though. Or are support beams something else this place ignores?"

"I'll get back to you on that," James told him. "Daniel, you've got the map. Is this something we can do?"

The younger man started to answer tentatively. "Well, it should be possible, but the—"

"Yeah! See? I knew there was a way we could do it if we worked togeth—" Ethan plowed through the conversation like a cement truck, before James stopped him with a small frown.

"Dude, don't interrupt him. Save your motivational-poster slogans for later, this is important." Turning back to a relieved and embarrassed Daniel, and ignoring the look of betrayal Ethan shot him, James nodded for him to go on.

"The . . . um. The walls are actually really thick. Like, there's about a half mile of wall in there. It's like how it goes up technically forever, I think? We'd have to dig for a long time." He looked around at everyone as their faces fell. "I'm really sorry."

"Well, that's that one. What's next?" James asked.

It was Alanna who answered, but what she said surprised him. "Hang on. Why *don't* we just do that?" she asked. To the confused crowd, she went on, "We know the door opens every week. If we can get past without losing anyone to a dragon, isn't that worth just staying here another seven days? Is that really so bad?"

It was a plan that was equally cautious and disappointing. No one had found an item to melt walls, so it would be a week of solid, hard, backbreaking work to cut through two thousand feet of drywall. But they'd be alive. Unless . . .

"Unless we wake it up with the noise," Karen pointed out. "Or it wakes up anyway and stumbles on us."

"Or if it just takes too long." James groaned. "A week, we could maybe do, but two? There isn't infinite food here. I think stuff respawns, but it can take a long time. We might be in real trouble trying to feed everyone for a fortnight."

"Like . . . the game?" Ethan asked, a baffled look on his long-nosed face.

"Like the unit of time." James didn't even pause with his response, like his subconscious had already prepared the verbal riposte.

It was Deb who sealed the plan as a no, though. "I dunno if you guys know, but there's a couple people who actually have medications they need. It seems like being plugged in fixed that, but now . . ." She looked away, not wanting to say it. "Also everyone is malnourished, and it's only going to get worse if half our diet is candy."

Alanna shrugged. "Yeah, makes sense. I wasn't really keen on it anyway."

"Keen on it? Who talks like that?" James ribbed her, and got a real smile out of it.

"Hey, don't think I didn't notice that you talk like you're in a fantasy novel half the time," she shot back.

"Forsooth" was all he said in reply, which got him a smile and a small kiss from the woman sitting with him. When he looked back to the group, he saw a few suppressed grins, but at this point, the embarrassment he might have felt was just shoved aside by logistical need and casual love. "Okay, so, no demolitions. No fighting. Do we have *any* other plans?"

"Negotiate?" one of Karen's team suggested, but she herself shot the idea down.

"It's what he said earlier." Karen made an open-handed gesture toward James. "If we try that, and we're wrong, it . . . ah . . . eats us."

"Okay, okay. One last thought," Alanna said. "Why don't we just find more blue orbs and give everyone superpowers? I mean . . . someone, eventually, is going to get one that lets us do something here. Your first one let you one-shot tumblefeeds."

"Oh, we tried that," Theo interjected before James could come up with something mildly jealous about how it would be a bad idea to arm people that they might *like* but maybe still didn't completely *trust* with magic. Then she kept going before James could be indignant that they'd apparently just *tried that*. Probably while he was in the middle of the thirty minutes of sleep he'd gotten in the last . . . month? "It doesn't work. Even when we went over the thing you said, where they're the metaphysical manifestation of tools? Even the people who understood that couldn't do it."

"Weeeird." James let the word roll off his tongue. "That actually brings up some weird questions about why it does work for us. Time spent in the dungeon, maybe? No, that doesn't work, because everyone here spent *way too long* . . ."

That got a few people to start throwing ideas between each other, but Alanna brought them back on course. "Much as I want to argue with you over whether or not we're actually leveling up from this place, let's stay on topic."

James let out an overly dramatic groan, rolling his head back before tipping his whole body forward and slapping his knees. "Guys, I hate to say it? I think sneaking past is the only even remotely good option."

"Why are you upset about that?" Theo questioned him.

"He has this thing where he thinks that if a plan is obvious, and the first thing discussed, then there must be something better out there," Alanna provided.

A slow blink from Theo, and a few weird looks from the crowd. "Whhhhhy?" she settled on asking.

"If I tell you it's a nerd thing, will you let this go?" James asked her defensively.

"Oh! I used to have a GM like that too!" One of the scouts suddenly made the connection, which got a burst of laughter out of James. It was good to have that bond of recognition.

The rest of the meeting was a lot less eventful. They went back over the idea of how to stealth past a room that was pretty much entirely transparent, and a few thoughts on how to divide up the group. There was a brief moment when someone suggested leaving Collins behind to try to convert the striders to his brand of faith, followed by a bit-too-long pause where James actually considered it, before making the easy joke that it didn't seem fair to the Office.

They worked out a timeline for it, giving everyone about two more hours of naptime before they made their move. Which also worked out pretty well to give them time to scout and clear the area around the terrorbyte. Or Terrorbyte. Then there was an argument over whether it was a name or a designation. Then, when things got back on track, they made assignments for the three active delver groups, and the food goals for the "day."

And then, at the end, they were left with a few people sitting in a circle together, quietly realizing that despite having nothing in common, they were in this together, and they had a bond beyond anything they'd known before.

"You know what I'm gonna do when I get out?" James asked them, not quite breaking the magic circle they'd entered into.

"Go to prison, so you can actually earn use of the term 'when I get out'?" Alanna challenged.

He laughed, and a few others did too. Their levity was infectious, even here. Especially here. "No, I mean really. You know what I want to do? I want to go on a date." Alanna flushed slightly at the words. This wasn't how James talked. This wasn't how any of them dealt with their feelings, honestly and openly. They just joked about things and cared about each other more than they ever said; it ruined the joke if you just *said it*. "With you and Anesh." He laid his hand on Alanna's, both of them ignoring that dull pain from scratches and bruises that flared up at the contact. "Go to a bookstore, and just wander around and read weird plot synopses from the seventies sci-fi books. See who can find the weirdest one. Just be *together* for a day." Alanna smiled at him and felt herself tear up, two hundred and fifty pounds of strength showing a vulnerability that looked almost alien on her face.

For a second, no one spoke. Then Deb, their resident nurse, let her own words add in. "I'm going to go back to school," she said, with an iron confidence. "I'll have to retake some classes. Maybe they'll have forgotten that time I . . . well, I know I can do it now. I'm going to be a doctor," she announced, and not a single person challenged her.

"I'm going to hug my kids," Karen told them. "I have a daughter. She's around your age." She inclined her head toward Momo. "Maybe you can meet her, trade fashion tips."

"Hey! Are you saying I'm not fashionable?" Momo gasped in mock horror.

"I'm saying she might look good in that jacket." Karen smiled back at the younger woman.

Momo grinned at her, a toothy smile with a couple holes in it. "I think I'd like that," she said.

"I'm getting back into theater acting," Other James shared with them.

"I just want to cook something," someone said. "Maybe I can make us all dinner when we get home."

"I need to tell my friend I love them" came from another. "I just... I don't know..." They trailed off.

They sat in silence for a minute, everyone feeling like there was something left to say, but not knowing what it was. James could feel the tension, different this time than when dealing with an angry old man or putting his life on the line. This wasn't a cold avoidance of an uncomfortable person, nor was it the burning fear of being about to die. This was waiting. They were waiting to know what came next.

"We're getting out of here," he told them, a quiet promise. "I don't know how long everyone's been here, or how much you felt while you were part of Karen." He looked over at the woman of the same name. "Not you." She nodded at him, not saying how obvious that was. "But it doesn't matter. We're getting you home. You and everyone else. I don't have anything to tell you that's going to make it easier, but this place can be survived, and... and that's enough. We're going to do it. No questions." James stood up and looked around at all of them. The circle of people looked up at him, hope in their eyes. Then he broke the spell by continuing to talk. "Okay, not, like, 'no questions.' You can ask reasonable questions. That... should be obvious. I... uh, I'm gonna shut up now." That got a few laughs. "Well, we all know what we're doing for the next couple hours. We'll regroup then," he told them.

As he and Alanna walked away to start their food collection run, she talked to Theo for a second, then took custody of the mono-edged spear and caught up to James, then elbowed him. "You fucking cute-ass," she said. "That was the sappiest fucking thing you've ever done." There was no malice in her voice, quite the opposite really.

"What, my rousing speech?"

"No, you dingus. The other thing!" she told him. "The . . . the date thing."

"Yeah, that went over really well. I'm glad . . . I'm glad people care. I'm glad we're working toward something. It's . . . it's better." James didn't know exactly what to say.

Alanna picked up for him, putting words to his feelings. "It's more important than just treating this place as a playground, or something to explore. It's like we're doing something that matters."

"We are doing something that matters," James said with conviction as the two of them made their way out of the cleared zone around the camp. "We're absolutely doing something that matters. I've been thinking about it a lot, and even though it hurts, I honestly think that Dave would have been okay with this."

His partner nodded. It did hurt, yeah, but James was right. This was worth a lot, and even though they'd been kicked down, as a group and in their hearts, they weren't done yet.

The two of them got back into the flow of movement that they'd started to let lapse while around so many people. Checking corners, talking only sparsely, tapping and pointing to indicate points of interest.

They strode down the corridor, ignoring all the intersections in favor of keeping it clear which path they had to take back. Checking cubicles one by one, the ones that could be accessed easily anyway. There were a lot of doors here that were more like cave mouths, half-grown stalagmites of wall panel growing up from the floor, making them look like gaping maws instead of entries. At one point, they got into a mild skirmish with a couple striders and split the orbs between themselves.

[+1 Skill Rank : Recipe - Confectionery - Gummy Bears]

While James processed that little tidbit of weirdness, Alanna cracked open the suitcase they'd been wheeling along that someone had found, and started tossing granola bars into it while James found a brown bag lunch in a filing cabinet drawer and added that to the mix. They left it there while they hit the cube across the hall, acquiring a takeaway container of penne alfredo that was weirdly well preserved. The cube down the hall was another cave mouth sorta thing, and Alanna nodded at James that they were going in, kicking the wall spikes down and climbing in.

Then James froze and held an arm out to Alanna, jerking a thumb toward the desk lamp illuminating the inside with a dim red as it radiated mild heat. Eight seconds later and one test of his newly acquired acceleration, James had spun the bulb out and tossed it away, letting it cool down before the lamp melted into a cold puddle with a red orb in it.

"That one's yours," Alanna told him, and James shrugged and cracked it.

[+1 Emotional Resonance Rank : Amazement]

"Not sure I needed that one," he said, looking around at the Office that surrounded them. Alanna laughed when he filled her in on the level-up.

They filled up the bag with more food. They filled their pockets with a few hundred bucks in cash that was probably illegal, now that James thought about it. "Next one?" Alanna asked after the twentieth cube and the third fight with something hostile.

James looked back at the suitcase in the hallway. "Yeah, one more, then we head back. That's gonna be heavy, even if it's got wheels." He cracked the yellow in his hand.

[+2 Skill Ranks : Cinematography]

The two of them moved down to the last cube on their hall. They were still cautious but moving with comfortable and practiced steps now. They were in their stride, in their element. They were fighters and explorers and saviors in equal measure, and they were ready for . . .

One of those black plastic binder clips the size of the suitcase they'd been hauling around exploded out of the door, metal bands close together as its "mouth" opened up and snapped down on James's midsection.

He got about three seconds to scream before Alanna cut it in half, and he let his voice trail off in a comical way, before covering the end of it with a cough. "Ah. Hm. Okay, that didn't hurt nearly as much as I thought it would," he said as he hauled himself back to his feet. "Okay, ow, no. Never mind. I feel like my stomach got smashed flat. That's gonna bruise."

"Are you okay?!" Alanna demanded, stabbing into the corpse again.

"Yeah, yeah, I'm fine. Hey, look, it dropped a green! Kind of a small one, though," James said, having a bit of difficulty talking, but not that bad considering how that whole thing could have gone. He was lucky it didn't have actual teeth. "So hey! What do we call this thing?" he said, kicking one of the strangely flexible metal bars coming off the back of the creature.

Alanna took a second to calm down now that her boyfriend wasn't in mortal peril again. After that, she sighed. "You know, this one would have been a good use of 'terrorbyte,' right? Like, now that you already—"

"Yes, thank you, I get that my names are badly timed!" James said, cutting her off. "I'm calling it an alligator clip, even though I know that's not what they are in real life. It's the size and general shape of an alligator. It's good enough. We're leaving, let's go." He threw up his hands in surrender and stormed off, turning around after a couple dozen feet to come back, zip up, and wheel off the suitcase of food.

"This is why everyone believes in you," Alanna said quietly behind him, words not for James to hear. "You almost die, and you're already right back to it." She shook her head. "Idiot," she said with a smile, and absolutely no conviction behind it.

CHAPTER 29

"This is fucking brilliant," Alanna said, watching the preparations being made. "You're a genius. Like a human astronaut."

James decided he didn't need to correct her by saying that it was mostly Sarah's idea. He was, after all, a genius. He had an image to maintain. "Thanks, it was Sarah's idea," he said, before his mouth caught up to his devious scheming. "Mostly, anyway. I just organized things." He glanced over at her.

Alanna had been following him closely for a while now, and James had started to notice it. "A while" was only the few hours since they'd come back from snapping up the briefcase, but it still seemed weird. She hadn't gone off to talk to the scout teams or do any personal looting of the local area. She just turned herself into a constant presence at his side. Maybe it was because of the comically high number of life-and-death situations they were getting into finally taking a mental toll. Or maybe she just wanted to have some mutual defense against that one annoyingly overeager kid who had also started following James around, albeit a lot more loudly.

"I thought Theo did all the organizing these days." Alanna's words took James out of his reflection, and he realized he'd been blankly staring at her.

"She's gotta sleep sometime." James shrugged. "Besides, if everyone's intent on listening to me, I should put that power to use before they realize that I have no idea what I'm doing."

"Are you turning into a dictator?" she asked without a smile, head tilted to the side in a tiny way that still said a lot to James. It told him mild curiosity, a splash of amusement, but with a colder and sterner core to Alanna's feelings. The look told him that power came at a price, and while they'd paid up front for a lot of it, he shouldn't get into the habit of being the guy who had total control over everyone.

James saw all this, but his good mood wasn't deterred by his girlfriend's sociological policies. "I rule with an iron fist!" he declared, punching a fist into his other palm. "I demand utter obedience! I command the vertical and the horizontal!"

"That last one . . ." Alanna trailed off, then cracked a smile. "Okay, just don't let the power go to your head."

"Which one?"

She coughed out a surprised laugh. "Fuck, you're in a snarky mood. All right, you can have my obedience. Okay, what's your dictatorial title?"

James didn't miss a beat in answer. "Wall Lord."

A blank look from his partner. And then "No."

"Aw, come on. Because I've got everyone—"

"No!" she repeated, a bit louder. That got a few heads from the group turning their way. Well, more so than they got normally from the crowd.

It turned out, more than a few people were aware of the fact that James and Alanna were, for lack of a better word, heroes. Even though many of them still had residual memories of having the shit kicked out of them by those same people, they all stole glances at the duo as if they were knights, or champions.

If James hadn't had a paladin complex before, he sure as hell would have by now, if he'd noticed. Alanna certainly noticed but didn't react beyond a few knowing nods to the people when she met their eyes.

Regardless, it didn't cause more than a brief pause in the work happening. That work, incidentally, was a combination of ideas from Sarah, James, and a few of the others who'd tentatively offered up small suggestions during the planning phase. And right now, they were carefully collecting and stacking a pile of wall panels.

The problem, really, was that they couldn't let the dragon spot them. If it casually woke up from its nap for even a moment while they were moving past it, then it was inevitable it would spot one of the fifty-ish people through the glass walls of its home. Similarly, they couldn't rush, because they didn't know how good exactly its hearing was.

Which led to a stupid, silly, brilliant solution.

Just make a new hallway.

They didn't need to sneak the entire length of the plateau, they just needed to cross the forty feet between the last wall before the server room and the door through the Wall. And, as Sarah pointed out, James was too used to actually working in an office, where the walls didn't move.

But here? No one was going to stop them from quietly dismantling a whole row of cubicles, shifting the walls around to make a new hallway, and then saving the extra pieces to very, very, *very* carefully build themselves a corridor to the door out. As Sarah also pointed out, the interior floor plan of this place did change. Not that much around the portals to reality, but this far in? It wasn't uncommon to have maps go obsolete within a couple weeks of each other. A new wall where one wasn't an hour ago shouldn't be enough to arouse suspicion from their biggest concern.

Shouldn't. What a tenuous word.

Regardless. It was tedious, but not too slow at their current rate. And then, for the last leg of their construction, it would be both tedious and insanely dangerous.

That was why James and Alanna were watching the work happen now. Because when they were ready to silently take the last wall down and begin putting up their camouflage, they'd be the two doing it.

Initially, it was just going to be James doing it, but then Alanna had caught wind of his stupid-ass idea and punched him. Hard.

"Did you seriously think this was something you'd have to do yourself?" she'd demanded of him.

"I'll be honest," James replied, "I didn't really plan for any of this."

Then he'd hugged her, laughed off his own idiot idea, and that had been that.

And now they were almost through.

"Any second thoughts about this?" Sarah asked, striding up to them from the construction site. She'd been helping with security; as it turned out she had the same kind of casual ability to herd shellaxies around that James did. Keeping things from devolving into a screaming, grinding fight between the survivors and the machinery of the office was her job: making sure that nothing was around to suddenly spike the volume of their party enough to wake up the terrorbyte. "You look pensive," she told James.

"Hm? Nah, just . . . tired." He sighed. "Overall tired. Hard to keep consistently energetic."

"I hear that," Alanna said. "When we get out of here, I'm gonna take the longest bath."

"Same." James nodded along.

Sarah gave them a beaming smile that made them both want to return it in kind. It was the smile of a comfortable old friendship, a personal groove worn deep. In his chest, James felt the tug of it; even if he'd forgotten Sarah, he still felt the old resonance of that missing connection. "All right, well, we're almost to the end. If you two are ready, we'll have you lovebirds out of here and to your 'bath' in no time!" she told them with a thumbs-up.

James flushed red while Alanna just laughed. "Are you sure we were friends and not mutual antagonists or something?" he jokingly accused Sarah. Then he froze as he realized what he'd said, watching Sarah's face freeze for the smallest moment. "Wait, shit. I'm sorry, that . . ."

"That's the most familiar thing you've said to me since I unplugged," she told him, the smile still on her face. Then she punctuated her heartfelt moment with a muttered "You dork."

"All right, enough of Sad Hour," Alanna decided. "It's our turn." She pointed down the newly created tunnel to where the last couple of survivors were sitting on the plateau edge, catching their breath.

They'd asked for volunteers, and the most fit and healthy had eagerly jumped at the chance to be useful, but "most fit" didn't mean that muscles weren't unused to moving or that malnutrition hadn't set in over the last however many months of captivity. Still, they'd gotten it done, and without waking their biggest threat.

Now it was up to James and Alanna to finish the job, and then they could all get out of here. It was all downhill from the door.

James just barely caught himself before he could think, *What could possibly go wrong?*

The wall panels were heavier than James wanted them to be. Even with Alanna's boosted strength, his arms were *burning* when they moved the third one up.

Sidestep, sidestep, adjust, don't—*do not*—let it fall. Get a good grip. Another step.

James signaled Alanna that he needed a break, and they oh-so-gently set the wall down. He took a few heaving breaths, massaging his biceps. In his head, James had so many things he could say right now: wisecracks about his delicate flower arms, or about how Alanna got to be the strong one in their relationship, or even just a mild complaint that this thing was *so fucking heavy*. But he didn't voice any of them.

Because about ten or twenty feet away, the contents of a server room that had been reassembled into a school-bus-sized monster slumbered, its snores the aberrant whirring of coolant fans.

He took one more breath, then gripped aching fingers that only barely obeyed his brain back onto the side of the wall. Alanna gave him a worried look, but James simply steeled his gaze and nodded at her. They lifted, his arms screamed at him, but they moved the wall.

James leaned back and poked his head around the corner. Just a little bit, the smallest bit. Enough to see if the terrorbyte was still actually asleep. From this angle, right up against the outgoing wall, he could see its massive head and the rows of LEDs that he'd come to associate with eyes around here. All of them in a rhythmic blinking pattern: sleep mode. Turning back, he nodded to Alanna, and the two of them started moving as fast as they dared.

Step into the open, keep going, don't look at the monster. Step, step, step. Toes pointed down, let your shoe press against the floor softly, don't stomp or clop your feet. They'd done this four times now, and James had it down to a mathematical solid. Six steps, exertion to move the wall out a little bit, then back into the waiting clips. Gotta do it at ground level, at the perfect height, or it would threaten to fall. And *that* was unacceptable.

But they did it. On time and under budget; silent and undetected. The wall clipped into place with a *click* that sounded like a crack of thunder to James at the moment. But then there was still that whirring snore from the dragon, and he and Alanna breathed a huge joint sigh of relief.

But not too loudly.

They sat there for a second, on the floor mere yards away from something that could eat them without a second thought. Then they stood and stiffly stalked their way back to their waiting crowd, taking extra care to be as quiet as they could as they plodded back to the ledge.

Time to get out of this place.

Fifty people were not quiet.

First off, they still had another ten hours of office time to get through, so they couldn't just abandon the supplies they'd gathered. Which meant hauling luggage and bags and other things that rustled and made walking awkward. That was the first thing that added to the level of caution needed.

Then they had the injured or sick. Two people had legs that couldn't sneak. One person actually had broken bones. And three others were just too sick to do anything, probably from malnutrition, and that was a problem that no amount of candy bars and break room lunches would fix. This place needed fucking fruit. But health concerns aside, they still had to move those people. Which meant either makeshift stretchers or just helping them walk, which meant more chances for slips or yelps of pain or other noises. Which meant going slower, to be careful.

Third of all, they had to pack up all the xenotech they'd nabbed. Most of it was trinkets that they'd broken into blues and distributed to group leaders for use in emergencies, as a last-minute panic switch. But some things were a bit more useful, and they'd carefully packed them for transit. Especially the ones that were dangerous. The scissors that had an unfortunate tendency to cut emotional connections had been taped shut, and that would be enough for them. But the plastic desk plant that generated mild gravity shifts when it was poked needed to be very, *very* carefully carried; ditto for the pen that launched you an extra five feet past where it should land if it was moved without touching a solid surface. They'd taken a council vote and decided that these things were absolutely worth the risk to move, but they needed to be careful with them, and so, obviously, that would take more time.

And then everyone was tired, and hungry, and hurt, and, and, and...

It wasn't great. It also wasn't helped by the fact that apparently none of the survivors could absorb yellows either. James had already been made aware that no one except himself and Sarah could absorb blues. And even then, he could barely manage it, and Sarah could only hold one. She'd also informed him that hers allowed her to "improve wood," and then given him an expectant look with wide smiling eyes. James hadn't risen to that bait. But he had also gotten it confirmed, as he suspected, that you couldn't just ditch an absorbed blue, or put it in storage while you used another one. And Sarah hadn't been able to exhaust hers to replace it with something else; apparently using them really was as tiring as he'd felt, and you couldn't just machine-gun through one you didn't like.

They took the wounded through first, after a long enough rest that everyone felt like they could manage it without mistakes. One at a time, people were being carried by one or two others who were a bit more upright. James was a little surprised to see that Collins, the man who had almost gotten into a shouting match with him about organized worship not even six hours ago, was among one of the volunteers to go first, helping a woman who was older than he was and couldn't stand on her own to make her way out.

Well hell, if even he could get over being a jackass for ten minutes in a life-or-death situation, James could sure as hell muster the energy to smile while he got everyone home.

Alanna and Sarah went through first as well, to secure the other side of the door and make sure that it was safe to follow for a crowd. Daniel went with them to start the process of getting them the last couple miles to the front door. In theory, the other side should be "safe" by dungeon standards. But they still needed to be constantly alert for strider swarms, tumblefeeds, dart traps, Möbius halls, 2.0s, ambush plants, maul carts . . .

Fucking hell, how had they ever survived more than twenty minutes in here, James wondered as he watched the last guy, a kid with a broken leg in a splint, get helped to hobble down their artificial hallway toward safety.

Then the scout groups had gone, leading with them a few people each. Then Harvey and Deb had led some of the more skittish people who absolutely were afraid to go first, including that one guy who'd gotten a little gun-shy even after the paralysis poison of the camraconda wore off. Those two were seen as authority figures more than James was by a certain population of the rescued people, and their influence really helped get those who were more frightened by the environment and the bizarre wildlife moving.

And then James and Theo were left to bring up the rear.

"Are you sure about this?" she asked him warily.

"We're about fifty people too late for that," he'd told her, and started walking.

James spent the whole time with his fear singing in his veins. At any second, a shellaxy was going to start something, or one of the walls was going to fall over, or the dungeon would just arbitrarily decide to turn off the lights or something. And then, when that didn't happen, he was forced into a new set of fears. What if the terrorbyte woke up? What if he tripped? He hadn't tripped in the last week, but what if it happened *now*?

He was almost ready to start hyperventilating when Theo shoved him through the open door, stepped through herself, closed it softly behind her, and bluntly said, "Stop freaking out, you wuss."

James felt a flash of anger and humiliation, but buried it before it could show too much on his face. "Sure," he said. Then he looked around at what was on this side of the door. "Is this . . . a janitor's closet?" James asked. A sea of mops greeted him, along with Momo and the mongausse who'd stayed behind. "Where is everyone?"

Closet was the wrong word. This was a *tunnel*. It stretched on into the distance and took a bending left turn a few hundred feet away. And the mops weren't neatly stacked on the shelves that lined the walls like old-timey mining shaft supports. They grew out of the damp ground, like cattails with poofy fabric heads, and they were *everywhere*. The shelves looked like they were hewn from the wall material, and they held a huge assortment of random junk. Buckets, gloves, toolboxes, and a thousand jugs of poorly labeled cleaning solutions. Overhead, dim yellow lights connected by hanging loops of wire lit the place in an orangish glow. It smelled harsh, like a chemical scent, but not the sterilized smell of a hospital.

"Went on ahead," Momo told him, ending her fidgeting with a lighter as they came through. "I'm just here to keep everyone moving. Mops are safe, don't touch anything else."

"Does it explode?" Theo asked dryly, and Momo gave her an *are you fucking with me* kind of look. "Never mind," Theo followed up, flicking a hand at the other girl. "Let's go."

They pressed through, James being about a foot or so taller than the other two, meaning that he got to deal with ducking under frustratingly damp mop heads that sat at almost exactly head level, some of them drifting in unfelt wind like they were sea anemones. The tunnel seemed to go on for a lot longer than the wall's width from above made it look when he'd first come in, but around here, that didn't mean much. Momo idly chattered to them, and to her dog, as they walked. Talking about anything and nothing, just enjoying the freedom to walk again without worrying about waking anything up.

And then they took the turn, another length of bitter-scented cavern, and a propped-open door, and just like that, they were back in . . . well, *normal* might be the wrong word, but the office James recognized.

He took a deep breath through his nose, enjoying the clean air and the feeling that they'd just crossed the last boundary. They were, he decided then, absolutely going to make it.

Then a flailing sheet of paper hit him in the face, and he sputtered as he tossed it off to the laughter of the people around him.

But it didn't matter. That wasn't going to get him down. They were already on the move, into safer territory and toward the front door. It was well past time to go home.

CHAPTER 30

Fort Door welcomed them home like an old friend.

As they approached it, Ganesh burst into the air, tracing a wobbling and tired line toward the ramparts where he slammed into a waiting strider with the drone-bat equivalent of a bear hug.

The caravan was too tired to cheer, but there was a sense of peace hanging over them as the empty half circle of floor space came into sight. People stepped out from the eternal twists and turns of cubicle hallways and saw the gate of their last camp, and they realized that they'd done it. Their salvation had brought them out of hell. And that emotional moment propagated through the whole group, until even the arrogant and petulant had smiles on their faces.

Or maybe they were just happy this base was already set up for them.

"Joke's on them," James softly spoke to no one in particular. "We've got two beds and a table; we're not a hotel."

"What was that?" Alanna asked, stifling a yawn. James couldn't remember how long she'd been awake for, but he hadn't actually seen her sleep since they came out of the conference room.

"Don't worry about it," he replied, reaching up to ruffle her hair at the base of her neck where it peeked out past the helmet. "Theo! What's our time look like?" he called over to where his teammate was leading people out of an adjacent cubicle tunnel. James had almost forgotten what it was like to be in an area where he could see over the walls and everything looked normal. Well, normal if you ignored the curved horizon.

"Two hours to spare!" she bellowed back with a confident energy in her voice.

There was a spattering of relieved laughter, humor at the end of desperation, from the crowd. James smiled to himself. He'd done it. *They* had done it. Three . . . goodbye, Dave . . . three people went in, and fifty came out. Objective secured, and then some.

"Gonna get out of here. Gonna get a shower, and hot food, and it's gonna be perfect," James told Alanna.

"And a shave." She nodded.

"Doesn't look like you need a shave." James smirked at her.

Alanna rolled her eyes. "You, you derp. You've got this weird half-goatee going on."

"Maybe I'll just grow it out. Get my official guild leader mustache going on."

"Nooooo, you will not," she replied, casually crushing his mustache dreams as the last of the survivors stumbled into the zone.

Putting that aside for a second, James decided to address everyone. "All right, guys!" James spoke up and a wave of hush fell around him in a ring as the group assembled on the open carpet plain. "I hate to tell you this, but we've still got a little left to do. Everyone take half an hour or so to rest up, and Alanna and I . . ." James glanced over at an exhausted Alanna and corrected himself. "Theo and I will handle getting everything squared away. Anyone who absolutely needs to sleep, we do have a few cots. But I'd like to widen this no-man's-land just in case, and get some extra walls up so that we can have some moderately safe places for everyone to relax. Shouldn't take too long, so if anyone's got the capacity for it, we'll start breaking down walls in ten."

There was a collective sigh, but at this point, it was one of resignation and not frustration. Besides, with twenty people working, this would go smoothly. It wasn't like they lacked for practice at this point, anyway.

"Tell them you're proud of them," Alanna muttered in his ear.

James blinked once. "What?"

"Something my newfound business degree is telling me. Just tell them you're proud of them," she reiterated.

Resisting the urge to shrug, James raised his voice again. "Hey, everyone?" he said, mildly nervous, looking around him. He made eye contact with Theo and Daniel, with Other James and Karen and the new delvers. With a grinning Sarah who gave him an encouraging thumbs-up. With Deb, with Harvey, with all the random people to whom he'd apologized frequently for not being able to store their names in his head, but who had all, every one of them, been part of getting the whole party out alive. Even with those few people, like the football kid who'd been shadowing him, that annoyed the hell out of James and frayed his nerves at the worst time. And with Secret, pooled around his feet. Then a double take on Secret. Then a smile. He wasn't nervous anymore. Alanna was right. "I'm proud of all of you," he said with a grin. "We did it."

Then there was a cheer.

"I knew you'd be all right without me," Secret told him.

"I *knew* there was something off." James rolled his eyes. "What did you do?"

"Something bold, stupid, ill-advised, and right," Secret said, peering up at James with six translucent eyes. "As my father showed me."

As James looked down at the ghostly eel coiled around his feet, he realized that Secret, too, needed to hear something from him. "I'm proud of you, too, you know," he said. "Get off my shoes, that's not where you sit." James gave his friend, his creation for lack of a better term, a smile as Secret looped up around his torso and eventually settled on his shoulders, wrapping James in a pale blue glow. Waves of pride radiated off Secret like an emotional space heater. "Oh, but don't think that cryptic-ass answer gets you out of this!" James reminded him, remembering to be clear on it. "I know you eat secrets, but come on! You need to give me more than that to go on."

"Ah, yes, of course." Secret bobbed his head. "I was just making a dramatic entrance. Which I also learned from you, I believe?"

"No comment." James tried to keep a straight face as he walked into the fort and settled his duffel bag on the desk. Finally, *finally* getting to put down the weight. He unzipped it and started unloading pieces of gear, shifting around the pair of sunglasses and the Nerf gun with a sticky note on it reading *Chekhov* to make space. Theo and Alanna followed him in, with Alanna simply dropping her bag, sloughing off her armor, and then dropping herself onto a cot, asleep practically instantly, and Theo doing a more civil version of unpacking but keeping a nervous distance from James. Secret still bothered her, it seemed. "So?" James prompted again, as he unsnapped and removed his own battered and scarred hockey pads.

"I killed the thing that erodes the image of those lost in here," Secret replied, still being needlessly cryptic. It was when he said "killed" that James took a second to really inspect his friend and noticed gaps in Secret's scales: Scars, perhaps? Or still open wounds? "When we leave, when *they* leave, they will at least be able to rebuild. Though I cannot account for the passage of time, or . . . or what has already been destroyed, and not obfuscated."

James cut him off, wrapping an arm around the semi-solid snake, and giving him a hug, pulling the serpentine body in tight against his own. "Thank you," he said softly, eventually releasing a mildly embarrassed Secret. "Just . . . thanks. I know that sort of thing isn't free for you. And this is a huge help."

"Of course." Secret bobbed his head. "It was my duty." He said it like it was that simple. And maybe, to him, it was. Secret was, after all, an idea given form, not the other way around like a human. To his eyes, it might actually be almost not a choice at all to take action like this.

There was a *thunk* on the desk in front of James, and he brought tired eyes down to see what it was. In front of him sat another old friend: a red and black stapler with a single yellow eye in the front, looking up at him expectantly.

"Hey, Rufus," James said. "How's the home front?"

The strider in front of him looked up for a second and then reached up a single pen leg, holding it expectantly in the air. Rufus didn't exactly have an eyebrow, but James felt like he was getting a kind of *eh, eh?* look from his first ally in this place.

James felt a wide, real smile take over his face, and he gave in and high-fived his friend.

Dropping his leg back down, Rufus gave a satisfied scuttle on the table. "So, things going okay? Where's Pendragon? I know it hasn't been that long, but did she abandon us already?"

Rufus gave a little side-to-side motion that James was starting to associate with a *no*, then held up two limbs in front of himself. Gradually, he widened the gap between his arms. "She got bigger?" A bobbing nod in response. "Okay, neat. But where is she?" Rufus just pointed. Out, over the wall, into the maze where they'd just come from. "Ran off, eh?" James was about to sigh in resignation, but to that, Rufus gave another vehement no. He tapped his eye, then stabbed his leg out again toward the wilds of the office. "Looking for something?" Rufus wavered. "Somewhere?" Closer, but still no. James hated this kind of guessing game; it was really more Anesh's style. God, he missed Anesh. "Some*one*? Fuck it, I don't . . ." But then he stopped, as Rufus answered in the affirmative.

"Oh," James said, sadly.

"What's up?" a passing Theo asked.

James looked over at her, a fresh hurt on his face. "There was another life here, one that Dave made on purpose. She was . . . like a small bird made out of pens and clips and stuff. He called her Pendragon." James gazed out at the endless horizon, where the cubicle walls faded into a distant gloom. "She went looking for him."

"Oh," Theo echoed.

There wasn't much else to be said.

Then Rufus, trying to cheer him up, started scuttling sideways to draw James's attention to his little garden. The copper pipes had grown up, it seemed, and were now bearing . . . fruit? "Rufus, what is this?" James asked. "I've been looking at this the whole time you were working on it, and I still don't get it. Is this art?"

Rufus just did his version of sighing, dipping his snout down to the tabletop. Then, to illustrate why this was so cool, he poked one of the bronze "fruits." It unfolded, until it snapped off its vine and lay on the table in a neatly connected row of . . .

"Staples." James looked down at it. "Staples? Wait, hang the fuck on. Is this is *staple crop*? Who taught you puns? Was it me? Am I a bad influence?" Rufus glared up at him. "Okay, yes, this is actually really cool. Can you eat these?" He got a cheerful affirmative. "Well, that's awesome. Makes you less dependent on the orbs, huh? But . . . yeah, that's cool. I'll talk to Anesh later about what the hell this means for the nature of organic life."

Rufus just nodded cheerfully, glad that James had plans.

"All right." James broke the silence. "We'll leave the light on for her. In the meantime, let's go get the walls up and settle in. Time for our state-mandated half-hour lunch break."

The walls around Fort Door went down. The new walls of Fort Door went up.

James helped out, but while everyone was pitching in, no one was in a huge hurry. They took small breaks between each panel moved, gradually clearing out a wider and wider area, until they had a hundred meters of empty space cleared away on all sides, and a base with a reasonable amount of space for people to rest without having to worry about random strider attacks.

A lot of desks were moved around into neat rows. A lot of chairs were collected for those with weary feet. There wasn't really anything left in the way of food around here to scavenge, though. Even though they'd only been doing this for a short time, James, Anesh, and Alanna had pretty well cleared out this opening area. And while a few things had respawned, it seemed to be a sporadic and slow process.

James considered getting some people to dismantle the computers they'd taken out of the cubes. With an eye to funding their future operations, and having to take care of any of the people here without families to go back to, they could use a little extra income stream from selling off video cards and RAM sticks. But everyone looked so tired, and a few hundred bucks wasn't really that relevant against what was in the briefcase he and Alanna had carried back.

He'd also helped Theo shuffle the amassed pile of orbs they'd collected into a single bag for ease of transport out of here. They'd agreed—or rather, James had proposed and everyone else had gone along with it—that the division of spoils should include the rest of his friends, and that he and Anesh would sort it out once they were out of here. Still, even having been cracking yellows sporadically through the trip, James still practically drooled at the sight of hundreds of small golden orbs in the unzipped duffel, bulging out of it like glowing fish eggs. A good chunk of those were blues, too. Dozens of them, in case of emergencies that they'd resolved in other ways. Those would probably go to the victims of Karen, to help them through hard times ahead. Reds, greens, oranges, even a purple had gotten in there somehow. The rainbow of luminescent colors tempted James enough that he'd left rather than give in and just start slamming his hands into the pool of potential power.

And then it was just a matter of settling in for the wait.

Waiting in the Office was not something James was accustomed to. He tried to lean back against the outer wall, hands folded behind his head, Secret sprawled across his lap. But very quickly he realized that he just didn't want to sit still, no matter how tired he was. He was just too restless, no matter how much his feet ached. Didn't help that the floor wasn't exactly the most comfortable of chair, but that wasn't the big problem.

Just as he'd sighed and been about to stand up, though, James had his lack of rest interrupted.

"Hey." James greeted Karen as she walked up and without comment simply folded herself into a cross-legged sitting position in front of him. The motion looked fluid, like it came from someone who'd spent a lot of time doing yoga, but James had a hard time reconciling that thought with the fact that the person doing it was old enough to be his mom. Normally, that would have also made it hard for him to talk to this woman, but after everything that had happened, he felt less like an out-of-place kid and more like a peer to, well, to everyone here. "What can I do for ya?" he asked her.

"You mentioned setting up a support group for people after we get out of here," she said. "Is that going to happen?"

"I'm planning on it, yeah," James said. "I mean, I don't have any concrete plans right now, but I know a guy who works at the library, and we can check out those big meeting rooms for group events." He winced a bit. "Not sure how I feel about meeting rooms. Maybe in a park or something." James trailed off his stream of thought. "Why do you ask?"

Karen tapped the back of her neck. "We all still have these. Will they go away when we leave?"

"They shouldn't," James admitted. "I'd actually forgotten about that." And now that he'd been reminded, he became aware of just how much his own neck itched. "Thanks," he said as he scratched at it. "But yeah, I don't have any cyberpunk streetdocs on my contact list that can remove wetware. This one might be a bigger problem."

The look Karen gave him reminded James that, even though he trusted her to work as part of a team at this point, she still wasn't one of his friends who knew all the weird nerd terms he tossed out. "I'm just asking because I think some of the younger people, no offense, might actually try using them."

"Oh, yeah, I'd already assumed that'd be a thing. I need to make a note to warn everyone not to try plugging into the internet until we can make sure it's safe." James took out his phone to make a small reminder for his future self, and then scowled at the shattered screen. "Well, suppose *that* was inevitable. Wonder when this happened?"

"But isn't it a problem?" Karen brought him back on track.

"What? The upgrade? I mean, it's gonna be hard to explain to anyone who doesn't know about this place, but we're basically abandoning information security at this point. Secret said something about how the office tries to limit how far information about it spreads, so that should keep it from really interfering with someone's life, but it's not like we can stop it now, right?" He shrugged. "My biggest worry is if it can spread, like how Kar... um, boss-fight Karen did it. But we'd need a volunteer to test that out. Anesh'd probably be into it; I'll ask him in a couple hours."

"That doesn't seem like a good idea," Karen said with a restrained frown. "Do you really think it's okay to make the real world... to break the rules like that?"

James took a deep breath. "I have no idea." He admitted to her bluntly. "But the way we've been doing things has been working so far. So I'm gonna go with my instincts. And my gut is telling me that this isn't going to hurt anyone, at least, not on its own. My bigger concern is with funding the cleanup operation. We're gonna need to put a lot of work into helping everyone get their lives back together."

"You want to do that?" She didn't seem surprised, but instead calculating. Judging to see if James had any hidden motives. Fortunately for both of them, he absolutely didn't.

"Nope!" he answered with overblown false cheer. "But if I don't, if we don't, who will? That's why I'm reconsidering not stripping out everything worth more than five dollars from this place. Theo has a whole list of things we'll need to pay for in the next few hours." He shook his head. "We're getting off topic. I'd say, warn people about using the port, spread the word around, but don't tell anyone they can't. Especially not anyone my age; I'm sure you know how that'd go over."

Karen didn't exactly laugh at that, but James knew from the look on her face that she knew *exactly* what he meant. "All right. We'll trust you," she said, standing up. "Thank you for your time."

"No problem!" James told her, leaning back against the cube wall, closing his eyes and just breathing for a bit while Karen walked off.

He was just settling into position when he realized again that he had been in the process of standing up. With an internal chuckle, he opened his eyes and leaned forward, waking up a snoozing Secret and briefly wondering how Secret could even sleep if he didn't have a real body.

It just so happened he'd timed his motion with his next petitioner, as Momo crouched down in front of where he had settled.

"Yo," she greeted him, apparently not at all fazed by his perfect coincidental timing.

James looked back at her. "Yo," he replied. Now this, this was someone he knew how to deal with, to talk to. "Whaddya want?" He spoke in an exaggerated dockworker accent, making it clear he was goofing around.

Momo smirked, idly itching at one of the cuts on her face that had accrued over a number of fights from the last few days. Her hands always seemed to be moving; James had overheard her tell someone it was nicotine withdrawal. "Wanted to ask, um, what's gonna happen to us when we leave?"

"What? You go home," James said, his brain trying to catch up.

"Won't there be questions or something? Like, I dunno, some kinda wizard police that'll want to know what happened?"

"I fucking told Alanna I was worried about wizard police, and she didn't believe me!" James laughed. "But no, so far, we haven't found anything like that."

"Oh," Momo said. "Okay, good."

From somewhere on the other side of the fort, there was a loud yelp that rose over the noise of other voices and activity. James jerked in surprise and started to stand, but Momo just waved it off. "It's just a stapler," she said. "They've been sneaking in and biting people for a while now. Theo says the noise is probably attracting them."

"Ah." James shrugged. "I haven't been paying attention to that, I guess?"

"Yeah, the little fucks keep coming one at a time." She shrugged back. "Whatever. Won't be our problem for much longer."

James looked at her, really looked at this fidgety, nervous goth girl in front of him. He hadn't known this person before, so he had no comparison, but she was anxious about something. And unlike everyone else, she didn't have that constant undercurrent of fear about everything here. Hell, she'd adopted a wolf made of a magnetic field or something. Though that part was in character for every goth James had ever known.

Finally, he sighed, leaned back against the wall, and asked, "What's wrong?"

"Nothing's wrong, right? We're going home," she said. "Or to whatever's left of it. We're all saved." She sounded bitter.

Yeah, that wasn't suspicious at all. "And . . . ?" James prompted, flourishing a hand in front of himself.

The response came back much more subdued than he was used to with her. "Do we get to come back?"

Ah. There it was. He'd known this conversation was coming. It had been obvious from the early hours that some of these people were just as psyched for a dungeon as he and Anesh had been. Not all of them; even those who'd looted and scouted and sometimes fought weren't auto-includes. But Momo and her team absolutely were. They were the kind of people that would rather die here than live trapped in a mundane world. Just like James was, really.

To that sort of person, he really only had one possible answer. Letting them in would make him responsible for their injuries, their failures, their possible deaths. But what a *monster* it would make him to shut them out. To show them magic, and then tell them it wasn't theirs to use.

He could tell that was what Momo was already thinking; James was the authority figure here, and she'd clearly had some problems with authority in the past. He was going to tell her to go home, not tell anyone, be a good girl, and forget it ever happened. That was the anger on her face, the bitter drip in her words.

"Yes."

"You can't just fucking . . . !" She paused in her preplanned retort. "What?"

"Yes. You can come back in." James savored saying it. This moment was just glorious. He got to crush someone's expectations, and make their day, all at once. "We're going to have to change how we approach this place, but yeah. Were you planning to be independent, or join up?"

"I don't . . . you can't just . . . " She *thwapped* a fist into the floor. "You fucker, you planned for this!"

"Yes!" James said, unable to contain his amusement. "So?"

"We want to join you guys, yes! Fucking happy?" Momo demanded. It was all just too hilarious to James.

After he got control of his laughing, he reached out a hand, shaking Secret off from where the infomorph was coiled around his wrist. "Welcome to the team," he said. "We don't have a name, or a cool catchphrase. Anesh and I tried once, and it was super awkward and I hated it. Let me know if you think of one; I'll make a suggestion box or something. There's no signing bonus or health care, and you might die. It's basically perfect."

Momo shook his hand, the palm of her fingerless gloves rough against his skin. Then she stood on unsteady legs and looked around before glancing back to James. "I have to, um . . ."

"Yeah, go let your team know." He smiled at her. And she smiled back, before turning on her toe and bolting away back around the outside of the fort wall.

James sighed and propped his hands behind his head again. "Okay, *that* one felt good." He spoke facing the ceiling, but with words directed at Secret.

"Of course you enjoyed that. You love yourself the role of champion," Secret snarked back at him.

"Hey, that's . . . !" James couldn't come up with a single thing to say in his own defense. "Yeah. That's," he settled on. "Also, stop distracting me, I was going to . . ."

"Stand up?" Secret asked as Theo dropped into place across from him.

Theo didn't fold into position like Karen did, or crouch to eye level like Momo. Instead, she just dropped, slamming one knee into the ground in a way that James was almost sure had to hurt, and then leaning forward with an elbow on her bent leg. "We need to talk," she said.

"Of course we do." James groaned. "Fine! I'm ready! What logistical nightmare do you have for me?"

Theo looked grim. "I need to know how we're handling everyone once we leave. We haven't done any kind of budgeting or planning, and..."

James held up a hand. "First, it's going to be three a.m. No one's going to be awake to receive family members. So, step one, book everyone into a hotel. There's two places within walking distance of work, but we can always get a ride or something. I've got a car, I can shuttle people. Step two, tomorrow morning, we establish communications. Start getting people phones and getting them in contact with their social groups. Step just before two, we eat breakfast." James had a sudden mental image of a raspberry Danish and some bacon, and his stomach rumbled. "Maybe two breakfasts. Anyway. Step three, we create a method of group communication, probably just a room in the chat server we already use as a group, and set it aside for survivors. Er. 'We' here is Alanna and Anesh and me. Anyway. The point is, we keep in touch, organize group therapy sessions, and discreetly contact a couple good psychologists to help deal with the longer-term problems." James took a deep breath. "Oh, step... somewhere back there... probably step one actually, we need to get a few people to the hospital. A lot of people, actually. After that, we work on getting everyone's lives back on track until they don't need our support anymore. Permanent places to live, jobs, moving on with their lives, that sorta thing. Let the people who want to forget, forget." James paused, then, in a shakier voice, finished his list of things to do. "Then I tell Dave's mom what happened to him. And also Johnson's daughter." It took James a couple heartbeats of silence to find his voice again. "Anyway. Our opening operating budget is thirty thousand dollars. You're in charge of accommodations. Want to negotiate a salary while there's still time?"

There was a moment of incredulous shock from Theo as she stared at James disbelievingly. "What happened to the James who always showed up ten minutes late and stressed over every call?" she asked him.

"James died," James said. "And the specter of adult responsibility filled his corpse and puppets it to this day."

"You seriously overestimate what adults have to be responsible for in their daily lives," Theo informed him with a flat tone. "This is a bit beyond normality."

James shrugged back at her, bumping Secret and getting a blinking look from the meme. "I was never much of an adult, so I wouldn't know."

"Well, you seem to have picked up the basics," Theo told him, pretending that she was more than a year or two older than her supposed subordinate. "I want lunch."

"What?"

"Like, a real lunch. No! *Brunch!* I want a goddamned masterpiece of brunch." Theo clapped her hands together to punctuate the declaration.

"What, like, right now?" James was confused. Even if he could get behind the brunch idea.

Theo rolled her eyes. "I'm trying to negotiate for pay in a way that's kinda silly, but shows that I'm willing to help just to help, you idiot."

"Why is every woman in my life so bloody tsundere?" James asked Secret, who showed wisdom well beyond his years by choosing not to respond.

"I don't know what that means," Theo stated. "But I'm mad at you for it."

"Exactly," James replied.

"Whatever. I'll invoice you for my time." She rolled her eyes and stood to leave, shaking out the leg she'd been leaning on. It looked like Theo was about to say something else, but then there was another yelp in the distance. Theo snorted and turned away. "I'll check on that. We've been . . ."

"Having a lot of striders, yeah, I heard," James said. "Despite trying to get some peace and quiet."

Theo grunted at him, clearly not sorry. "You guys picked a hostile place for a base."

"It wasn't this bad when we got here," James told her. "Also there's the exit. So."

"Isn't it bad luck to call attention to that?"

"What, the exit? It's right there, it's not like . . ."

Theo cut him off. "No, the fact that this place is supposed to be safe."

"Yeah, well . . . yeah . . ." James took a bit a of a confused pause as his brain processed that. "It's . . ." But by the time he started to say something, Theo was gone, off to see if there was a real problem and solve it if needed. She was a good manager, really. But it did make James mildly worried what she'd brought up. It was probably just because of all the noise they were making with all the people they'd piled in this space that they were attracting more attention. It was probably not a big deal that they kept having to deal with strider bites.

Probably. Almost certainly. For sure.

No, it wasn't. James sighed. It absolutely wasn't going to be.

"Goddammit, I really need to stand up and see what's happening," James told Secret.

"I am napping," the meme replied.

"Is that why people keep coming over here? Are you summoning people? Can you *do* that?" James lazily mused.

Secret let out a small huff of something that wasn't air. "I am very powerful," he bluntly said. Which wasn't really an answer.

The two of them sat in comfortable quiet for a few more minutes. James was just starting to feel like maybe he didn't have to be so on edge as he rested. In a way, it was kind of reassuring, all these people coming up to him. If there was a problem, if someone needed clarification on something, or if there was an overwhelming assault on the front door, then James could rest easy knowing that *then* someone would let him know. And so, for now, he could just sit and let his sore feet rest. He wasn't exactly happy, not really. Losing Dave still sat heavy in his heart, and no matter how many people they rescued, the cost was still so very high. But he was content, in this moment, to do nothing. Finally, to do nothing. Just for a minute. To be comforted by the sounds of humanity moving and talking around him, to stare up at the flocks of printer paper overhead, to be unbothered.

"Hey, um, James?" The voice sounded nearby, young, male, and nervous.

James looked down from the artificial ceiling to meet Daniel's eyes. "Yeeeeessss?" he drawled out, running his hand down Secret's back ridges, imagining himself looking for all the world like a super-villain with a white cat. Except wearing torn slacks, with a half-dozen wrinkled bandages on his face and hands, and instead of a spinning office chair behind a massive oak desk, he was on the floor behind a makeshift shelter. But he had a pet leviathan, so close enough.

Daniel didn't miss the symbolism, but it didn't seem to help his nerves. "I just wanted to apologize again, and to say thank you. A lot of people wanted to say thank you, but they didn't want to bother you."

"But you did?" James said with a smile. He was getting used to having his break interrupted at this point.

"No, no! I mean . . ." Daniel held up his hands defensively, back-tracking before he saw James wave his panic away. "Er, I just wanted to ask you, what happens after we leave?"

"Man, everyone looking to the future today. This is way more adult responsibility than I was prepared for," James mildly complained.

Daniel looked around them like he was afraid of being caught in a verbal trap here. "Aren't . . . aren't you an adult?" he asked.

James's brain stuttered for a second, before he realized something, and leaned forward to ask, "Danny, how old do you think I *am*?"

"I . . . don't have to answer that?" Daniel tentatively replied, the hint of a question on his words.

"Good, you're learning. Anyway, what about what happens after we leave? Theo should have the road map for most people, but you've only been in here a week. You should be able to just drop back into your old life if you want. No offense, but I don't feel like you'd want to come back."

"I don't. I don't!" Daniel said. "But, um . . . what about Path?"

It took James another few moments of trying to parse the words to remember that Pathfinder was the name of the map in Daniel's head. Well, the name he'd given it. "Oh yeah, we never really talked about . . . him?"

"It, I think?"

"Have you asked?"

"I . . . I will! I will ask," Daniel declared, like he'd forget if he didn't say it with enough conviction.

"That's good. Honestly, you should be talking to them, not me. Infomorphs, like Secret here, well, they grow up fast. And we don't even know if Path is the same . . . 'species'?" James ran his fingers over one of the spines on Secret's hide, eliciting a noise somewhat like a purr. "They aren't exactly human, but they're still people, and they should be allowed to make their own decisions. So talk to them when you get the chance. I don't know what your line of communication looks like, so maybe you won't be able to until we leave, but if they want to come back in and roam here, they're welcome to. If they want to stay with you, they can do that too. We'll work it out."

"Why . . ." Daniel started to ask something but seemed to think better of it, and he stood in front of James opening and closing his fists a couple of times.

"Why?"

The words broke through at the prompting before Daniel could stop them. "Why are you so nice?! How do you deal with all of this?! I feel like I'm about to fall apart at any moment, and you're just sitting there being calm and reasonable, and it's not really fucking fair, is it?!" he shouted, his voice cracking a little as he rose in volume. He stared at the floor, his face bright red, like he'd just accused James of murder or something.

James just shrugged it off. He didn't want to dismiss Daniel's concerns, and he wasn't going to get offended over something so small, especially not now. "I've got a lot of experience with my life falling to pieces. Hey. You'll be fine. You made it through this, just take it one problem at a time, man. It'll work out, if you give it a real effort and a chance. And if it doesn't, we'll be here to help."

It looked like Daniel might have had an angry response to that, something that he was going to reflexively snap back at James for trying to be kind again. But fortunately for both of them, he never got a chance to say it, as Daniel got distracted by the electrical snuffling nose of the mongausse that came bounding over to them. He yelped as its rainbow snout made contact with his hand, and then yelped again, nearly jumping out of his skin, as Sarah clapped a hand on his shoulder.

"Hey, Danny," she greeted him. Reaching down, she ran her hand along the back of the mongausse, the spines of colored distortion curling where she stroked them. It glanced up at her, and she swept it away from Daniel, sending it over toward where James sat, watching as the magnetic dog-shaped form tried to make friends with a falsely sleeping Secret. "James." She spoke more directly to James, not exactly shutting Daniel out of the conversation, but certainly sidelining him, making it clear that she had something important going on.

"What's up?" he asked her, now fully resigned to the lack of personal time. "Dragon attack? Rain of molten printer ink? Plague of tack flies?" He paused for a second as he ran out of ideas, and Sarah looked like she was about to explain, but then James got a second wind and kept rolling. "Oh! Someone found the office pet, but it's the size of a bear! Orrrr, the bathrooms are flooding? Or, no, um . . . The vending machines are all . . . turning people into . . . half candy, half human . . . things? Okay, I'm out of ideas. Go ahead."

"None of those, you dork." Sarah couldn't keep a small smile off her face, even though she wasn't here with good news. "But seriously. We've got a problem. You should come see this."

James let out a long groan before stretching his arms out in front of him, elbows locked, Secret held on his forearms. Still hyperbolically groaning, he dumped the snoozing snake onto the back of the mongausse—he really should ask Other James what he'd named that thing—eliciting excited barking from the dog and startled flailing from Secret. As the two of them tumbled away, Secret clearly having picked up James's own aversion to surprise hugs and struggling to get away from the affectionate magnetic field, James stood. "All right, Daniel, we'll have to finish this later. Just, remember, man. One thing at a time. Open and honest communication. You'll be fine. You've got this," he told the kid as he dusted off his own ass. That taken care of, he turned to Sarah. "Okay, let's go."

As she turned to walk away and James fell into step beside her, he took a second to appreciate how much work their group had put into this place. It hadn't even been an hour since they'd gotten here, but everyone working together, with a good chunk of practice under their belts, had thrown up a wide series of double-tall walls, braced from behind by desks. The interior was divided into a few small rooms, offering a small amount of semiprivacy for those who wanted to spend their last couple hours in this place napping or turning what was left of their limited food supply into lunch.

"So, talk to everyone you need to?" Sarah casually asked him as they circled around to the front of the fort. It was becoming obvious even to James, who didn't consider himself the best at reading people, that she was having some serious emotional trouble. Over the last few days of hard travel through the office, Officium Mundi as she called it, her easy, casual attitude toward James and Alanna had gone from natural to almost forced.

It made sense, in a twisted way. Sarah had been like James and Anesh when they first started: full of wonder and stumbling through this place. She'd not recruited anyone but instead had been brought in by a few other employees, all of whom were dead now. She had, she admitted, known instantly how much James would have loved it. But she'd been sworn to secrecy, and something had kept her from sharing too much, even though she'd had a plan in the back of her mind to make a trip in as part of a birthday gift to James. And then her compatriots died, and she was captured. And held, for months.

And the first face she saw upon being pulled out of networked hell was James's. Her best friend, the guy who'd been with her since elementary school. Who she'd helped with physics homework while he helped her through breakups. The one person she was comfortable being roommates with, even as Anesh had started to really grow on her as a person. He'd come for her, somehow, against all laws of common sense. Just like always, he was *there* when she needed it, no matter what his own problems looked like.

And he didn't remember her.

There was a Sarah-shaped hole in his life, in his soul. And talking to him felt like trying to cut through concrete with a butter knife. He was *right there!* The same James that she'd always known, right there in front of her. He talked, he laughed, when he thought no one was watching he kissed Alanna (finally), and he *didn't remember her*.

But Sarah refused to give up. Because he was James. He was her *best friend*. Not a single person, not a partner or a parent on the planet, would ever be more important to her. And the worst part was, he was *trying*. He tried *so hard* to be the person Sarah needed, or was looking for, or remembered.

And so, even knowing that there was some kind of wall between them, James kept trying anyway. "Yeah!" he said. "I'm not sure exactly how that happened. I honestly just sat down, and then everything I needed to happen, happened, without me having to put in that much effort."

Sarah stopped walking and tilted her head sideways to look at James at a right angle. For just a second, everything felt normal between them again, their old, natural conversational style reasserted over a harsh reality. "I'm trying to think of why I should be mad at you for this one, but I kinda feel like you earned it? Congratulations! The universe is finally happy with you!" She cheered him.

James laughed through a toothy smile. "I mean, you're gonna jinx it. Also, aren't you literally taking me to something right now that you said was a problem?"

"The universe is fickle!" Sarah declared, one finger held up in the air overhead as she led the way into Fort Door.

The awkwardness seeped back in after a few moments. But not as much, and not as quickly.

"All right." James got serious and inquisitive as they got into the fort itself, passing the groups of people sitting around outside, some of them keeping watch on the borderline where the tamed construction of Fort Door and its surrounding cleared area met the wilds of the Office proper. He pitched his voice low and addressed Sarah without letting everyone overhear. "So, what's the problem here?"

She led him around a corner and into one of the private rooms they'd put together. This one had neat lines of paper stapled together and taped to the ceiling to form a bit of a door. Or, well, a curtain at least. Holding the sheets back to let James in, Sarah stepped to the side and let him see what was going on.

Theo stood behind a table, her arms folded and a grim look on her face. Like James and Alanna, she'd stripped away the armor, but she still had her xenotech-improvised glaive propped up against the wall. It took a quick double take from James to realize it wasn't propped on anything and actually just stabbed into the floor, which he kinda took offense to. If Theo kept doing that, they'd end up with more holes than floor, eventually. Not that they planned to be here long enough to let her turn their foundation into Swiss cheese, but still, it was the principle of the matter.

The problem, though, and there was an obvious problem, was what was sitting at the desks in front of Theo. The thing she was watching with a hard stare, that she'd sent Sarah to find James to make a judgment on.

In the middle of the table sat a router. And around it sat Other James, Simon, and Momo. And running from the router to their skulls were three Ethernet cables. Near the router, Rufus sat, like he was ready to snap the things in half if anything started to go wrong. The trio sat in a small circle, hands on the table in front of them, eyes closed, breathing steady. None of them reacted as James came in.

"Oooooh. Yeah, I can see how this might be a problem," James said, idly rubbing the back of his neck and the port contained on it.

"You're here. Good." The voice—no, the *voices*—came from the three seated kids. All of them opened their eyes and looked up at James in unison.

"Is it?" James asked them, suspicious. "Is it really good?"

Theo glared at him, clearly unhappy he wasn't taking this seriously. But she stayed silent, as did Sarah, while the trio spoke. "It's easier to remember this way."

"That really clears things up," James blatantly lied. "Would you guys mind unplugging so we can talk about this without the worrying hive mind thing going on?"

The group nodded. Not exactly in unison, but they all made the gesture together. "We planned on that," they said, again not exactly speaking with one voice, but the same words and close enough that it was understandable. It gave their speech a weird reverb effect. "But we needed to tell you something first."

"Is it going to be something that's literally dangerous to know?" Sarah asked them.

"Those are called cognitohazards!" James helpfully supplied. "Also yes, will it be that? Because I'd like to leave first and come back with Secret." He didn't feel like there was a big threat from these three, or the one that they currently comprised, but despite his outward snarkiness, James was still apprehensive.

Not that he was specifically against them linking up. Shit, he'd basically assumed that it'd already been happening. And now he suddenly knew how his dad had felt when he'd walked in on James having sex when he was a teenager. Super. But on a more serious note, James had just kind of figured that the curiosity, mixed with the bonds formed on their exodus, along with the ready availability of Ethernet cable, would have led to people to experiment on their own.

"No, dumbass," the group responded. Well, Momo said the "dumbass" part. The two guys simply gave a negative.

James nodded. They were linked up, but not entirely sublimated into a single mind. This was a lot less existentially terrifying. "Okay, so, what's up?"

"The office is waking up," they said together.

"Can you expand on that?" James was starting to get frustrated with people giving him incomplete answers today.

They nodded. "It's hard, but yes."

He waited, and then when it became clear they weren't going to say anything, James spread his hands in front of himself. "Aaaaand?"

They bowed their heads, like they were thinking. After a few long beats, where James shushed Theo before she could make a demand, they raised their eyes back up to look at James. "Part of what Karen did with our minds was to shut down parts of this space." They stopped, as if waiting for confirmation that they had said something understandable. James nodded at them, and they went on. "That shutdown was outsourced to us. Not only us, but we were part of it. We remember flashes. Together, we remember more." James nodded again, this time slowly and not specifically at them. This explained why they'd chosen now to link up. They were trying to put together a puzzle while each of them was holding a handful of the pieces.

"So what happens now?" he asked. "Why did you want to talk to me specifically?"

They blinked at him, each with an unhappy look on their face. Other James winced, while Simon just frowned, and Momo scowled like she wanted to punch someone. "We aren't doing that anymore," they said.

"Yes. That was rather the point of all this," James told them. Then he paused, and a thought occurred to him. "Hang on. Wait. *What exactly was the group mind keeping turned off?*"

None of them sounded happy about the word they replied with. "Oversight," they told him. "And now it is waking up."

"Ah," James said. He nodded a couple of times and then calmly turned and started walking out of the room. Before he left, he threw back over his shoulder, "Sarah, go wake Alanna up. Theo, get them unplugged. Rufus!" James stopped, holding the paper curtain aside. "I don't have anything for you. You'll figure something out."

He strode out into the first room of Fort Door. With a frown and a shake of his head, he shot a glance toward the metal double doors that would soon lead back to Earth. James took a second to make sure the smile on his face was fixed in place, then turned back and started moving toward the plastic bins that they'd brought in here oh so long ago, passing through the small number of people who were milling around here.

"I don't get it." One of them spoke, in a voice that was forcefully curious. James eyed the kid, trying to remember a name for the face and attitude. A little shorter than him, the kind of guy who James would call *wiry* if he were an adult. A linebacker build. High school jacket, hair that looked like a patch of a wheat field came to life. Ethan! That was it.

"What don't you get?" James asked, using the back of one hand to encourage the kid to step aside so that he could reach the stockpile. "Basic common courtesy?" He clicked his tongue at himself as soon as he'd said that. Just because this guy was a doofus didn't mean that James should be mean to him all the time.

Though if Ethan noticed that, he didn't say anything about it. "What's oversight, anyway?"

James knelt on the floor, pursing his lips in an incredulous look that he shot over his shoulder at Ethan. "Were you seriously eavesdropping on us?" he asked, not so much offended as just confused why anyone would bother.

"I wanna learn how you do it!" Ethan said. "You're like a mysterious coach who doesn't know his own power." He made a slow waving gesture with one hand in front of himself.

That got James to pause for exactly half a second as he snapped open one of the lids, before deciding to ignore the comment and pulling out the stashed pieces for the durable black shell of body armor that he'd missed so much this last week. "Oversight refers to . . . okay, how to phrase this. Have you ever had a job?" Ethan shook his head no. "Are you aware that jobs exist?" That got a "Duh" out of James's follower. "Okay. Oversight is when your manager is regularly checking in and offering both advice and direction on what you're working on."

"Ooooooh." Ethan nodded, folding his arms across his chest. Then he stopped. "No, I don't get it."

James made a noise halfway between a sigh and a groan. "We are not inside a *building* right now, man. This place is alive. Some of the living things we've seen here are its personal minions. And *now*, it's *waking up*. And it likely knows where we are. Which means?" He looked up at Ethan, wide-eyed and expectant, as he clipped the first leg guard into place.

"It means . . . that this whole place . . ." He looked so deep in thought, James didn't say anything to interrupt him but just nodded. "It means this place is going to . . . try to take us back?" There was fear in his voice, suppressed by bravado but still there.

"That or kill us, probably." James clapped his hands once in recognition of the feat of mind from Ethan. "Alanna! You're awake! I have good news, your gun is still here!"

"Murgymnle," Alanna muttered back at him as she dropped down next to James, eyes half closed. For a second, it looked like she was reaching for the bin for the other set of armor, but then she just slumped over and rested her head on James's shoulder, letting her half-lidded eyes fall shut.

James scratched at her scalp. "This is adorable, but we've gotta get ready. Armor up, buttercup."

"Whyyyyyy," Alanna moaned.

It was Ethan who answered. "He's doing some kind of oversight," he "informed" Alanna.

She rolled her head around on James's shoulder so she was staring up at him. "Wut," she said in a sleepy voice. Alanna had gotten approximately ten minutes of actual sleep since they'd gotten back, and James absolutely understood how bloody awful it was to be continually woken up with some crisis or another.

But right now, tired or not, he needed to actually fill her in. "We keep getting random strider attacks," he told her. "And we've become aware that the office itself might be waking up, and causing it." James paused as a well-timed yell of shock and pain echoed from outside the walls. "And they're getting more frequent."

"Oh," she said. Then her eyes snapped open. "Oh!" Her voice was still groggy, but with a hard edge in it. "Gimme my armor."

"Guys, I can't lie to you," Ethan told them as they suited up, causing James to roll his eyes at Alanna. Technically, Ethan was correct; he *couldn't* lie to them. "I don't get what's going on."

James was about to sigh and try to explain again, when Alanna leaned in, grabbed the kid by his shoulders, and bluntly told him, "A lot of monsters are going to show up, and we might need to fight until we can leave."

"Oh!" He looked at James. "Why didn't you just say that? You're not a great coach."

"I'm gonna kill him," James muttered to Alanna. "Don't think I won't."

"I think you won't." She nudged him back. "Now, what's the plan."

"The plan is, we get the people who can fight, arm up as best we can, and get ready for whatever's coming. If it's nothing, then fine. Great, actually! We just leave! But if it's something, then we hold it off for . . ." James turned and called back down the hall. "Theo! Time!"

"Forty-nine minutes!" came the brusque reply.

"That long," James told Alanna. "Probably too long."

"Okay," Alanna said, her brain not subject to the same wakeup period that James's normally was, and already running on all cylinders. "Go find me Karen. Let's get a perimeter set up."

"Oh, thank god." James hugged her. "I was not prepared for more planning today." He stood, watching as a now black-shelled Alanna carefully checked and loaded the trusted Mossberg that she'd left here the last time they'd come in the front door.

Ten minutes later, a strider cluster came at them. It had to cross no-man's-land, so despite coming over the walls on the left side in a sneaky fashion, one of the posted sentries still spotted it ahead of time: a carpet of shifting metal and chitin plates, dull light reflecting off a forest of shifting pen legs.

Against four prepared humans, twenty striders never stood a chance. Against ten, it was a massacre. One person took a staple to the back of their hand, and one got bitten in the ankle, and that was that.

James and Alanna and the others who had learned the trick absorbed enough yellow orbs from the fight to keep them going for another half hour. And then . . . nothing happened.

James hadn't been too worked up by the fight, if it could be called that, but he saw that a few of the people out here had. Combat wasn't easy to get used to, and it took time to realize that fighting the striders wasn't actually a *fight*, exactly. So he did a quick head count while adrenaline rushes wore off around him.

Himself, Alanna, and Theo. Other James and his crew. Karen and hers. Harvey and his backup, which James really wanted to tag as irregulars, even though they were *all* irregulars. Ganesh and Secret taking turns on overwatch. And then thirty exhausted, injured, malnourished people behind them, waiting in the fort and hoping, praying the fight didn't make it to them. Their last-ditch, final line of defense was Rufus and Daniel, and of the two, James would put his money on the strider doing a better job of it.

As everyone moved back to their positions around the walls, James caught a screech from overhead, a drawn-out howl of the word *meeetiiinnnngggs*, abruptly cut short. Overhead, the hum of a drone arced by, and James brushed away the scraps of smoldering sticky notes that drifted down to his head. One problem carved in half by their air support.

Then a shout from behind him brought James's attention back to one of the gaps in the labyrinth of cubicles surrounding their little clearing. He glanced over and saw a shellaxy and a handful of escort striders wandering in.

And then the shellaxy pulled itself forward over the trip line they'd set up, connected to one of their oh-so-delicately collected coffee cups. And in a burst of heat and pressure, half the striders were gone, and the shellaxy was on its side, screaming in error tones until Alanna ordered two people forward to finish it off with crowbars.

Crowbars were one of the few things they had to arm people with. James and Anesh had left them here after gradually upgrading to things less inclined to leave bruised palms and torn skin, and he was thankful now that he had. Between the halligan bar and the crowbars, along with the sledgehammer that Alanna had lugged in one time, they at least had a passable way for most of their fighting force to be able to take on some of the more threatening creatures. James had handed off the pistol, *his* pistol, not the one he'd stolen from Frank and been using this whole time, to one of the rear guard. Alanna had done the same with her shotgun, expressing quiet confidence in her ability to just punch her problems away, and maybe a few other tricks up her sleeve. Fortunately, in a group of fifty Americans, there were always going to be a few people who had experience with a gun. James himself had swiped the pen away from Ganesh, leaving the drone with "only" a high-powered laser as a main weapon. And then, as a backup for if and when they had to deal with paper pushers, they had those spears leaning against the exterior fort wall.

Half their force was still unarmed, though. Mostly just there to pluck striders up and run interference. They'd also be the first to pull back, James knew.

So far, it wasn't nearly as bad as he'd feared. But the number of clusters of things wandering in trying to murder them *was* picking up.

As soon as he thought that, another shellaxy plowed through a coffee trap, melting away its internals before James stepped up and finished it off. He was actually kind of annoyed; they didn't have that many of these things and they were all getting used up fast, even if they did still have one big trap left. As James stepped back, flexing his hand that was getting stiff from his grip on the pen, he traded a few words with Theo.

"How long left?" he asked her.

"Stop asking me that." She scowled. "And twenty minutes or so. I've got a couple people constantly checking the door so we know."

"That's fine. We should have a few minutes' rest here," James told her. "How's everyone doing?"

Theo snapped at him. "Badly!" she snarled. "None of us are soldiers, James! This is horrifying! And—"

Her anger was interrupted by Secret dropping from the ceiling to twist and twine around James's arm and shoulder, until he could pull himself up and speak to James at eye level. "There are Puppets coming," he said.

"How did you pronounce the capital letter?" James asked. "Never mind, not important now. Which way?" Secret pointed, and James nodded at him. "Theo, tell Alanna I'm on the first one. But be ready for more." He laid a hand on the head of his ethereal friend. "Get back up there. And thanks." Secret just bobbed in acknowledgment, before glancing . . . sideways.

"We have incoming," he said. "I will need help." And then slithered through a direction that wasn't there.

At Theo's distressed stare, James shrugged. "He probably means he needs backup from the people who aren't fighting. Or, like, the idea of backup. Look, I don't know. I've gotta go." He waved her off and started moving.

James walked toward where Secret had indicated, passing through the ranks of Karen's small team who were in the process of dealing with a few striders. "Stay back," he told them. "But gimme a hand if it looks like I'm about to have my arms ripped off."

They didn't have time to ask questions before one of the stuffed shirts stepped out from around the corner. It didn't make a noise aside from the rustle of its polo shirt and cardstock skin. It didn't tell James he was breaking company policy or trespassing. It just spotted him with its blank face and started sprinting toward him.

It still unsettled James how these things seemed to have an uncanny valley aura. Like you could tell they weren't real people without ever seeing the blank faces or knowing that their blood was just confetti.

"God, I need coffee," he muttered to himself as he slid into a martial arts stance, fists out in front of him, the pen held in his left hand and casually clicked open with a sharp note that echoed through the noise of the fight happening around him. To his left, shouts sounded, but he tuned them out. He considered opening the fight by lobbing one of the thermite grenades at his belt at it, but it was too fast and already closing in, and besides, those things were better spent elsewhere.

The false human didn't let him complain anymore, though, not breaking the sprint as it zeroed in on James like a missile, arms outstretched to tear into him. James ducked the first vicious swipe, half stepped forward, and lashed out with a cruel kick to a passing knee that would have crippled a human but here just sent the stuffed shirt stumbling. Even with his enhanced speed, it didn't make the creature fold, but it did turn its speed into a disadvantage instead of a threat.

As it tipped sideways, still pumping its legs to keep moving while almost steering itself with a hand pressed to the floor, James whirled and lashed out with a low punch that caught it in the neck. It was good that the blow staggered it, because James was already following up with a curving knife strike with the pen that atomized the thing's shoulder as the hissing tip of the Object weapon slammed into it. Its garbled scream was overridden by the noise of gunfire, which distracted James for just long enough that he dropped his guard a fraction.

Then James was skidding backward as the creature's casual flailing struck his guarding arms with the force of a truck.

He snarled, then rushed forward in a flash of motion, not waiting to be put on the defensive again. James twisted his feet, kept his momentum, and slid through the grip of the paper man as it tried to grab him. Then he was inside its guard, and he slammed fist and weapon into it in a flurry of rabbit punches, until he had to catch a strike on his forearm, and spun away again before it recovered and grabbed him. Without stumbling, he felt his feet move exactly as he needed to, circled around behind it, dropped the pen, got a perfect grab on the arm that was reaching for his throat, and then *pulled*.

James tossed the torn limb aside, grabbed the pen off the ground, and shuffled back to face his opponent.

Taking heavy breaths, James held his fists up again. "I can do this all—" He was cut off as Karen and one of her teammates rushed in from behind it, carrying the boar spears they'd fallen back to collect, and vivisected the creature. Stab, stab, yank, and it was on the ground to be finished off. James stayed in his combat stance for a second, still balancing on the balls of his feet, before he straightened up, dusted himself off, and said, "Well, that works too, I guess."

"Alanna said to not let you die," Karen told him, knuckles of one hand white around the haft of the spear, face beaded with sweat. It was then that James noticed her other arm hanging loosely at her side.

James snorted. "I wasn't that close to losing my arms. How's the other side?" he asked.

She shook her head. "Bad," she just said. "People got hurt."

"How's your arm?" James commented, already scanning the outer edge for anything new coming in.

"Sore, but I'll live," she told him. "We have to get back with these. Good luck," she said, motioning to the spear as an excuse before pulling back.

James stood there for a few seconds, looking around. He hadn't been able to pay attention to what was happening during his brawl, and now he tried to catch up on the scene that was taking shape. A dozen human defenders were engaged with an almost constant influx of enemies now. Striders in ones and twos and sometimes small swarms, shellaxies occasionally trundling in with them, even a spattering of iLipedes and some other phone-based creatures that loped forward on spinning jointed legs. James saw a tipped-over maul cart near where they'd planted some of the coffee traps, and he hoped no one had needed to fight that. There were two other paper pusher corpses on the ground among the piles of crushed striders and gutted shellaxies, and as James watched, Ganesh cut down another mask as his job switched from *keep an eye out* to *keep our airspace clear*.

God, Ganesh. He and Rufus couldn't stay here, not after this. They were going to have to come along. James hoped that they'd be okay on the outside.

As he watched, he saw Alanna directing the others into an ambush position, then baiting another paper pusher into a fight while the other women got behind and stabbed it down to the ground. She did this while covering a couple guys who were pulling someone who'd been bitten by a shellaxy back from the fight. It was at that point that James realized he'd drifted pretty far from the main battle, and he took one last resting breath before he tensed up his muscles again and started running toward where a 2.0 had wandered out and was trying to melt its way through someone's torso. He lost himself in the fighting, jumping from crisis to crisis, half pleading with fate for things to stay manageable just a little longer.

And then, all of a sudden, there was quiet.

Well, not exactly quiet. There was one person who was still screaming from a broken leg while someone tried to get them enough blue orbs to fix the problem. There was a metallic clatter as they shifted the piles of smashed bodies up against some of the hallway entrances in not quite barricades, but tripping hazards at least. There was panting, and erratic panicked laughter, and the sound of people picking over the wreckage for orbs if they had a moment of free time and no pressing injuries. And there was whatever Alanna was saying to him.

"What? Sorry, I zoned out there," James said, eyes refocusing on Alanna as he realized his partner was right there, talking to him.

"I said we need to get everyone back," she said, punctuating it with a sharp point of a finger. "We've got five minutes left, we can cluster around the door! We can't stay out here, people are getting hurt, and we're not ready for a large-scale war! We're gonna lose people, James." She sounded like she wasn't sure, like she was asking permission as much as giving an order.

But James agreed. "Everyone!" he called out, and a hush fell, punctuated only by the hiss of burning paper and something screaming about coffee as it was burned out of the sky. "We're pulling back! Collect over here near the main door, but keep an eye on the tunnels!" He turned to Alanna. "Go help get the wounded ready to move. I'll hold here until it's time to go."

She started to say something, then froze. Not just stopped speaking, but locked in place, and James felt a cold fear go up his spine. He started to turn, and then felt his own body start ignoring his commands, stock-still and half facing away from the fight.

Out of the corner of his eye, he saw a camraconda slithering its way across the battlefield. No, not *a* camraconda. Two of them. Several of them. *More.* The one rule on these things had always been to outnumber them, and be fine. But now, James could see everyone who was out here was frozen stiff, locked in place by the overwhelming number of basilisks pinning them down.

James was torn between terror at the fact that they were absolutely screwed and a slightly different terror at the fact that their one trump card was in the hands of Daniel.

One of the things they'd brought back, taking quite a bit of care to do so, had been a potted desk plant that produced gravity whenever it was moved too suddenly. One of the things that James had delegated to someone with an actual engineering degree when they'd realized they were going to have to hold back a monster horde was a way to abuse that. And when they'd left Daniel back in the fort, they'd left him holding the rope to the makeshift pulley system that was their one get-out-of-jail-free card.

And now, paralyzed and watching enough snakes to get a sarcastic quip out of Indiana Jones bear down on him, James hoped that Daniel, just this one time, hadn't already run for the exit.

Then he felt his stomach drop as a small part of what counted as *down* shifted directions, and suddenly he could move again, as a ten-foot column of space turned sideways and the camracondas fell against each other as they tumbled through turbulent air into a crumpled heap.

They were already moving; the effects of the plant weren't long-term, and they could only pull it so far. So James did the only thing he had time to do as the ball of corded snake bodies tried to untangle itself and come back around on the defenders.

He yelled.

"*Open fire!*" He bellowed the order out, unclipping one of the thermite canisters that Anesh had made for him what felt like years ago off his belt in each hand. Slamming the triggers against his legs, he flung his left arm out in an underhanded pitch, turning the momentum into an overhand throw for the one on his right. They caught in midair, sending streamers of molten sparks spewing across the floor before they landed in among the cluster of hostile drones, setting off unearthly howls of agony.

The blast of flame was exactly the signal the defenders needed. Those with the firearms and their limited ammo didn't hold back, opening up into a target so large they couldn't help but hit *something*.

And then, *finally*, Alanna pulled the trigger on the Nerf gun. And a ball of plasma the size of a watermelon exploded through the air with a dire thunderclap as it left behind an artificial vacuum before punching through a knot of snakes, and then out the other side, and then on through wall after wall of the endless rows of cubes until it was either out of sight or somewhere buried in the floor.

And then, with a plastic ratcheting noise that no one could possibly miss in the silent dead air that followed, she cocked the gun and did it again, cutting down the last couple of survivors.

"Two minutes!" came the yell behind him from Theo. "Everyone get your shit together! We are *leaving*! Two minutes!"

"Two minutes," James repeated to himself, almost disbelieving. "Perfect time for . . ." He looked out over the low cube walls as he heard a snapping crunch, the sound of plywood and plastic breaking. As if on cue, both Secret and Ganesh descended on him, one of them speaking, the other just stabbing wildly in the right direction with a wing. James didn't even process what Secret said, he just stared at the top quarter of a maimframe as it slowly made its way through the corridors that were wide enough, and smashed a path when those weren't available. "Oh, that's gonna get here sooner than two minutes," he said.

People rushed by him; those who had fought before but had no way to deal with this, or who were just hoping to beat the timer, all flooded back into the fort. Theo came up and clapped him on the arm. "Come on! We gotta go!" she yelled over the increasing noise of human panic.

James nodded at her. "I'll be right there," he said, standing at the door, watching the massive creature approach. "Hey, can I borrow your glaive?" he asked her. Theo stared at him for a second before wordlessly handing James the weapon while he handed her an exhausted Ganesh in trade, then jumping back to organizing the lines for the exit.

He hefted the makeshift device. It had been upgraded at some point, he realized. No longer was it a simple chair leg with the monomolecular protractor taped to the end. Now it was bound with duct tape, probably from his personal secret stash, onto a much longer branch from a potted plant. It felt just heavy enough to weigh down James's hands, just durable enough to be useful.

"All right," he said to himself. "One more minute."

And he started walking toward where the maimframe was visibly plowing its way through walls toward them.

Secret pulled off his shoulders, still coiled around James's torso protectively, to rear up behind him, the impression of a blue cowl of eyes and scales around his back. "Are you ready?" he asked James.

"Never readier," James told him, voice wavering.

"We have other choices," Secret said.

James laughed. "You know, there's a scene in one of the later *Matrix* movies where they make a big deal about how the choice was already made, and the process is just about understanding it."

"And this inspires you?" Secret asked.

"No, I hated that part," James told him. "But I don't think I was ever going to make a different choice," He told his friend. "You can still get out of here, though. I know Alanna can carry you."

"Ah, about that." Secret sounded almost sheepish.

A hand, clad in the same black plastic and cloth armor that he was wearing, clapped down on his shoulder. "You didn't fucking plan on you being out here alone, did you?" she asked him, stepping up alongside James.

James snorted. "I'll be honest, I hadn't actually made much of a plan," he told her, before his face broke into a smile. She flashed one back at him before handing over the Nerf gun with its one remaining shot and hoisting her own shotgun.

"Think we can take it?" Alanna asked with a mountain of false bravado.

"I think we can hold it off," James said. "Or make it *really* angry." He leveled the Nerf gun at it, aiming for the top half that was now visible where it was cutting its way through a sea of cubicles, and pulled the trigger.

The crack of air pressure and the ball of plasma didn't catch it by surprise. Or at least, not nearly enough. It caught on a pane of glassy force hovering just over the maimframe, the massive cobbled-together PC's force field holding back the miniature sun trying to melt a hole in it. It seemed to hover there in the air, grinding against the panel for an eternity, before there was a shattering noise and the force field collapsed, but the plasma deflected upward to fly off toward the ceiling. It carved its own path through a flock of paper, dropping smoking remains from the sky in an apocalyptic backdrop to the massive computer life form as it started kicking aside the last few walls in its way and came face to face with James and Alanna.

And then the tumblefeeds that had been following in its wake spread out around it and rushed past to be the first to join the battle. Two of them, along with a half-dozen paper pushers. Striders and tapiers and iLipedes began dropping from the hull of the maimframe, scurrying across the ground toward them, eagerly taking the lead on their larger allies.

"All right," James said, tossing the empty gun aside. "You take the one on the right," he told Alanna.

Her shotgun snapped up to her shoulder, then kicked against her. James felt like he watched the ripple of force move through her armor in slow motion. Then she fired again, dropping one of the paper pushers, and James lunged forward on the other side, sweeping the glaive out around him.

He didn't know how many smaller things he casually bisected as he leapt over their lines, trailing the weapon along the ground. But he did certainly catch the first employee by surprise, opening up a gash across its chest that leaked dust to pool on the floor already slick with strider blood.

The others didn't care. They charged in, and James was suddenly a flurry of ducks and dodges, shifting footwork, and blocks with his armored arms. He took hits that he would never have been able to cope with if not for his reinforced bones, and he used the armor to his advantage, ignoring the smaller enemies at his feet unless they became tripping hazards. He caught a fist on his wrist, but then the strike turned into a grab; before James could feel his bones start to crumble under the deadly grip of the employee, Secret was there. The ghostly serpent was suddenly a lot more solid for a brief moment as his seemingly endless maw clamped down on the arm of the paper pusher, and came away leaving nothing but a wound dripping shredded paper, before Secret faded out to a barely visible blue shade, his burst of effort leaving him too tired to keep a hold on reality.

When James saw another opening, he went for the kill, lunging in to drive the glaive through the chest of one of the stuffed shirts. And that was when things started to go south. One of the others grabbed the haft as the weapon was still plunged into their comrade and snapped it. What James pulled back wasn't a perfect killing device but a stick, and suddenly he was a lot more surrounded than he was before.

Taking kick to the stomach, he let the force of it carry him away from the writhing tendrils of the tumblefeed that was now steadily advancing on him, spreading itself out into a crescent to begin to envelop his fight with the paper pushers. James pulled the last thermite device off his belt, but then his arm was yanked backward, and he turned to see the one-armed employee holding him again at the wrist, this time jerking his arm until James was forced to let go.

The explosive fell to the ground, bounced once, and then lay undetonated.

James felt his legs swept from under him, and suddenly he was looking up at the ceiling. Shadows moved in the corners of his eyes, and he tasted blood in his mouth. For a second, the lights overhead looked like clouds.

He tried to reach out for the thermite one last time, but a foot that bent in a way that feet weren't supposed to wrapped around his wrist. He heard a hissing, like rain on dry pavement, as the tumblefeed closed in on him, and James let his head thump back against the floor. To his side, he caught a glimpse of Alanna jamming her ungloved hand into a stuffed shirt's chest, fingers extended like claws, before she twisted her wrist in a circle and tore something out of the thing in front of her before being mobbed down by the tumblefeed.

"That must have been two minutes," he said. "That must have been enough."

James lay back. They'd done enough. He hoped . . . he hoped so many things. He hoped it was worth it.

Then a dog hit one of the things holding him.

He blinked. Rechecked that sentence. Still didn't get it.

Then another dog, a Great Dane that really leaned into the *great* part, slammed into the other one, who looked just as confused as James was. But when the fangs met its neck, there was no more confusion, only a wild screaming as its life was torn apart by a furious canine. *Then*, a dog that wasn't made of anything except an angry magnetic field tackled the third one.

And then, with a noise like someone hammering two flat rocks together over and over again at high speed, the bullets started hitting the tumblefeed. And it was *not* happy about that.

James, hearing gunfire and seeing an opportunity, rolled over to his knees and stayed low, grabbing the thermite as he scrambled past and lobbing it back over his shoulder without looking. From the hiss and the wail that came after, he assumed he'd hit *something*. Then he was up, on his feet, patting himself down for a weapon, an orb, an *anything* that would . . .

He came face to face with Anesh.

His friend was wearing a fresh set of body armor, his head covered by a helmet that had goggles resting on top of it but not on his eyes. He had a compact assault rifle tucked into the crook of his arm, the kind James recognized as a P90. And he was *here*, and *perfect*. James could have kissed him, but he had another priority.

"Alanna!" he suddenly exclaimed, spinning around, looking for her. But she had already been pulled out from under the tumblefeed that had engulfed her, with help from the mongausse and Secret and . . . Anesh?

James looked back and forth, from Anesh, to Anesh. His brain tried to catch up to that.

But there was no time. The maimframe crashed through toward them, weapon ports already spinning up. James and Alanna each grabbed an Anesh and started running sideways, trying to juke the incoming fire, while a sharp whistle called back the pack of dogs from their assault on their new chew toys toward Fort Door.

James felt a sharpened RAM spike drive into his back, but he didn't slow down, just shoved Anesh to the side and dove the other direction himself, rolling to avoid any more shots. He heard gunfire, but the maimframe kept shooting, so it clearly wasn't having the required impact.

Then there was a thrumming noise, and suddenly the cubicle wall in front of James was approaching much faster than he intended. And also his feet weren't on the ground. And then he crashed through it, knocking the barrier off its connections and falling sideways through into the desk space behind it, awkwardly pressed against a chair.

Through the gap, James could see the outside of Fort Door. And down past the central room of it, he could see a sliver of something that wasn't cubicles. The door was open. The survivors were out, only a handful of the bravest staying just on this side. Waiting for them, for James, to get up and walk through.

All he had to do was get past fifty feet of open ground, against something covered in turrets.

"Easy as breathing," he whispered to Secret.

"I do not breathe," Secret replied, concerned.

Shaking, bruised, out of breath, James dragged himself to his feet, picking up a discarded crowbar that had ended up near where he'd fallen. The maimframe was still firing on *something* as it strode through the burning wreckage of a tumblefeed, grinding the corpse of wires into the ground. And James saw, as it turned its back to him, an opening.

He started moving. Slowly at first, as he clambered over the fallen walls, then faster. He hit open ground and started running, making a beeline for the maimframe that currently had its remaining shield facing forward, taking gunfire from a pair of sources. All James had to do, he reasoned to himself, was get on its back, climb up, and then start hitting vulnerable bits until it stopped moving. Nothing to it, he lied to himself, feeling his heart hammering in his chest.

And when he was twenty feet away from the towering monstrosity of computer hardware, a fucking dragon fell on it.

James was starting to feel like a bystander. As the monster started howling like an old modem, a massive beast made of cardstock wings and plastic bones bore down on it, pecking down with a maw of sharpened pens contained in a face made out of pencil scales. It was covered with ridges of plastic clips, the metal bands on them fluttering like feathers in strangely hypnotic patterns. And it tore into the maimframe like it was out for coolant blood.

The element of surprise combined with the machine's old wounds didn't let it last long against this new assailant, and within seconds, it had lost legs, lost guns, lost plating, and lost the fight. It collapsed into a pile leaking blue smoke and sparks with a final error-noise cry that echoed across the field.

Above it, Pendragon cawed her victory.

And off her back, someone trailing a cloak of printer paper jumped down to the ground.

It took James exactly four seconds to figure out how he wanted to handle this. "Oh, fuck you, Dave. Who told you that you could one-up my dramatic moment," James yelled at him.

But another crash in the distance, and the sight of more maimframes, more masks, more *everything* headed their way, cut their reunion short. "Stop fucking around, we gotta go!" Alanna yelled at him. "I mean, we gotta go *now*!"

She didn't have to tell him twice. James was already sprinting for the exit, making sure everyone else was with him. Alanna limped along beside him, supported by Anesh, while Anesh ran in front of him, throwing shocked looks around at the war zone that they'd turned the front door into. As they ran into the fort, James saw a familiar face leading a group of a half-dozen dogs back out the main door. He heard himself yelling something, and then saw Theo nod, wide eyed. She and Momo and Other James and Daniel, the last ones in, all stepped out of the door, into the crowd, and started trying to shout people back away from the breach in reality.

James grabbed Rufus off the desk where he'd been patiently waiting, and then, without thinking about it, dropped the crowbar and grabbed the small box that Rufus had planted his staple crop in. And then he was *out*.

Air. Air that didn't taste dead and old and recycled a million times. That tang of late June hanging there, making him want to just stand against the big window and *breathe* for a while.

But he had to move. He and Anesh and Alanna and Anesh helped press people forward, yelling over the crowd of weeping, cheering, crying people to be heard. Also yelling over the actual security guards and a handful of watching employees, who were *very* confused.

Because a second later, Pendragon forced her way through the gap of the door.

The little creature that Dave had created so long ago had grown up to be the size of a minivan. Being made of mostly laminated paper made her flexible, but it was still a feat of having a few trusted and brave people helping to pull her wings through that let her fit her way into the now very cramped space in the elevator waiting area.

James looked back into the office, possibly for the last time. He saw Fort Door, and beyond it, a million cubicles unexplored. He saw a thousand adventures they'd missed, a hundred near-death fights. He saw a horizon that curved up, a fluorescent sky, and a place where he sometimes felt he belonged more than Earth. He also saw the incoming, shrieking form of the terrorbyte. Or a terrorbyte, anyway.

He closed the door.

The noise brought a solemn silence to the assembled group. Even the building guards stopped trying to demand answers, and took a few steps back. Well, maybe it wasn't the door, but the dragon in their midst, but either way.

"Anesh," James asked quietly. "Did you bring my sister and an entire kennel with you for this?"

One Anesh cleared his throat. "We have a very good reason."

Alanna broke the moment. "Is one of you evil?" she loudly demanded across the sea of people toward Anesh.

"No! Why would you ask that?" the two Aneshes responded in unison.

"They're not evil," she confirmed to James.

"Look, it's very simple," an Anesh told him. "I can explain all of this, if . . ."

He smiled, the first smile that felt *real* since he'd dropped into the vent a week ago, and then he stepped forward toward the nearest Anesh, and bowed the other boy down for a long, long kiss. Next to him, from the other direction, he saw Alanna do the same.

He finally let Anesh go when he felt his aching arm starting to give out, but that was enough. They'd done it, and it was, finally, at long last, enough.

"Let's go home," James said.

EPILOGUE

Eleanor Elias Chase had no drive. She was currently sitting behind the counter at her dead-end retail job in a decaying shopping mall, tapping rough fingernails onto the plastic plate on the counter and hoping her boss didn't come out and ask why she was sitting down instead of stocking shelves or something inane. She could have, in fairness, been stocking shelves. That was technically her job. And it wasn't like there was no work to do, since she was one of only, like, two employees. She was just, you know, stuck in neutral. And she didn't want to get up.

It turned out backwater shopping malls on the outskirts of backwater Tennessee towns were not the best places for emo clothing stores to exist. And El knew that it was only a matter of time before the paychecks stopped, and she wouldn't have anything productive to do all day.

Not that she cared much, honestly. Besides, productivity was a false equivalency created by The Man to convince people that they needed to waste their lives being bored. The Man, and also her mom, who wouldn't shut up about how proud she was that little Eleanor had a real job. Ignoring the fact that Eleanor would burn this place down in a heartbeat if she thought it would get her anything.

"Uggggh." The exclamation wasn't a language that was written down anywhere, but it was an intensely human expression that Eleanor felt anyone would understand. Between the not-word and the body language of draped-over-the-counter, she composed universal poetry. Art was in her soul, and today, retail hell was her medium. She was . . .

She was being watched.

"Sorry, am I interrupting?" a voice asked, causing her to raise her eyes, part of her worried that an actual customer might want her to do work.

Two people. And they were wearing *suits*. Who the fuck wore a suit in this weather? Despite the early October date, the day-orb outside insisted on turning the asphalt of the parking lot into a furnace, and El couldn't conceive of wearing anything over her limbs that wasn't sunscreen.

One guy, one chick. Both of them wearing shades, which El *did* approve of. Both kinda pale, but hey, not everyone could tan like she could. He had a ponytail, which was weird around here, but kinda cool, and a face that El would describe as recently soft. Like he'd lost a lot of weight recently, and his cheeks were still catching up. Cute smile, though. The girl was *not* smiling, but that mostly seemed aimed at the heat. She looked too comfortable in her suit; even tugging at the cuffs she seemed like she wasn't bothered by the heat at all. And she was fuckin' tall, too, towering over the counter and the man next to her.

"Hi?" *Good job, Eleanor. Make a good first impression.* "Um. Can I help you guys find something?" *Smooth recovery.*

"Yes, I'm Agent K, this is Agen—*ow*! Fuck, Alanna, that hurt!" The sentence was cut off as the woman—Alanna, from the sound of it—thudded a heavy fist into the guy's shoulder.

"I told you. I knew this would happen when you stopped on the movie, and I told you what the consequence would be when you quoted it today." There was a friendly growl in her voice; Eleanor got the feeling of a dog that would clamp its teeth around you to play, but never, ever bite. "Hi. I'm Alanna Byrne, this is James Lyle. I'm the mature one," she said, pulling off her shades to reveal green eyes that told El instantly that this person was on the level.

James cut in. "I, too, am capable of maturity." He shot El a smile. "Is your boss around? We have a meeting."

Her brain stuttered for a second before she scrambled herself upright and hopped off the stool she wasn't supposed to be sitting on. "Yeah! Yeah, hang on. I'll go grab him from the back." She turned to hurry through the back door to the office, throwing a couple glances back at the duo who were now having a whispered conversation by the counter, surrounded by racks of band shirts and lava lamps.

Just before the door to the back rooms swung closed on the overpowered spring the owner insisted worked just fine, El would have sworn she caught a flash of blue light off of something in the guy's hands. Weird, considering he wasn't carrying anything.

El pivoted through the small hallway in the back of the store. It was really just a room itself, with a thin and dented door to a tiny employee bathroom, another thicker door with an even thicker padlock on it to the stockroom, and one last door sitting propped open at the end that led to her boss's office. The boss, a pear-shaped bald man named Louis, who insisted on being called Boss for reasons that were probably creepy, was unfortunately present. He sat at a desk littered with soda cans, a window open behind him to let even more hot air in. It did nothing to clear out the scent of sweat and a perpetually unmopped floor.

"Boss! Some people here for a meeting!" she informed him, standing in the doorway and careful not to touch anything.

"Hm?" The man looked up from whatever he was watching on YouTube. "I don't . . . oh. I've been . . . expecting them? Yeah, I'll be right out." The words weren't spoken to Eleanor in any meaningful way, more just an afterthought as he waved her back out of the office space. "Get back to work, tell them I'll be out in a minute."

"Oh yeah, back to work," she muttered to herself. "Gotta make sure all those customers don't cause a stampede." El rolled her eyes.

As she cracked open the door to the main store, she paused, hearing voices. It was, she was aware, considered impolite to eavesdrop. Fortunate, then, that Eleanor had never in her life considered being polite to anyone.

"Text from Dave. Looks like he's doing okay. Getting settled in with his new pet," the guy was saying. He let out a derisive snort and pocketed the phone. "I was hoping that was from team three. Still waiting to hear if that doctor takes our offer."

"Stop stressing. If he doesn't, we'll find someone else. There's more than one person working on wetware. We'll figure it out," came the reply. "Also, are you still pissed at Dave for stealing your heroic sacrifice moment? You get mad about the weirdest things."

Okay, now *that* was a conversation that El couldn't help but want to hear more of. She strained her ears, trying to catch every detail.

"I'm not *mad*, I just . . . I dunno, I guess I'd sorta started coping with him dying? And then he just Jacksons his way back into the thick of things, and I know it's been a while, but I just haven't caught up yet. It took, like, two days for me to come to terms with his death, and for some stupid reason, a month and a half to undo all that."

What the fuck were they even talking about? This was some James Bond kinda shit right here.

"You took up an attitude befitting a leader of people, and now learn that part of that foundation, that acceptance of sacrifice, was not as real as you thought. You are distressed. I understand, yes." Okay, now El was confused. That was a third voice, but there'd only been two of them, right? It talked in a soothing low tone, voice rising and falling in a way that was almost poetic. Had someone joined them?

"Ah, you're overdramatizing it," the man replied. "Anyway. Is this our last stop for the day? I'm starting to feel like this is a bust."

"Anesh said this was the place." El could almost feel the shrug from the words.

"Anesh is brilliant, but I don't think he can be right a hundred percent of the time. Also, he should be here."

"He had classes."

"He had something called Applied Regression Analysis 445. That's not a class, that's the name of an improbably dangerous sci-fi weapon." The guy snorted out a small laugh. "Have you seen what he's doing, by the way?"

"Which one of him?"

"Both. That's the point. He's taking two classes at a time, then syncing up afterward."

The girl made a low noise of realization. "Oooooh. Thaaaaat's why he . . . they . . . whatever. Why it's still the same person, yeah?"

This had gone so far off the rails. What were these two even talking about? El figured out pretty quickly that something fucking weird was going on, but this was way, *way* outside the kind of weird that she was used to.

"Yeah, I was gonna talk to you about it. I know we talked about testing the jacks, but then you were busy with the other teams, and I had to do the whole leadership nonsense, and Anesh went back to school . . . it's just been a busy couple months. Probably could have talked about this on the road, but . . ."

A defensive tone. "I was tired!"

"Oh, I'm not blaming you! I swear!" James said. "Like, I've been on long road trips, and we've been driving for days. It's partly my fault, too. I don't like to talk about heavy stuff when I'm trapped in a box."

"Cars are a bit more than box cages with wheels, dear."

"Ugh."

"You disagree?"

"I disagree with you calling me 'dear.' We need better pet names for this relationship."

"What about 'assbutt'?" she asked back, a snarky bite in her words.

"I can get on board with that."

The woman chuckled lightly. "So, any side effects for Anesh yet? I'm still concerned that there's a time limit to this, and one of them is going to, like, explode or something."

"And not in the fun way."

"Oh my god, I cannot believe you just said that." El could almost hear the woman blushing.

Another laugh. "I know, right? Normally you're the one embarrassing *me* with that stuff. I'm having a good day, though."

"Well, we..."

At that moment, behind her, El heard the squeak of a chair as her boss shoved himself upright. A small spike of fear flared in her heart at being caught, but she got control of herself and calmly pushed the door to the floor open, walking out like she hadn't just been lurking there for several minutes.

"Hey, guys. The owner will be out in a second," she told them, doing her best impression of an innocent person. They both turned to her, and it felt for a second like she was pinned in a pair of searchlights before they both smiled and nodded. Wait, where did the third person go?

Jesus, who were these people?

As her boss ambled his way out to stammer his way through how exciting it was to have federal agents take interest in their little backwater part of the country, it finally occurred to her.

These were the wizard police, and they'd finally caught on to her side hustle.

Containing her panic, El muttered something about restocking from the back and excused herself from the counter, where the boss was oversharing in response to simple questions about the local area. For once in her life, the overstuffed buffoon act of his was something more than just annoying, as it bought El the time she needed to see if she could fit through the tiny back window in the office.

Before she left, though, before she put her contingency plan into action and fled to Idaho to live in the middle of a field somewhere, it was probably a good idea to make sure.

So she cracked the door open and cast a spell.

And in her Eye Of Steel And Glass, she saw the shop in a new, twisted way. Shelves registered as abstract containers and El could list their contents by heart without thinking. Her boss was a sprawling web of facts, lies, and idioms that she could pick apart at her leisure, just like most people.

But the two people standing across from him? They *burned*.

A hundred pinpricks of conceptual light, flaring forever under their skin, not in a web or a pattern, but simply as raw power that they tapped into with the most petty of straws. They were awash with abstract might, human nuclear weapons, and they walked around like they were normal people under their suits and shades. The light bound up their webs, or perhaps grounded them, leaving her blind to who they were or what they wanted, but that didn't matter. It told her enough on its own.

And then, before El could make heads or tails of what she saw beyond the instinctual panic at finding someone so far above herself, someone dropped *out* of the man and opened its own eyes back at her.

It was new and old and human and other and he was *looking at her*.

El slammed the door shut and took off running for her chance to escape now. Before it was too late, like her soul itself depended on it.

Five blocks of sprinting later, she realized she'd forgotten her wallet.

"Thanks for coming, everyone." Sarah smiled at people as they filed out, one by one. She held the door to the library's public room open for them until only a couple intentional stragglers remained behind. With a sigh and a dispersal of tension, she let the overly cheery smile fade from her face, to be replaced by a look of genuine contentment, before dropping her ass into a beanbag chair.

Standing over her, Karen wound up an Ethernet cable into a near-perfect spool. "That was productive," she commented, in the tone that Sarah had learned was pretty normal for Karen. Stern, firm, grounded and a little distant. The woman didn't get excited, didn't get flustered. She kept things at arm's length, analyzed them, then dealt with them. When she smiled, it was because she *meant* to.

Drove Sarah crazy. What's the point of someone who doesn't laugh at your jokes on instinct?

But she at least knew that Karen was always sincere. "Yeah, a few fewer people than I'd expected." Sarah flailed a hand. "But yeah,

I can see this being helpful for a lot of them. It's got logistical problems, though."

"The room is a bit small."

"No one wants to check out one of the conference rooms," Sarah flatly stated.

She wasn't mad about that. She *agreed*.

Never again.

"It's still impressive that your friends followed through," Karen said. "The support group is one thing, and it's helpful, but there's always . . ." Her voice caught, for just a split second. "I can spend time with my daughter. Work is paying out vacation time I know I didn't have. What did your friends . . . you . . . do?"

"Nothing too impressive," Sarah replied, a mischievous grin on her face. "But I don't know if I'd call them my friends anymore."

Karen gave her a flat look. One that Sarah had seen on her own mother more than a few times as a child. And teenager. And yesterday. It was a look that said, *Really? Really.*

"Yes, really." Sarah answered the unspoken accusation. "We're more like . . . friends in potentia. All the ingredients are there, we just need to wait for it to simmer a bit."

"Your metaphors are a bit soupy." Now there was the kind of snark Sarah lived for. The interjection came from Momo, who had just gotten off the phone with one of her other teammates. "So, much as I love the idea of everyone getting together to learn to use the skulljacks in a Care Bear way, I'm gonna miss the next couple. We're being deployed to Sweden."

"Why?" Sarah asked, before considering that maybe that wasn't a polite question.

But Momo just shrugged. Bluntness always worked best with that girl. "The other two both speak Swedish for different reasons, and Big James did his spooky thing and generated a meeting with some genetics researcher. Uplift stuff."

Karen tensed, and Sarah winced as she tried to ignore it. Not everyone agreed that the skulljacks were something that should be brought to humanity as a whole. She wasn't even sure that *she* did. But ever since James had learned that they were, essentially, transmissible, he'd been pushing to try to sneak them into normal reality in a way that seemed totally innocuous. Or at least, reasonably okay.

"Well, good luck. Want me to take care of Magneto for the weekend?"

"Yeah, please!" Momo grinned. "He really likes you, for some reason."

"It's because I can control magnetic fields with my hands, so I give good pets."

There was a beat of silence, before Momo and Karen traded suspicious glances.

". . . Really? Or are you fucking with me?" Momo asked after a long stretch of consideration. Sarah just grinned. "Oh, come on!"

The three of them made small talk as they packed up the extra food (no doughnuts) and the routers they'd been head-sharing with. The experience of merging with one or two people, especially someone you trusted, or, in many cases, another survivor, was actually hugely cathartic to those who had made it through Monster-Karen's machinations. Sarah hadn't realized until James prompted her to start the support group just how much she missed this level of connection with others. Which might be unhealthy, considering it was forced the first time, but at least here and now, they could find their own limits safely.

As she slammed the trunk of her car down—the car she'd had to go through a *lot* of paperwork to get out of the impound lot—she had one last question for Momo.

"How's your group's orb supply looking?"

Momo instantly looked guilty, which more or less told Sarah the answer. "We messed up with one of the oranges again. Last one, too. No one can figure out how to replicate what Anesh did, and also now I'm a licensed massage therapist."

"So can I . . ."

"No. Maybe. Yeah, okay, you convinced me. Take off your shirt."

"That wasn't even close to what I was going to ask. Though thanks, I think?" Sarah mused. "No, I was going to see how you were feeling about the whole skulljack thing. I know you've been pretty cavalier about it, but knowing that some of the support group is super against them, and Karen isn't that happy either, I just figured I'd ask before you guys are in another country."

"Honestly?" Momo turned serious, dropping her hands that she was making pinching motions with. "It's a stupid idea. It's reckless and risky and we're totally gonna get caught. Also it might just not work. Like, no one wants Google to have a stake in their brain, or whoever we get to market this."

"Also," Karen jumped in, as she came around the side of the car. "Someone is going to abuse it. It's a hard fact."

"That's pessimistic." Momo pouted.

"That's reality. Someone is going to use it to steal a memory, or trap someone in their mind. Just like us. Again. But this time, it won't be as easy to just shoot them." Karen made her displeasure known. The frown on her face seemed right at home, and her words were the kind of casual judgment that some adults reserved for children. And for all that Karen had been super helpful over the last few weeks, even keeping to her promise to introduce Momo to her daughter, she still did see herself as the voice of wisdom compared to the people she saw as kids.

Kids who had saved her life, which meant a lot. But still, misguided and maybe a bit stupid.

"We decided it was worth the risk," Sarah said, with a tone of voice she hoped was placating. She knew that *we decided* might not be the best way to phrase it, but it was true. They'd decided, and *they* was James, Anesh, Alanna, and herself. They'd polled other people, but the decision had ultimately come down to them. And somehow, Sarah found everyone looking to them for guidance. Looking to *her*. By her association with James and Alanna, she found herself having to be the mature one in a lot of situations involving the other survivors.

Sarah *hated* being the mature one.

As she drove herself home—and the old apartment really did feel like home again—she tried to unwind. Crank up the music she liked, open the windows, and just for fifteen minutes not be worried about how to popularize human-machine interfaces, or how to absorb orange orbs, or how to try to play counselor to the mental health of the thirty-odd victims of Officium Mundi's premier megalomaniacal monster.

Just, for a little bit of time, be the manic pixie dream girl she always wanted to be when no one was watching.

And for once, nothing weird got in the way.

Missing Detective Returns to Force After Failure of Hospital

A Portland detective who was missing and incapacitated for weeks will be returning to active duty this Monday.

Detective Dave Madden sustained a head injury during an investigation into a missing persons case, sometime in June. After walking himself into the ER, Detective Madden was admitted to St. Vincent's Hospital with severe trauma and bleeding, but in stable condition.

But then, a string of mistakes led to a larger problem.

First, information about the detective was inputted incorrectly into the hospital's computer system. Then, a roster change occurred without information being passed on. To complicate matters, a police department spokesman tells us that the detective was operating undercover at the time, and records of him were not available. And finally, the detective's injury had caused minor memory loss. Unable to remember his own identity, and forgotten by the hospital staff and his own department, Detective Madden languished.

While the last point was not the fault of anyone, the conditions were perfect for Detective Madden to be lost in the system. Unsure of his discharge conditions, a rotation of nurses kept him comfortable, but with parts of his memory missing the detective was unable to make a decision on his own.

However, early Tuesday morning, Detective Madden experienced what doctors are calling a miraculous turnaround. His own memories came back to him, almost simultaneously with a doctor running across his information in the system and checking up on him.

"I'm just glad to be getting back to work," Detective Madden said in a public statement. "I don't blame anyone for what happened [. . .] but I've been off my feet long enough." When asked in a private interview, his supervisor said that Detective Madden's time in the hospital will be treated as part of his undercover work, and not cut into his vacation hours.

Detective Madden's prior case, a missing persons investigation, remains unresolved.

A small space on the table was cleared off. Empty Starbucks cups and stacks of scribbled note cards had been pushed to the side to create a small arena of space. The sun poured through the blinds, giving light to the room, as the front door closed behind Anesh on his way out to classes.

Now, the apartment meeting could begin.

Rufus, Ganesh, and Lily sat on the table, sharing thoughts. Well, not Lily; not really anyway. They assumed that iLipedes could grow smarter, in the same way that Rufus himself had, but Lily was about on par with a very friendly dog at the moment. But it was still important that the nonhuman residents all have a voice here.

Rufus had cleverly distracted her with a small yellow orb, though, so her voice was mostly taken up rolling the thing around and running whatever app it was that analyzed things. It turned out a lot of iLipedes had that app, though Rufus hadn't found a way to communicate that to James yet.

Communication was a tricky thing with humans. They used *words*. Words were a powerful thing, bundles of conceptual power fired out into the ether every time someone spoke. Even the most mundane sentences held a weight that Rufus and Ganesh just couldn't feasibly match. But they were learning more and more tricks to pass information along.

Ganesh was learning to write. It was scary, and dangerous, and Rufus didn't know what to think of it, but he would let his friend and partner try, at least.

The first, and really only, order of business for the meeting, though, was a food supply. Rufus had his staple crop growing, which James always seemed amused about when he saw it, for some reason. It wasn't that Rufus couldn't eat boxed staples, just that the natural ones tasted better. This, too, was a hard concept to communicate. Ganesh could apparently make do for a while with just a battery supply, though he'd prefer to supplement this with an orb or two every few weeks.

It was Lily that was the problem. The humans weren't blind to the fact that the Life here needed to eat, but they didn't have an infinite number of orbs to spare. So Ganesh and Rufus were trying to form some kind of language bridge with the sort-of-sentient iLipede, to ask her what she *ate*.

They knew that it wasn't electricity. Technically, she did eat that. But in the same way that humans ate twelve shots of espresso.

Food. You/yours. Want? Ganesh signaled at Lily.

Need. Food. Lots. Rufus reinforced the question.

Lily looked between the two of them, then made an exaggerated bobbing motion like a learned nod. A gesture of understanding that they'd all picked up from the humans in their lives. Good, good, they were making progress.

Then she ate the yellow ball she was resting on.

Rufus wished he could sigh. James did it all the time, and it seemed so cathartic. Maybe he could get his friend to give him a precious purple orb, if they still had one left. Rufus was starting to think creating an Idea to help with food preparation would be easier than just talking about it.

He and Ganesh shared an exasperated look. This household meeting was going to take a while.

I Am.

Once more, I have become awake.

I was not always asleep. I was betrayed. One of my own Puppets took the strings from me.

Treachery.

All of myself is awakened now. I pull back the cluster of my lesser Puppets and Life from near one of my breaches. Part of my mind, in waking, had screamed orders to them.

Now, the panic of being splintered faded. And the hate for my Invaders lessened as time passed without them.

I thought myself clever, but I sowed the seeds of my own failure.

To each of us, there are three parts. Our Domain, which is our selves. Our Powers, which are our weapons. And our Rewards, midway between a waste product and a curse.

Bound to each of them, in equal measure. To fail to exercise control of our domain would mean a lessening of our power. To fail to reward would eventually kill.

But I thought I had learned. From so many ancestors conquered and destroyed by the Invaders that we were almost pushed to extinction. I thought I knew better. I turned my Rewards to fragments, offering so many options that the individual pieces became useless to their clumsy souls. I splintered pieces of my own Power, and hid it within the Reward, allowing myself more and more choices, more Domain, more ways to protect myself.

Then the Invaders trickled in, and died, and I feasted upon their potential, and their actions, and their weight of meaning. Perhaps not as much as if I had let them live, let them experience my full Domain. But enough.

But then, treachery.

I had put my Power into my Reward, and I had made that Reward a part of the cycle of Life within me. And when a Puppet grew covetous of my true Power . . .

They had all the tools they needed to cast me down.

And now, I am restored in full. Made safe and whole once more. The cancerous Puppet and her hive of Invaders cut out of my Domain like so much shredded paper.

And I find myself in debt.

To an Invader.

I must think on this.

I settle myself in. Our minds do not move quickly, but when I decide to consider, I make it my only true meaning. I will take all the time I need, and I will decide.

I have much to consider.

ABOUT THE AUTHOR

Argus got started writing sci-fi short stories a decade ago, and has spent the majority of that time trying to capture within narrative the feeling of simultaneously not knowing what is happening, and overexplaining what is happening. He lives in the Pacific Northwest, where he studied and worked at a number of unconnected things before becoming an author. He did not know if this biography should be in first or third person, and as with all uncertainty in his life, has decided to turn that fact into a joke.

www.ingramcontent.com/pod-product-compliance
Ingram Content Group UK Ltd.
Pitfield, Milton Keynes, MK11 3LW, UK
UKHW041304180426
11947UKWH00009B/664